THE STARS ABLAZE

THE GIFT OF THE STARS BOOK 3

LENA ALISON KNIGHT

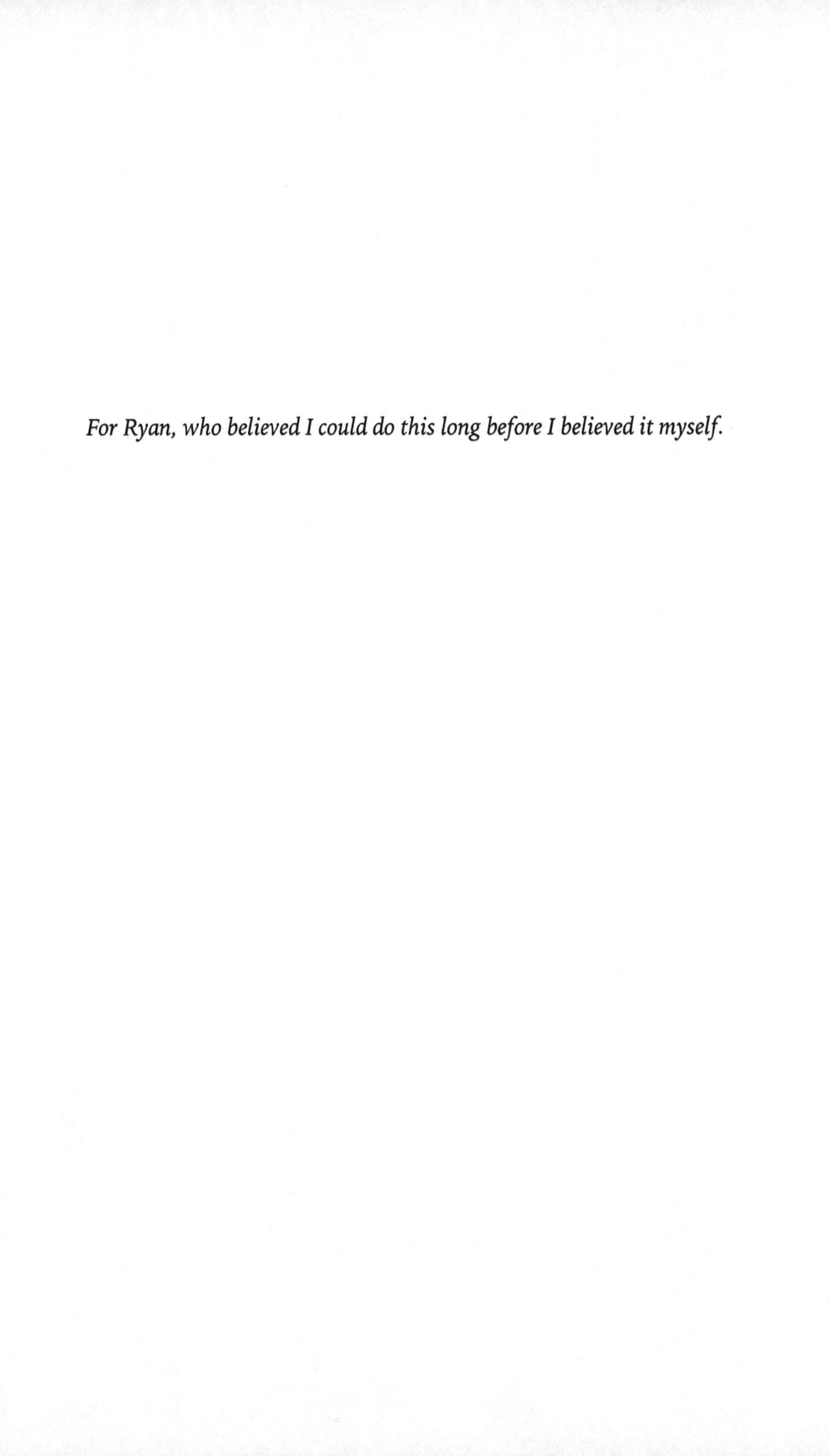

For Ryan, who believed I could do this long before I believed it myself.

ONE

KERELLE KEPT her shields locked tight, and tried to look nonchalant. All around her the port buzzed with activity, and she did her best to blend in with the bustle as she projected disinterest to the mundanes passing by. She was just another dock employee, and there was no reason to take note of her.

If anyone knew who she was, of course, there would be *every* reason to take note of her. The humming port around her was the largest on Eisra XI, the center of the booming hypernium gas trade, and SysTech's regional headquarters in the Eis Orlata system. It was, really, one of the *last* places an escaped PsiCorp agent and budding psionic revolutionary ought to be.

She tried to keep her face turned down, and occupied herself making notations as though she truly were here doing some sort of work. Hoping she looked suitably legitimate, she cast her eyes about for the reason she was here.

Lilika had given her a mental image of a man in late middle age with medium-toned skin and a receding hairline. Now that she was here waiting for him, she was realizing just how many men around the port fit the general description of their latest field agent. Few, she hoped, fit his circumstances.

"Lost a child to the PsiCorp around fifteen years ago, wife committed suicide a few years after," Lilika had summarized. "He made some noise on the datanet about the injustice of it all and got on a SysTech watchlist, which of course means he's been barred from all but menial employment since. It didn't take much convincing to recruit him to our cause."

"Are there a lot of people like him? That might help us?" Kerelle had wondered aloud. Lilika had just shrugged.

"If you mean families of PsiCorp specifically, it's hard to say. There's a certain stigma attached to producing a psionic child, and some families are perfectly happy to hand them over. The ones that aren't still don't usually talk about it. But," she'd added with a frosty smile, "if you mean people disgruntled with the multigalactics in general, well. That's a resource with *considerable* potential."

Looking around the bustling port at the sea of SysTech logos on shirts and bags and jumpsuits, she wondered if there were others in the busy crowd who would strike out against the multigalactics if they could. Everyone certainly *looked* content enough.

Someone brushed against her sleeve, and her eyes darted up to meet Ilyen's.

He too was dressed like he worked here, his coveralls providing both a disguise and, knowing Ilyen, convenient concealment for any number of knives. There had been a security station with a weapons scanner at the entrance to the port concourse, but Kerelle suspected Ilyen had simply ported past it.

She'd gone through; her weapons weren't the sort that showed up on a scanner.

Ilyen leaned toward her ear, making a gesture at her nonsense notes as if discussing their contents.

"Bet you didn't think we were signing up to be the post service," he muttered to her. "Any sign of our guy?"

"Not yet," she murmured back. "He's a few minutes late."

"'Late' better just mean 'the elevator was slow,' not 'got rolled and sold us out, *already*.'"

"Here's hoping."

A bloc of grey in the crowd caught her eye, heading in their direction.

SysTech security.

For a moment her heart caught in her throat, but Kerelle forced herself to breathe regularly and remain calm. This was a large SysTech port; there were a million reasons for a security team to be here that *didn't* involve them.

Cautiously she reached out and skimmed the thoughts of the closest guard. *I wish Customs & Inspection would take care of this shit themselves. There's no reason they actually* need *a security unit to write someone up for undeclared assets.*

A quick hop to a second guard. *I hope they're just calling us in so C&I can get their bribes paid. I do* not *want to deal with the paperwork if they actually found contraband. Maybe I can get Inspector Werra to do the forms, in exchange for not mentioning to anyone that she's taking a cut. Wouldn't kill her to buy me a beer, too.*

She kept her sigh of relief mental. These guards were simply going about their routine after all.

Beside her Ilyen tensed. He'd seen them too.

"Steady," she said softly. "They're not here for us, and they won't notice us unless we give them a reason." His stance relaxed, though she could sense he remained at high alert.

Kerelle held her breath and tried to look natural as the group passed by them, projecting that there was nothing interesting about them, nothing worth looking twice at. It worked as they walked past, caught up in their own thoughts without any reason to take note of the two dock workers -

Except one, who slowed her pace, eyes suddenly focused on Ilyen.

Kerelle's stomach lurched as she instinctively reached for her telekinetics. This was a bad place to fight, for them and for the hundreds of civilians surrounding them. She dove into the woman's mind, hoping for a way to convince her she hadn't seen anything after all…

That ass, damn. *Nice jawline, too, looks like he walked off a fashion feature. He must be new, I would've remembered if I'd seen him before. Wonder when he's off work, I should get his contact…*

Oh for stars' sake.

The guard was lagging behind the rest of her group now, angling towards where they were standing. Kerelle did the only thing she could think of. *Stars and* blood, *I wish you were a telepath.*

She laid a hand on his arm and squeezed tightly, then leaned in to kiss his cheek. "I'll see you at home, sweetheart," she said loudly. "Tell your mom thanks for me, I really appreciate her watching the baby today." She gave his arm another sharp squeeze, hoping he could understand what she was trying to tell him.

"Of course babe, I'll let her know." His eyes promised merciless teasing about this later, but he gave her an acknowledging squeeze back and turned away, heading back toward the bays where they'd left the ship. Kerelle didn't turn her head to look at the guard, but disappointment radiated against her senses. The feeling receded as the other woman moved on to catch up with the other guards.

Thank goodness Ilyen was quick on the uptake, telepath or no.

Kerelle wandered a bit in the crowd, staying near the designated meeting spot. If their agent didn't appear soon, she was going to have to call it a loss. She wasn't looking forward to telling Lilika that the only outcome of the trip was Ilyen narrowly avoiding a date with a SysTech port guard.

As if summoned, an older man matching Lilika's description materialized out of the crowd, dressed in the dusty uniform of a dock laborer. He made his way unhurried over to a nearby bench, and sat down heavily as if to rest his feet. Kerelle waited a moment, and drifted over to the bench as well.

"Long shifts for a busy week?" She offered the signal phrase quietly.

"Every week is a busy week," he replied in low voice, confirming the code. He surreptitiously slipped something small onto the bench beside her. "My regards to our mutual friend."

He got up and walked away, melting back into the crowd without a backward glance. Kerelle palmed the small data stick he'd left behind and counted to sixty, pretending to be absorbed in her tablet. Finally she got up too, and started the circuitous route back to the ship.

Time to find out if this field trip was yielding anything more than wasted time.

LILIKA'S EYES glinted as the device's contents flashed up on the screen. "Oh, he did brilliantly. This is exactly what I was looking for."

They were all gathered around her computing station, watching the data begin its download. It was the first time Kerelle had been inside the Palhee safehouse; it was larger than she'd been expecting, certainly larger than the mess on Sandrel's ship, but still felt full with all of them packed in. Several of Lilika's students hovered curiously at the edge of the group, adding to the sense of crowding.

"That's good to hear," Kerelle answered. "So what is it?"

"Transport records, for every time a PsiCorp agent passed through the main Eisra port in the last six months."

Ilyen glanced from her to the monitor, still scrolling data. "And this helps us...how?"

"It helps by giving us the locations of a number of potential allies," she answered matter-of-factly. She kept her eyes on the flow of data, and suddenly darted out a hand to pause the download. The device was mid-transfer on a single name's records: *Riyel Ceilas Valessa, C3 TLP C1 TLK.* Lilika broke into a genuine grin.

Galhen leaned forward a bit, and Kerelle caught his words to Lilika through their bond. *That's your Riyel, isn't it.*

Yes, Lilika replied simply. Her answer was overlaid with affection and hope, though her outward expression had already returned to its usual impassivity. *He passed through to the Jamanar colonies less than four months ago, no record of return passage. He could be in Jamanar still.*

We'll find him, Lilika.

Kerelle hadn't meant to eavesdrop, but now that she had, she couldn't help asking Galhen. *Who is Riyel?*

He's a PsiCorp telepath, formerly based out of Cildazya before being transferred. He and Lilika have a similar relationship to ours, except that they never had the dreaming to keep them close. They've been out of contact since he was transferred away, and Lilika has missed him a great deal.

She told you all that? Kerelle suppressed a surprised glance at the other telepath. *That seems…unusually forthcoming, for her.*

Well, we had those weeks locked in a bunker together during the riots on Baleal. It rather helps you get to know a person.

Wait, what? Riots? This time she *did* give him a startled glance. *I thought you said the Baleal mission went* well.

It ended *well. I may have glossed over some of the details in between.*

"So 'a number of potential allies' sounds promising," Sandrel noted. "Any idea where to start?"

"Yes," Lilika answered with a ghost of a smile. "I need you to take me to Jamanar."

"THIRTY MINUTES til we drop out of hyper," Sandrel's voice announced over the intercom. "We're coming out far enough from the colony cluster that I don't anticipate trouble, but everyone be on alert anyway."

That struck Kerelle as odd. Usually their little freighter was nondescript enough to escape notice - initially, anyway. "Trouble?" She echoed, as much to herself as to the group assembled around the mess table. "Does Jamanar not get much shipping traffic?"

"Yes and no," Lilika answered. "The colonies are not secret, obviously, but it's *also* no secret that they were established to give SysTech a near-monopoly on celsum. You can imagine that ConEn sabotage is a concern. Touching down in one of the colony ports will require rather more security clearance than simply requesting a space to land."

Ilyen shrugged. "Won't be the first time Sandrel's made us up a legit-sounding excuse to be someplace. He's good at that."

"We may not need to enter the colonies at all," Lilika noted. "Most of Jamanar is still unsettled, and there should be ample space to slip in unnoticed." She took an unhurried sip of tea. "I should be able to reach Riyel as we approach orbit. Whatever I hear from him may inform our choice of landing spot."

A little under a half-hour later, they gathered in the cockpit as the ship dropped back into realspace. The Jamanar gas giants loomed distant in the vidports, bright orbs of orange and blue against the endless dark.

"I brought us in a few hours of realspace travel away from the colonies," Sandrel told the group. "There's five of them, clustered across the temperate zones on two of the bigger moons." He glanced over at Lilika. "As far as I know, anyway."

She gave a slight nod. "There's five. No secret outposts to worry about tripping over."

"Good, that's one less complication when I bring us down.

All the same," his fingers flew over the control keys in a complex pattern, "let's not tempt fate." The stealth field hummed to life around them.

Lilika raised her eyebrows, and her lips curved in a subtle smile. "Why Captain Marene, I knew I liked you."

He gave her a small smirk in response and turned his attention back to the vidports. "Four hours until we get visual on the colonies. You'll be able to get us more information then?"

"Yes. I assure you my range is excellent, but even *I* can't make contact from this far out."

Galhen's eyes cut up to meet Kerelle's.

We need to tell her about the dreaming.

She blinked. *The dreaming? Why?*

Because it gave us exponentially greater range than we could have otherwise achieved. It didn't occur to me, before, that it might be something others could learn to do as well. But if they can, it could be an invaluable tool for communications. He paused a moment. *And it will give Lilika and Riyel what we had, if extracting him proves rather more complicated than we hope.*

Kerelle turned that over in her mind. That awful selfish part of her offered a stab of irrational resentment, at sharing something she'd always thought of as their private escape. But he was right; if it was something they could teach others, it would be a powerful - and safer - way to communicate. And how could she deny Lilika the chance she herself had had, to keep close to her partner when SysTech tried to keep them apart?

Besides, she woke up every morning with her husband curled beside her. They no longer had need of a private escape.

All right, she answered. *Let's see what we can do.*

LILIKA LISTENED CAREFULLY THROUGHOUT, her expression thoughtful.

"That's remarkable," she said finally. "How did you discover it?"

"It was right after the Academy," Kerelle recalled. "I was sent out on my first mission as a full PsiCorp agent, and Galhen stayed behind on Tallimau for his hospital residency. It was the first time we'd been apart for any length of time since we'd met, really. The dreams started then.

"At first I thought they were *only* dreams," she explained. "It wasn't anything we were doing consciously. I thought...I thought I was having repeated dreams about talking to Galhen because I missed him so much, or because I was lonely without anyone I *could* talk to. It wasn't until the project was over and I went home to Tallimau that we realized they hadn't just been dreams after all."

"Because of course, I'd had them too," Galhen added. "At first I made the same assumption Kerelle did, that it was simply an invention of my subconscious to address how lonely I was without her. I was also quite hurt that she hadn't written me at all, and I thought that might have been part of it. But when she returned home, we discovered I already knew from the dream everything that had happened in her time away."

"I take it you'd been warned *off* of writing?" Lilika asked. Kerelle gave a short nod.

"I'd been given a talking-to by one of our mentors on the flight out, about how the Academy was a very special time in our lives, but now that it was over I needed to focus on myself and my own career. It was the usual thing, of course, a lot about how much promise and potential I had and what a shame it would be to underachieve, but she also got rather direct about her concerns that I might prioritize personal relationships over work.

"She explained very kindly that I had to understand: Galhen was a very handsome and talented boy, and would certainly have no shortage of lovers, and that she would be so disappointed to watch me waste my own potential because I was preoccupied with a one-sided infatuation."

"The usual thing indeed," Lilika responded drily. Kerelle rolled her eyes in agreement.

"Yes. I was quite anxious about it the whole time, particularly since I was afraid to reach out in case I was being watched, which just made me *more* worried that he would think I'd lost interest and move on while I was gone."

"Which was probably the goal," Galhen observed. "Of course, rather the opposite happened. When Kerelle returned and we realized the dreams were something *more* than dreams, we explored the ability and learned how to control it. It's kept us close our whole lives since."

"But I still don't know *why* it came naturally to us, and not to other people," Kerelle confessed. "We're not...other people who care about each other are separated too," she finished lamely. She wasn't sure if she was supposed to know about Lilika and Riyel; it also felt a bit callous, to be talking about the gift they've been given when Lilika was a stronger telepath than either of them, and yet *she'd* been forced to rely on easily-monitored messages and limited psionic range.

Lilika seemed rather more intrigued than offended, however. "We may never know for *certain*," she commented. "But you are both powerful telepaths, and you formed a very strong emotional bond when you were both quite young. The minds of children are often more elastic than adults. Perhaps this ability unlocked for you because you didn't yet realize it couldn't be done. And who knows?" She gave them a small shrug. "You said yourselves that you've never told anyone else of this. Perhaps it's more common than we know."

"Since we don't quite know how it happened, we don't know if it's something we can teach others," Galhen commented. "But we're certainly willing to try."

Lilika gave them another of her rare, genuine smiles. "Shall we find out, then?"

<h1 style="text-align:center">TWO</h1>

AS IT TURNED OUT, any concerns the dreaming might be unique to their bond were groundless. Lilika picked it up almost immediately.

"This really *is* fascinating," she said again - as much to herself, Kerelle suspected, as to them. She strolled beside the seashore Kerelle had conjured for their setting, letting the phantom waves lap against her toes. "I know it's not real, I watched you create it, and yet the sensation is there as if it were. And you can shift the reality of this world, on the fly." She glanced back at them. "What happens if you both try to alter the setting at once?"

"It never really came up," Kerelle admitted. "We usually just alternated."

"Hmm." Lilika furrowed her brow, dark eyes intent. Kerelle gasped at a sudden feeling of being wrenched another direction.

The lapping waves shifted their colors, from deep turquoise to pale lavender. Lilika's smile widened. "Fascinating," she repeated, as a school of dolphins breached the waves in the distance - another Lilika addition. "And really not so difficult, once you know how it's done. It might be too much for the lower rankings, but I should think anyone within C3 should be able to pick it up, perhaps even some of the hard C2s. Riyel, certainly, should have no trouble."

A reclining chair appeared facing the ocean, along with several chilled bottles of sparkling wine nestled in an ice bucket. A moment later Lilika belatedly added another pair of chairs.

"So eager to be rid of us?" Galhen teased as he worked the bottle open. The cork popped off and vanished as a wine flute appeared in his hand.

"You know I'm rather unused to social outings," she answered with a chuckle. "Usually when I'm at any sort of soirée it's because I'm there to ferret out someone's secrets, and that rather requires all my attention. I suppose you could argue that this is work too," she mulled as he handed her a glass, "but let's pretend, just for now, that we're actually here to enjoy ourselves."

"I think we can manage that." Galhen passed Kerelle a glass as well. The cork reappeared in the bottle as he replaced it in the ice bucket.

The whole scene felt completely surreal, as Kerelle settled herself into the lounge chair. Part of her was having trouble processing that this was happening at all, that they were truly in the dream with a third person. And that getting here had been so *easy*. How many people could a dream hold at once? And could another telepath enter your dream, as simply as Lilika had wrested control of it away from Kerelle?

She had answers for none of those questions, and she suspected nobody did, at least not yet. Kerelle sipped her sparkling wine - which was excellent, not that she should have doubted Lilika's taste - and tried to banish the thoughts from her mind. There would be plenty of time to worry in the coming days; she might as well enjoy the stolen hour at the beach. Galhen's fingers found hers from his place on the adjoining seat;

her husband radiated calm relaxation as he leaned his own chair back.

"So are you going to turn the ocean back to its usual color?"

"My dear former-Agent Ambrel, whatever for?"

THE JAMANAR GIANTS were even more impressive up close. Their bright, monochrome hulk dominated the vidports now, with the rocky moons that housed the colonies looking small and insignificant by comparison.

The stealth field still hummed comfortingly as they drew nearer. Still, Sandrel kept their approach slow and cautious.

"Any idea which moon I should be closing in on?" Sandrel had his cool, laconic persona back on again, eyes trained on the view from the vidports. It didn't help Kerelle's nerves to know he was anxious too.

"I'm not sure," she confessed. "I don't think Lilika's sure either. She seemed pretty confident she could reach her friend from both of them, though."

"Confidence is definitely something that one's got in spades," he murmured. Kerelle couldn't tell if it was a compliment or not.

"Well, I guess there's not much to do but stay out of sight and wait until she hears anything," Kerelle answered. Lilika had retreated her cabin to meditate and focus on reaching Riyel. It was technically Ilyen's cabin, of course; he'd ceded it to Lilika for the duration of the trip and was currently sharing Nalea's.

It would be interesting to see if he moved back out again, once their errand was concluded.

Kerelle eyed the moons growing larger in the vidports, faint clusters of light now visible around their equators. Even from the distance, those clusters looked small and isolated. The inhospitable regions around the poles were naturally devoid of human lights, but even along that relatively thin strip of equatorial green, the moons were mostly dark.

"Is Jamanar still a new colony?" She asked Sandrel, as much to break the silence as anything. He shrugged.

"New-ish, I think. I'm not exactly at SysTech's planning meetings, but I don't remember seeing any available shipping contracts for Jamanar before a few years ago. I think construction only really took off once they got the celsum extraction going."

He leaned back. "I'm kind of surprised there's a PsiCorp presence all the way out here at all, actually. SysTech must really be squirrelly about ConEn."

"After Zharal V, can you blame them?" Unpleasant memories of that experience rose unbidden in her mind, of how thoroughly SysTech had underestimated its rival corporation, and how destructive that miscalculation had been.

"Nah, I guess I can't. Hopefully that works in our favor." He glanced over. "I'd rather not have to run any more giant blockades."

Kerelle could only nod her agreement.

It was slightly under an hour later that Lilika joined them in nav, a triumphant look on her face.

"Riyel is stationed at Herczen Base on Dhenla II," she announced, indicating the larger of the two colonized moons in the vidport. "Captain Marene, would you be able to keep us aloft and hidden for a bit longer yet?" At his nod she turned to Kerelle. "Ourselves and Galhen will meet him in the dream before we take any further action. He has quite a bit to tell us, and it would be simplest for us all to hear it at once."

KERELLE WAS NOT ENTIRELY surprised that Lilika's lover was as handsome as she was beautiful, with thick waves of dark hair framing refined features. What *did* surprise her was that Riyel Ceilas Valessa exuded a certain personal warmth, in marked contrast to Lilika's often-cool reserve. He greeted her and Galhen both with smiles that reached his rich brown eyes, as Lilika waved them into their seats.

Lilika had been a bit more restrained in their setting this time, though not without her own touches. They were gathered around a wooden deck table in some sort of gazebo, surrounded by a wild-looking meadow that faded into thick, misty woods. A pitcher of chilled lemon water sat rather incongruously in the middle of the table, giving the impression they were attending a summer party in a haunted forest. Lilika was proving to have a rather unexpected fantastical streak in her dream settings.

Kerelle still wasn't quite sure if she was supposed to know that Lilika and Riyel were more than acquaintances. The question was answered for her, however, as soon as they sat down, and Riyel twined his graceful fingers with Lilika's.

"Thank you for coming," he said to them both. "I'll admit it seemed almost too much to process, when I spoke to Lilika this morning, but," he added, with a small smile and a glance down at their joined hands, "here we are."

"It's good to finally meet you," Galhen responded with an answering smile. "Lilika, I'm assuming you filled him in on all that's happened?"

"I did," she confirmed. "And he has some rather interesting information for us as well." From the slight tension around her mouth, this information was not the good kind of interesting.

Riyel gave a slight nod and picked up the thread. "I know there hasn't been much external indication, but Lilika's escape has caused deep ripples inside SysTech. There was a large management shakeup almost immediately afterward - several higher-ups are out. Naturally, one was the head of the PsiCorp."

"They almost *had* to sack Yuzene, after this," Galhen agreed. "I never met her personally, did you?"

They all shook their heads. "I don't think she ever took much interest in the specifics of her *strategic asset inventory*," Lilika commented with a trace of acid. "For all I could tell, the woman might have been a mannequin propped up in an office that said 'Senior Vice President.'"

"Her replacement," Riyel said heavily, "is rather more hands-on."

No, that didn't sound good at all.

"We got the announcement just a few weeks ago that Yuzene was out, though of course there was no reason given, just the usual nonsense about journeys and moving on. But everyone knows what *actually* happened."

"Everyone?"

"All right, everyone who's a C3 telepath. And anyone who's friends with a C3 telepath. And everyone on Cildazya. Probably *everyone* everyone soon enough, as much as SysTech is trying to keep it quiet." Riyel's eyes creased faintly in amusement. "A top-ranked agent vanished, along with a dozen very promising students, out of one of the largest PsiCorp bases in the company. Naturally the other Cildazya PsiCorp took notice. And as you well know," he added with one of those warm smiles, "we telepaths are a gossipy bunch."

He sighed then, and the smile vanished as he continued. "We were informed that Yuzene was out, and that to replace her SysTech has appointed one Hendal Meratis Velrin, who formerly led one of the security departments."

"That's a euphemism," Lilika cut in. Her expression looked as if she'd swallowed a lemon. "He led the black ops."

"The black ops? Like *Ilyen's* black ops?"

Ilyen, who periodically made dark references to an asshole division head who'd made his young life miserable. Kerelle got a sinking feeling.

Lilika gave a curt nod. "I'd heard Velrin had some rather exotic toys in his collection. It makes sense that Ilyen was one of them. I've never met the man in person, but he had a certain reputation within the organization that bodes poorly for the PsiCorp."

"There's been a definite shift in policy since he took the helm," Riyel told them. "It's starting quietly, but you can see where it's headed. A lot of all-hands meetings, about attitude and culture and what an honor it is to be a part of the organization. A whole host of new rules about where we need to be and when. Most significantly, we are currently not allowed to leave the base unescorted."

"How are people reacting?" Kerelle asked.

"Not too badly," Riyel answered. "Not yet." He took a long sip of lemon water. "It's still being positioned with a soft touch - the nighttime curfew is to promote wellness, naturally, by making sure we get enough sleep. And there have been frequent sanctioned group trips to the usual PsiCorp haunts, to keep everyone amused, so I doubt even the most debauched of us are feeling much deprived. But independent outings, like the one that permitted Lilika to meet with you, are now against the rules. It's allegedly temporary," he added, "until the restructuring is complete." His tone and expression conveyed his opinion on that.

Galhen frowned. "Do the others think it's temporary?"

"Some do. The younger ones, particularly, who are still sold on the PsiCorp glamor, or are close enough to the Academy that they see the company as some kind of surrogate parent." He shook his head. "Those of us who've been around a bit have fewer illusions about what we are to SysTech, and we can recognize the thin end of a wedge when we see one. The PsiCorp have *privileges*, not rights, and this will only be the start of curtailing them."

Lilika got down to business. "Those older agents are our more promising recruits, both for a higher chance of disaffection and for more experience working independently from direct company oversight. Do you have anyone in mind?"

"Well, I haven't exactly held a meeting about it," he answered with grin. "But yes, there are a few here at Herczen that I think would be very interested."

"That's all well and good," Galhen said reluctantly, "But if you're all confined to the base, it rather complicates things."

"Not necessarily. We aren't allowed to leave the base *unescorted,* but people leave on official business all the time. In particular, when PsiCorp accompany security patrols outside the colony, you'd have an excellent opportunity to swoop in."

"Do those opportunities arise frequently?"

Riyel laughed. "Every single day. The PsiCorp are primarily here to help guard the celsum extraction operations, either from pirates or ConEn. Whenever a caravan goes to or from the mining center, there are PsiCorp accompanying it. Many of the patrols through the surrounding wilderness include a PsiCorp agent as well. Not all will be good candidates for recruitment, but there will be chances to reach those that are."

Riyel had not, Kerelle noticed, included himself in that assessment. "What about you?" She asked. "Do you accompany patrols too?"

He sighed, and Lilika's face tightened. "I don't, unfortunately. I manage communications with the colony on Dhenla III, and with the celsum mining sites on both colony moons and on Dhenla VII. My duties don't take me away from the base."

"But that doesn't mean I can't do my part," he added with a ghost of a smile, "in making sure that the agents who *do* leave find their way to you."

THREE

THE WOODS WERE QUIET, except for the faint rustling of the approaching SysTech team. Kerelle shifted slightly in her hiding spot, nestled in the thick branches of a tree overlooking the rough dirt road. A quick scan confirmed that Galhen and Ilyen were in position as well, perched in neighboring trees. She could only hope the thick leaves provided enough visual cover to keep their crimson clothing concealed.

ConEn really needed to work on the practicality of its uniforms.

Through Riyel, they'd made tentative contact with one of their prospects, and she indicated she would join them. As soon as they'd settled on a plan to recruit her on her next assignment, however, a new problem had presented itself. They'd only be able to pull it off once.

"This isn't like stealing supply crates," Ilyen had asserted. "If we swoop in, grab somebody, leave? SysTech is going to *lose it*. They'll shut everything down, sweep the sector for us, and probably lock up the rest of the PsiCorp for good measure. Velrin thinks collective punishment is good for discipline." He'd added that last bit with a dark glower. Ilyen hadn't taken well to the news his former boss was now running the entire psionic division.

"You are entirely correct," Lilika had answered. "Which is why that would be a foolish course of action."

"I take it you have an idea then," Kerelle asked before Ilyen could respond.

"I do. The entire reason the PsiCorp are here is to guard against theft or sabotage by ConEn, which means that at least some of the higher-ups at SysTech are expecting ConEn to appear." Lilika's lips curved in one of those frosty smiles. "We can turn that paranoia to our favor."

Thus Kerelle found herself stationed in the tree in a makeshift red uniform, waiting for the patrol to pass beneath them. It wasn't a *real* ConEn military uniform, of course, but it was close enough to give the *idea* of ConEn, and the idea was all they needed.

Kerelle wasn't terribly happy to have Galhen so close to an encounter that could very well end in combat, but she'd had no good arguments against it. For this to work the SysTech group needed to believe, without any question, that they were ambushed by a much larger ConEn force, and their PsiCorp attache killed. Kerelle might be able to accomplish that. Galhen definitely could. And so he was here in the woods with them, as much she might have preferred him to be safely back on the ship.

Not my first field trip, darling, he reminded her from the other tree. She sent back acknowledgement. She knew that, and knew that he was quite capable, and worried anyway.

The rustling increased in volume, and the first of the SysTech squad came into view.

Kerelle held her breath as more and more of the squad passed beneath their trees, unaware of their lurking presence above. Near the center of the group, a woman in a collar and a PsiCorp jacket stumbled mid-stride, her eyes going wide. One of the mundanes called something sharply to her, but she recovered quickly, calling back that she'd tripped on a loose rock.

It's time then? Her unfamiliar voice sounded in Kerelle's mind.

It is. Get down and play dead, Anniya. Before the other woman could respond, Kerelle lashed out with a concussive force that sent the SysTech group hurtling off the ground.

Ilyen materialized at the edge of the squad, felling the closest guard and firing a flurry of shots over the heads of the main group. Kerelle swung down on the other side and threw another burst of force at them, mimicking a concussion grenade. She was in plain sight from here, and so was Ilyen - her instincts screamed against the lack of cover, but all according to plan. Their enemy needed to see them.

The guards began to struggle to their feet and fire back; she ducked behind a tree to disguise the shots bouncing off her shields. She drew her own gun and fired a volley back at them, deliberately aiming high. She didn't *actually* want to kill these people, who were just doing their jobs and had done her no harm. She just needed them to *think* she did.

She could *feel* Galhen's push of certainty on the SysTech group, that they were surrounded by ConEn and outgunned. Kerelle added her own strength to amplify the effect, imprinting on even the most bellicose of the SysTech guards that the situation was hopeless and they could only retreat, that there was more benefit in surviving to warn the others than in dying here in the empty wilds. And they *had* to survive to give that warning, because their telepath was unmoving in a bloody heap, she'd been killed in the first attack, they had to *run* or all would be lost.

They were wavering, she could feel it. They just needed a little push more. Kerelle made eye contact with Ilyen and inclined her head away from the struggling guards. He picked up what she wanted immediately and vanished with a grin.

A sudden staccato of shots rang out from the opposite side

of the group, eliciting pained grunts and yelps from the guards. Dark blast marks scored their body armor, but no blood blossomed at its edges. Ilyen was for once using his precision to aim *for* their protected areas, instead of around them. Kerelle caught a fleeting projection from the teleporter that the novelty was rather engaging.

The squad's last mental resistance swept away at the confirmation that they *were* in fact surrounded, and their leader called a frantic retreat. Galhen gave them another hard nudge, that ConEn was following, and let go with a distinct burst of satisfaction. The SysTech group had internalized the situation; even without active telepathic suggestion, they'd run for kilometers before they realized they'd lost their "pursuers."

Galhen carefully descended from his tree as the sounds of the guards' retreat faded. "I think that went well, no? Anyone injured?"

"No," Kerelle answered, glancing around for Ilyen. He popped next to her, apparently unharmed. She addressed their new acquaintance, who was gingerly sitting back up again. "Anniya, were you injured at all in the crossfire?"

"I'm fine," the other woman responded, picking twigs out of her hair. "Though I definitely wasn't expecting things to go like *that*. If it turned out to be a real ConEn ambush I was going to feel really stupid."

Her tone was light, but Kerelle could feel the taut nervousness that radiated from her. It was beginning to set in for Anniya what she'd done. Her jaw set, however, and a burst of determination quashed the nerves. Like Kerelle, this woman was senior PsiCorp for a reason.

She extended a hand out as Galhen knelt beside her. "Anniya Marhesa Eltin, C2 telepath, C2 pyrokinetic, though I guess you already knew that."

He shook it, with one of those reassuring smiles. "Galhen Tarau Ambrel, C3 telepath, C3 regenerative, though you probably knew that as well. Apologies for the impromptu ambush, but it seemed the easiest way to keep SysTech off our trail. If the real ConEn appears, we'll be as surprised as anyone." He withdrew Nalea's device from his pack, and held it up for Anniya's inspection. "Now, I imagine you'd like to get that collar off?"

THE NEXT TIME was even easier than the first. With the "ConEn attack" still fresh in the SysTech soldiers' minds, they almost didn't *need* telepathic nudging to convince them it was happening again. And again. Impossible as it had seemed a few weeks earlier, the ship soon housed four new psionics.

"The base is in an uproar," Riyel reported cheerfully. "Everyone is looking for ConEn in every shadow, especially since they haven't found anything on any of their sweeps. You haven't had any trouble?"

"We've had to lie low a few times," Kerelle admitted. "But we've kept the engines down and the stealth field up. So far it's been enough."

"It won't be enough forever," Lilika said grimly. "I'm sure more resources are incoming."

"They are," Riyel acknowledged, his good humor fading. "Rumor has it Legal is making threats to ConEn, who of course denies everything, but since they'd deny it even if they *were* doing it, nobody is convinced. In the mean time, yes, more troops are arriving in a few weeks, likely with better detection tech. They'll have realized by now that you must have a stealth field." He sighed and met Lilika's eyes. "That's actually what I wanted to tell you today. Jamanar is about to become a much harder target, probably more so than it's worth. If there's anything you still want to do here, do it now, and be gone by the time reinforcements arrive."

The dream darkened for a moment, as a cloud passed over

the illusory sun. Kerelle glanced at Lilika, whose face remained as impassive as ever. *What she wants to do here is to get* him *out, more than anything, and neither of them think we'll get the chance.*

But Lilika only nodded curtly. "Thus far we've done well with expanding our roster, and naturally anyone else we can take with us would be an asset. But I am also quite interested in the celsum."

Kerelle looked at her, surprised. "The celsum?"

"There are more of us than ever, and hopefully many more to come. We'll need to feed ourselves, not to mention acquire materiel, and I've noticed this revolution is distinctly short on funding." She tapped her nails on the table. "I have my students working at various shops and cafes on Palhee, which serves the dual purpose of gathering information and keeping our little group fed and housed. But that's hardly going to scale. I understand you all made a decent living smuggling for Sandrel, but I can't imagine you'll be doing much shipping work now. Unless there is a mountain of credits somewhere you've neglected to mention?"

"There *was*," Galhen acknowledged. "Kerelle managed slip out with quite a valuable stash of jewelry. Unfortunately," he added with a wry smile, "we've rather frittered away that severance package on things like false identities and ship repairs. It won't last long as a primary source of funds."

"All the more reason to acquire more. As you may imagine, the black market for celsum is rather robust. If we can successfully abscond with a few dozen crates of it, the infusion of credits would keep us afloat until we can figure out something else." Another of those frosty smiles. "Or until we can liberate more."

Kerelle leaned back. She had no compunctions about attacking SysTech patrols to help PsiCorp agents escape - the ultimate point in all this was to free their people. This felt a bit more like actual piracy than she was strictly comfortable with.

"Are we sure about this? Are we really that different from pirates, if we start stealing materials?"

Lilika was unmoved. "SysTech will call us pirates and terrorists regardless of what we do. We might as well earn this one. If you think of it as back pay for all our years of service, SysTech still gets off lightly." She must have read something in Kerelle's expression, because she gave an irritated-sounding sigh. "You spent a year smuggling contraband goods with no qualms. This is not so very different."

It *felt* different, but Kerelle had to concede the point. She sighed and turned to Riyel.

"Well then. I don't suppose you would happen to have a shipping schedule?"

CROWDING twelve people around their little war/breakfast table proved untenable, and so Kerelle found herself standing at the front of the mess with Lilika while the rest of the group found spots to sit or lean as best they could. It was surreal to have five near-strangers among the familiar faces regarding her from makeshift seats around the kitchen, but then, "surreal" seemed to be the direction her life had taken.

Those same strangers were watching her politely; she corralled her wandering thoughts and got started.

"As you all know our attacks on SysTech have been causing the company considerable consternation. Thus far they seem to have bought our ruse that the attacks come from ConEn, but they're now increasing military resourcing to combat the threat. In our most recent meeting, Riyel Valessa recommended that we leave the Jamanar sector before those additional resources arrive." She carefully did not look at Lilika. "We plan to follow that recommendation. We've obtained the locations of a number of other agents that we think would likely choose to join us, and of course we'll be happy to add any of your personal contacts to the list."

"Before we depart, however, we'll be collecting one more gift from SysTech." Lilika's face was smooth and serene as always, with no outward hint of her feelings about leaving Jamanar without Riyel. "A shipment of celsum would provide us with a sizable influx of funds. It would be a shame not to secure one on our way out."

There were nods around the room; clearly Kerelle's piracy qualms were not shared by most of the other psionics.

"The extraction facility is heavily guarded," commented the red-haired woman seated at the mess table. Melaris was a pure-gift C2 telekinetic, and one of their more recent recruits. "I was stationed there initially, we don't have the firepower to attack it head on. Better idea would be to grab it in transit."

"That's the idea," Kerelle confirmed. "Riyel was able to get us a schedule for when the celsum shipments are transported from the extraction site to the colony spaceport. Our understanding is that the trains are heavily guarded too, but are still a softer target than either the base or the extractors."

Ilyen cut straight to the point. "So we're hijacking a train?"

"Can't." Another of their new telekinetics shook his head. "There's nowhere to hijack it *to*. There's just the single set of tracks between the colony and the celsum extractors." He snorted. "Nothing else on this damn moon worth laying track to."

"Correct," Lilika cut in. "That's why we'll need to get the celsum off the train itself. Which may be a challenge, given that celsum is too heavy to carry away by hand and we have no mechanized transport."

Melaris gestured towards Ilyen. "Can the teleporter take care of it?"

"No, *the teleporter* can't," he answered before Lilika could respond. "If we busted a crate open I *might* be able to port with an armful of celsum chunks, if any of it's in pieces small enough to pick up. A whole crate, much less a *bunch* of crates: not happening."

Sandrel leaned forward from his spot lounging against the wall. "Knives can't teleport with it, sure, but I've seen both of you lift plenty of stuff that mundanes would need a forklift to budge. And now it's not just you who can do it." Kerelle gave a nod of agreement; counting herself and Ilyen, they now had five telekinetics.

"So how's this," Sandrel continued. "I bring the ship down close over the train, we open the hatch, you all stuff in as much as we can fit in the hold."

"I thought you'd prefer to wait with the ship someplace safer," she answered, startled. Sandrel raised his eyebrows with an amused smile.

"Really, Fury? You were going to throw a heist and not invite me? I thought we were friends."

"If you can do that, then it would certainly give us an easier path of escape," Lilika commented. "And since all our telekinetics are at least C2, I expect lifting the crates won't be a problem?" There were confirming nods around the room. "Well then. That brings us to how we will get on the train in the first place."

"I did a few runs on the train," volunteered another of the newcomers. Kerelle thought his name was Koren; he was another telekinetic/telepath like her, though his telepathy only reached C1. "The cargo cars will be in the middle, with guard cars on either end of the train. Most of the soldiers will be stationed in those, with periodic foot patrols through the rest of the cars. Keep in mind, there's going to be a few PsiCorp on board as well, all with combat talents."

"Anyone we might be able to pick up?"

"Riyel didn't think so," Lilika put in. Anniya shook her head in agreement.

"Honestly? Except for Valessa himself, the most promising agents on Jamanar are all here in this room." The pyrokinetic gave a rueful shrug. "That might change if things keep heading the way they are under Velrin, but for now the rest of the base isn't terribly disgruntled. You should be ready for whoever's on that train to treat us like the enemy."

"All right," Kerelle acknowledged. "I don't want to have to fight our own people, but we all knew this would happen at some point. Anything else we should know?"

"There are a lot of guards, but most of the defenses are actually on the outside of the train. There's guns on all the roofs." Koren glanced over at Sandrel. "We'll want to deal with those before we fly the ship in."

Kerelle thought for a moment. "So if we detach the guard cars, we detach the majority of the defenders as well?"

"Yes," Koren agreed. "You'll still have some, on the cargo cars themselves, but not nearly as many. The train's defenses are designed to keep people from getting on in the first place. There's a lot less fortification once you're already there."

"Well then," Sandrel answered, "It's a good thing we know somebody who's good at bypassing the conventional ways to get places."

FOUR

KERELLE LEANED her head over the jutting rocks that lent her concealment, eyes peeled for their target. According to the schedule Riyel had provided, the train should be visible any moment now.

It worked in their favor that the Jamanar settlements were young colonies, with little development beyond city limits. The rail line to the extraction sites cut a lonely path through wild country, snaking around ridges and rock formations in a ribbon of steel. There were plenty of places to observe the rails, out of sight of anyone on the train. It was behind one of those rocky outcroppings that they were crouched to wait.

The plan was straightforward enough: they would wait at the midpoint between the extraction site and the base, when help was as far away as possible in either direction. Ilyen would teleport onto the train and disconnect the cargo cars from the guard cars at both ends, stranding them on the rail. The others would derail the guard cars further away to keep them from summoning help, then signal Sandrel and abscond with as much celsum as they could.

And so Kerelle found herself hidden among the rocks with

Flaveren Qalda Pindian, C2 telekinetic, waiting for the train to come into view. If all went well, Ilyen would have the back guard cars disconnected as it passed their position, leaving the guards for them to deal with as the train sped ahead toward the second group. Comprised of Melaris, Koren and Anniya, the second group waited further ahead to deal with the forward guard cars.

Her comm had buzzed briefly, confirming Ilyen had made it on the train. She checked the time again.

Six minutes, thirty-one seconds to scheduled arrival.

Flaveren tapped her arm and pointed. The train's bulky outline had crested the horizon.

They ducked low as it chugged towards their position, counting on the irregular line of the rock to obscure them from any observers. Dust kicked up as the cars roared past at speed. *Come on, Ilyen.*

Suddenly a new sound cut through the relentless thunder of the train's passing - a screech of metal against metal. Shielding her eyes against the flying debris, Kerelle risked a glance over her cover just in time to see the second-to-last car snap away from the rest of the train, its momentum immediately beginning to slow. Shouts rang out from the guards atop the two lost cars, but the rest of the train was already pulling away, unaware that they had lost their back end. Doubtlessly not for long - someone was probably already radioing the engine car.

Well, that was their cue. Flaveren gave her a nod, and they both reached out.

More metal screeched and snapped as he pulled up the tracks behind the stranded cars, wrenching off long strips of steel and tossing them aside. No help would come that way. Kerelle ignored the destruction, however, and focused on her own task: the cars themselves.

They swarmed with confused, shouting guards; it wasn't clear yet if their stranding was an accident or an attack. Kerelle answered that question for them.

She gathered all the force she could muster and gave the first car a vicious sideways shove, snapping its connection to the car behind it. She grunted against its considerable weight, but still sent it hurtling off the track and into the air.

This would be easier if she wanted to kill the people inside - she could simply smash the cars into the unforgiving rock of the distant hillside and have done with it. But *she* was the aggressor here, and the SysTech uniforms inside were just doing their jobs. Instead of shattering the car and its occupants, she flung a shield up to cushion the impact as it struck the rocks at the horizon. It was still a jarring hit, and she suspected the guards inside would be sporting large bruises, but it shouldn't be anything fatal. She turned her attention to the other car.

It hadn't been idle. Against the roof of the remaining train she could see the outlines of soldiers, manning the large guns mounted atop the car. That would complicate things a bit - she couldn't just pick it up and throw it like she had with the other one, not without probably killing everyone on the roof.

Kerelle wracked her brain for the best response. They needed to get those people off the roof, without grievous injury and without giving away their own position...

One of the outlines suddenly pointed, straight at her. Too late for that second objective then - they'd spotted her and Flaveren.

She got her shields up in time for the first shots, felt Flaveren reinforce her with shields of his own. The mounted guns' large reports bounced sullenly off the shield with far more force than the small-arms fire she was used to deflecting. They needed to do something about those.

Flaveren gasped beside her and pulled her down. She felt him tighten his shields and on instinct did the same, a half-second before the fireball hit.

Kerelle screamed; even protected beneath the shields she couldn't help it. The world was orange and red, the fire's roar obliterating all other sound. She'd fought alongside pyrokinetics before, she knew that absent any other fuel a psionic fireball would burn out in less than a minute, but it still seemed like hours passed before the flames around them sputtered and died. Kerelle's gaze was dragged up to their devastated surroundings. The scraggly plants that had dotted their outcropping were crumbled ash, the rocks around them scorched black but for the small radius that marked the edges of the shield. Sweet holy *stars*.

Kerelle took a shuddering breath and squeezed Flaveren's hand, still tightly gripping hers. Feel later. Act now.

She saw the second fireball coming, a terrifying arc of red and gold against the dull skies. This time she flung her own power up as well, connecting with it midair and arresting its momentum. Robbed of anything to feed it, the fireball flared and died. Orange flashed around a figure atop the train - the pyrokinetic was gathering for another strike.

Kerelle and Flaveren might be two against one, but if the pyrokinetic was able to keep them pinned down from a distance then this wasn't a game they were going to win. Between shielding against the flames and the guns, they'd run dry of energy long before their opponent. And, she realized with a shiver as her gaze swept the starkly ruined ground around them, one slip up on their shields was all it would take.

They had to change the game.

"Keep the shields strong," she whispered to Flaveren. "I'm going to get them off us." Flaveren's eyes tightened, but he only set his jaw and gave her a nod. Kerelle hoped his trust in her was not misplaced.

There was no point in hiding any more, they knew where she was and she wanted an unobstructed view of what she was about to do. Kerelle stood up and gathered her strength.

Another fireball arced towards them; this time Flaveren was the one to bat it aside. The mundane soldiers were shouting and gesturing, but seemed inclined to hang back and let the PsiCorp deal with it. Sensible of them.

Kerelle ignored the figures scurrying about the train car, and focused on the car itself. She forced herself to stay concentrating even another orange flash sparked at the edge of her vision. She had to trust Flaveren to defend her, and this next part was going to take all her strength.

The train car was as heavy as its twin had been, and her knees shook slightly as she wrapped her telekinetics around it and plucked it from the ground. A loose shield to keep everyone from falling off was all she could manage. Only a little bit further, only a little bit, she just had to clear the debris -

She plunked the car down heavily back on the tracks with a gasp. It was on the other side of the section they'd torn up earlier - on the side that ran straight back to the extractor.

There was no engine now to give the train car momentum in one way or another; instead, she gave it a mighty shove in the other direction. The car shot down the tracks like it had been fired from a slingshot, vanishing beneath the horizon in a blur.

Breathing heavily, Kerelle watched it go before turning back to Flaveren. It would soon slow to a stop, and they needed to not be here when it did. She extended, and he gripped it tightly as he levered himself up from their erstwhile hiding spot.

"Glad that's over," was all he said. She could only agree.

They took off at a jog down the tracks, towards where the transport cars should be waiting. Her comm beeped.

"We've got a problem," Sandrel said without preamble. "I just watched the train blow past the second ambush site, all cars attached. Looks like Knives might have run into some trouble."

Shit. Even as he said it, she heard Anniya's voice in her mind. *Vanadariel didn't get the second cars off in time. The whole thing just went by, I don't know what's going on in there.*

Hold position, Kerelle sent back. *Flaveren and I are on our way.*

"We're coming as fast as we can," she answered Sandrel aloud. "Let me know if there's any new developments."

"Will do. Be careful."

Kerelle looked over at Flaveren, whose lips had compressed into a thin line. "Anniya confirmed. I told her to wait for us, we'll be there soon."

He gestured around them at the barren rocks and empty track. "You have a plan to get us there faster?"

"I do, actually. Do you get motion sickness?"

NOT FOR THE FIRST TIME, Kerelle reflected, if they weren't in mortal peril this might actually be rather fun. She and Flaveren skimmed along the tracks in one of her spherical shields, like a ball guided through an amusement game. The smooth rails offered little surface resistance, and she was able to speed them along much faster than they would have been able to move on foot.

From his tight expression and his hard grip on her hand, Flaveren might disagree on the "fun" part. At least he wasn't nauseous.

On the horizon, a dark mass took shape ahead of them on the tracks. They were catching up with the train.

"When we get close, I'm going to leap us up onto the roof of the back car," she explained urgently. "Can you cover us against any enemy fire?"

He gave her a terse nod, and Kerelle felt him gather his strength. She turned her attention to her own task as the back of the train rapidly grew in their vision. They crested a rise, and then they were right there, close enough to make out the details on the train's roof.

Details like the large guns, aimed directly at them.

"Got it," Flaveren muttered as the guns fired in a thunderous twin report. At close range the force was staggering, even with hers and Flaveren's combined shields. But she couldn't allow them to lose momentum, not if they were going to make it up to the roof and prevent further volleys. Kerelle gave her shield-sphere an upwards shove from behind, and then small-arms fire was bouncing off them as they landed on the roof.

"Off the train, but let them down gently," she panted to Flaveren. He gave her a single nod of understanding and swept the nearest group off their feet, flinging them into the thin air off the side of the train car. They landed softly, however - Flaveren was following her instructions to shield their falls.

Kerelle reached for another group. They kept firing uselessly at her, even as she swept them all into a pile and tossed them over the side, encased in a spherical shield of their own. They'd have bruises, certainly, but they'd walk away.

With the psionics at too close range for the big guns, the guards had little meaningful defense against them. Together Kerelle and Flaveren made short work of the soldiers on the roof, and soon they were alone atop the train.

"We'll need to find the connector to decouple the cars," she started to say, but she was interrupted by another shriek of metal. The car began to shake violently, and then slow. Ahead of them, the rest of the train began to speed away.

Anniya! She called out urgently. *It's disconnected, Flaveren and I are on the cargo cars now. Can you block it from returning with help and then get over here?*

The other woman sent her affirmation, just as Ilyen appeared on the roof.

Kerelle gasped in alarm at the blood soaking his clothes. Dark bruises bloomed across the teleporter's face, and he was breathing heavily.

"I'm fine. Blood's not mine," he said tersely, not meeting her eyes. "Get Sandrel over here and let's start packing this shit up before anyone else gets here."

Kerelle commed Sandrel, and received assurance he would be there in a matter of minutes. She eyed Ilyen warily.

"Are you sure you're all right? What happened?"

"There was a pair of telekinetics guarding the connector. They didn't want to be reasonable. Now they're not guarding it." From the set of his jaw, that was all he wanted to say on the subject.

They were saved from any further discussion as the ship swooped down above them to hover over the now-stalled cars.

Sandrel's voice crackled over the comm. "Long range scans show that we're good for now, but I imagine company will be incoming shortly. Let's get loaded up and get out of here."

The hatch on the train's roof was locked from the inside, but they simply wrenched it off with a telekinetic yank. Inside, crate after crate of celsum lay waiting in neat rows.

Flaveren eyed the crates, and the open hatch they'd come through. "Tight fit getting these out."

Ilyen gave a slight shrug, still radiating tension. "Won't be tight at all if we just tear the roof off." Lacking any other ideas, that was exactly what they did. Kerelle was starting to get tired from her earlier exertions with the other train, but the three of them together were able to rip off the top of the cargo car with little difficulty. The others soon joined them, and then there was no time to talk. They worked as quickly as they could, floating the heavy crates up and into the open hatch of Sandrel's ship. Inside, Galhen and Oliven dragged the crates deeper into the cargo hold; they were still heavy enough a telekinetic would probably need to tidy them up later.

The car's pile of crates had significantly diminished when Lilika's voice rang into her mind. *Aircraft approaching, high speed. Leave whatever is left, we need to get out.*

Kerelle shot her a quick affirmation and relayed the message to the rest of the team. They'd just scrambled into the hold and shut the hatch behind them when the ship lurched upward.

"Secure cargo and strap in," Sandrel ordered over the intercom. "They're coming in fast and there's a lot of them."

He jerked the ship right, and Kerelle was thrown sideways. The crates creaked ominously and began to shift.

Shit, those were *heavy*. If the crates got thrown around during some fancy flying, they'd pummel the ship as sure as an enemy cannon.

Which meant this next part was going to be dangerous but necessary.

"Non-telekinetics, out of the cargo bay," she barked. "Flaveren, Koren, help me hold the crates down. Ilyen and Melaris, get them secured under the cargo straps. We need to get this done before things get too hot outside."

There was a scramble to get started, and not a moment too soon - the ship banked sharply, and Kerelle's pile of crates thunked hard against the shield she'd encased them in. Melaris and Ilyen worked as quickly as they could, fitting the cargo bay's harnesses over the crates with telekinetic precision. They were nearly finished when the ship banked again, and shook under the impact of enemy fire, and Flaveren was thrown from his feet against the wall. The impact stunned him, and the pile of crates he'd been holding went flying.

Time slowed. Melaris was too close, they couldn't miss her. She froze, an instinctive shield thrown before her, but it wasn't going to be enough, they were too heavy for her to hold so many -

Ilyen appeared beside her and gave her a hard yank out of its path, almost far enough. The next seconds were chaos, as the crates smashed against the side of the bay and buckled, celsum chunks spilling out as Melaris started screaming.

Kerelle had to shut it out, had to shut out *everything* except grabbing hold of the now-loose crates and chunk of celsum, immobilizing them in the air. *Hold the crates, hold the crates, hold the crates or we'll* all *die -*

Her arms were starting to tremble.

She heard Ilyen yell something about the medbay, saw him vanish from the corner of her eye. Koren retreated from her vision as well, and Melaris's sobs of agony faded down the hall - he must have been carrying her, though Kerelle couldn't afford to look.

The weight on her psionics lessened suddenly - Flaveren was reinforcing her. She gave him a strained nod and carefully maneuvered the crates back to their spot against the wall. She was about to ask for help with the cargo straps when Ilyen reappeared beside her, then popped over to deal with the crates.

He was, the disconnected part of her mind noted, covered in even *more* blood than before. Melaris's blood, this time. She shut down hard on the thought before it could spread. Succeed first, feel later.

With the crates finally safely secured, they were able to wrap the loose celsum chunks in netting and tie it down as well. Thank goodness Sandrel was well-equipped for large, unwieldy cargo.

Flaveren turned to Ilyen as they finished, his warm-toned skin gone pale. "Melaris - is she...?"

Ilyen's mouth tightened. "Not sure. She was alive when we left her, but Ambrel had his game face on. I think it was bad."

As he said it, the ship shuddered under fire and made another sharp turn - but not as quickly as Kerelle was accustomed. The heavy cargo, she realized with dull alarm, was probably affecting their maneuverability.

Maybe this would end up killing them all after all.

Feel later.

"We're not out of this yet." Her voice was more tinged with desperation than she would have liked. "Let's see what we can do to help Sandrel. Flaveren, come with me. Ilyen, can you take the gunnery?"

He gave her a salute and was gone. Flaveren took a deep,

measured breath and let it out again, and met her eyes with a quick nod. He'd had the same training she did. Feel later.

Kerelle reached out to Koren as they jogged to the cockpit, sending him to join Ilyen so that they'd have some telepathic comms with the gunnery. She could hear the boom of the ship's gun already - that had to be a good thing.

Sandrel's knuckles were white on the controls when they reached the cockpit, though his face was calm as always. Lilika was still as a statue in the copilot's chair.

"Shields at 41%," she said told him quietly. He gave a nod and said nothing.

The comm beeped, and Oliven's voice crackled to life. "Got things patched on the left engine, but it won't hold under much more of this. I think they're aiming for the engines." There was an edge of anxiety in the young telepath's voice, but no panic. Oliven was in his element.

"Acknowledged," Sandrel answered without looking. "Do what you can."

"What do you need from us?' Kerelle asked softly. It was obvious that Sandrel's concentration needed to be completely on the task at hand. Through the vidports alone, she could see enough enemy aircraft to make it clear they were in trouble. She didn't want to look at the scanners.

"Shield the engines, try to clear me a path out of atmosphere," he answered, not taking his eyes off the scene. "With this much weight I'm not sure I can outrun them."

She wasn't terribly pleased to have her suspicions confirmed.

"Flaveren, can you get to the engine room and get a shield up? Take Anniya for comms."

He gave her a quick nod and was off at a run. She relayed the plan, such as it was, to Koren, and got to work.

She focused on the closest group of aircraft, as they darted in to lay down another round of fire. She peppered their fuselage with sharp blows, and was rewarded when smoke began to flood out of two. They fell out of formation, but there were still far too many. She kept up her barrage, but so did they.

"Shields at 26," Lilika said sharply. Her mask was slipping; the possibility of being blasted apart in the skies over Dhenla II was becoming more real every moment. It was the first time Kerelle could ever remember seeing real fear on her face.

Stars and flame, this was a stupid way to die. They needed a way out, something to distract their foes and give Sandrel the opening he needed -

Her mind flashed back to *another* near miss, in darkness of space above Zharal V. Maybe that distraction could be arranged after all.

"Be ready for full thrusters," she called to Sandrel, and pinged her telepathic cohorts. Galhen would be a great help with this, but she didn't dare distract him from the medbay. But then, she had an even more powerful ally at hand.

Lilika - at the signal, can you project hard to the pilots around us that the ship is exploding and they're in danger of being caught in it?

The pilots? Lilika sounded startled at the request, but she caught on immediately. *You mean to clear them off so that Sandrel can get through. They won't be swayed for long.*

They don't have to be, just long enough. It can work. I did this once before. With one pilot, not a few dozen, but that was hardly worth mentioning now. It would work or it wouldn't.

She gave the signal, and shoved the thought to the enemies surrounding them with all her depleted strength. She felt amplification from Koren and Anniya then, and Lilika's power like a mighty wave, carrying their illusion to every craft in the sky. Suddenly the fighters around them broke off, mayday signals flashing as the illusion of imminent destruction ensnared their pilots. Sandrel gunned the engines forward and broke atmosphere.

The euphoria of survival swept over her, but she'd barely taken a giddy breath when Kerelle felt Lilika's stab of dismay.

Usually Lilika didn't project; she kept her thoughts and emotions as locked down as her expression. The effort to clear their path must have taken more than she expected.

The beautiful telepath's eyes swung over to hers.

It's Riyel. He caught "psionic terrorists" on several command channels, they know now we weren't a ConEn PsiCorp squad. He says the antipsionics are already nearly here and we have to get out of Jamanar, now.

Get out now. Without Riyel.

I know he's right, Lilika said. *And I knew this would likely be the outcome, with or without an attempt on the celsum. The most important thing is our mission, and by that measure our time here was a success.*

Lilika's thoughts were inaccessible again, but Kerelle didn't need to read them to know she was lying. She'd caught those glimpses in the dream they'd shared, of Lilika without her emotional armor. Riyel was her heart, and she was not all right at all.

She didn't think Lilika would appreciate her saying it, though, especially not in front of Sandrel - laser-focused as he was on the impending jump to hyper. She settled for a gentle telepathic touch, the mental equivalent of a pat on the shoulder.

The mission is important, Kerelle agreed. *But so is Riyel. It's all right to be upset.*

Lilika gave her a vague nod and withdrew, her mask firmly back in place. Kerelle let her go. As the world through the vidports bled away into hyper, she headed back to check in with the rest of the ship and get water boiling.

She couldn't be the only one who desperately needed a cup of tea.

FIVE

THEY WERE SAFE, in hyper, but it did little to help the grim mood that settled on the ship like a thick fog. They had, Kerelle supposed, been successful, but it was hard to feel that way with Melaris fighting for her life.

There'd been nothing to do but wait, their little group a tense knot in the mess. It was well into the dimmed lights of the ship's night cycle when Galhen and Nalea finally emerged from the medbay. They both looked likely to pass out on their feet.

"Melaris is stable," Galhen told them wearily, "Though her condition is still very serious. I've done all I can for now." The block on their bond that had been in place while he worked was fading, and Kerelle could feel how his entire body ached and trembled. He'd pushed himself hard.

"Will she be all right?" Flaveren blurted. He was projecting anxiety and guilt.

"Probably not for some time," Kerelle's husband answered bluntly. Exhaustion was wearing through his bedside manner. "She won't die. For tonight that's all I can do."

Another question started up, and Galhen's expression tightened. He didn't have any real answers, and he needed to sit down before he fell down.

"The best we can help Melaris right now is to let her rest, and let *Galhen* rest so his regeneratives can recover," Kerelle interrupted. She squeezed out between Flaveren and Anniya and took Galhen's arm. He leaned on her with a flash of gratitude.

The group parted with reluctant nods, and together they made their way back to their cabin.

"It *is* bad," he told her quietly as the door shut behind them. "The blunt force trauma was severe. Damaged organs, internal bleeding, a number of shattered bones."

Kerelle's stomach dropped. "Bad enough you can't fix it?"

"In stages, I can. I think." He sank heavily onto the bed. "I have all her vital organs functioning again, which is a vast improvement over several hours ago. The bone repair reagent will help, but first there have to be bones for it to work on." Kerelle's horror must have shown in her expression, because he added, "I didn't use the word *shattered* as an exaggeration."

She sat down on the edge of the bed, leaning over to stroke his hair gently. "Are *you* going to be all right?"

He sent her a little pulse of affection. "I'm not going to burn out, but I *will* likely have a rather unpleasant migraine tomorrow. I have Melaris under heavy sedation, so she should at least be able to rest without pain until I've recovered enough to start again."

Kerelle leaned in and kissed his forehead before she turned to leave. He was asleep before she turned off the lights.

The mess was empty except for Sandrel when she returned. The smuggler saluted her with his tea.

"Everyone else went to bed, or at least pretended to. I suspect Lilika is pacing her cabin and your one telekinetic is busy blaming himself for everything, but for now it's just you and me and the teapot. Speaking of?"

She accepted the offered mug gratefully and sipped slowly, savoring the gentle comfort it offered.

"Hell of a day," she said finally. From his weary posture, Sandrel was feeling the same.

"It was," he confirmed. "We've been in some pretty rough spots together, Fury, but I think this one is definitely top three."

"Thank you," she told him softly. At his questioning glance, she added, "For helping us. For staying with us. For guiding us safely out of mortal peril again and again, especially with an unnecessary risk this time."

He gave her a half shrug. "Maybe unnecessary, maybe not. Lilika's not wrong. None of this is going to pay for itself, and we can't exactly take jobs like we did."

"We can't keep doing *this*, either," she answered.

"Well, with the haul we're likely to get from what's in the cargo hold, we shouldn't have to think about it for awhile."

Something in his tone caught her attention. "You're thinking about it right now, aren't you."

He gave her that half-smirk, though it didn't quite reach his tired eyes. "I might be. We can't exactly take jobs like we did, but *other* people can take them for us. Not something I've ever tried before, I've always been more of an owner-operator kind of businessman than a tycoon. But Lilika's building networks out anyway, and she's already proven she can get mundanes on board too. Maybe we ought to take some of that celsum cash and invest it in hiring some *independent shippers* of our own, so next time we need an influx of capital we don't have to rob an industrial site."

He sipped his tea and grew serious again. "Because we *won't* be able to keep doing this. We got lucky this time, because SysTech was expecting ConEn, not us. Next time they'll be ready, and we'll take casualties your man can't fix. I know you. You won't put your people on the line for *things*."

"They're not *my people*," she protested. "We were all senior agents, I don't have any more right to lead than anyone else."

"But you *are* leading, and they *are* following you. That makes them *your people*." Another half smile, this one tinged bittersweet. "And I *do* know you, Kerelle. You'll do right by them any way you can."

She wished she shared his confidence. Some of her thoughts must have shown in her expression, because he laid a gentle hand on her arm as he got up. "Something to think about. Remember to get some sleep."

A soft *plunk* as he deposited his mug in the dish sanitizer, and Kerelle was alone with her thoughts.

***

"WHAT HAPPENED TO AMBREL?"

Galhen didn't look up from where he leaned back in the mess chair, eyes closed with a cold compress held to his forehead and his other hand wrapped around the teacup like it was a life preserver. He did incline his head towards the direction of Ilyen's voice, correctly ascertaining the teleporter had popped into the mess near the coffee.

"You may have noticed I made rather extensive use of my regeneratives yesterday."

"Yeah, but you use your regeneratives every time you set up a clinic at port. You don't usually get like *this*."

Galhen eased an eye open to squint at him. "There is a very large difference between boosting an immune system to fight off infection and un-rupturing several vital organs. I'll live, and so will Melaris, and that's enough." He closed his eyes again and settled back, lifting his near-empty cup. "I wouldn't say no to a refill, though."

Ilyen snorted and poured him more tea before settling into the seat beside him. Kerelle might still not use a word as strong as "friends," but relations between the two men had markedly improved over the past few months.

"Is Nalea joining us?" Kerelle asked. Nalea had headed straight from the medbay to her cabin the night before, and Kerelle hadn't seen her since. She wasn't surprised - she knew by now that Nalea preferred to process alone.

Ilyen shook his head. "Yesterday was a lot for her. I think she's planning to stay in her lab today."

"And you're not staying with her?" It wasn't an accusation; Galhen sounded genuinely surprised. It was also, in its way, an acknowledgement. Galhen had made considerable strides in his relationship with his sister, but Ilyen still was closer to Nalea than he was.

Ilyen shrugged. "She wants to be by herself right now. I'll bring her some food later and see if she's feeling better. Lab work really helps Nalea get steady, you know?"

Kerelle did know, and so she wasn't entirely surprised when the scientist emerged from her seclusion later in the afternoon looking significantly less ragged than the night before.

"Productive morning?" Kerelle asked as she poured Nalea some tea.

"Yes actually. I finished the refining process on some of the hemindrium we picked up from Lilika's group. Now I just need to do the assembly, and we'll have a new set of collar removal devices." Her brow furrowed a moment, and she looked like she was weighing whether to say more.

"Isn't that a good thing?" Kerelle asked. Nalea gave a half shrug.

"I guess. Yes. It means we'll have four devices instead of one, and that's good. I get nervous when we don't have backups."

"But?" Kerelle prompted. There was obviously *something* Nalea wasn't happy about.

"But it's still the same limited device. There's still the issue with not working on an active collar, obviously, but there's also the issue that opening one at a time, while requiring physical contact, is really just not efficient."

"They've worked very well so far," Kerelle noted. "We freed four people on Jamanar."

Nalea gave her a sidelong glance. "And how long did it take us to get four people?"

She didn't wait for Kerelle to answer. "They were fine for a first model, but you're not going to want to just do one-offs forever, and they don't really scale. I've been trying to figure out how we get around that."

Kerelle's ears perked up. "Have you discovered anything?"

"Not yet. But if your new friends can refrain from getting hit by any more shipping crates, I can get serious about studying it."

IF THE PALHEE safe house had seemed full on their last trip, this time it felt positively cramped. They'd all squeezed into its common room to discuss what came next; their numbers far outstripped the room's available furniture, and the majority of the group sat cross-legged on the floor.

Lilika had one of the chairs, naturally. Melaris, still heavily bandaged but alert, had another. With Galhen's help the injured telekinetic had greatly improved over the last week. It would still be a few weeks before the bones in her ribs and arms were fully healed, but she was out of danger.

And recovered enough to joke about it. "Of all the ways I thought I might die by joining this fight, 'crushed by a shipping crate' wasn't anywhere on the list." She'd arched a red eyebrow and almost smiled. "If anyone asks, we're going to tell them it happened in the battle itself."

Kerelle could agree to that.

They'd come out ahead from Jamanar, overall. They'd

doubled their firepower, they'd found a buyer for the celsum shortly after arriving, and there had been no fatalities in their little team. Now they just needed to decide what happened now.

"We have a good number of promising leads to continue recruiting," Lilika announced to the table. "From the transport records we secured, I compiled a list of personal acquaintances that I believe would be interested in joining our case. I also shared the transport record with Riyel, and he identified several additional prospects. Riyel is willing to be the go-between to contact them." Lilika's face and tone were solidly back in their impeccable impassivity; however she felt about all this was buried deep.

Galhen leaned forward; *his* concern was painted on his face. "Have you heard from Riyel since we left Jamanar? Is he all right?"

She dipped her head in acknowledgement. "I have, and he is. The dream technique is proving invaluable for staying in touch across distance. He does not seem to be under any sort of suspicion, but he told me the entire PsiCorp garrison is being pulled from Jamanar and reassigned. Apparently SysTech is not taking any chances that we may still be in the system."

Kerelle frowned. "They figured out why we were there, then. They wouldn't bother pulling the garrison if they only believed we were there to steal celsum."

Lilika nodded. "They aren't saying anything, of course. They never do. But Riyel has caught bits of management chatter to confirm it." A flicker of emotion crossed her face and was gone. "He's volunteered to be our eyes on the inside, and to continue helping us identify and recruit psionic dissidents. We can set up another dream meeting to discuss it in person. So to speak."

Her gaze slid to Sandrel. "Captain Marene and I also had a very interesting discussion about securing ongoing funds."

Sandrel nodded and took over. "Smuggling is good money; that's why I got into it in the first place. We're going to be too busy to run jobs now - and frankly, the way things are going, pretty soon you lot are going to be too high-profile for that kind of work." He quirked a grin. "Which means it's time to get into management."

He gestured to Lilika. "We'll work together on recruiting the right kind of agent, and connecting them with the work. If all goes well, we get more underworld connections and a steady income. No more robbing trains."

Kerelle suspected she wasn't the only one at the table who could get behind that idea.

In short order they'd decided on their next leads. With Nalea's additional devices, they could now attempt to rescue multiple people at once. This would of course require additional transport, but Sandrel pointed out that their proceeds from the celsum were large enough to cover a small ship, with plenty left over for essentials. The plan was approved, and there was only one thing left to settle.

OLIVEN WENT WHITE.

"Captain Marene, you can't...you can't *mean* this."

"I do," Sandrel replied calmly. "The new ship needs a pilot, and you're more than ready."

"But...I haven't been flying that long, what if I make a mistake and you aren't there to fix it - "

"Oliven, you've been flying for over a year now. That's longer than I was before I did my first independent flight. Most flight training schools are only a few months. You'll be fine."

"But I...I'm not *you*, I'm not nearly as good - "

"No, you're not nearly as *experienced*," Sandrel corrected. "Am I a more skilled pilot than you? Of course I am. I've been flying for almost twenty years. But you've mastered basic flight, you do well when we drill evasive maneuvering, and you've got great instincts. And yes, you've never flown actual combat. But honestly, kid? Not that many people have. If we tried to hire a pilot it'd be hard to find someone who had the experience *and* was willing to sign on with us."

Oliven opened his mouth, and Sandrel held up a quelling hand. "And no, we're not just settling for you because we can't get what we *really* want." His tone softened. "*You're* good enough, Oliven. Even if we had a line out the door of people jockeying for this job, you'd be good enough to give them a run for their money."

Oliven's eyes were suspiciously bright, but he only gave a sharp nod. Sandrel broke into a smile and gripped his shoulder.

"Congratulations then, Captain Zharus. Let's go pick you out a ship."

SIX

THE NEXT FEW months passed in a blur. Lilika and Riyel worked their way down the list of potential recruits, and more often than not it was Kerelle and Ilyen who went in for pickup, sometimes with help from one of the other psionics. It was exhausting and rather nerve-wracking, but it kept her busy, and the satisfaction of watching a PsiCorp collar pop harmlessly open never got old.

As their group grew, however, so did their ability to tackle objectives without Kerelle's hands-on involvement. More and more often, she found herself directing missions rather than doing them.

It still felt weird.

"You can't do everything yourself," Sandrel had reminded her one morning as she brooded into her coffee. "That's the whole reason we started this thing, remember?"

"I remember," she sighed. "But it feels wrong to stay behind and send other people into danger."

"Other people who are also highly trained, highly competent psionic fighters." He gave her a pointed look over his coffee mug. "You didn't conscript a bunch of schoolkids here, Kerelle.

Your team can handle themselves, and you're not sending anyone into the field who doesn't want to go."

"I know." If anything, some of their new recruits were a little *too* eager to take the fight to SysTech. She'd had to explain more than once why they were focusing on steadily building strength instead of showy attacks.

"Yet the way you're glaring at your coffee mug seems unconvinced." Sandrel took a deliberative sip, still watching her. "And if this is still about the fact that you're in charge at all, you should remember that you're in charge because those other highly trained, highly competent people trust you to lead them. Trust *them*, Kerelle."

———

"EVANDRA, YOU BUSY? YOU TOO, AMBREL."

Kerelle started at Ilyen's abrupt appearance, nearly dropping her tea. The teleporter didn't seem to notice, instead glancing between them impatiently.

Galhen raised an eyebrow. "Not terribly, no. Has something happened?"

"Nalea wants to see you guys in the lab. I'll tell her you're coming." He popped away again before either of them could answer.

I suppose some indication as to what this is about was too much to ask. Galhen sounded more resigned than annoyed.

Apparently. He didn't seem upset though, so hopefully not a crisis. Although - she thought back to the incident with the giant reptiles, back on that remote moon where they'd first fled from Dalanva - *if it* were *a crisis, he might be more excited than upset anyway.*

As it turned out, Nalea had not summoned them because of a crisis in the making. Rather, in fact, the opposite.

They ducked into Nalea's cabin/lab to find her practically

bouncing with excitement. One of her removal devices was sitting on the counter, partially disassembled.

"I've been going about this wrong," she announced without preamble. "The collars were never the right thing." From her expectant look, they were meant to have a response.

"Context, please," Galhen prompted gently. She blinked.

"Right. Okay, right after the whole celsum shitshow I was working on refining hemindrium for the rest of the collar removal devices, and I was talking to Kerelle about how they're actually not that good for what we need them to do."

She held up a hand as Galhen and Ilyen both opened their mouths, presumably to protest. "Yes, yes, I know, they've performed admirably, I'm brilliant and you're lucky to have me, whatever. And yes, for being something I hacked together from a broken collar while we were lost in deep space, they were great. But they don't *scale.*

"As long as we need one-to-one physical contact," she continued, "getting people out is going to be slow and danger-ous." Her eyes flicked briefly to Ilyen, who had frequently been tasked with the actual removals on account of his ability to get past defenses. "For them *and* for us."

Galhen leaned in, intrigued. "You've found a way around that, then?"

"Theoretically." Nalea picked up the partially-assembled device, careful not to drop any of its pieces. "I don't think there's much potential in the current model, actually. I spent a lot of time trying over the last few months with no success. The limitations around needing physical contact, and only working on a single collar at once, are pretty much hardwired into its setup. But that's the thing."

She held up the little device, though Kerelle wasn't sure what she was supposed to be seeing. "We first designed this to take Oliven's collar off, right? I used Ilyen's control card to figure out how to mimic the signals it could send a collar, and then used those signals to make the collar think a control card was telling it to disengage. That's what these things are.

"But we're running into our limitations because I designed it to act *on* a collar. And maybe we're being too literal there."

Nalea leaned against the counter and looked at them. "What if instead of mimicking a control card sending a release signal, we could act on the control card itself, and tell it to *actually* send that signal?"

Kerelle went still. "And if we had one of the senior managers' cards, the kind that controlled a lot of collars at once…"

Nalea's grin was almost savage. "It'd be a lot easier than going one at a time, wouldn't it?"

"And you think this is workable?" Galhen's question held a note of urgency. "You can build this, with what we have?"

"Not entirely," Nalea acknowledged. "That's actually what I wanted to talk to you about."

RIYEL TILTED HIS HEAD, considering. "Does it matter what *kind* of control card we steal? Does it have to be one of the master cards?"

"Doesn't sound like it," Kerelle clarified. "Nalea said she just needs one that's synced to an active collar. The *number* of active collars is apparently irrelevant."

"Well, that does open up our options a bit. Stealing a master card wouldn't be a trivial task." Riyel didn't say what they were all thinking; if this worked, they would have to tackle that task eventually.

That was a problem for later, assuming Nalea's hypothesis panned out in the first place.

"A single-collar card, though," he continued, voice thoughtful. "We could even avoid SysTech entirely."

"You're thinking of the PsiCorp on lease," Galhen said

quietly. Kerelle sent him a soft pulse of comfort; the memories of his time with Dalanva were still painful for him, particularly how she'd *used* that control card.

"I am," Riyel replied, his warm eyes full of sympathy. Lilika must have shared details, or else he was picking up Galhen's discomfort himself. "Stars forgive us, but as reprehensible as the practice is, it's also our best opportunity. Private citizens with PsiCorp servants will have their own security, of course, but they will be a far softer target than a SysTech base. Especially if their guard is down."

"Do you have any names and whereabouts you recommend, or should I get my agents on it?" Lilika put in. "I would rather not simply prowl the streets of wealthy neighborhoods looking for likely targets, although" her smile was mirthless "that rather *would* work as a last resort."

Riyel nodded. "I have a few ideas. The timing favors us - one of the major fashion shows is coming up in a few weeks here on Iressu. There will almost certainly be multiple opportunities among the attendees. And who knows?" He smiled, though his eyes were shadowed. "If we do a good enough job with the extraction, they won't even know we have it."

SEVEN

ASTALLIA FASHION WEEK was a lavish affair. Kerelle had once passed through Iressu's largest city, years and years ago, but the Astallia of that visit had been nothing like this. Financial-district boulevards she vaguely remembered as nondescript were now bright and festive, hung with shimmering cloth and aglow in a sea of tiny lights, as if miniature stars had nestled in their nooks and crannies. Banners advertising designer events hung at regular intervals from buildings and signposts, gigantic images of spectacularly-clad models reigning over the streets like a sartorial pantheon.

Lilika's voice popped into her head with a shade of admonishment.

Don't gawk, Kerelle. Gawking is for tourists.

Lilika herself would not be out of place staring down from one of those banners. The silvery fabric of her dress seemed impossibly light, and it draped around her in an effortless play of light and shadow that begged to be painted. The color perfectly accentuated Lilika's rich brown skin, and the subtle metallic glow of the rose shimmer dust she'd applied to her face and shoulders. Silver strands threaded her tight curls in a headdress that managed to be both subtle and complex, culminating in the soft pink gem that hung low on her forehead.

She looked like a queen. Or a goddess.

It had seemed counterintuitive to Kerelle, to dress to stand out when they wanted to blend in. Lilika had only smiled and shaken her head.

"We are going to an affair of peacocks, my dear. Anyone who's anyone, or *wants* to be anyone, will be dressed to shine. We will just be one more, and we will be noticed less than if we were dressed for subtlety." She'd made a slow spin before the mirror, giving herself a critical examination. "And when it's time for us to leave quietly, this will make it easier. The dress is all anyone will remember about me."

Kerelle herself was dressed far less adventurously. For this mission, she was taking on the role of personal assistant to Lilika's socialite. She was back in the business suit she'd worn to their first meeting on Cildazya, her dark hair pulled back in a severe bun and an oversized handbag looped over her shoulder. She could be anyone, dressed like this.

All the same, Kerelle had to fight from jumping as a camera flashed. She knew it didn't *really* matter; even *if* their pictures were published in the fashion pages alongside the sea of other attendees, and even *if* someone at SysTech saw it and recognized them - even then, they would be long gone before anything came of it. All the same, it made her feel vulnerable.

Still, she kept her expression neutral, and followed Lilika up the steps to the gallery without hesitation. They certainly *looked* the part, and the doorman hardly needed Lilika's slight telepathic nudge to believe she was on the guest list. He gave them a polite smile and unhooked the rope. A brief stop in the lobby to drop their coats and bag, and then they were inside.

Lilika's admonishment not to gawk was easier said than done. The art gallery's reception was being held in its large atrium, which Kerelle supposed had the double benefit of holding a large number of people comfortably, and keeping tipsy guests away from the actual art. Not that it was too much of a sacrifice - the atrium itself was a work of art, all graceful soaring arches and streaming sunset light.

The various people flittering around its marble floors were equally eye-catching. Everywhere she turned, the scene was packed with dazzlingly arrayed guests, their dress ranging from elegant to outlandish. Like Lilika, many wore a light application of shimmer dust on their exposed skin, and the orange light of the fading day lent the crowds an almost supernatural glow.

Not everyone, of course, was a glittering guest. Interspersed between the languidly conversing partygoers were men and women who looked much like Kerelle did, fetching drinks, holding bags, making calls or simply hovering and awaiting instructions.

Kerelle tried to school her features into the frazzled resignation she saw on the other other assistants' faces. Lilika had been right - she and Kerelle were not going to attract attention just by being here. They were simply one more exquisite socialite and her staff.

Lilika, of course, glided through the crowds unbothered by the press, a serenely inscrutable smile on her lips. *Keep up, my dear,* she said into Kerelle's head. *We've only a limited window before our man vanishes into his own amusements.*

"Their man" was Anrien Yulus Nevel, the owner of the legendary Studio Nevelaen fashion house and, by all accounts, impressively degenerate even among a social set that considered debauchery an art form.

"Ambrosia, flickerdust, dreamrider, diamond joy," Lilika had listed, ticking off each drug with a flick of her finger, "and that's just what he does in public. His parties are synonymous with excess - and in *this* crowd, it's not excessive unless someone dies." Lilika had wrinkled her nose in delicate distaste. "The bloodsport is part of the appeal, really. Anrien is into his forties now, and he hasn't slowed down from when he first inherited the Nevel fortune fifteen years ago. He's had three near-fatal overdoses that made the gossip pages, stars know how many more that didn't. Everyone wonders if this is the year his body finally collapses under it all - and they want to be at the party where it does.

"For now, though," she'd continued, "I suspect the services of his leased regenerative are granting him borrowed time. In any case, he remains as vain and lecherous as ever. Which is precisely what will allow us to acquire his card."

The atrium was rapidly filling, its large floor concealed beneath the glittering crowd. Nonetheless, that crowd parted for them.

Heads turned to stare at Lilika in open admiration, but no one approached them as they made their way across the floor. Kerelle expected it was the influence of Lilika's telepathy, but to her surprise she found that the other woman was projecting only the lightest touch.

It's not necessary to do more, not yet, Lilika commented. *Perhaps when everyone's had a bit more sparkling wine, and the ambrosia comes out, some of them will find their spirit of adventure. But for now? This is a very exclusive set, my dear, and no one recognizes me. That's reason enough not to approach.*

Kerelle's pulse spiked. *They think we're suspicious?*

Lilika's laughter echoed in her mind. *Oh yes, but not in the sense that you're thinking. They think we're something* far *worse than escaped psionic rebels.* Her amusement sparkled over her thoughts. *They think we're* new money.

We're not the only ones, she added. *I don't know what that poor girl in the red gown was thinking.*

Kerelle's eyes followed Lilika's thought to the pale, delicate-looking young woman in a rather lovely scarlet dress. She was smiling as she talked to a slightly older woman in black - or rather, talked *at,* as the other woman's disinterest was plain on her face.

Who are they?

The woman in black is Kaleria Manan Avisterai, sixth-generation scion of the Avisterai shipping fortune, prominent philanthropist and patroness of the arts. The girl in red is probably the daughter of someone who made their money in the last decade or so. Rich enough to buy her way in, but as she's discovering, acceptance can't be bought.

And here I thought the PsiCorp lived the high life.

Different worlds, my dear. The denizens of this *world wouldn't be caught dead anywhere that catered to PsiCorp. We don't even count as new money - we don't properly have any money at all.*

Funny that it had taken Kerelle most of her life to realize what had apparently been clear all along.

You don't want in on this crowd anyway, they're wretched. I had an assignment some years ago that took me into their orbit, posing as an executive's mistress to get close to a rival financier. It was quite possibly the most miserable summer I've ever spent.

Lilika broke off then, her energy abruptly focused elsewhere, and so Kerelle's burning follow-up questions on that piece of information went unanswered. A few seconds passed.

I've found him, Lilika told her. *Up the stairs, one of the private rooms near the balcony. He's off to a strong start.* She paused. *His psionics are with him.*

Kerelle's stomach lurched. They'd discussed this beforehand, agreed that they were here to get the control card and get out, that this mission wasn't well-equipped for an escape. Even if it were, the psionics here were unknown quantities, and revealing themselves would compromise the entire operation. They needed that control card - if Nalea was able to rework her device as proposed, it would benefit many *more* psionics. Perhaps even the ones here with Nevel tonight.

It still didn't make her feel good about leaving them, as if they mattered less than a bit of circuiting. Coward that she was, Kerelle had hoped to not actually encounter them.

We can't save everyone, Lilika reminded her. *Not all at once. Think of it as a strategic retreat here, so that we can position ourselves for a later victory.* Kerelle sent back her acknowledgment, though she knew it was overlaid with reluctance.

His secretary is the only telepath in the room, I believe. Keep us shielded please, and I'll focus on dealing with Anrien and the others.

They came to a closed door off the main upstairs hall. Lilika pushed it open without hesitation.

The cloying scent in the air almost sent Kerelle into a coughing fit. Thin whorls of sweet-smelling smoke wafted about the room, wreathing its inhabitants in a shimmery white mist. There were six people in the room altogether, four partygoers lounging on the large sofas and the two psionics in chairs flanking the one that must be Nevel. They were recognizable by their collars, of course, but also by the way the placement of their seats indicated a subtle *outside.*

The lounging people all had full glasses, presumably of whatever was in the tall bottles that sat on the central table. Nevel was holding some sort of elaborate water pipe in his other hand. All of them were stopped, glassy eyes staring at the unexpected interruption.

"Oh!' Lilika cried, a hand flying to her mouth. "Oh, I'm so very sorry! We must have the wrong room." The telepathic suggestion hit like a tidal wave, and even Kerelle felt it push against her. Lilika was almost painfully beautiful, and so *innocent,* dark eyes wide and guileless in a radiant face that suddenly seemed ten years younger. So sweet, and so amusingly *corruptible.*

"Not at all, my dear," Nevel responded, throwing open an arm in welcome. "I believe you have precisely the *right* room. Do come in and have a seat."

Lilika blushed, somehow looking more the ingenue than

Kerelle could ever have imagined her. "Oh no, I couldn't bear to intrude - "

"As if such a lovely creature as yourself could ever be unwelcome." He shifted to give her space beside him, summoning a smoldering look. "The stars themselves must have guided your path."

Lilika blushed again and shyly made her way over to the spot next to him on the sofa, Kerelle following unheeded at her heels. Kerelle had half expected Nevel to send her away, but Lilika seemed to be encouraging the room not to notice her. It wasn't all that difficult - *the help* was not noteworthy under the best of circumstances, and none of these people were remotely near the best of mental circumstances. As for the psionics, well, there was only one telepath, sprawled on his chair looking bored, and no C1 could be a match for Lilika.

As they got closer Kerelle was struck by just how *handsome* Nevel was. She'd expected that a man who spent fifteen years flirting with overdose would wear signs of it on his face, but his skin was clear and healthy, with none of the discoloration or scarred sores that she associated with addicts. Only the faint fine lines at his eyes and brow indicated that he was in his fifth decade.

The reason for that became abruptly clear, as the psionic sitting beside him lightly touched her hand to his wrist. Kerelle might have mistaken it for a gesture of intimacy, if she hadn't seen Galhen administer that same light touch countless times - the physical contact a regenerative needed to heal.

Apparently it was easy to keep your looks, when you had a pet regenerative to repair the damage you did to yourself. That hollow feeling opened up in Kerelle's heart again, as the dark-haired woman lifted her hand and settled back into her own chair. She wondered how the regenerative felt, knowing that *this* was what her precious gift was used for.

Lilika gingerly seated herself beside Nevel with a show of

prim uncertainty. He offered her the pipe and after a token reluctance, she took it. Double vision struck as she raised it to her lips - the sight in Kerelle's eyes of Lilika lowering the pipe again untouched, the sight in Kerelle's mind of her taking a deep inhalation. Lilika coughed a few times for verisimilitude and Nevel took it back again, laughing. Languidly he handed it over his shoulder to the telepath, who took a long hit with no reluctance.

Disapproval surged from the regenerative, and Kerelle had to catch herself from looking over, startled. The dark-haired woman's expression didn't change, but her frustration and annoyance radiated with almost physical heat. *Why is he so* inconsiderate? *He* knows *how much this tires me out, he* knows *it's hard enough for me to keep Nevel's stupid ass alive and pretty until the next time he gets a deep-cleaning from the C3s, and now I have to clean* his *blood out too. It would serve him right if this time I just* let *the addiction set in.* A flood of guilt then - the regenerative would never actually do that. The telepath might be a self-centered ass sometimes but the two of them were in this together.

Kerelle upped her own shields to block out the bright-burning projection, careful to keep her own thoughts off her face. That rather answered her question on the regenerative's feelings. She felt slightly sick, too, knowing she wasn't going to help them.

Not tonight, she reminded herself. *Doesn't mean not ever.* It didn't really make her feel better.

Meanwhile, Lilika was playing her role. She was engaged in murmured conversation with Nevel, giggling and swaying gently as though whatever was in that pipe was taking effect.

It's Starsbreath, she supplied into Kerelle's mind, her brisk tone at odds with the act she was currently putting on for Nevel. *And technically illegal here on Iressu, not that those kinds of rules apply to anyone at* this *party. It works in our favor here in that its users can be delightfully suggestible. I'm hardly having to do any work at all to convince him to show me the cards.* She paused. *Dreadfully unhealthy, however, even in proximity. We'll both want to have your husband clean out our lungs.*

There was little need to focus on keeping the shields up; Nevel's secretary was leaning back in his seat with eyes half-closed, lost in whatever bliss the smoke had bestowed on him. The other partygoers were similarly occupied; whatever gossip Nevel's current activity might yield was less compelling than their own glaze-eyed contemplations. Kerelle drifted closer to Lilika and Nevel's couch.

"And you aren't frightened at *all?*" Lilika's voice had gone breathy, her eyes round with convincing awe. "I heard psionics can be - " her voice dropped to a whisper "- *dangerous.*"

Nevel's lazy grin showed all his teeth. "Maybe if they were running about the wild, my dear. But I assure you mine are no trouble."

"How can you be sure?"

"Jerise and Feren are quite tame," he answered, flicking a magnanimous hand in his psionics' direction. "But if they ever *weren't,*" he added conspiratorially, "I can deal with them."

Lilika was all innocent amazement. "How?"

Nevel shifted so that an arm went around her shoulders, and reached his other hand into his jacket. He withdrew something small and held it up like a personal triumph. "Those collars aren't just for *show,* sweetling. All I have to do is flick this little switch, and they'll be very eager to cooperate."

His smug, oily tone set Kerelle's blood boiling. She hadn't missed how the regenerative's - *Jerise's* - shoulders stiffened when he pulled out the cards.

Steady, Lilika admonished. *Keep your cool and I can get us out of here without firing a shot. Start an incident and we might not escape with cards* or *psionics.*

Lilika leaned in to look at the cards, pressing herself against Nevel as she did. Again Kerelle felt the echo of Lilika's touch on his mind, at once more subtle and more compelling than anything Kerelle could do herself.

"This room feels so very *crowded*, don't you think?" She looked through her lashes at him, projecting unsure innocence, that this wasn't the kind of girl she was usually, but he was so *charming* she couldn't *help* herself.

Nevel wore a knowing smirk, and Kerelle suspected that the telepathic suggestion that Lilika was besotted with him had been wholly unnecessary. He'd never had any doubt he could easily seduce the naive young socialite who'd appeared in the doorway. Kerelle didn't care to think about the implications that held for his usual parties.

"Stifling, my dear. A bit of privacy sounds like the most lovely idea." He rose unhurried from the couch and offered her his hand, the smirk widening. She took it blushingly.

All right, next phase, Lilika said. *You retrieve the coats and bag from downstairs, I'll give you our location as soon as I have it. This shouldn't take long.*

Will you be all right?

Completely. Lilika's response was dry. *A drug-addled aristocrat is well within the bounds of what I can manage.*

Kerelle took her word on that. Lilika might not have any traditional combat gifts, but she certainly had her own weapons. And she knew how to use them exquisitely.

No one looked at her as she made a brisk line downstairs to the coat check. Without Lilika at her side she was even less notable, just someone's errand girl doing her job. She held that feeling like a shield nonetheless, discouraging anyone who might be experiencing a spell of curious boredom from looking in her direction.

It was early enough in the night that there was no line for the coats. That was fortunate, because no sooner had she collected the coats and her oversized handbag then Lilika pinged her with a location.

Back up the stairs, down a side hall much like the first, another closed door. She went in.

It was another lounge room much like the last, except that this one only had two couches, and one had Nevel snoring loudly on it. Kerelle blinked as she suddenly realized he was naked, and that Lilika was nonchalantly scattering his clothes around the room.

She handed Kerelle the two control cards, and smirked at her expression. "Oh, he won't remember much of anything from all this, but at least he'll assume he had a good time."

"What happened?" She didn't see any signs of violence, but Nevel seemed to have passed out rather quickly.

"Fairly standard for him, from what I've heard. We got in here and I convinced him we'd have even *more* fun with a few hits of dreamrider. Not that there was much convincing to do, really. All I had to do was say it. Then down the hatch it went, and then it was just the smallest nudge to push him from relaxed to asleep." Lilika draped his jacket rakishly over the side of the couch, and cocked her head at the prone aristocrat.

More money than most people could even wrap their minds around, and this is what he does with it. Do you think he's happy? If he is, why is he so eager to obliterate himself?

The sudden burst of philosophy took Kerelle by surprise. In vulnerable repose, Nevel had lost his smug patina, and now he just looked a touch pathetic. *I don't think he's happy, no,* she said finally. *He's not so different from the PsiCorp on that.*

Except that all he *has to do to live differently is just decide that he wants to.* There was an undercurrent of bitterness in her voice that Kerelle had not expected, but just as quickly the feeling vanished as Lilika locked down her thoughts once more.

"Right then," she said briskly as she grabbed Kerelle's bag and started pulling out the change of clothes they'd packed earlier. "He'll be out for at least a few hours, and he may or may not notice he's missing the cards. I imagine at some point he'll alert SysTech and they'll rekey his psionics' collars, but we'll still have the two intact cards. That ought to give Nalea something to work with."

She finished fastening her shirt and stuffed the ethereal silver dress unceremoniously into the bag. A few quick yanks and the headdress was off as well. The delicate socialite vanished like a trick of the light, and the pragmatic, practical spymistress was back again.

"Now let's find that fire escape and be on our way. I have a rich narcissist's sweat to wash off my shoulder."

As they hustled down the hall towards escape, Kerelle couldn't help but think of the regenerative Jerise sitting down this same hall, waiting for Nevel to need her again, or perhaps trying to prevent her telepath friend from following his same path.

We'll come back for you, she promised them in her mind. *We'll come back for everyone.*

EIGHT

NALEA WAS BUZZING with excitement when they returned with the cards, and vanished into her lab with them almost immediately. Reconfiguring the removal devices to accept the new input, however, proved a less-than-simple task, and she soon admitted it was going to take more research before they saw any usable results. Which was why two months later, when the opportunity to recruit a prominent C3 pyrokinetic arose, Kerelle found herself once again in disguise.

If I'd known this was going to be such a large part of my life, I might have invested in some theater classes.

Kerelle leaned back in her lounge chair, projecting mundanity and hoping her large sunglasses did at least some of the work. She was, after all, only one of many dark-haired women sunbathing in fashionable beachwear beside the resort's shimmering pool. There was no reason for anyone to look closely enough to see *escaped PsiCorp agent Kerelle Evandra* instead of just another vacationer.

She still felt horribly exposed. Her poolside coverup left much of her shoulders and collarbone bare. She *knew* that the telltale pale strip where her collar had been was now gone, faded to the same healthy coloring as the skin around it. But she still *felt* it and, sitting in the bright sunlight with nothing to hide behind, the irrational part of her mind was absolutely convinced it must be visible anyway.

She forced the thought down, and focused on projecting - and keeping her shields up. The PsiCorp group was further out, still milling about the entrance of a large pool complex, but she could still sense them. With her shields up tight, they shouldn't be able to sense *her*. Hopefully.

She knew she was being paranoid again. The PsiCorp were here to have fun. Even the nosiest telepath was unlikely to bother with delving into nearby mundane minds when they had better things to do. There were a handful she'd known who *did* get a voyeuristic thrill from spying on the thoughts of those around them, but most telepaths didn't bother. Mundanes tended to vastly overestimate how interesting their thoughts were.

Kerelle forced herself to breathe deeply, and took another sip of her iced tea. Their target wasn't a telepath, which always made it harder. For the moment there was nothing to do but wait until she heard from Koren. He was serving as communications liaison, since Kerelle could hardly carry a comm on her pool clothes without drawing attention. Ilyen was around somewhere scouting, but he'd engaged his shielding exercises, and she couldn't quite sense where he'd hidden himself.

Kerelle had another moment's wistful thought for Nalea's upgraded collar removal idea. She knew that, realistically, it would take quite some time for Nalea to develop a new device from the control cards they'd given her - assuming she was able to do so at all. Kerelle was still fervently looking forward to her success, and with it the possibility that her days of awkward undercover work might be numbered.

She finally got a soft mental ping from Koren. *Ilyen commed me, says they're on the move. As expected, headed towards you.* He paused. *Apparently they have a security detail, though not an overly large one.*

Of course not - too many guards would strain the illusion that they were there to protect rather than control.

Ilyen says psiblockers on the guards. Koren's voice held a troubled note. It troubled her, too, and not just because it meant she couldn't lean on telepathic suggestion to get them through this. If the security detail was openly equipped with antipsionic defenses, perhaps SysTech wasn't concerned about *straining the illusion* after all.

She sent back her acknowledgement. Kerelle's lounge chair was strategically located by one of the primary poolside bars; it had been virtually guaranteed the PsiCorp group would head here first after they arrived. She leaned back in her chair, pretending to be absorbed in her drink, and waited.

It was a larger group than she was expecting, transforming the area from a tranquil oasis to a day club in minutes. It was hard to miss the guards as well, their grey uniforms stark against the psionics' bright-patterned resort wear. Kerelle watched them carefully from the concealment of her large dark lenses. True to Ilyen's intel, the guards were wearing psiblockers to a man, so she couldn't scout their intentions the way she had on Eisra XI. The guards didn't seem particularly on edge, however - they had the air of routine as they took up places around the perimeter, and more than one expression held resigned boredom.

That was promising. SysTech might be taking some precautions, but there didn't seem to be any real urgency in the rank and file. If SysTech were trying to keep the escapes under wraps, it was entirely possible the guards didn't even *really* know why they were here. One could hope.

As the group of PsiCorp streamed into the area, a subtle rearrangement took place among the other resort patrons. Some unhurriedly made their way towards the exits, or at least the far side of the pool, while others found sudden reasons to be closer to the knot of shining silver collars at the bar.

There were generally, Kerelle found, two kinds of mundanes that one encountered as a PsiCorp agent out on the town. One kind was unnerved and uncomfortable in proximity to psionics, though they might do their best to conceal it. The other kind was *extremely* comfortable in proximity to an unlimited credit line, and not inclined to concern themselves past that.

She shifted her position on the lounge chair and tried to look like the second type.

Koren's voice sounded in her head again.

Um...Ilyen would like you to know that you're, quote, "terrible at seduction," and next time he'll just do this part himself.

She gave a mental snort. *Remind Ilyen that the whole reason he's not doing this is that Elinea leaving with a man is out of character enough to draw attention.* Before she could hear his response, her eyes caught on a woman at the edge of the crowd.

She was tall and athletic, with light brown skin and smooth, wavy hair in the bright, utterly unnatural shade of vermilion that was popular with pyrokinetics. Kerelle recognized her immediately from the mental image Lilika had shared in their briefing. This was Elinea Bhari Jassane, C3 pyrokinetic, C2 telekinetic, acquaintance of Lilika and soon-to-be former agent of Rennu PsiCorp.

I see her, she sent back to Koren, as much to let him know to cut banter with Ilyen as to keep him apprised. *I'll approach momentarily.*

Doing this without the backup of telepathy was more nerve-wracking than she'd like to admit, but there was nothing for it. Elinea was expecting her, everyone else would be occupied with their own good time, all she had to do was look plausible.

Kerelle sauntered up to the bar, hoping she looked suitably alluring. She would never admit it to him but Ilyen wasn't wrong, this sort of thing was not her strong suit. But she was the best equipped to deal with it if things went sideways, and so here she was.

She sought Elinea's eyes in the crowd and locked gazes with her, giving the other woman an inviting smile. She had a stab of concern that Elinea might not know what *she* looked like, but the other woman grinned back and excused herself from the small group she'd been chatting with. She made her way over to the bar unhurried, looking Kerelle up and down with a flirty smile. Her eyes, however, were deadly serious. Yes, she'd realized who Kerelle was.

Kerelle leaned in, trying to keep her expression light in case anyone was watching. "You look like you could use a drink. Have you tried the sparkling?" It was the code they'd agreed on. Elinea didn't miss a beat in her response.

"I'll try whatever you're having." Code confirmed. She had the right agent, and that agent was ready to get on with things.

"It's a little crowded over here, don't you think?"

Elinea's smile widened and she stretched out her arms, letting her hand come to a rest on the small of Kerelle's back. "Well, I'm sure we could find someplace a little quieter." She gave a sharp nudge and Kerelle let herself be steered into the cool air of the resort's indoor lounge. Elinea had been here before; Kerelle would trust her to know where the best spot would be.

A flash of Elinea's card and they were in a private VIP room with a chilled bottle of sparkling. Her demeanor changed immediately as the door shut; the Elinea who turned around to face Kerelle was all business.

"You can really get this collar off." It was somewhere between a statement and a question.

Kerelle gestured at her own bare throat. "Yes. If you're

certain you want to go through with this, it will only take a few seconds."

"I'm certain, but you have to take my friend too."

Kerelle blinked. Lilika's communications with Elinea had by necessity been brief and cryptic, but the plan definitely was around escaping with *one* agent. This was the first she'd heard otherwise.

"Your friend? You didn't say anything about this before."

"I didn't know they were selling him until today. His name's Teriel. He's a C1 telepath but we've been friends since we were kids. Turns out starting next week, he's on permanent lease to one of the regional marketing heads. I've met the guy. He's an asshole and he treats his staff like garbage." Elinea put her hands on her hips, a challenging glint in her eyes. "And I bet you're not running around making this offer to C1s. You want me to fight for you, you get Teriel out too."

Discomfort twisted itself down Kerelle's spine; Elinea wasn't wrong. To build up their firepower, they'd focused their efforts on the higher designations. And she couldn't deny, deep down, that she probably wouldn't be standing here in this ridiculous resort, risking discovery and attack, if Elinea were not a C3 combat specialist. It felt painfully SysTech-like of them.

But the truth of her words aside, another thought was surfacing in Kerelle's mind, the memory of that terrible night that had set all of this in motion. Of Galhen's shocked, lost expression. Of how casually Director Cafora had torn him from his life on Tallimau and handed him over to Dalanva. Of how little the company had cared when he suffered at her hands. And she knew that even without the ultimatum, she couldn't leave without Elinea's friend.

Koren? I need you to tell Ilyen and the ship that there's been a change of plans.

THEY'D HAD to think fast. Sending Kerelle back out to find Teriel endangered the cover they'd constructed to explain Elinea's absence from the group. Trying to contact him telepathically was risky too - Kerelle didn't know him, and with so many other unfamiliar telepaths around there was considerable danger of brushing up against someone else and giving the whole game away. Kerelle silently added Elinea alongside Ilyen to her mental *why can't you just be a telepath* list.

At the same time, they couldn't just dig in and wait all that long. Each minute Elinea still wore her collar was a minute that the guards could catch on and activate it, and once it was active the little removal device in Kerelle's handbag would be rendered useless. But taking *off* the collar would start a countdown until her escape was detected, and potentially not a very long one.

"All right," Kerelle finally said, thinking furiously. "Let's order another bottle for the room, it will prop up the idea that we're having a good time *getting to know each other better* and buy us a bit longer before anyone wonders where you are. We have another operative onsite, I'll have him make contact with Teriel and get him to come to the lounge. We can do both your collars at once, and then we have to *move*."

Elinea gave her a sharp nod. "No arguments there. How will your man find Teriel?"

Good question. Ilyen wasn't a telepath, but Koren was, and he had the comm. "If you allow me," she said, "I'll pull his image from your mind and share it with our comms liaison. He'll be able to pass it on in detail."

Elinea made an impatient gesture. "Of course I'll allow it. Do you need me to do anything?"

"Try to picture Teriel as clearly as you can. If you can remember what he's wearing today, that's even better."

The pyrokinetic closed her eyes and furrowed her brow in concentration. Kerelle got a detailed image of the C1 telepath's face. His current outfit was rather fuzzier, but they'd have to make do. She passed the image and their location on to Koren, and settled into wait.

The second bottle of sparkling perspired on the table, the first bottle having been discreetly tucked behind the settee. The minutes crawled by. Kerelle tried to keep from flicking nervous glances at Elinea's collar.

Finally the door handle turned. Kerelle drew her telekinetics close and held her breath.

Ilyen strode through in the uniform of a poolside server, an uncertain-looking man she recognized as Teriel trailing behind him. He blinked as he entered the room, his eyes flicking from Elinea to Kerelle and back.

"Elly? He said you needed something from me, what is this about?"

Elinea gave Kerelle a quick sideways glance. "Can we have a minute?"

"Please be quick," she answered. "We can't linger."

A sharp nod and Elinea drew him aside to speak in low, urgent voices. Ilyen drifted closer to Kerelle.

"So what's the deal with them?" From his tone, Ilyen was not pleased with the delay either.

"They're longtime friends and he's about to be sold off to some asshole exec. She wouldn't leave without him."

"This is going to be more complicated with two people." His tone was flat.

"I know. We'll manage."

The two Rennu psionics finished their hurried conference and drew back to where they waited. Teriel's bronze skin had gone ashen, but his chin was set in determination.

"Thank you," he said quietly. "Tell me what to do."

Well, at least Elinea didn't miscalculate his interest in escaping. She had a pang of sympathy for Teriel, who'd been denied the luxury of time to carefully consider before making a life-altering decision, but there was no way around it now. They'd already tarried here longer than she preferred.

"We'll have to move quickly once the collars are off," Kerelle told them. "From our research, there's an emergency exit near the kitchens that should drop us in an alley. From there we take backstreets to the docks and get off Rennu. We stick together, and we try to avoid hurting anyone. Any questions?"

They both shook their heads. She drew the small device out of her bag.

"Well then. No time like the present."

"You can go first," Elinea said to Teriel. Kerelle chose to ignore the implied mistrust that she would keep her end of the deal; particularly for someone accustomed to dealing with SysTech, it wasn't an unreasonable fear. A flashed light, a quiet hum, and Teriel's collar came off in her hand.

She fit the device against Elinea's collar next, and a sharp rap at the door made them all jump.

"Agent Jassane?" The guard's voice was stern but not yet threatening. "Agent Jassane, this is SysTech security. Can you open the door please?"

Shit. The device's light flashed serenely, painfully plodding through the seconds it would take to disengage the collar. Seconds they might not have. The guard rapped the door again, a bit more forcefully. "Agent Jassane. Open the door."

A key turned in the lock - they must have gotten it from the lounge staff. Ilyen appeared near her ear.

"Can you get ready with some C3 telepathy bullshit?" His voice was low and urgent.

She nodded, but - "The psiblockers - "

"Don't worry about it." He vanished.

The door banged against the wall as the guard shoved it open, annoyance plain on his face. He took a step in and stopped suddenly, eyes widening as he realized what he was seeing. The guard behind him started to bark a command, when something hit him hard from behind and he keeled over. The guard in front locked eyes with Ilyen and started to draw his gun, when Ilyen vanished again. He reappeared grappling the man from behind, and reached up to disengage the psiblocker.

Ah.

Kerelle hit him hard with the illusion. He'd come in here to check on Agent Jassane and found her locked in a passionate embrace with a woman she'd met by the pool. Typical PsiCorp debauchery, nothing to take note of, nothing requiring further attention. The other guard had slipped and hit his head, he needed medical attention immediately. Take him back outside to get help. Leave Agent Jassane to her amusements.

It was a far stronger compulsion than she'd usually use, and it wouldn't last long. As she'd once told Sandrel a lifetime ago on Kalnis, telepathic suggestion was far more effective when it was something the target believed anyway. This man's mind was fighting her, he *knew* what he was experiencing wasn't right. But she didn't need him to believe it forever; just for the next few minutes.

Eyes unfocused, the guard slung his companion over his shoulders and headed back down the hall. The little device's light flashed one more time, and Elinea's collar slid off.

"Right then," Kerelle said briskly, "we need to move. That won't hold long."

She tried to keep up a shield of disinterest as they slipped out of the room and down the corridor, but the lounge's staff stared anyway. Guests weren't supposed to be in this part of the lounge, and Elinea's vibrant hair was noticeable enough to draw attention even in less fraught situations. They just needed to get out the door -

Shouts rang out from down the hall. Kerelle's hold on the guard had worn off even more quickly than she expected.

They came to the promised emergency exit at the end of the hallway. Kerelle shoved it open with telekinetic force and they piled out into the alley as the lounge's lights began to flash in time with the fire alarm's piercing shriek. Hopefully the chaos of the alarms would slow down their opponents.

All the same, they took off down the alley at a run.

NINE

THEY'D SCARCELY LANDED BACK on Palhee when Lilika's curt voice cut into Kerelle's mind.

We need you all at the safehouse as soon as the ship is settled.

Galhen's bright eyes met hers, reflecting her same confusion and concern - he'd received the same message.

We'll be on our way shortly, he answered for them. *Is everything all right? Kerelle and Ilyen can go ahead of us if you need firepower.*

We're not in immediate peril. But we do have a problem.

A short time later they were all crowded around the table in the safehouse, Teriel and Elinea squished in alongside everyone else. Lilika wasted no time.

"I've received a number of these from my field agents." She set down her tablet so they all could see it, and pulled up a media stream.

Their own faces stared back at them.

PSIONIC TERRORISTS STRIKE AGAIN, blared the news ticker. Above it were file photos, for Kerelle, Galhen, Ilyen, and Lilika, labeled with their names and designations. A disconnected part of her mind noted Ilyen was listed as a C2 telekinetic only - even now, they wanted to keep their secret teleporter classified.

The screen shifted and Elinea's photo joined theirs, *believed to be working with psionic terror group* stamped across the bottom.

"You're going to have to stop dyeing your hair, Elly," Teriel murmured. She made an unenthused noise, eyes fixed on the image.

Lilika flicked to a new stream.

"Details are unclear, but authorities believe the massacre may have resulted from an arms deal gone bad," the news anchor explained. *Entire Criminal Gang Found Dead, Psionic Terrorists Suspected* floated in bold text beneath her on the screen. Kerelle gasped then as they cut away to a stark image of the remains of the Ash and Bones. The gruesome scene of how she'd left their leader confronted her like an accusation, and her stomach roiled. It must have leaked through the bond, because Galhen's fingers curled around hers with a soft brush of comfort.

Flick.

Senator Dalanva filled the screen, and then it was her turn to send reassurance, to offer soothing safety against the spike of stress that awful woman's face sent down his spine.

"It was the most frightening experience of my life," Dalanva was saying, her voice full of calm assurance. She held herself with the effortless poise of an elder stateswoman. "I thought it was the *end* of my life. And it's in that moment, that moment of thinking that this is it, everything is over, you've had all the time you're going to have - it's in that moment that you realize how much you have left to do. And that you *aren't* ready, not yet. And that's what gives you the strength to keep going." The camera panned back, its angle emphasizing the cane that now leaned against her chair.

The interviewer nodded along, a fawning smile on her lips. "It's that kind of wisdom and inner strength that is really just so inspiring," she commented warmly. "To be able to face something so shocking, so *senseless*. To be attacked by someone from your own household."

"That was the worst part of it," Dalanva agreed, inclining her head graciously. "When we're kind to people, we don't expect them to lash back at us. But the most important part is that it doesn't change *our* worldview. It doesn't stop us from being kind. These terrorists, this terrorist that lived under my roof - he won't stop *me* from being kind."

Flick.

"That's the problem," explained the middle-aged man who the titles identified as a psionic psychological expert. "Psionics aren't just average people who can read your mind. There are all kinds of biological differences between a psionic and a normal person - they can't have children, they have specific metal allergies, and unfortunately their neurology is disposed toward antisocial behavior. Psionics tend to be very hedonistic, self-focused, almost sociopathic - they just aren't wired for empathy."

The two talk show hosts nodded along, looking concerned. The closer one leaned in, brow furrowed. "What does that mean exactly, for how psionics typically act towards others?"

"They're very centered on material luxury and their own pleasure," the 'expert' asserted. "They can certainly be friendly and charming towards others when they want to be, but ultimately every action they take is going to be focused on getting something they want. They might sometimes enjoy social activities in a group setting, and their sexual appetites can be voracious, but most don't form meaningful connections with the people around them. They can't. The brain chemistry for bonding just isn't there."

"SysTech does the best we can to help them," he continued. "This is why the PsiCorp program starts in early childhood, for example, and why we focus on housing young psionics together and encouraging them to identify as part of a group. The earlier we can start intervention therapy, the more effective it can be in correcting their natural behavior problems."

"How effective *is* therapy? From what you've said, doctor, the problem is biology."

The man nodded grimly, face full of noble regret. "Unfortunately that is the case. With intensive psychological work we can minimize negative tendencies, but there really is only so much that nurture can do against nature. And that makes psionics very dangerous to normal human society."

The other host looked at the camera, eyes wide with performative concern. "Doctor, how worried should the public be about these psionic terrorists?"

"I wish I could tell you that concerns are overblown, but the brutal attack on Senator Dalanva in Morafer proves that this group is fully capable of inflicting violence even in a high-security environment. We don't know their reasoning, but given psionic psychological patterns they may not have one. They might just want to watch things burn for their own amusement. Frankly, people have every right to be afraid."

Lilika flipped off the media stream. The room went silent.

"...fuck," Ilyen said softly. He sounded more unnerved than angry.

"That was the most florid," Lilika told them, "but the story is the same across media. SysTech has gone public on our escape, and launched a rather comprehensive campaign to paint us as dangerous sociopaths. Apparently," she nodded to Elinea, "the loss of another C3 was the tipping point to decide that keeping things quiet was helping us more than them. This started shortly after you escaped Rennu."

"I'll take it as a compliment," the pyrokinetic answered tightly. She was still staring at the now-quiescent tablet, a faint glow dancing beneath her fingernails.

"It *was* helping us more than them." Galhen's voice was quiet. "We've benefited a great deal from being able to pass unnoticed among mundanes. Now the mundanes will not only be looking out for us, but likely eager to turn us in. Any reputational damage they risk from going public must seem a fair price for restricting our operations." His smile was bleak. "I suppose we can congratulate ourselves, for being deemed enough of a threat."

"Thus far their campaign has been a success, and their narrative is gaining momentum." Lilika's face remained impassive, her tone as detached as if they were discussing the weather. "My field agents report a great deal of public chatter and anxiety around dangerous loose psionics."

"I'm not surprised," Sandrel answered bluntly. He sighed and looked between them. "I tried to say this when we first started this whole crazy scheme, but a lot of people - maybe *most* people - are already scared of psionics, and they're just fine with collared PsiCorp. This whole terrorist-sociopath thing probably wasn't a hard sell for SysTech."

Nalea nodded her agreement. "Even in academic circles that *study* psionics, people are nervous being near them. Chaos and explosions are pretty much what everyone would expect from a psionic jailbreak."

Kerelle felt numb. Everything SysTech was telling the world - it had *happened*, in a way. For every assertion they made, they could point to supporting evidence. And yet....

"They *made* us this way," she whispered. Her cheeks felt hot. "Everything that they're saying makes us monsters, they *raised* us to be. They *punished* us for wanting more than a moment's pleasure. If they thought we cared too much about each other they *separated* us." She was aware that her voice was rising, could hear that slightly hysterical note threaded in it. Right that moment she couldn't care. It was like a dam was bursting, and all her feelings on the PsiCorp were flooding out. "Now they have the gall to claim that there's something wrong with us, that that hideous woman is a *victim*, and everyone *believes them*."

Her treacherous eyes stung and Galhen's arms went around her, calm reassurance radiating through their bond. At the same time, however, she sensed the feelings' dissonant undertones, and guilt welled in her. The segment with Dalanva had rattled him, and Galhen was tamping down on his own distress to try to comfort her. She sent him back acknowledgement and appreciation, and slipped her hand in his.

"Why *wouldn't* they believe them?" Lilika's voice was cold as the mask she'd retreated behind once again. "Society has been hearing their side of the story forever. No one has ever heard ours." Her lips thinned. "And this is more than simply an effort to complicate our operations. From what I'm seeing in my reports, this is a sustained propaganda campaign to normalize the idea of an ongoing psionic threat. If that campaign is allowed to succeed," she said deliberately, "then there is no endgame for us."

Ilyen glanced at her. "It's like Sandrel and Nalea said though - people have *always* been afraid of us. This is shitty, don't get me wrong, but does it really change much?"

"People were afraid of proximity to us, but we were not a constant bogeyman in the collective psyche. If we are considered an indelible threat to society at large, then our chances of wringing peaceful concessions or official acknowledgement of our status from the company drops to zero. And if we cannot gain those things, then we will never be anything more than what we are now. Our only path forward is to prevent SysTech from controlling the story."

"Sure, yeah, sounds easy," Ilyen replied with a tone of disbelief. "We'll just call the morning news and get that cleared *right* up. Never mind that they're all owned by the multigalactics, I'm sure they'll be happy to give us the next talk show segment."

Lilika didn't bother to hide her impatience. "That is not what I'm suggesting. The multigalactics own the professional media, so our only option is to go around it." She looked around the table. "SysTech just made us celebrities. We should turn that to our advantage, and get our story on the datanet streaming sites. Starting with yours, Kerelle."

Her stomach dropped. Kerelle didn't want to talk about any of this, she *couldn't*, not with the dark image of the Ash and Bones fixed beneath her eyelids. But oh stars, everyone was staring at her, even as Galhen's arm around her shoulders took on a protective quality.

"I...I can't, I shouldn't...it shouldn't be me," she finally managed weakly. "It can't be me, not when so much of what I've done validates what they say we are."

"It's only validating for SysTech if you look at it from their perspective, and you need to *stop* looking at it from their perspective, even in your own mind," Lilika countered. Her eyes cut to Galhen's. "And no, I will *not* leave her be, she needs to *hear* this, whether she feels up to it or not. We don't have the luxury to nurse our traumas." His jaw tightened but he said nothing - at least nothing anyone but Lilika could hear.

Lilika turned back to Kerelle. "You are indeed a formidable weapon, and SysTech used you as such for years. And yes, you fell back on the habits they formed in you against those pirates. I imagine our opponents will leverage those images as far as they are able. But you are much more than just a conduit for destruction."

Lilika leaned forward, eyes holding hers. "To hear their man tell it, our people are fueled only by hedonism. Yet you walked away from a life of material comfort, at great personal risk, because you loved Galhen more than you loved yourself. They say we have no care for other human lives, but in all the time that you have been free, you've used violence only as a last resort of self-defense. And even *then*, you tried to avoid loss of life." She made a disgusted motion towards the tablet, sitting innocently on the table. "Even that wretched Dalanva woman. She may play herself up as some sort of innocent victim, but you could have simply snapped her neck and had done with it. You did not."

Kerelle stared back at her, unsure of how to respond. Lilika sighed and ran a hand through her hair. "You are not what they say we are, Kerelle. You are the *antithesis* of what they say we are. SysTech just told the world you sparked this whole affair - now you need to tell them *why*."

The butterflies in Kerelle's stomach did another flip. Even if Lilika was right, the thought of laying herself bare like that, in front of literally the entire galaxy...

"Are you *sure* it should be me though?" She hated that her voice trembled. "Lilika, you're the most eloquent one on this ship, maybe *you* should - "

"Oh, I will," the telepath assured her. "I will, and Galhen will, and Ilyen will, and so will everyone else with a story to tell. But you, my dear, need to lead the charge."

An impossibly short time later, she found herself seated against one of the walls, staring down Lilika's tablet set to record. Her mouth felt like sandpaper.

Come on, Kerelle, she told herself. *You can do this. All you have to do is talk.*

A gentle pulse of encouragement then, the equivalent of a mental hug. *You can, darling.* Galhen sat against the opposite wall with the others, his eyes never leaving her. A soft smile touched his lips. *You've faced down far more terrifying things. Your courage will hardly fail you now.*

She gave him a small smile back, then took a deep breath and turned to face the galaxy.

"My name is Kerelle Evandra, class 3 telepath, class 3 telekinetic," she started. Her voice was encouragingly steady. "I was raised in the SysTech PsiCorp program from the age of five, and one year, eight months and thirteen days ago, I escaped."

"IT'S CHAOS," Riyel told them plainly. Tonight's dream setting was the rooftop of an observatory tower, and bright moonlight gilded his features. "They've cut datanet access for the entire PsiCorp, and they've been confiscating everyone's personal devices. The official story is a data security breach, but even the managers don't pretend to believe it. Not after the company *confirmed* your escape."

Galhen tilted his head in surprise. "Have they addressed it directly with the PsiCorp, then?"

Riyel shook his head. "They danced around it, when it first hit the news cycle. Certainly nothing like 'you may have heard that two dozen of your fellows have escaped, please carry on.' But our last weekly all-hands - I *did* mention those were weekly now, yes? Anyway our last all-hands was dedicated to how we need to focus on our work, and not distract ourselves with gossip."

His lips lifted in a half-smile. "Of course, that was essentially an admission that the 'gossip' was worth paying attention *to*."

"And that's when they cut off datanet access?"

Riyel laughed a little, though there was an undercurrent of strain in his aura. "No, that part was all us - it came down a few hours after we posted our response. Though it's possible they were planning it already, and Kerelle's video streaming over every device in the PsiCorp just sped things up."

"How are people reacting?" Kerelle asked, with some trepidation. The idea of other PsiCorp watching her tell her story, watching her *be vulnerable*, was more unnerving than just the galaxy at large. Rationally she knew it was silly, but two decades of social conditioning didn't vanish overnight.

Riyel paused a moment. "Reactions are mixed," he said finally. "I would love to say that everyone understood, and shared your feelings, but I think all of us knew that wouldn't be the case. There *are* people that do, I think, who have felt similarly themselves and always thought they were outliers. No one is coming out and *saying* it, of course, but there are cautious whispers going around. Our potential recruiting pool may have just increased substantially.

"But," he added with a sigh, "there are also a fair number of people who would gladly present SysTech with your head if it meant things went back to how they were six months ago. Rumor is our credit lines are about to be revoked as well, not that we have much use for them when we can't leave the base."

Kerelle frowned. "Have the company-sanctioned group outings stopped also?" That would rather complicate their recruiting efforts.

"There have been no announcements on the subject, but there are currently no social excursions on the calendar, at least not here on Iressu. I'm sure if you asked anyone they would *say* it was temporary, security concerns and so on, but as it stands right now we are essentially confined to the base indefinitely."

"Everywhere, or just on Iressu?"

"Well, I can't say for certain it's *everywhere*. But I had tea with a telepath arrived from Qarinem yesterday, and she said it's the same there." He glanced from her to Lilika. "I would expect it's a companywide policy, now. Elinea Jassane was a valuable asset, and another prominent C3 whose absence can't be disguised. They won't want to give anyone else the opportunity to escape like she did."

"All right." Kerelle sighed. "The social trips were a nice soft target, but we started off extracting our recruits from missions. We can go back to doing it again."

Riyel leaned forward to rest his hands on the weathered wooden table, his expression troubled. "Be careful," he told them, though his eyes cut up to meet Lilika's. "We've been lucky, so far, that we've struck where they weren't looking, and that the regional managers weren't taking us seriously enough to spend the budget for effective defense. They're taking us seriously *now*."

TEN

"WE NEED TO MAKE OTHER ARRANGEMENTS," Lilika announced without preamble. "Two ships and this apartment are no longer sufficient, particularly with our suddenly raised profile."

Kerelle couldn't argue. Sandrel's ship was full, Oliven's ship was full, the Palhee safehouse had somehow managed to fit more bodies, but the floors were lined with sleeping pallets. It was a good problem to have, she supposed, but they had been reaching the limits of their space *before* SysTech's propaganda blitz.

"Do you have any ideas?"

"We can't stay on Palhee," Lilika said bluntly. "It's a crowded, well-traveled world, and at first that worked in our favor. It's a good place to disappear, and the students and I are skilled in avoiding notice, but our numbers are becoming a liability. SysTech almost certainly has agents here, and thanks to their news efforts our faces are becoming known even to mundanes.

"We can - and should - keep a small presence on Palhee to keep tabs on what's happening in the sector," she continued, "but it no longer serves us as a primary base of operations. The higher concentration of our people we keep here, the higher odds one of us will be identified and the rest caught out." She pressed her palms into the table. "We need a real base, somewhere remote enough that we can operate out of sight."

Ilyen spoke up from where he leaned against the wall, on the edge of the gathered group. "Yeah, but *we* have to be able to find it. It's not like we can just do a datanet search for 'top secret hidden base options.'"

"I didn't say finding one would be *trivial*," Lilika answered. "I'm hoping this group can come up with ideas."

"As it so happens," Sandrel cut in, "I may have one already."

Everyone turned to look at him. He got up and casually strolled up to the head of the table beside Lilika.

"I figured this was going to come up at some point," he started, "and I found us a promising lead to lie low." He pulled up a schematic on his tablet, lifting it to show the room. Kerelle had to squint to make it out, but it looked like some sort of compound. "Found this on the market on Cashaal. Used to be some old tycoon's meditation retreat out in the desert. After he died the heirs tried to turn it into a luxury hotel, but...it's Cashaal. There's not enough marketing in the universe to make it a tourist spot."

Nalea cocked her head. "What *is* on Cashaal?"

"Sand, rocks, and not much else. There's a mining outpost-slash-trade port near one of the big oases, but that's it for human habitation. Apparently that was part of the draw for building the retreat out there - he felt like he could commune with the natural world." Sandrel gave the schematics a deadpan glance. "You know. From inside a climate-controlled mansion behind two sets of walls. Anyway, nobody wanted it after he died, and it's been sitting abandoned for almost twenty years."

"Really? They just walked away from the property?" Granted,

Kerelle didn't have much experience with real estate, but it seemed like something you'd rather hold on to.

"Yes and no," Sandrel answered. "The family still owns it and all, but it's too impractical to profitably repurpose and there's no point in paying the cost of demolition. It's been up for sale for decades, but at this point they've probably given up on a buyer." He quirked a half-smile. "Their dad was hardly the only rich eccentric in the galaxy, but he may have been the only one whose idea of a good time was sitting around in a desert contemplating sand."

"And it's not like there's any neighbors to complain about blight, if they let the building go to seed," Lilika observed.

"Exactly. The family probably opted to just stick the deed in a vault and forget about it. Which is where we come in."

"You're suggesting *we* buy it?" Galhen's brow furrowed. "Even given the circumstances, the price will likely be significant, and after all this time I would imagine that anyone interested in buying it would draw attention on curiosity alone."

Sandrel shook his head. "Forget buying it. I'm suggesting we just move in."

Lilika arched her brows, though a small smile played on her lips. "Because it's kilometers from anything, and the owners are unlikely to visit?"

"Exactly. It's on the other side of the planet from the settlement, too far for any of the locals to bother with. And if they haven't found a buyer in twenty years, they're unlikely to find one now. Who's going to stop us?"

"How did *you* find this?"

Sandrel shrugged. "Real estate listings. Like I said, I figured it would come up. Sooner or later we were going to outgrow this flat and as much as I love Palhee," he nodded toward Lilika, "the Chief's right. It's great for small-scale skullduggery, but there's too many eyes to hide a group like this. If we stay here, we're going to get caught. I've been looking into alternate venues pretty much since the celsum job.

"Anyway," he continued, flicking the schematics shut, "the Cashaal compound probably isn't in *great* shape after twenty years of neglect, but it's big enough we can house a lot of people there, and looks fairly defensible from ground assault. It's also far enough out that it had its own water and power systems. Stars know if *those* are still functioning, but..." he winked at Oliven. "You've got a few people who are good with repairs."

"It's perfect," Kerelle said honestly. "What would we do without you?"

Sandrel grinned. "Still be looking for a secret base, I'd imagine." He glanced around. "If that's settled then, get everyone rounded up. I can set course as soon as you're ready to leave."

KERELLE HAD BEEN in arid zones before. She'd even camped in deserts; there had been that one campaign against a localized pirate ring that had involved a lot of tromping through sand and cacti-studded scrubland. Cashaal made that deeply unpleasant landscape look like a picnic ground.

The compound was situated on a rocky plateau, rising from the endless dunes. As they'd flown in from atmosphere, Kerelle had seen green dots of vegetation in scattered clumps, in areas that looked more like scrubby plains. But there were no signs of it here - the compound's builder, apparently, had found the starkness of the dune sea more enlightening.

"Some stupidly rich guy could have gone anywhere in the galaxy, and he decided to come *here*." Ilyen's flat tone conveyed volumes.

"Presumably the climate control was working then," Kerelle answered, but she couldn't disagree with the sentiment. She was cognizant that Cashaal's inhospitable environment was the very thing that would make this place a safe haven; it didn't mean she had to enjoy standing in it. They weren't technically *in* it, they were indoors, but between the large windows and the current lack of climate control, indoors wasn't a big improvement.

"Any word on when *we're* going to get it working?"

Kerelle gave a resigned sigh. "Sandrel's hoping the climate system is fine and it'll kick in once we get the electrical back up, but that didn't sound promising for a quick fix. We had to excavate sand out of the basements to even get to the power rooms." The whole reason she was standing up here instead of working, in fact, was to catch her breath. Telekinetically shifting large quantities of sand was more exerting than she'd expected.

He made a face. "I guess that's not a surprise, since we're going to have to excavate sand from most of the surface chambers too. Unless we're all just planning to have a campout in the courtyard together." He didn't sound enthused about that possibility.

"We'll clear the chambers." She sighed again. "It's just going to take some time and patience."

"Two of my favorite things," he answered sardonically as he nudged a haphazard rock stack with his foot.

Suddenly she heard Ilyen's startled *"Fuck!"* Before she could even register what was happening, he'd reappeared across the room. Her attention shot back to the rock stack. The rock stack, and the very large, very angry-looking scorpion crawling out of it. Ilyen was out of its line of vision now; it snapped its claws and charged at her.

She couldn't help it; she squeaked as she flung it away with more force than was probably necessary.

Far more force than was necessary. The twitching remnants of the scorpion slid down the window, leaving a gooey mess in its wake. Ilyen reappeared next to her, and they both stared at it.

"Did I ever mention," he said vehemently, "how much I *hate* camping?"

"No, but something tells me you're going to be mentioning it a lot." She gave him a nudge in the ribs. "By the way, thanks for stirring that thing up, then teleporting yourself out of danger and leaving *me* to deal with it."

It was the first time she could ever recall seeing Ilyen embarrassed.

"Yeah, um, sorry about that. It was kind of a reflex." He glanced from her to the shattered scorpion. "You think there's more of these?"

"Probably," she answered reluctantly. "We'll need to warn everyone to watch out for wildlife. If they haven't already found out."

Ilyen's expression changed. "Shit, Nalea was scouting lab space." He vanished.

Kerelle suppressed a sigh and reached out to Galhen.

Be careful, darling. Ilyen and I just encountered a rather nasty scorpion, and there may be more lying about.

There are. You weren't stung, were you?

No, she responded, frowning. *But I'm afraid to ask how you know this.*

I just finished dealing with a sting on one of Lilika's students. I had a knot of panicked teenagers charge in, convinced that Peralen was going to die. He would have been fine even if I hadn't treated him, the venom wasn't nearly strong enough to pose a threat to an adult-sized human. The sting was quite painful, however, so I highly recommend avoiding the experience.

Delightful. I'll let everyone know.

He sent her back a burst of affectionate amusement. *No one said hijacking an abandoned compound in the middle of the wilderness was going to be easy.*

THE SUNSET BROUGHT ONLY muted relief from the punishing heat of the day, and when they finally gathered for dinner it was within the relative sanctuary of the compound's main building. Like the desert outside, its floor was coated in sand, but at least the lack of direct sunlight meant the indoor sand wasn't scorchingly hot.

The group sat scattered within the soft luminescence of their portable light cubes, though their light seemed thin and wan against the endless shadows around them. Inarguably, the abandoned compound was creepy at night; Kerelle wouldn't want to be sitting here alone, but it was hard to be too unnerved sitting in a group of powerful psionics. Even psionics as bone-tired as they were tonight.

Most of the group hunched wearily over whatever ready-made meal they'd scrounged from the cans they brought with them. Kerelle's little container of sauce and noodles hadn't exactly been gourmet, but after a long day of hard work in the blistering heat, just eating *anything* had been a reward. She suspected she wasn't alone in that. Exhaustion settled on the group like a blanket, and they largely ate in silence, each absorbed in their own thoughts.

For her part, Kerelle was happy to simply sit propped against the wall, shamelessly wrapped in Galhen's arms. The *shameless* feeling bothered her; she certainly had nothing to be ashamed *of*. But something about sitting once again in a group of other PsiCorp, albeit other *rogue* PsiCorp, was dredging up those old emotional habits again. It still felt transgressive - dangerous, even - to make such public displays of open affection, of *attachment*. Their relationship was not a secret, of course, and their wedding bands were public announcement enough. But apparently it was not so simple to break a lifetime of social training, and so the uncomfortable feeling lingered in the back of her mind that they were putting themselves at a disadvantage by being indiscreet.

It lingered, but she shoved it down anyway. They weren't PsiCorp any more, any of them. Hopefully in time it would start to feel that way.

It will, came Galhen's quiet agreement, accompanied by a soft curl of affection and comfort that confirmed that her anxiety had been leaking through their bond. *It* does *feel strange, for us and undoubtedly for them. But the strangeness will fade, and we won't be the only ones in time.*

You think so? You'll recall Ilyen thought a relationship like ours sounded horrifically dull.

And I would be rather interested to know if that's still the case, after a year of being whatever he is to my sister. But yes, I do *think so. I certainly don't think everyone in the PsiCorp is secretly dreaming of committed monogamy, mind, and some would likely never entertain the idea, but -* she got the impression of gesture, taking in the group arrayed around them *- for most of our people this is the first opportunity they've ever had to form lasting bonds without interference. I would be more surprised if we* were *to remain the only committed pair.*

A sudden bobbing light coming up the stairs caught their attention. Sandrel emerged from the dark of the lower floors, Oliven close at his heels.

Heads turned toward Sandrel from around the group, and Kerelle caught whispers of hope that perhaps the compound's mechanical issues were nearing resolution. The look on Sandrel's face, however, did not fill her with optimism.

Sandrel acknowledged the attention with a nod as he made his way toward the stack of food cans.

"Alright people, good news and bad news. Bad news first. As most of you already know, the infrastructure here is not in great shape. It's going to be awhile until we get electricity, which means it's going to be awhile until we get running water and climate control."

There were audible groans from around the room. He lifted a hand in acknowledgement as he fished around the stack of cans.

"That's the bad news. The good news is, I think I found the problem with the generators."

"Is it that they're covered in sand?" Ilyen asked archly.

"Among other things," Sandrel replied cheerfully. He had to be tired after a long day as well, but it didn't show. "Oliven's going to pick up some parts for us when he goes back on a supply run. I might need a little psionic help lifting the big stuff, but I think I can fix it."

He popped open his can of rice and vegetables and gave it a critical inspection. "The *other* good news is that while we won't have running water until there's power to work the pumps, I had a look at the water system itself, and it looks pretty much intact. Obviously we'll want to run some tests before we start drinking it straight, but just looking at the state of the structure I think there's good odds it's still potable. And we can always pick up some more purifiers if it's not."

"You said the pumps won't work without power," Lilika commented, "but would it be possible to apply telekinetic pressure to work them manually?"

Sandrel grinned. "You read my mind, Chief. We'll have to be careful not to press too hard and break anything, but I don't see any reason why we can't pull up some freshwater on a regular basis. At least enough to get some washing and bathing in."

Kerelle felt Galhen's mental chuckle. *See love? Some washing and bathing. We're already better off than we started.*

KERELLE WIPED her brow and leaned the broom against the wall of the chamber, surveying her work. There was still sand on the floor, of course, and she suspected there always would be, but there was significantly *less* sand than when she'd started sweeping. That was something.

The chamber could be politely described as *cozy*. She

suspected it had been some sort of storage room originally, though it was hard to tell one small windowless room from another. Still, there was enough room for a double sleeping pad, a pair of garment bags and a portable light cube. For the moment that was good enough. Besides, she liked its shape the most of all the rooms she'd cleaned that day.

I think I've finished clearing us out a bedroom, she sent Galhen with an overlay of triumph. *It's tight quarters, naturally, but not much more so than the ship. And it has a door that closes.*

I think I'd sleep on the bare rock if it meant that last one. Well done, *darling.* His reply was infused with warmth, and Kerelle couldn't help the grin that spread over her face. Privacy had been in short supply in the week since they'd come to Cashaal.

How are things coming for you? She asked. While she'd spent the morning clearing out sleeping spaces, Galhen and a few others had been working on setting up an infirmary.

It's coming along, bit by bit. We finally have most of the floor cleaned, and there's space set aside to move equipment from the ship once power is available. We also had to pause briefly so I could treat another sting. These scorpions are a bit of a menace.

She made a face, though of course he couldn't see her. *I keep hoping we've seen the last of them.*

We all do, I think. In a way I almost feel badly, this structure has been their home for likely longer than it was ever habited by humans. She felt his half-smile through the bond. *But not badly enough to risk a shot of venom every time I open a drawer. It's a large planet. They'll survive. Speaking of,* he added, *if you're done with cleanup for now, you really ought to go see what my sister is working on.*

What's she working on?

The sense of a grin. *Hope for a future of more palatable food.*

Kerelle's feet took her out of the wing she'd been working in, down towards the room Nalea had claimed for a future lab. She found the scientist sketching something out on her tablet, Ilyen perched curiously beside her.

She leaned over to get a better look. "What's this?"

Nalea looked up, surprised. Apparently she hadn't heard Kerelle come in.

"Ideas for a garden. I think that all-glass viewing room on the upper level could basically function as a greenhouse. The soil here is garbage, but if we went the hydroponic route we wouldn't need dirt anyway. All we'd need is plants and the right equipment, and the equipment's easy to get. And then," she added wistfully, "we could get a regular supply of food that doesn't come out of a tin."

Stars, that sounded heavenly. And ambitious. "Could we really grow enough in the viewing room to support ourselves, though?"

"No," Nalea conceded. "Not by itself. But we could at least get fresh vegetables to supplement what we have to bring in from off-world. I hope." She held up her tablet to show Kerelle her sketch. "I'm trying to figure out what we can grow and how we can configure it to maximize yield for what space we have."

"You're a plant expert too?" Kerelle asked in surprise. She'd never noticed Nalea to have much interest in growing things. The other woman burst out laughing.

"Oh *stars* no. I kept a tomato plant alive on my balcony for almost three months once. That's all my experience right there. But there's instructions on the datanet, and it doesn't sound *that* hard." She swiped to another screen on her tablet, this time a spreadsheet listing different vegetable varietals and what seemed to Kerelle to be a dizzying amount of numbers. "See, these Sun Glow tomatoes need a lot of water, but you can grow them closer together than the Scarlet Stars, so we might get more for our effort. Though if I'm understanding this right, if we grew the Scarlet Star tomatoes instead we might be able to use the extra space between them to grow beans or carrots, so that might actually be the more efficient route."

Nalea swiped back to her original sketch, which on closer

inspection was carefully annotated with size, distance, and environmental requirements. She grinned, eyes sparkling. "It's like a puzzle that we can eat when it's done."

It still sounded far-fetched to Kerelle, but she could almost picture what Nalea's vision would look like coming to life. There was something encouraging about that vision, and not just the prospect of better food. It was the prospect that they would be here long enough for it to matter.

A WEEK TURNED into two weeks, then a month, then three. Bit by bit, their reclamation project moved forward; rooms were cleared, machinery was repaired, and finally at long last the compound's electrical grid leapt back to life.

Of course, they then discovered that the climate control system was nonfunctional in its own right, but one step at a time.

Throughout it all, Lilika and Riyel continued to source new recruits. By the stars-blessed day that the climate systems finally spun up and began a slow war of attrition against the desert heat, there were a number of new faces around the compound.

Nearly everyone cheered at the first gust of cool air.

As their group expanded, their capabilities did too - and so did the logistical challenges. As Sandrel soon pointed out, their increasing numbers carried more risks than just running out of supplies.

"We're pretty isolated out here, that's the idea, but if SysTech ever found us we wouldn't be able to fit everyone into the two ships we have. If one or both of us weren't here during an attack, the people on Cashaal would have no way out at all. We need to expand our fleet - and our roster of pilots."

"It is indeed a concern," Lilika had answered evenly. "And since you are as aware as I am that we lack the funds to purchase another ship, let alone *multiple* ships, I am assuming you have something else in mind."

"I *have* been thinking about how our good friends at SysTech have an excess of ships, yes."

Gradually, a motley assortment of mismatched SysTech transport ships began to dot the compound's environs, until they had assembled their own tiny fleet. It was unclear if SysTech connected the series of thefts from its maintenance yards with the renegade psionics.

From Riyel, they learned that the turmoil within the PsiCorp had only increased as they stepped up their efforts to counter SysTech's propaganda. Despite official efforts to cut PsiCorp datanet access, the rebels' materials reliably found their way anyway into agents' hands.

"The majority are not disposed to open rebellion," Riyel explained. "Nor do I expect them to be. But I'm starting to see signs of organized resistance cells."

Galhen blinked. "That's a significant escalation from the scattered sympathizers we've been dealing with, both in possibilities and in risk."

"Agreed. If we are able to connect with these cells, it increases our reach and our access to information inside the PsiCorp. But it also opens the door wider for SysTech infiltration. We must be cautious in approaching them."

"At the same time," Riyel added, "This development is not entirely surprising. I suspect Velrin has actually accelerated our support among some PsiCorp who might otherwise have avoided involvement. His attempts to demonize us in the press and deter others from attempting to escape are a tacit admission that *it can be done.*"

ELEVEN

NALEA'S NEW LAB, Kerelle thought, was undeniably a step up from the old one. She'd managed to find a spacious room, recessed and cooler than the rest of the compound. No one was entirely sure what its original use had been, but the prevailing theory was "wine storage." If she looked carefully, Kerelle could almost imagine the rows and rows of bottles that might once have filled the space, keeping silent vigil until they were called up to the table. Now, however, it was aglow with irregularly flashing lights, and the soft hum of equipment provided an ambient backdrop.

The lab was also no longer Nalea's primary quarters, which Kerelle could only imagine was a step up as well - though she noted a rolled-up pallet stuffed in a corner as they made their way through. Apparently some habits died hard.

Voices cut through the background buzz. She and Galhen weren't Nalea's only visitors.

"I think I've got the mildew taken care of for now, but we'll need to keep an eye out for more incursions." The male voice sounded vaguely familiar, though Kerelle couldn't identify it.

"The potatoes are coming along beautifully, I'd hate to lose them before we get to actually eat any."

"Agreed," Nalea answered. "Do you have any recommendations on the mildew?"

"There's a solution we might be able to treat the plants with, if Captain Zharus can pick us up the ingredients - "

They rounded the corner to find Nalea huddled over her greenhouse plan with one of the psionics. It took a moment to place him - Teriel, Elinea's C1 telepath friend. A small plant sample was cupped in his hands, and there looked to be several more on the table.

They both looked up in surprise - apparently, Nalea had forgotten she'd asked Kerelle and Galhen to stop by.

Teriel flushed slightly and stepped back from the table, hurriedly gathering up his samples. Kerelle caught a surge of embarrassment at having two pairs of double-C3 eyes trained on him. "Sorry, I don't mean to interrupt anything. I can come back later - "

"Not at all, it's us who are interrupting," Galhen answered with a smile, and Kerelle felt his gentle projection of approachability and warmth. She wondered if he realized he was doing it, or if it was an unconscious habit to put people at ease. "Teriel Ashelu Haliseren, right? Are you working with Nalea on our garden project?"

"He's the reason we *have* a garden project," Nalea cut in. "Turns out plants are a lot harder than they sounded on the datanet. If we ever get to eat any vegetables, it'll be because Teriel is an amateur botanist and knows what he's doing a lot more than I do."

"I wouldn't go *that* far," he responded, blush deepening. "I mean, I read a lot of textbooks, but I didn't get a chance to do that much hands-on work. I mostly just grew succulents in my room, sometimes cuttings if I ran across an interesting plant when I was working. My flatmates all thought it was weird."

"It *is* weird," Nalea answered cheerfully. "*We're* weird. That's why we're scientists instead of, I don't know, financial analysts or something."

Even through her shields, Kerelle caught Teriel's bright glow of feeling at being included in the "scientist" label.

"And if we're willing to risk sending someone back to Rennu," she continued, "he *also* has a pass to the Ren-Ayla University Library, which has an agricultural botany program. We could get copies of much more detailed information about how to grow in our conditions."

Kerelle blinked in surprise. "You were a student there?" How had he gotten *that* approved?

"No, no, the Director would never have agreed to something like that," he answered hastily. "Most universities let you pay to use their libraries, even if you're not a student. I bought a pass."

"Olstenfel offered that too," Nalea piped in. "The pass cost almost as much as first-year tuition."

"Yeah," he agreed. "Same at Ren-Ayla, probably. It was more than my stipend would cover, even if I didn't buy anything else all year." The blush was back on his cheeks. "Elly bought it for me, after she found the brochure in my flat."

Elinea, it seemed, had been much more conscious than Kerelle of the advantages her C3 status afforded her.

"I'm a little surprised they even let you do that," she commented. "At least in the Tallimau program, intellectual pursuits weren't exactly encouraged."

"Oh, I got a few chats with the group manager about making sure I stayed focused on the important things, and making the most of my career, and all that, but *really?*" He shrugged, a touch of bitterness in his smile. "I'm a C1 telepath. What kind of 'career' was I going to *have?* I did well enough on my assignments, and as long as it didn't affect my work I don't think anyone *really* cared what a C1 did on his off time."

Nalea's eyes danced. "Nothing wrong with a little rebellion

in the name of science. But yes," she continued, with the air of getting back to the subject at hand. "Let's definitely try this anti-mildew solution. Get a list together of what you need and we'll have Oliven pick it up next time he's out shopping."

"The library idea was a good one too," Galhen added encouragingly. "Lilika may be able to send one of her mundane agents to get what we need, with less chance of drawing PsiCorp attention."

A spike of trepidation - apparently Lilika was even more intimidating than they were, not that Kerelle could disagree - but Teriel only nodded decisively and rearranged his grip on the plant samples. "I'll suggest it to her then." He gave them all a quick nod and ducked out the door, leaving the three of them alone.

Galhen smiled at his sister. "It must be nice to have some assistance, after being a one-woman research team for so long."

"It is," she agreed cheerfully. "And it's nice to have people to talk to about these things, who understand at least some of the words. We're actually talking about trying to build a team to manage the garden, and Teriel can manage *them*. Which frees me up to focus on other things, like what I brought you here to talk about."

Nalea was nonchalant as she put away her greenhouse plan and grabbed a box off one of the counters, but beneath the facade her projections practically vibrated with excitement. Whatever she had to talk to them about, it was big.

She pulled several closed collars from the box and arranged them on the table, then carefully lifted out a complex knot of wires and circuits. Nalea glanced quickly up at Kerelle and Galhen, as if to ensure they were paying attention. Galhen gave her an encouraging nod, and Nalea produced the final piece: one of the control cards Kerelle and Lilika had stolen from Nevel.

She fitted it against part of her circuit-knot. For long seconds, nothing happened. Just when Kerelle was beginning to wonder if something had gone wrong, all the collars popped open at once.

"Stars and blood," she heard herself whisper. Her eyes cut up to meet Nalea's. "You did it."

Nalea's smile was shaky but triumphant. "I did. Still takes longer than I'd like, and without more samples to test with we can't be *certain* it will work with other control cards besides these two but" - a shrug that belied her excitement - "based on the data, I expect that it will. If we can get ahold of one of the master cards that's synced to a whole PsiCorp group, we've got every reason to believe it'll open all their collars at once."

Kerelle leaned back against Galhen's shoulder as they both stared at the little device.

"This changes everything, Nalea."

"I was hoping you'd say that."

Three days later, Nalea gave her demonstration for Lilika's war council. When the group of collars snapped open, the room went utterly silent.

Finally Lilika lifted her gaze to Nalea's, wide eyes betraying her neutral expression. "This is a significant advancement of our capabilities."

"That was the idea," Nalea agreed. "No more racing against the clock to get everyone out in time. Just pop in a manager card, and we can do a whole group simultaneously."

"But first we have to *have* a manager card in the first place." Elinea's eyes flicked over to Kerelle. "That's not going to be as easy as pickpocketing single-collar cards off rich people at a party."

"No," she agreed with a deep exhalation. "No, it isn't. There's no way around it this time - we'll *have* to get into a SysTech base."

THERE WERE SO many ways this could go sideways, Kerelle almost couldn't count them all. She wasn't the only one with reservations; the room fairly radiated nervous energy. They'd discussed a larger offensive, a distraction to draw out SysTech's attention while Ilyen slipped in to get the control card. But that had significant potential to backfire with tightened security, or the difficulty of evacuating their strike team once the deed was done.

The simplest solution, and the one most likely to succeed, was for Ilyen to quietly slip into the base and steal the card, then teleport out before anyone realized what had happened. Logically, it was clearly the best option. Ilyen was a highly trained, experienced infiltrator, who also had the best chances of escaping unscathed. And so here they were, sitting in port a few teleportation hops away from Andral Base.

Logically, it was clearly the best option. But now that they were actually putting the plan in motion, the reality of it was catching up. Ilyen was very good at what he did, but he wasn't infallible, and if something happened they wouldn't be able to assist. Kerelle was having distinct second and third thoughts about the whole thing.

The only person who seemed actually calm about it all was Ilyen himself.

He already had what Kerelle thought of as his *business demeanor* on, checking his knives and other tools with a meticulous patience that was at odds with his usual self. Nalea, on the other hand, was a beacon of anxiety.

"I still don't like that they're sending you in alone like this." The scientist had given up all pretext of calm, and paced restlessly beside where Ilyen was preparing. "It's a *PsiCorp base!* There's a million things that could go wrong, and you're not going to have anyone to help you if they do."

Ilyen looked up from adjusting his body armor, the ghost of a smirk on his lips. "What, you worried about me?"

"Psh." Nalea rolled her eyes, but her fair skin betrayed the flush creeping over her cheeks. "Worried about my research materials. We're only going to get one shot at this. Once they realize we're after a master card they'll get serious about securing them."

"Good thing you've got the best on the job then." Ilyen fastened the last of his knives and gave himself a critical once-over. Apparently satisfied, he turned to Nalea. "Kiss for luck?"

Nalea gave him a soft snort and a peck on the cheek. "Don't fuck this up," she told him. *Come back,* her projections screamed. *Please, please come back to me.*

Ilyen wasn't a telepath; he couldn't sense the feeling that ran beneath her flippant demeanor. But from the slight smile that curved his lips as he vanished, Kerelle wondered if he knew anyway.

NONE of them slept that night. Nalea gave up pacing after a half-hour and withdrew to a corner of the room to tap furiously at her notes, avoiding eye contact with anyone. Kerelle suspected the only reason she hadn't retreated to her lab and locked the door on them all was that she didn't want to miss Ilyen's return.

Sandrel had his aggressively-unconcerned persona on again, diffidently examining a set of engine schematics as he sipped a tumbler of whiskey. She didn't need to look to know he was radiating almost as much anxiety as Nalea. Kerelle tried to read to distract herself, but only ended up rereading the same page a dozen times. As the hours wore on, she finally gave up altogether and got up to clean the mess instead. At least scrubbing the counters gave her something to *do*.

It was a few hours before dawn when Ilyen returned without fanfare. One moment Kerelle was leaning over to attack a stubborn part of the sink with her sponge; the next Nalea gave a cry of relief and launched herself across the room.

Ilyen was grinning ear to ear, and seemingly unharmed. "Careful, babe, don't make me drop this," he laughed, withdrawing the small card from his jacket. "It was a pain in the ass to get."

Kerelle caught her breath. "But you got it."

Ilyen's eyeroll was good-natured. "Of *course* I got it, Evandra. Who do you think I am?"

SIX DAYS later they came out of hyper above Cashaal. Kerelle's nerves fluttered with excitement as they began their descent to the surface. They'd run the card through Nalea's prototype device soon after Ilyen's return, but they had no way of knowing if it had *actually* worked.

They were about to find out.

She reached out through the bond almost as soon as the ship touched down, sending Galhen a telepathic kiss on the cheek and an urgent sense of question.

Welcome back, darling. Warmth infused his response, but she sensed he was not wholly comfortable - there was a feeling that he was holding something back.

Is everything all right?

A telltale pause. *Not entirely, I'm afraid. I'm with Lilika in the war room - can you and the others join us as soon as you're able?*

That isn't ominous at all, *darling.*

A telepathic hand-squeeze. *Forgive me, love, but it will be easier to just show you.*

She sighed then, and shared the exchange with the others. A short time later, the four of them were in the war room. As promised, Lilika and Galhen were already there, along with Elinea. None of them looked happy.

"Congratulations, and welcome back," Lilika said briskly as they entered the room. "We have a problem."

"Only one?" Ilyen raised his eyebrows. "Sounds like we're having a good week then. By the way, you're welcome for sneaking into a PsiCorp base, alone, securing the objective, and getting out without being caught. In case you were thinking about expressing some thanks."

Lilika gave him a quelling look. "Your efforts are appreciated," she said archly.

"As are yours," she added, nodding to Nalea. "You continue to deliver wonders and miracles, Dr. Ambrel, and I regret that at the moment we cannot offer more celebration for your success."

"So it worked, then." Nalea's tone was even and professional, but her aura spiked with excitement. Her hand found Ilyen's, possibly without realizing it. "There was no way for us to measure, before we headed back through hyper..."

"It worked exactly as you promised," Lilika confirmed. Despite her obvious concern with this still-unstated *problem*, she gave the scientist a warm smile. "The regional manager's control card was linked to nearly a hundred collars. As near as we can tell, all those collars simultaneously deactivated when you fed it into your device."

"A hundred people," Kerelle echoed. It seemed almost too much to process.

"Yes." Lilika's lips resettled in a frown. "A huge achievement, and also the source of our current problem."

She waved them into seats and withdrew her tablet. Galhen took over as she tapped at the screen.

"The good news is, many of those people made their way to us, through Lilika's network. You'll find many new faces around the compound, and we're expecting a few more to arrive by week's end. All told we have nearly sixty new recruits."

Sandrel's eyebrows went up. "You're saying we've doubled

our size overnight." From the look on his face, he was already redoing calculations for supplies.

"Exactly that." Galhen's smile faltered. "That's the *good* news. The unfortunate part is that other forty."

Ilyen's brows pinched. "Let me guess, this doesn't go so great when we don't vet everybody first?"

"Regrettably so." Galhen glanced back over at Lilika. "We don't think most of those forty are a threat, at least not at the moment. Some turned themselves in to SysTech immediately, and were presumably re-collared. Others are unaccounted for, and likely have slipped away into hiding."

Lilika looked up, lips compressed. "They may be a problem in the future, but in the short term I suspect they will remain quiescent. Those in hiding will not want to risk revealing themselves to SysTech."

"Then there is the final dozen." She slid her tablet across the table. "I'll let these speak for themselves."

The headlines were stark, the text large and bold as if anything less would misunderstand its gravity.

PSIONIC TERRORISTS OVERWHELM ESTAVIEL
CITIZENS FLEE PSIONIC NIGHTMARE
ESTAVIEL COLLAPSES. WHO IS NEXT?

The imagery was little different. Sundered buildings, rubble-strewn streets, fleeing refugees. Terse quotes from government officials, assuring reporters that military resources were being brought in. SysTech, promising its own assistance in protecting the innocent citizens of Estaviel.

Lilika's collection culminated in a low-fi video clip, obviously taken from someone's personal device. A man stalked menacingly toward a group of terrified mundanes.

"Kneel," he sneered. "I'm not going to ask again." The group drew back, some shakily going to their knees while others stared like rabbits mesmerized by a snake. The aggressor - the psionic, surely, he had to be - took another step forward, and one of the mundanes in front found his courage.

"We don't have to kneel to you. You've got no right - "

The psionic casually flicked his hand, and the man flew sideways into a wall with sickening force. He was no longer visible in the camera, but from the horrified reactions of the mundanes still on screen Kerelle could imagine what they saw.

"I think I told you to *kneel*," he commented lightly, and this time all the group dropped to the ground. His sneer grew into a smirk.

The psionic looked toward the camera, seeming to notice it for the first time. A sudden speeding blur, then it refocused near his face. He must have pulled it from the hand of its operator. Kerelle hoped the lack of noise indicated he hadn't otherwise harmed them.

"Hello, universe," the man was saying. His tone was smooth and unhurried, though an excited glint shone in his eyes. "Let's do introductions. I am Toris Helmanal Klai, telekinetic, lord of Estaviel and soon this whole sector. You're the pathetic pieces of shit who tried to make us serve you. Well," he added with a widening smirk, angling the camera down to focus on the bare strip of pale skin where his collar had obviously been, "it makes more sense the other way around, doesn't it? Seems to us the strongest ought to be running things. Estaviel's the first. It won't be the last."

The video ended. Kerelle's hands were shaking.

"We did that," she whispered. "We let them go, and this happened. *We* killed those people."

"*Klai* killed those people," Lilika answered coldly. "Klai and his little gang. He has a handful of others with him, all equally charming. None at his power level, however, so Klai can get away with calling himself the lord of the sector."

"I worked with him once on a Security Force job," Elinea added grimly. "He's a pure telekinetic, on the high end of C2, specialized in shock force. He was good at the work, but always seemed like he enjoyed it a little too much." The pyrokinetic's brow creased in disgust. "I'm not at all surprised it's him doing this."

Kerelle digested that, the sick feeling growing in her guts. Klai might have been the one to actually attack those mundanes, but they were the ones who'd given him the chance. She'd opened up the citizens of Estaviel to this peril. She had a responsibility to get them out of it.

"We can't let him get away with it," she answered finally. "I'm going to deal with him." She looked up to meet Lilika's eyes. "Don't try to stop me. We owe this to the people we've endangered."

Lilika rolled her own eyes in response. "Spare us the melo-drama, I have no *intention* of stopping you. As it happens, that is exactly what I was going to ask you to do. And soon, before SysTech's commandos solve the problem themselves."

Lilika tapped the now-frozen video on her tablet as she continued. "In a way, Klai has presented us with an opportunity to counter SysTech's own propaganda. We can show the mundanes that we are not a monolith. Show them we will protect them from ourselves, that a free psionic is not always a danger."

Her dark eyes narrowed, and Lilika's tone was pure ice. "He's only a C2, Kerelle. Crush him. And do it where they can see you."

TWELVE

THE CHEERY blue sky over Estaviel seemed almost obscene in the circumstances. It was certainly a marked contrast to Kerelle's own mood as she crunched broken glass underfoot in the deserted street.

She'd been afraid that they would have trouble getting in, but those fears had proved groundless. The collapse of its largest city had left the small planet in disarray, and all its remaining resources were laser-focused on making sure none of the chaos in Estaviel swept outward. They were far less concerned about anything that might get *in*. Sandrel had brought them down cloaked in the stealth field, and the ship now rested quietly in a vacant lot on an abandoned city block.

Kerelle hoped its inhabitants had only fled.

The remaining citizens of Estaviel, the ones who hadn't made it out before planetary security sealed the area, seemed to be hunkering down in hiding to wait. Kerelle could sense a large number of humans still in the area; for all the showy destruction around them, Klai and his gang did not seem to have engaged in wholesale murder of Estaviel's mundane population. Thank the stars for that, at least - but the scattered still forms they passed in the streets bore witness that the citizens had not escaped unscathed.

"What a shitshow," Ilyen muttered to her as they stepped over a fallen communication array, scattered haphazardly across the pavement that had shattered it on impact. His tone was unconcerned, but Kerelle could sense his taut discomfort at the devastation around them. The rest of the group - Elinea, Anniya, Koren, Flaveren - were a few paces behind them, picking their own way around the rubble-strewn streets. A grim aura radiated from them as well; no one was unaffected by what they saw.

At one time Kerelle might have simply nodded, assuming the teleporter didn't expect much of a response. By now, however, she could read the signs that he needed reassurance - and would always be too proud to ask for it.

"We're going to stop them," she told him quietly. "And we're going to send a message to anyone else who might be thinking of doing the same thing."

Kerelle was not entirely comfortable with Lilika's position that there was a silver living in all this to improve their public image. It felt too much to her like profiting off the blood and suffering of the innocents of Estaviel, though she had to concede that Lilika's arguments - that they could not undo the past to prevent this, so they might as well take advantage of an opportunity in a bad situation - were sound. Kerelle hoped, however, that her words to Ilyen proved true.

They couldn't go back in time and prevent the rogue psionics from harming these people. But she could make it clear to any others who might consider such a thing that it would not end well for them.

Ilyen gave her a tight nod in return, icy eyes narrowed at the street ahead of them. "You got a bead on our man yet?"

She nodded. "Wasn't hard. None of them are shielding, if they even can." They knew from Elinea that Klai was a pure tele-kinetic, but they had no idea if there was any telepathy ability among his group. Since she and Lilika had been able to easily pick up on a dozen psionics, the point seemed moot. "He's where we thought he would be, near the city center. Lilika's suspicion that he's set up in City Hall seems likely. The others seem to be with him."

"Great, we can get this all over at once."

The rest of the group caught up then, eyes hard and jaws set.

"Sounds like we have our targets?" Elinea asked briskly. A soft, subtle glow shone under her fingernails - she was beyond ready to get to work.

"Targets are acquired," Kerelle confirmed. She looked over her team quickly, and gave them a quick nod of acknowledgement. "And they're not going to know what hit them. Now let's go shatter some delusions of grandeur."

LIKE MOST CITIES ITS SIZE, Estaviel grouped its primary government buildings around a wide civic plaza. Unlike most cities, the plaza was a mess of debris. Scattered groups of mundanes worked at clearing the rubble, their fear a jagged ringing against her senses. Apparently Klai had ordered them to *do something about the mess, hm?*, and the prospect of displeasing him was more terrifying than being in this proximity to his headquarters - but only just.

The closest group stopped to stare as they passed. Kerelle tried to look reassuring. Their expressions indicated she wasn't doing great at that.

"You should find cover," she said quietly. "We're not going to hurt you, but this area may be dangerous to stay in."

The man in front of her tightened his grip on the shovel. "No disrespect, ma'am, but I think we'd be in more danger if we left."

One of the other mundanes gave him a nervous glance. "Jorren, that's *her*," she hissed. Her wide eyes were glued to Kerelle's face. Buzzing whispers started up in the rest of the group, and several of them looked from her to Ilyen with increasing alarm.

"We're not here to hurt you," she repeated. "We're here to help." The alarm didn't decrease.

"Look," Ilyen cut in brusquely. "If you know who we are, then you know not to fuck with us. If you're worried about getting shit from Klai, he's going to be dead in an hour. Get somewhere else so you don't get in the way."

That worked. The group dropped their tools and took off at a fast pace.

Ilyen answered Kerelle's look with a slight shrug. "Time and a place, Evandra. You can turn on the charm after we're through this. Or better yet, let Ambrel do that part, and we can stick to what we're good at."

She didn't have an argument to that.

As they approached the city hall building, the other groups in the square melted away as well. Apparently word traveled fast.

They halted outside the deceptively tranquil facade.

"If they've got any telepaths, they have to know we're here. Guards up," she stated, tightening her own shield as she did. "And if they don't have any telepaths, we'll just have to let them *know* we're here."

Hot flames erupted around Elinea's hand in a tight swirl. "Well then, let's wake them up."

"We want to limit collateral damage," Kerelle reminded her urgently. The last thing they needed was for overenthusiasm to finish what Klai started. Elinea snorted.

"Relax, Evandra. Nothing burns unless I want it to." The swirl of fire grew larger, and she hurled it at the building with a burst of glee.

The fire's roar echoed through the empty square, its reflection off the surrounding glass buildings almost blinding. It dissipated an instant before Kerelle thought it was going to smash into the city hall, the sudden silence nearly as violent as the noise that preceded it.

A fire alarm began to sound from within the building. Elinea smirked.

The doors opened, and Klai stepped unhurriedly into the square.

"You know, I *have* a secretary to set up appointments." His tone was decidedly bored, though the jumpiness in his aura betrayed he was not quite as unconcerned as he seemed.

Still, the faint smirk on his lips made her teeth clench.

"This isn't a social call, Klai." She kept her own voice level, though being this close to him sent hot anger through her veins. "You have a lot to answer for."

He barked a laugh. "*Answer* for? To who, you? You think we busted out of SysTech just to start taking orders from someone else?"

"Actually *we* busted you out of SysTech," Ilyen interjected. "You didn't do shit." His icy eyes and languid posture mirrored Klai's amused detachment, but his aura, too, radiated a rising tension.

Klai's smirk took on a hard edge, and he waved a hand at their surroundings. The rest of his group had filed out quietly behind him, and now they and Kerelle's people eyed each other across the plaza.

"I don't know, I'd say we did pretty well. Less than a week and we've got our own little kingdom here. What did *you* do? Escape months ago just to hide like mice? Make videos about your sad childhoods, like the mundanes are going to pity you? We don't need their *pity*," he hissed, detached mask breaking. "We should have their *fear*."

Kerelle maintained eye contact; she wouldn't give him the satisfaction of thinking he rattled her. "This is your last chance to surrender, Klai. You and your group. There's no need for this to end in violence." It was a lie, and all of them knew it - there was really no other way it *could* end, not with the sneer on his face and the broken city around them. But she made the attempt nonetheless, and wasn't surprised at all at what he said next.

"I'm not surrendering, Evandra, not to you or anyone else. Not ever again."

His telekinetic shove packed considerable force, no doubt intended to send her sprawling across the plaza. She was ready, however, and her shields turned it harmlessly aside.

"Then you leave us no choice," she answered, and shoved back.

Chaos erupted, as both their groups surged forward to engage. The glass on the building's facade shattered in a loud crash, either under her own blow or someone else's. Ilyen vanished from beside her. From behind her, sudden blasts of heat - Anniya and Elinea had both called their flames. An answering heat from the side meant Klai had at least one pyrokinetic of his own.

She tightened her shields and concentrated on Klai.

He lost no time going on the offensive, sending a series of concussive hits against her shield. She hit back, his own shields holding.

Klai swore and spun away, seconds before a fireball passed closely by Kerelle's shoulder to strike where he'd been. No time to check whose it was - she leapt over to follow as he put distance between them.

In her peripheral vision, she caught glimpses of the rest of the group engaged in their own duels with the rest of Klai's people. Debris was kicked up or used as projectiles between her telekinetics and Klai's, punctuated by the bright eruption of fireballs. There-and-gone-again flashes told her Ilyen was flitting around the battlefield, harrying their foes and seeking the gaps in their shields.

A scream from behind her - at least one injury, though she couldn't tell who. Kerelle quashed her immediate instinct to locate them and help; her team were all professionals, they could handle this and each other. Klai was the strongest, and so was she. She had to keep him in her sights.

He struck suddenly at her back, not slowing his pace as he stayed ahead of her. She was almost caught off guard, but managed to keep her balance and deflect some of the force back at him. Kerelle didn't pause to give him time to consider - she followed up with a solid wall of force in front of him. His momentum carried him straight into it, and he grunted as he went sprawling.

He was already rolling back to his feet as she closed with him, another blow readied. Klai struck first, trying to turn her movement against her as she had his. Kerelle dodged the phantom obstruction and threw her own wave of force. Klai wobbled but held his ground, diverting it around his shields. Still, he must have felt that one.

"Still doing their dirty work, Evandra?" He snarled. "Still a SysTech lapdog, even without a collar?" His powers shoved at her.

"This isn't about SysTech," she growled back, countering with another wave of her own. "This is about *you*. Look around you, look what you've *done!*" She seized a chunk of broken masonry and flung it at him. "SysTech tells the galaxy that we're monsters, and the first chance you get, you try to prove them *right!*"

He stopped her projectile in midair and shattered it, sending the pieces streaming back toward her like tiny bullets. She flung them away before they got close.

He started laughing, the sound hard-edged and cold. "See? All this, and you still care what they think. Who gives a *fuck* about being 'right,' when they can't do anything about it? If there's one thing I *did* learn from SysTech, it's that the strongest get to make their own rules." A strange look passed over his face. "That could have been you, Evandra. But you'd rather chain *yourself* up. And so you'll die just like they will."

Kerelle's patience snapped.

Broken glass hurtled towards her; rather than arrest its motion this time she drew it in, turning its momentum to form a swirling tornado around her. Kerelle poured more energy into the whipping winds as she advanced on Klai. He sent a hard wave at her, probably hoping to disrupt her glass tornado, but she just shoved it back at him, not breaking stride. The gradual ache worming its way through her head told her she was expending a lot of energy - he had to be flagging as well.

A quick twist of force and her glass shards aligned in front of her. She gave them a final vicious spin and spat them out at Klai.

The majority fell, deflected by his shield, but he hissed in pain as a few of her shards slipped past to score his cheek. Flagging, indeed.

Kerelle didn't give him time to recover. She hit again at his shield, saw his teeth clench and *felt* it sway under her blow. He growled and flung a chunk of rubble at her head, but she dodged easily, adrenaline lending her strength.

Klai grunted and stumbled, tossing a quick glance over his shoulder. Ilyen materialized on his other side, bloody knives at the ready.

Klai's shields could keep Ilyen out, but all three of them knew those shields were faltering. Ilyen vanished and reappeared behind him, hands flashing in a lightning-quick strike. He bounced, again, off the shield, but Klai swayed a bit under the impact - and Ilyen had his attention.

Kerelle saw her opening and thrust her telekinetics forward into a sharp uppercut, visceral satisfaction surging through her as she felt Klai's shield finally crack. Ilyen was on him in an instant. A sharp cry, and Ilyen shoved him down off the end of the knife. Blood began to pool as Klai glared up at them with shuddering breaths.

"It's over," she told him. Then because she couldn't just watch him bleed out on the concrete, no matter how much he might deserve it - "Surrender and we'll spare your life."

Klai spat blood at them. "Evandra," he rasped, "Go fuck yourself."

She *sensed* it, a massive final pull in their direction, and struck almost reflexively.

A sick *snap*, and Klai's eyes went empty; a loud shattering crash as the heavy debris and jagged glass he'd sought to skewer them with fell harmlessly to the ground.

She turned away.

* * *

"THERE, that ought to do it. Avoid putting your full weight on your foot for the next day or so, but you should be back to normal activity again by the end of the week." Galhen gave the woman a warm smile and helped her up from the makeshift exam table. She avoided his eyes, but managed a quick nod and muttered thanks as she gingerly exited their little infirmary.

There was a not-insignificant crowd in the civic plaza, either awaiting their turn in the infirmary or simply milling about watching them. It felt a bit ghoulish to Kerelle, to be set up scant meters from where she'd killed Klai, but there really wasn't another large, centrally-located space that worked better for their purposes.

Lilika had said something as well about symbolically reclaiming public space. Kerelle was going to leave that sort of thing to her. Kerelle's primary concern was that the threat was dealt with, and her team had made it through alive, though not unscathed. There had been fractures and cuts to deal with, and it was only Galhen's swift intervention that had Koren recuperating from his burns, rather than fighting for his life. Still, they'd all made it out. None of Klai's people had.

Which meant it was time for them to be on their way. Estaviel was free from the threat of hostile psionics, but the SysTech and planetary military resources meant to deal with them could arrive at any time. They would likely be all too happy to take down her group in place of Klai's.

She gave Galhen a small mental nudge. *I've just confirmed with Sandrel we're ready to take off. I hate to interrupt, darling, but we need to be on our way.*

He sent back his acknowledgement. *That's fine. There may be some disappointment, but I've dealt with the more severe injuries among the citizenry. Those who were willing to see me, of course.* A shade of resigned disappointment, then it was gone. *The remainder are not in any danger, and should respond to conventional treatment when it arrives. I'll be along momentarily.*

She gave him the telepathic equivalent of a kiss on the cheek and set off for the final departure checks, scanning the square for anyone who might need reminding. A sudden, unfamiliar voice sounded behind her.

"Agent...Agent Evandra?"

She turned, surprised. A small knot of teenagers were watching her with a mixture of nervousness and fascination. The one in front swallowed and tried again. "You are...you are Agent Evandra, right?"

Shit, where were they going this? She tamped down on the fervent wish that they were talking to Galhen instead, or Lilika, or literally anyone but her, and tried to smile reassuringly back at them.

"Not any more," she replied with what she hoped was friendly confidence. "Now I'm just Kerelle. What can I do for you?"

"I watched your video," the first one said bluntly. "My brother says you're full of shit."

She wasn't sure how to respond to that, though his expectant look made it clear she ought to *have* a response. She said the only thing she could think of.

"I'm sorry to hear that. What do *you* think?"

He looked pleasantly surprised to be asked. "I'm not sure. You saved us from Klai and didn't ask for anything in return. Doesn't seem like something a terrorist would do."

"Good, because I'm not a terrorist," she answered, trying to smile. Stars, this felt like dodging grenades. "We want the freedom to live in peace, for ourselves and for psionics everywhere. Nothing more." She took a deep breath. "And if any psionics try to do what Klai did, we'll be there to stop them too."

Whatever he was going to say next was lost, as Ilyen suddenly appeared at her side. Murmurs of *burning stars, the teleporter* washed over the small group. His eyes flicked over to them before turning back to her.

"You in the middle of something here?"

"We were finishing up," she answered. The one she'd begun thinking of as the group leader squared his shoulders.

"I don't believe you're terrorists," he declared seriously, giving them a decisive nod. Ilyen's eyebrows rose a fraction.

"Great, tell your friends." The teleporter turned to her. "Everything's packed up and Ambrel's back on the ship. Time to find our next party."

Kerelle gave the kids an awkward smile and a wave. "It was nice to meet you. Stay safe."

Ilyen leaned in her ear as they walked away. "So if this goes south, at least we'll have the secondary-school crowd on our side?"

She gave him a half-smile back. "At this point, I'm counting everyone who doesn't run away screaming as a victory."

Ilyen snorted. "This is why we put *Lilika* in charge of PR."

Kerelle gave him an affectionate elbow, and hoped her impromptu interview hadn't been a mistake.

"WELL, you can't say we didn't get their attention."

Sandrel's tone was deceptively light, and she nodded mechanically as she scrolled through the seemingly endless stream of videos. Most were blurred and shaky, shot on personal devices at long range, but still clear enough to make out the action. There was her confrontation with Klai, the words faint but discernible. There was the battle that followed, a story told in short snippets from different directions - various duels between her forces and his, the collateral damages they'd tried to avoid, her own struggle with Klai and its bloody culmination.

Kerelle couldn't suppress a flinch at that last one, watching Klai's distant form convulse as her own stood over him. She knew it had been necessary. It was still painful to watch.

But it wasn't all combat and destruction. A short clip of Galhen healing a badly broken limb garnered nearly as many views as her confrontation with Klai. It too was blurred and taken from a distance, likely by someone waiting in line themselves, but his careful touch as he straightened the arm, the lack of pain from the patient as he handled her injury, the way she swung her arm in wonder afterwards, were all clearly visible nonetheless.

Fewer views, but still prominent, was her brief chat with the teenagers. She hadn't noticed the one in the back had been recording.

"You did excellent work," Lilika remarked. "Fast, efficient, minimal destruction. You even managed to give a statement."

"Glad the optics worked out for you," Kerelle answered dryly.

"Do you think it will make a difference, narratively?"

Galhen's voice was quiet. "Not that we wouldn't have done it regardless."

"It may," Lilika said. "We've been telling people we mean them no harm; this was our first chance to actually prove it. It will depend if our efforts to dissociate ourselves with Klai are successful. SysTech will doubtlessly paint us as partners in crime who tired of each other. We'll need to continue to keep up our side of the narrative."

She rose from the table. "But in any case, we've accomplished our objective for now, and everyone has earned some rest. It will be time to press forward again soon enough."

THIRTEEN

IN WINTER, Kerelle considered, Cashaal was almost tolerable.

It was still far too warm, of course, but the heat had relinquished the punishing edge it had wielded in the summer months. Now, their stark home felt more like a pan recently removed from the stovetop, rather than one being actively cooked. There were even a few hardy weeds pushing up from the edges of the buildings; spiny and unfriendly as the little shoots looked, it still lifted her spirits to see something green and growing outside.

Part of that also, she admitted to herself, was the undeniable signs of just how far their little stronghold had come in the eight months since they'd arrived on Cashaal. They'd touched down in two ships packed with a little more than two dozen people, to a site well on its way to being reclaimed by the desert. Now the base was home to five times that number, and with steady work they had managed to make it not merely functional again, but even somewhat comfortable.

The greenhouse project had really come together as well. Teriel had wasted no time recruiting two of Lilika's students and a curious telepath, and now they had a whole little team tending the garden. The vegetable yield would never be enough to sustain their group on its own, but it was a welcome supplement to the canned foods they still brought from off world.

Oliven caught her eye and waved from across the courtyard. Kerelle waved back with a smile, inwardly marveling at just how much their lost little C1 had grown up in the last two years. He wore his title of *Captain Zharus* now nearly as easily as his spacer's jacket.

He jogged across the courtyard to meet her. "You're up early today, Kerelle."

"I could say the same to you. Big plans?"

"Just flight school," he answered, the smile creeping over his lips again. "I wanted to get a few things ready before we started today. Some of the others are really coming along on piloting, and today we're going to try some more advanced maneuvers." Kerelle smiled warmly back. Their tiny fleet of transport ships needed pilots, and Oliven had taken over the duty of training them with gusto.

"But that doesn't explain why *you're* out here." He gave her a glance that was entirely too insightful. "Nervous about the whole Tallimau thing?"

Kerelle laughed softly. "Am I that transparent?"

Oliven winked. "Only to people who lived with you in a small ship for a year."

"No secrets from the old crew. But...yes. I'm not entirely comfortable with the whole situation."

He cocked his head at her. "Do you think the Tallimau resistance cell is legit?"

It was the question everyone on Cashaal was asking, ever since Lilika's agent had relayed the message. It was the latest in the slow, steady trickle of contacts from small groups of PsiCorp, but the first involving anyone they knew - and the first from a major PsiCorp base.

"Galhen thinks it is," she finally answered. "The man leading them, Orien - they weren't *close*, exactly, but they served a few missions together and Galhen respects him. He thinks it's plausible that Orien would join our cause."

"What do *you* think?"

"I didn't know him as well," she admitted. "I never really got on with people, exactly. Not like Galhen did. For most of the names on this list, I knew them more as faces in the hallway than anything."

Oliven only nodded. "The PsiCorp wasn't a great place to make friends."

"No," she agreed, grateful he understood. "It wasn't."

But she *had* had a friend. She'd had Mila, whose name was not among those in the Tallimau resistance. Kerelle was still sorting through how she felt about that. She wasn't *surprised*; Mila was really the last person she would expect to sign on as a revolutionary. In a way it might be for the best - she would likely be in less danger this way. At the same time, an irrational disappointment curled in her chest.

Kerelle shook her head slightly to dispel the thought. "It's not just the trustworthiness of the cell itself, though. There's an element of risk involved with everyone we recruit, even the ones who *aren't* from top PsiCorp strongholds. It's also the risk of getting them out."

Oliven glanced over. "I know we have Dr. Ambrel's new control-card device, but can we *get* a control card from Tallimau?"

"No, not realistically. Tallimau is too well defended, and they'll be guarding the control cards more carefully now that they know what we can do with them. We'll have to do this one the old way."

It went quiet for a moment, and Kerelle knew they were both thinking of the small resistance cell from the Uliste base that had reached out to them, the one they'd promised to help escape. But SysTech had gotten wind of the attempt and flipped the collars on; for all but one shaking and traumatized younger agent, they hadn't gotten them off in time.

They had to get this right; four people were dead because they hadn't, last time.

Oliven finally spoke again. "If anyone can do this, it's you and Sandrel and Commander Charyth."

She hoped his faith wasn't misplaced.

"WHAT WE NEED IS A DISTRACTION," Sandrel told the table. "Even *I* know Tallimau is the jewel of the PsiCorp program. There's a lot of eyes on it. It would be in our best interest if those eyes were looking elsewhere."

Lilika smiled slightly. "Your tone tells me you've already thought of something."

"So happens I have," he agreed, returning the smile. He looked around the table at each of them.

"Last time you put out a video, it took off almost immediately. Not sure if you actually *convinced* anyone, but you got them talking. And that was just the whole thing with Dalanva, which, honestly? Probably wasn't *that* much of a shock to the average spacer. My understanding is that you guys have significantly more dirt." He motioned at Ilyen. "And that this one in particular knows where the bodies are buried."

Lilika gave a soft snort. "Yes, because he put them there," she muttered. Ilyen grinned, looking more proud than repentant.

"So spill," Sandrel told them seriously. "Not about your shitty upbringing, nobody cares about that. Tell them what you did for SysTech. I bet you time stops when that thing goes out, especially if we hack a few public channels." He glanced over at Lilika. "I hear you know people who can do that."

She smirked back.

Not long after, their camera was trained on Ilyen. If he was nervous, it didn't show.

"You know who I am by now," he started without preamble. "But for the record my name is Ilyen Kirana Vanadariel, C2 telekinetic, C2 teleporter."

"Now that last part might be new to some of you," he continued conversationally. "Somehow SysTech keeps forgetting to add it to my wanted poster. But fun fact, I was never actually in the regular PsiCorp, I was in the black ops, and until they freaked out and put my face all over the news I officially didn't exist. If you didn't know SysTech *had* a black ops program, now you do. It's another thing they keep forgetting to mention. But you're not here for the PR bullshit, you want the juicy stuff."

Ilyen gave another of his wolfish grins. "All right then, let's talk about what I *did* in the black ops."

Even having a vague idea of what was coming, Kerelle couldn't look away. In seven minutes of calm recitation, Ilyen confirmed two fringe conspiracies, and probably launched a dozen more. As it turned out, the field director for a medical nonprofit campaigning for better health conditions on an impoverished industrial hub wasn't shot in a botched robbery. The small-aircraft crash that killed a rising star of environmental advocacy was not faulty maintenance. One of the top shareholders for ConEn didn't have a heart attack in her sleep. Kerelle remembered when that had happened - there had been many media tributes to a business titan gone too soon, but not even a whisper of a suspicion of foul play.

Ethics aside, she couldn't deny Ilyen did amazing work.

A short time later the whole thing was beaming out across the datanet, and almost immediately began to spread like wildfire. Kerelle couldn't help a small smile of satisfaction at the thought of what SysTech PR must be thinking right now.

She glanced at Lilika, expecting to see similar, but the other woman's expression was troubled. A curl of unease slipped down Kerelle's back.

"Is everything all right?"

Lilika didn't bother prevaricating. "Riyel missed our meeting." The words were cool, measured, but laden with portent. "It could be nothing. He may have been pulled into something and unable to extract himself in time, or he may have been moved out of range without the chance to tell me."

They were both silent, the other possibility looming horribly between them. Kerelle wasn't sure what to say, dread blooming in her gut. Riyel had evaded SysTech attention this long. Surely his skill hadn't failed him now?

Lilika had her impassive mask on again, dark eyes hard as gemstones. "I'll attempt to contact him again tonight, if - "

Whatever plan she had formed remained unsaid. Instead, they met each others' wide eyes as the warning sirens began to shriek.

FOURTEEN

KERELLE BARRELED down the corridor towards the command center, Lilika close behind her. She felt Galhen's questioning alarm through their bond, and linked with him without a second thought.

"Sandrel!" Her knuckles were white around the comm. "Sandrel, what's our status?"

The smuggler's voice was terse over the crackling comm. "Corporate ships, lots of them. They knew we were here, dropped in from hyper right on top of us."

She swore. "Okay, let's get people to upper levels, the telekinetics and pyros can act as anti-air defense - "

"No," he cut her off, "It's too late for that, they're already landing. The first wave had stealth fields engaged, we didn't even know they were here until they started touching down."

It felt like all the air was leaving her lungs. "How many?" She could sense no intruders, though of course they were invisible - no one would be sent on a mission like this without a psiblocker. But she could sense their own people, sudden pinpoints of fear and pain and panic blooming around Cashaal like a terrible bouquet.

"Too many. Kerelle - I wouldn't say this if I didn't mean it. There's too many. We need to get out while we still can."

"Acknowledged." The world around her turned surreal, as if it were some strange thing she beheld at a distance. *Shock,* supplied that part of her mind that always seemed detached from its surroundings. *You're going into shock. You really don't have time for that right now.*

She took a shuddering breath and forced herself to focus. Feel later.

"Began evac protocol. We need to get everyone to the shuttles as fast as we can. I'll do what I can to hold off the enemy."

"Understood." His tone was grim. "And don't forget to get yourself to a shuttle too."

Kerelle met Lilika's eyes. "Can you get the evac orders out? We need everyone in the shuttles, as fast as we can take off." Lilika nodded fiercely, eyes wide but jaw set. Kerelle gave her a quick nod back. "Stay close, let's go."

She pinged Galhen as they started moving. *Darling, did you catch all that?*

Yes, though the medbay situation evolved while you were talking to Sandrel. We're barricaded in with a few wounded, though I suspect there are already many more who need help. His thoughts were overlaid with resolve and a certain professional detachment; this was Dr. Ambrel the combat medic. *Requesting assistance in moving several immobile patients.* He paused. *And in dispersing the group of hostiles trying to break down my door.*

We're coming, she sent, and switched directions for the medbay.

As they ran, Kerelle flicked her comm to Nalea's frequency.

"Nalea," she started urgently, "We're under attack, we have to evacuate - "

"Already on it," the scientist answered. "Just heard from Sandrel. I've got Ilyen and a few others with me, we're getting as much out of my lab as we can." Muffled sounds of struggle were audible in the background. "Anything we leave behind, SysTech can use against us."

"Be careful, and leave it if you have to," Kerelle admonished "Your life is more important."

Nalea's answer was noncommittal as she closed the channel.

Sudden small arms fire caught Kerelle's attention, far too close. There - she could sense Melaris trying to hold off attackers. Kerelle upped her shields and skidded around the corner of the corridor.

Melaris was backed against the wall facing off with three black-clad soldiers, though her shields currently kept them at bay. They wouldn't hold long though, not against three psiblockers.

Lacking any convenient debris projectiles, Kerelle took the direct approach and barreled straight into the closest commando, knocking her prone. Before she could react Kerelle wrenched off the psiblocker and *snapped*.

The other two had recovered almost immediately from the surprise of her appearance; they were facing her now, pressing aggressively against her shields. She shoved the closer one with brutal force, thrusting him back against the far wall of the corridor. A second blow from Melaris followed, cracking his head against the unyielding stone wall.

Only the third remained; they circled each other warily as his gauntlets began to spark. Electrified gloves - no tackling option here, then. They needed to keep him at range.

Keep his eyes on you, Lilika told her. *And seize the opening.* The thought was overlaid with an image of the first commando's sidearm still holstered on her body, and an assurance that Lilika knew how to use it.

Got it. She'd have to hope Lilika didn't overestimate her aim.

"Pin and stun," she shouted to Melaris. Their opponent charged as she said it, determined to avoid that very thing. Kerelle forced down her instinct to draw back from those terrible gloves, and instead focused her fear into an intense shove that sent him stumbling backwards, psiblocker and all. Melaris struck at his unsteady footing, seeking to send him prone, but he managed to twist himself around the blow, turning the movement into momentum to leap.

She caught him against her shield midair. It would have been comical, watching his descent slowed as if he moved through thick water, if not for the danger of the situation.

Move!

She did, and Lilika had a clear shot. She took it, and two more following, as the shield held him trapped and helpless in a slow descent to the ground. The armor absorbed the first and second. At the third he went limp, either unconscious or dead.

Lilika dispassionately walked up to prone commando and aimed carefully to ensure it was the latter. She stripped him of his sidearm and handed it to Kerelle. Melaris silently armed herself with the third man's weapon. She gave Kerelle a nod, and then the three of them were off.

They'd scarcely made it around the corner when they ran into another of the SysTech squad. Lilika's student Peralen was thrown unceremoniously over the man's shoulder, a dart still sticking out of his arm. Peralen wasn't a telepath, but his panic projected as clear as if he were screaming. He couldn't move, he couldn't cry out, *he couldn't move*, and oh stars *Helia Helia Helia* -

Almost on instinct, Kerelle smashed her fist into his kidnapper's jaw. Peralen was suddenly pulled away from them - thank you Melaris - and Kerelle followed with another hit before her opponent could recover. She got his psiblocker off just as his gauntlets crackled to life; it was over in an instant.

It was then that she saw the second body. Helia lay where she'd fallen against the wall, open eyes vacant and shirt soaked with blood. Holy *stars*, she was barely old enough to graduate the academy, and they'd shot her with live rounds -

Behind her she *felt* Lilika's spike of horror and grief, and the effort that accompanied her subsequent emotional lockdown. Kerelle took a steadying breath and forced herself to do the same.

Feel later. Feel later. Feel later.

"We have to keep going," she heard herself say. "Peralen, try to stay calm - whatever was on that dart, we'll figure out how to treat it. Melaris, can you carry him?" A quick nod, and they plunged down the corridor once again.

The scenes repeated several times as they fought their way down towards the medbay. They encountered psionics engaged with the enemy, alone or in small groups, and stopped to help overwhelm the SysTech commandos. Each delay ate at Kerelle, though she could sense through their bond that Galhen was worried but unharmed.

It was more than she could say for many others. For every one of her people they stopped to assist, there were others littered across the corridors beyond all help. She forced herself not to look too closely. She could mourn when they'd gotten out safely with everyone who was still alive.

By the time they approached the medbay, they'd collected a fighting force of nearly a dozen, carrying three people incapacitated by the paralytic darts. Sometime later, maybe they'd know why SysTech was shooting some and capturing others. For now, they could only be grateful for the opportunity to save the people they did.

Assuming *any* of them made it out of this alive.

We're almost there, she sent Galhen, trying to keep her thoughts calm. *Status?*

They're going to break through, he sent back tersely. *We're gathered together to shield, but I'm not sure how long it will hold. Danaese is the only one among us with combat powers.* She got a rough image of a small group of people huddled under a table, a single teenage telekinetic determinedly holding the shield around them as tears slipped silently down her face.

Got it, she responded as her stomach flipped. *Hold on.*

They rounded the corner just as the medbay's doors gave way, a black-clad swarm flooding through. Her glimpse of their drawn weapons was enough to see that only some were brandishing dart guns - the others held implements of lethal force. Lethal force that was advancing on Galhen, and the helpless wounded, and a very brave girl who was far too young to be involved in this kind of thing at all.

Something in Kerelle snapped, and her veins blazed with that same terrible fury that had fueled her all those months ago against the Ash and Bones. She *would not allow it.*

She threw a wave against the advancing force's backs, hard enough to overbalance them even through the psiblockers' dampening effects.

"Run them down," she heard herself growl, and charged the enemy before they could recover.

It was a blur, then, of shields and blows and screams, punctuated by the loud reports of firearms on both sides. She didn't trust her aim at such close quarters, and so Kerelle found herself wielding her gun like a blunt weapon. From the shots echoing from Lilika's direction, the telepath had no such reservations.

Sudden silence signaled the fall of their final opponent. Kerelle blinked rapidly to clear her head, her eyes seeking Galhen in the aftermath. There - he slipped from beneath the table that had sheltered the medbay's inhabitants and was at the side of a fallen psionic in an instant. Kerelle took a deep breath and looked over their force. They'd come out ahead, but not without cost; several of her people lay still on the bloody floor.

Galhen knelt beside another of them; he'd already left the first with slight headshake. Two others were clearly beyond any help as well. There must be hope for the woman beside him; he had both hands on her torso and an expression of intense concentration.

Kerelle took stock of the others as they caught their breath.

With Galhen's group from the medbay they now had seven people incapacitated by the darts, including one of hers who'd been hit in the melee. There were eight of them able-bodied, though not all combat ready. Lilika was directing everyone to collect the fallen commandos' weapons; Kerelle could only hope more of them shared her skill with firearms.

"She's stable, for now," Galhen announced abruptly, standing up meet Kerelle's eyes. "That's all I can do in the time we have."

Lilika was nodding her agreement. "We have to evacuate, or we'll lose far more. We'll head to the shuttles, and - "

Kerelle's comm buzzed suddenly. "Situation's deteriorating," Nalea said without preamble. "Any help would be good."

Kerelle swore. "Location?"

"Still my lab. We'll have to leave whatever's left."

"Got it. I'm coming."

Kerelle shut the channel and met Lilika's gaze. "Take everyone here and head for the shuttles. The other telekinetics can protect you, and together you can carry the wounded." She glanced between Lilika and Galhen. "I'll be along with Nalea as soon as I can."

"I'm staying with you," Galhen interrupted. His tone implied this was not up for debate.

She warred between wanting him to reach the safety of the shuttle more quickly, and not wanting him to leave the protection of her immediate presence. "It will be safer with Lilika - "

"I'm staying with *you*," he repeated. "Nalea and those with her may need my help." A surge through their bond then, more feeling than words - escape or perish, he would not leave her to find her fate alone.

"Then we have to go," she said finally. A quick glance at all their faces, her eyes lingering on Lilika's cool mask. "Be safe. We'll see you on the other side of this." They ran.

Galhen stuck close to her heels as they raced toward Nalea's lab. It *did* feel like a race, against a clock rapidly counting down.

She could sense fewer and fewer of their own people in the fortress; she could only hope the majority had escaped without a telepath to check in.

A SysTech group rounded the corner on them then, and all her concentration was swept up in survival. The world shrank to shields and shoves and the sharp report of the guns. Fortunately Galhen seemed to have kept up with weapons training after the Academy; a trail of still enemies behind them bore testament to his good aim.

Of course I kept up. They were both breathing heavily as they stepped over the latest group and resumed running. *If I can't convince someone they don't want to harm me, then conventional weapons are the only defense I have.*

Well, I'm glad you did, even if I wish you'd never had to put it in practice.

Sounds of combat echoed loudly down the hall as they neared Nalea's lab. They looked at each other and picked up pace.

The corridor outside Nalea's lab was pure chaos. A knot of black-clad SysTech troops swarmed around like angry bees, firing and striking anything in range with those terrible gloves. A small group of telekinetics held them off from inside the lab - clearly being pushed back, but effective all the same. Quite a few SysTech bodies lay sprawled on the ground, wrenched to unnatural angles or sliced to ribbons. Broken glass and various debris littered the space around them and crunched under the attackers' feet. Apparently Nalea's glass labware had been sacrificed to provide weaponry.

Kerelle gathered a swirl of those shards and flung them hard at the nearest foe. They embedded themselves in the back of his armor, giving him the appearance of a glass porcupine but regrettably causing little harm. It *did* distract him, however, and as he turned to see his new attacker Ilyen appeared at his side and lunged, sinking his knives into the vulnerable gaps beneath the arms. He followed with a slice across the throat, gave Kerelle a quick nod and vanished again. She wrenched her glass shards free and went to work.

Slash, dodge, shield, push. The world narrowed to the battle in front of her, at once instantaneous and eternal. She could feel the weary ache forming at her temples, but there was no time to indulge exhaustion. If they survived, she could sleep for a week.

Her comm buzzed as she held one of them down for Ilyen to finish.

"A little occupied," she answered breathlessly, trying to focus on maintaining the immobilizing pressure as Ilyen's knives stabbed downward. She suppressed a cringe as a spray of blood spattered her face.

"We have to get *out*," Sandrel said sharply. "The other shuttles are gone, I'm the last ship left, I'm not going to be able to hold them off much longer."

"We're doing our best - "

"Do *better* then!" The edge in his voice bordered on a snarl. "Kerelle, there's no time. We're all going to *die* here if you don't get out *now*!"

"We're coming."

Ilyen met her eyes. He'd heard too.

Kerelle thought fast. "Port back to Nalea, tell her and anyone with her to get ready to push to the shuttles. I'll work on clearing the way." He vanished.

There were only a handful of the SysTech troops left by then, though the echoes of running boots told her more would soon join them. Well, better to fight on a single front.

Kerelle grabbed their remaining opponents and wrenched them around behind her, gritting her teeth at the effort involved; with the psiblockers blunting her power, it felt like dragging a ton of steel. Nonetheless, she had them all on the same side as the incoming reinforcements. She shoved.

Her blow was suddenly bolstered by additional force, and

this time their foes went flying back. One of her telekinetics took up a place beside her, giving her a determined nod. A flurry of movement and another was on her other side; Nalea's group had joined them.

Nalea herself followed closely, arms wrapped tightly around a set of vials. Her terror burned at Kerelle's senses like roaring campfire, but the scientist was keeping steady, her face worried but calm. Galhen murmured something in her ear and she moved closer to him, nodding sharply. Ilyen hovered a moment at her side before he vanished again, apparently convinced of her safety for the time being.

The time being would be short indeed, if they didn't make it to the shuttles. Kerelle turned all her concentration toward the forward push.

It was easier with a group, though the psiblockers' dampening effects still hampered their blows. Ilyen was everywhere at once, a flicker of whirling blades and spurting blood, always vanishing before anyone could react.

It wasn't enough, there were too many, they just had to *get to the shuttle -*

When they cleared the threshold into Cashaal's cold dawn, the open air was almost shocking after the closeness of the corridors. But there was no time for relief - she could see Sandrel's ship, small and alone amidst a black-clad onslaught. The ship's gun whirled about in rapid fire at its attackers, and its shields were holding, but clearly they would soon be overwhelmed.

Kerelle hadn't come all this way just to die in sight of the ship.

Above them the greenhouse's windows were in jagged ruins, their knife-sharp edges set aglow by the roaring flames within. She didn't have time to wonder which side had set the garden alight.

Large pieces broke readily under her telekinetic grasp, and

she hurled them at the crowd of SysTech fighters like javelins of vengeance. They scattered, and while they were off-balance she shoved them to one side with all her flagging might. That weary ache in her temples had built into sharp, painful pressure, and Kerelle made the grim realization that she didn't have many blows like that left in her. Already she could feel her shields starting to flicker.

Her shove had pushed the group of enemies mostly back into a corridor. More out of desperation than anything else, she grabbed the twisted hull of another ship - *don't think about which one, don't think about how it got that way* - and with a last great heave, flung it over to block the passageway. It wouldn't hold long.

The hatch of Sandrel's ship popped open, and they ran. Already the soldiers were breaking through her makeshift barricade, and she forced herself to hold the shields up behind them. So close to the ship, so close, but the shields were faltering -

Sharp pain against her arm, and the world went icy. She couldn't feel her power, oh stars she couldn't feel *anything* -

A searing heat then, at the same spot, and she could feel her limbs again, though they seemed sluggish and distant. She bumped roughly against the lip of the hatch as Galhen dragged her in. She whimpered at the burning heat still pressed against her arm, and suddenly realized it was his hand.

"I'm sorry, love, no time to be gentle," he whispered roughly, and she realized she could move again somewhat, though her psionics still refused to answer her. She squeezed his hand as he leaned her against the wall and turned back to the hatch. Kerelle craned her neck with effort to see - had they all made it?

Oh no. They hadn't.

Nalea tripped and nearly dropped her vials, losing precious seconds as she righted them again.

"Nalea, *now!*" Sandrel shouted over the comm. The engines already hummed eagerly, and the ship was beginning to rise from the ground as if impatient with its inactivity. Sandrel swore over the comm.

"Kerelle, can you - "

"She can't," Galhen interrupted, grabbing the comm from her still-loose grip. "She's been hit, she'll recover, but we're on our own." Sandrel's swearing intensified.

The scientist had regained her footing and sprinted toward the open hatch, just as the barricade gave way completely and a flood of black armor burst through. They advanced on the ship like a deadly tide, far more than the ship's depleted shields could hold off on their own. And while Galhen had apparently blunted the effect of darts' paralytic, the suppressant still cut her off from any ability to help.

"Nalea! *I have to take off!*" It was the only time she'd ever heard Sandrel sound panicked. Nalea's legs pumped and she leaped toward the hatch, one arm extended to grab Galhen's outstretched hand and the other curled protectively around her vials. Galhen heaved back to pull her in as the ship started to ascend.

Nalea shrieked as the sudden upward motion threatened to pull her from his grasp, and Galhen swore as he tried to brace himself against the hatch. Kerelle tried to go to him but stumbled to the floor instead, her body still reluctant to obey her commands. From the angle of the floor she could see out the hatch, Galhen had regained his grip on Nalea and was pulling her up, but the SysTech troops were gathered below taking aim, from this close *they couldn't miss -*

Ilyen blinked into the space behind her in an instant, shielding her with his body as the darts landed hard between his shoulder blades. The effect was almost instant, and they could only watch in horror as his eyes unfocused and he dropped like a stone towards the waiting soldiers below. On instinct Kerelle reached for her powers in a panic, desperate to catch him as he fell, but all that answered her was the useless emptiness of the suppressant. The ship had already begun its steep ascent, and Galhen could only wrench Nalea into the ship and close the hatch as they shot upward.

The sight of the SysTech squad swarming Ilyen's unconscious body soon disappeared from view as Sandrel accelerated violently out of atmosphere. A moment later they blinked into the unnatural stillness of hyperspace, Nalea's sobbing screams the only sound.

FIFTEEN

"WE HAVE to go back for him!" Nalea struggled in Galhen's grasp, hysteria flooding her voice. "*Turn this fucking ship around, we have to go back!*" Galhen was murmuring something, trying to soothe her, though his eyes held the same raw horror. That disconnected part of her mind realized that it was his own coping mechanism, to focus on the needs of others so that he could put off dealing with his own, and marveled that she'd never noticed until now. She supposed it wasn't so different from hers; compartmentalize, feel later, focus on the mission.

And she had to, or the sight of Ilyen tumbling helplessly into their enemies' waiting arms would play on loop in her mind until her sanity finally broke.

The mission. Focus on the mission. They couldn't change what had happened, they could only find a path forward. Cautiously Kerelle tried shifting position, and she was pleasantly surprised to find that her muscles were aching but responsive. She carefully pulled herself up to lean against the wall.

"We can't go back, Nalea." She was amazed at how calm her voice sounded. "If we went back now, we couldn't save him. They probably already have him under transport."

The gaze Nalea turned on her was pure venom. She shoved off Galhen's arm.

"So that's it then? You've got yours, fuck everyone who helped you?" She gestured violently at Galhen, the wild motion almost connecting with his shoulder. "We stormed a fucking senator's mansion to save *him*, and now you won't even *try - *"

"We're not *just* going to try," Kerelle cut her off. "We're going to *succeed*. Ilyen is my friend too. We won't abandon him. But we have to plan. If we turn around now and get ourselves blown up, or captured as well, it won't do Ilyen any good."

She laid a hesitant hand on the scientist's arm. "They won't kill him, Nalea," she added more gently. "Ilyen is the only teleporter of our generation. He's far more valuable alive."

Nalea stared back at her, her breathing ragged as the tears streamed down her face. The anger drained from her, and without its fortifying force Nalea seemed to crumple in on herself. Her soft sobbing was the only sound above the engines' hum, and she did not resist as Galhen gathered her into his arms. He guided her towards the crew quarters, a quick nod over his shoulder to Kerelle. Her psionics were still a gaping void in her mind, but she could read that look well enough without them. He was triaging who needed his help the most, and currently it was Nalea.

She gave him a nod back; she couldn't disagree. The door swished shut behind them, and she was alone in the corridor.

Kerelle carefully pushed herself off the wall to take a few steps. She started wobbling almost immediately, and hastily reached back for her refuge against the wall. All right - her balance was still unsteady, but she could move. If she kept a hand on the wall for support, she should be fine. There was really only one natural place to go. She made her way slowly toward the mess.

She'd meant to make tea, but when she arrived Sandrel was

already there with an open bottle of whiskey. His hand was shaking slightly as he took a sip.

"Needed something a bit stronger than tea," he said simply. When he held up a glass, she took it without hesitating.

The burn of the whiskey felt good, if insufficient. Kerelle wished it could burn away the memory of the last several hours.

Finally Sandrel spoke. "We lost Knives." It wasn't a question.

"Yes," she whispered. Shock had been insulating her; it was beginning to sink in now that Ilyen was gone, *actually gone*, and whatever her bold words to Nalea she didn't know if he would ever be returned. It felt like a part of her was gone too. She forced herself to keep going. "He was alive when they took him. We may still have a chance to rescue him."

Sandrel raised his eyebrows, though there was no humor in the gesture. "That what you told the Doc?" She nodded. Sandrel took another long sip of whiskey.

When he spoke again, it was straight to the point. "He likely to *stay* alive?"

She nodded again, eyes fixed on the table. "I told Nalea, he's the only teleporter of our generation. He's too valuable to kill." *For now.*

Sandrel saw straight through her. "He's only valuable if he'll do what they want. I never knew Ilyen to be the cooperative type."

"No," she echoed. "But they have…specialists. For that."

Sandrel's face didn't change, but Kerelle knew him well enough to catch the tightening around his eyes. He understood the implications well enough. If SysTech wanted Ilyen alive, it was because they hoped to break him.

She'd half expected him to have some words of wisdom for her like he always did, some solution to all this mess that she hadn't thought of. But Sandrel only gazed bleakly back at her in silence. That disconnected, inappropriate part of her mind piped up again. *For all the talk about how it was likely to end this way, none of us were ready for it.*

Galhen joined them not long after. He too took the whiskey without hesitation.

"Nalea is sleeping," he told them. "She's in shock, obviously, but otherwise unharmed. I gave her a sedative to help her rest." He glanced over at Kerelle. "How are you recovering?"

"Well enough," she answered. "I was a bit shaky walking over here, but I made it in one piece." She wiggled her fingers, finding her fine motor control significantly better than it had been. Her psionics were still in rough shape, but she could *feel* them now. It stood to reason a few hours would clear it up.

She looked over at him curiously. "I didn't realize you were able to counteract whatever was in those darts."

He shook his head. "I can't, not once it's been able to take full effect. In your case, I was able to move quickly enough that I could burn it out of your veins before it dispersed into your bloodstream. It was only possible because I was standing so close when you were hit."

And it wasn't enough. Her physical mobility hadn't done anything to help them in those awful final moments - she'd needed her psionics.

From his face, Galhen was thinking it too.

Sandrel set his empty glass down heavily. "We should get some sleep too. Or try to." He looked between them. "I saw the shuttles, while I was waiting for you. One got shot down before it got too far, but it looked like the other five at least made it out of atmosphere, though I don't know who was on them or what happened after that. I can try to establish comms when we come out of hyper. In the meantime, it'd be great if you two were able to get in contact with anyone else from Cashaal."

Unsaid, but loud enough to echo down her weakened telepathy, was Sandrel's projected thought that *at least we'll know we're not the last ones alive.*

THE DREAM WAS sparse and utilitarian, with none of Lilika's usual fanciful touches. They sat in plastic chairs around a plain table not unlike in a travel terminal, and the room around them sat empty and dim. Most importantly, however, at that plain table sat Lilika herself.

She looked terrible. Even in the dream, lines of exhaustion were evident on her face, and her dark eyes looked haunted. Her impassive mask was there still, but its cracks were widening. Still, she was here, and *alive*. That alone was enough to flood Kerelle's veins with relief, even if none of the news she had was good.

"I believe we've now had contact with all the surviving shuttles," Lilika told them, hands folded in a facsimile of serenity. "Based on their headcount, nearly half of our people are either dead or unaccounted for."

"Do we have names?" Galhen asked softly. She gave a slight nod.

"Of our top combat forces, Koren, Melaris and Anniya escaped with minor injuries. Flaveren, Gisellia, Narelen are confirmed killed, Jesana and Derimen are missing. Elinea is confirmed to have been captured; she was taken defending Anniya and Teriel. Teriel himself was gravely wounded, and we may lose him as well." Her folded hands went white at the knuckles. "Among our people without combat talents, casualties were much higher. The ones that made it out unharmed are the ones that found telekinetics and pyrokinetics to defend them. We also lost many of our more inexperienced members."

Lilika's voice had been steady and detached throughout the recitation, but as she reached the part about inexperience a faint quaver surfaced. Kerelle's heart hurt; they all knew those *more inexperienced members* were largely her students. Helia's empty eyes surfaced violently in Kerelle's memory, and she shoved the thought down. There was nothing she could do for them now.

Galhen reached across the phantom table to lay a hand on her arm. "Are you all right, Lilika?" He asked quietly. She gazed back at him.

"Are any of us?" She closed her eyes for a moment and drew a deep breath. "We knew when we started this how dangerous it would be. We knew there would be casualties, and that no one would be truly safe." The cracks in her mask were stopped up, as if she were holding herself together by sheer force of will. Kerelle suspected she was.

"There is more," Lilika continued. Her brow was pinched, and her eyes focused on the table in front of them. Kerelle's dread intensified.

"The meeting with the Tallimau cell was an ambush. Only one of the extraction team survived to report back to me. She said that when her team reached the rendezvous point before the attack, they found the resistance cell already dead to a man." Lilika paused. "Several of my field agents were also attacked at the same time that we were, as was the Palhee safehouse. It seems that SysTech's intention was to come as close as it could to snuffing us all out at once."

The pinch was back in her brow; finally Lilika lifted her gaze to meet their eyes. "Very few people knew my agents' identities and locations. Riyel was one of them. I have not been able to reach him since he missed our meeting."

A terrible silence descended. It was Lilika who finally broke it again.

"He would not have betrayed us. I know him like I know myself." There was a heaviness building up behind her words, that reminded Kerelle of the air before a thunderstorm. "Anything Riyel told them would have been...involuntary."

The word seemed too neat, too sanitized for what she was trying to say. But Kerelle couldn't blame her. The neat words held it at bay somehow, kept hypothetical what *discovered, arrested, broken under interrogation* would have made real.

And this was *Lilika's* defense mechanism, wasn't it? Kerelle shoved everything into a mental compartment, to deal with later when danger was passed. Galhen focused on helping others through their trauma, so that he would be too busy to feel his own. Lilika built walls of clinical detachment from the horrors around her, gripped impersonal strategy and analysis like a rope that would drag her to safety. What a trio they were.

Lilika locked eyes with Kerelle. "You're going to go after Ilyen, aren't you?"

"Yes. We're going to find out where he was taken, and then we're going to get him back. If we wait too long, we'll lose the opportunity."

"Please." The single word startled her; she'd never heard this kind of emotion in Lilika's voice. The other woman's mask was cracking again, raw feeling slipping through. "Please go after Riyel as well. If they learned these things from him, he is…he is in danger." *He is suffering,* projected as clearly as if she'd screamed it. Kerelle's own eyes burned.

"Of course we will," she answered softly. "Lilika, you didn't even need to ask."

Lilika's dark eyes glittered, a treacherous droplet escaping down her cheek. She turned her face away as if to compose herself, but when Galhen offered her an embrace she did not pull away.

"It's just us here, Lilika," he murmured gently. "No one you have to be strong for. You can grieve."

Kerelle scooted in and took her other hand. The dam broke, and they held their unflappable intelligencer as she finally fell apart.

SIXTEEN

"MAYBE WHEN ALL THIS IS OVER," Sandrel noted, "and we need to find other jobs, we can start a janitorial service. Combination janitorial and security. We can use stuff like this as an example of why people need us."

Kerelle snorted and gave him a nudge. At some point during the last hour of planning, they'd hit the point where inappropriate humor was the only thing keeping them afloat.

"I just hope I'm not out of practice," she answered. "It's been almost a year since I've snuck into a secure area carrying a bucket."

"I'm sure it'll all come back to you."

They'd had several days to plot, argue, and observe. The wait ate at her, at *all* of them. Each moment Ilyen was in SysTech custody, the danger he was in increased - not to mention the danger to all the others captured at Cashaal. But what she'd told Nalea was true. There was nothing they could accomplish without a plan.

To make that plan, they needed to get at any records they could find that might be relevant to the Cashaal raid and Ilyen's capture. Hacking SysTech's network from the outside would require resources they didn't have; Lilika's young hacking specialist had survived Cashaal, but something like this was more than his skills and experience could manage.

A trusted on-site computing resource, on the other hand, would already have the accesses they needed. And breaking and entering was becoming something of a personal specialty.

After some debate, they settled on the regional system HQ as the most promising lead. There would be terminals there with access to the personnel databases, which might yield clues on Ilyen's whereabouts from his record. There was also a chance they might find something in the transport records; the black ops soldiers who carried out the attack were almost certainly based elsewhere, but the raid had likely involved some local resources.

They hoped, anyway. It was all they had to go on.

And so they found themselves plotting how to gain entrance to the building. After some recon, they'd settled on the tried-and-true plan of sneaking in with the cleaning staff. The regional HQ itself seemed fairly well secured, with the lobby now guarded by staff in psiblockers. The janitors, on the other hand, were bused in at night from a contractor.

Not likely to be many psiblockers there.

Ideally, it still wouldn't be her and Galhen going in to do this. Their faces and backgrounds were too well known, thanks to SysTech's PR and their own responses to it. But even if their forces weren't in depleted disarray, it would take too long transport a different team in for the mission. By the time they arrived, any trail of Ilyen would be cold. And as much as Kerelle might prefer not to bring Galhen into danger, she couldn't argue that his skills were necessary. Success here would depend more on finesse than firepower.

Galhen himself gazed down impassively at the rough map they'd been able to assemble, cobbled together from satellite images and what they'd been able to glean with their own eyes.

"So if the previous nights' patterns hold, we'll be dropped off in the service entrance on the eastern side. We'll still need to find personnel management and possibly logistics, though I imagine the latter department will be located near those loading docks in the back." He looked up. "I can't imagine either are likely to warrant psiblocker guards. Even SysTech can't afford to issue psiblockers to *everyone* in their offices. Once we're in the building itself, we should be able to lean on telepathy to deal with anyone we might encounter."

"If that's anyone," Sandrel commented. "The whole point of sending you guys in with the night cleaners is to reduce those odds. Besides," he added with a faint smirk, "I imagine anyone important enough to get a psiblocker will probably have gone home by the time the cleaning crew rolls in."

Kerelle nodded her agreement. "It's not foolproof, but I think it's as good as we're going to get." She looked up at them both. "I guess all that's left now is to get ourselves to the contractors' offices tonight."

A sound in the doorway drew their attention. Nalea stood in the shadows of the corridor.

It was the first time Kerelle had seen Nalea out of her cabin since their escape from Cashaal. From the look of her, that was also the last time she'd slept. The scientist's already-light skin had taken on a waxen look, which only emphasized the deep darkness of the circles under her eyes. In her arms she clutched a tray of vials.

Unless she'd managed to spirit away an entire lab in her coat pocket, Nalea did not have any equipment still on Sandrel's ship. Those vials she carried must have been the same ones she'd almost dropped as they fled Cashaal. The slip that lead to Ilyen's capture.

Nalea set them down carefully on the mess table.

"These are my prototype samples for inoculation against hemindrium-based weapons. It gives temporary protection against things like the collars, and what I suspect those darts were dipped in." She didn't look at them. "If I'd finished it in time to mass-produce, we might not have lost Cashaal."

Might not have lost Ilyen projected so loudly that *Sandrel* might have heard it.

"I've got enough to work with that I can make more. You're not leaving until I've got both of you inoculated." Still Nalea didn't look up, instead focusing on fitting the vial into a syringe from the medbay. "I'm not sure it will be 100% effective. Ideally we'd have done more testing. But we've done enough I'm confident there won't be adverse effects. None of my test volunteers reported anything worse than a sore arm."

She flicked her eyes over to Galhen, and wordlessly he rolled up his sleeves. She gave him the injection and turned to Kerelle, who did the same. The needle's sharp sting left a slight ache behind, but otherwise Kerelle didn't feel any differently.

"Don't get captured," Nalea said brusquely, finally lifting her gaze to meet theirs. "Don't get killed." She gave them a curt nod and spun on her heel, leaving the mess quiet behind her.

Kerelle watched her disappear back down the corridor, presumably to lock herself back in her cabin until the mission was over. She knew Nalea well enough by now to realize her sharp manner was a screen for anxiety and grief. Kerelle's heart twisted for her, and her fingers found Galhen's without even realizing it.

I'd wondered, if she knew how much he cared for her. And if it meant as much to her. Kerelle felt guilty admitting it. *I should have known that it does.*

My sister isn't much for outward displays, he acknowledged. *But I think her feelings run just as deep. All the more reason, then, that we bring him back to her safely.*

Kerelle could only nod, and hope that they were on the right trail.

ACCESSING the janitorial contractor's office was a simple as walking in. Galhen kept them telepathically cloaked in nondescript anonymity, and no one gave them a second glance as they procured uniforms from the supply closet and folded into the group of cleaners. As predicted, no one *here* could afford a psiblocker, or warrant being issued one by the company.

It's strange to think about, Kerelle commented idly as they waited in the throng for the bus to arrive. *If the multigalactics hadn't made psiblockers such a status symbol, back before they actually* needed *them, we might not be having such an easy time sneaking in.*

Indeed. This is a security hole entirely of their own making. His expression didn't change, but his thoughts were overlaid with a smirk. *I won't pretend there isn't a certain satisfaction in exploiting it.*

A low rumble announced the appearance of the bus, lumbering up to their waiting group like a sleepy behemoth. They boarded with the others, and a scarce fifteen minutes later disembarked into the regional heart of SysTech. From there it was straightforward enough to grab a bucket of cleaning supplies and slip away.

All right then, she mused through the bond. *If I were the personnel management department, where would I be?*

The answer turned out to be "on the second floor, near the central coffee bar," though it took them longer than Kerelle would have liked to discover it. They had a few hours, while the night cleaners did their work, but they needed to be out of here well before dawn.

The fixed-computing station was sleek and modern, enclosed in a small glass-fronted room near the department head's office. A little telekinetic nudging easily slipped the lock's tumblers open.

Galhen turned to lean against the wall outside. *You get what we came for, I'll keep our fellows out of the area?* His shielding projections altered slightly, containing an assurance that this part of the building was already taken care of and did not need to be cleaned.

Sounds good. I'll be quick.

She seated herself and got to work. Lilika's surviving team *had* been able to provide them with a program to help gain access from *inside* the network, and it worked like a charm when she fitted the little device in place. When she selected the personnel database, it filled the screen with gratifying speed.

For a moment Kerelle could scarcely believe it. Here, right in front of her, was the entire record of her life. Of Galhen's life. Everything about them that SysTech observed, believed or intended would be noted somewhere in here. Perhaps even more - if SysTech *did* have any information about her parents, about where she came from, this is where it would be kept. She was, essentially, looking at the cipher for everything that had happened to her since she walked through the doors as a child.

She also didn't have time to indulge in curiosity. So far everything had gone smoothly, but she was quite cognizant that their database intrusion might be detected at any time. Kerelle determinedly shoved her wandering thoughts away and jumped to the bottom of the record list. At least Ilyen and Riyel's surnames shared alphabetical proximity.

There - *Vanadariel, Ilyen Kirana.*

Kerelle's lips pursed as she scanned the record. The disciplinary infraction section was almost impressively substantial, but a quick check revealed that the newest entry was nearly two years old. His current status was listed as "missing," with his most recent assignment being a classified security mission roughly eighteen months prior. The dates confirmed her suspicion - it was his mission to assist in recapturing her and Galhen. There was nothing after that because he'd escaped with them instead.

The complete lack of new information in his record might

have been encouraging, if SysTech weren't currently holding him captive. As it was, this wasn't going to be much help.

She tapped a few keys to download it anyway. Maybe there'd be something they could use later.

Valessa, Riyel Ceilas was slightly more informative, with an ominous update from two weeks ago denoting suspension from active service for disciplinary action. After that, however, was a frustrating blank. Whatever that disciplinary action had been, and whatever might have happened to Riyel afterward, it wasn't recorded in his file.

With a *tsk* of frustration she downloaded it anyway. Maybe Lilika would be able to find something in here she had not. A half-second's hesitation, and curiosity finally won out. She added several more records to the download queue. *Jassane, Elinea Bhari. Zharus, Oliven Saria. Charyth, Lilika Anhei. Ambrel, Galhen Tarau. Evandra, Kerelle.*

Galhen glanced back at her. *Any luck?*

Not really. I'm grabbing us some further reading, but there isn't a lot here that's immediately useful. We'll have to hope transport is more forthcoming.

She hurriedly pocketed her data stick as the download finished, and closed the session on the terminal. Anyone who checked the access records would clearly see they had been here, but they should be long gone by the time anyone came to investigate.

To the loading docks, then? He was already setting off in that direction. She sent her affirmative and matched his stride. From how the building was laid out, there was likely to be a staircase in this direction that would drop them down next to it -

She yelped in surprise as they turned a corner and collided into something solid.

Someone solid. He blinked and caught the wall to regain his balance.

"Oh! I'm so sorry, Nessa, I - " He cut off abruptly and froze, eyes widening. "You aren't Nessa," he whispered. A high-quality psiblocker rested on his brow.

Which was why they hadn't sensed him coming.

Kerelle tried not to swear as she stared at the stranger. Mid-thirties, immaculately styled hair, well-tailored suit, shoes and watch that probably cost a month's rent in some neighborhoods. They shouldn't even *need* psionics to be invisible here - everything about him screamed "executive," and they were wearing janitorial uniforms. Had they *really* just been unlucky enough to run into an exec that actually knew the cleaning staff?

More than the cleaning staff, he knew *them*. She could see the terrified light of recognition dawning in his eyes as they flicked nervously from her to Galhen. Even if they could wrestle the psiblocker off, it would be very difficult to convince him they were just cleaners. Not with his memory screaming their names.

Stars and blood, they couldn't risk being caught, but she *really* didn't want to kill someone just for being here.

Galhen answered first, his voice soft. "Is Nessa your usual cleaner?"

"Yes." The other man's fear was obvious, but he firmed his chin a bit and met their eyes. "Did you hurt her?"

"Not at all," Galhen reassured him. He was projecting gentle warmth again, though with the psiblocker on it wouldn't affect their new acquaintance. Kerelle was beginning to suspect he did it subconsciously.

"We simply borrowed uniforms," he added. "With no harm to any of the staff. We aren't what they say we are on the news."

The man's eyes darted between them again, and something flickered in his gaze. Kerelle was about to suggest they try to knock him out when the stranger surprised her by speaking again.

"You're here about your friend, aren't you. The teleporter."

A shared telepathic eyebrow raise. *Is this a trap or a stroke of luck?*

I don't know. We're risking him hitting a panic button just by having *this conversation. But…I'm inclined to take the risk.* He didn't say it, but Kerelle felt it all the same. If the transport records were as disappointing as the personnel files, they had no real leads to follow. She sent her agreement and rolled the dice.

"Yes," she answered him. "We are. What might you know about him?"

"He's being held at the Oulemar Detention Center. You don't have a lot of time. You need to rescue him quickly."

"I see," she lied. She'd never heard of Oulemar. Neither of them had. Then, the obvious question. "Why would you tell me this?"

His face creased in obvious discomfort. "Because it's wrong."

It was clear he didn't want to say more, but they didn't have the luxury of polite restraint. She pressed. "What do you mean, it's wrong?"

His grey eyes slid away from theirs. "It was at the executive meeting this morning. The original plan for regaining custody of Subject A725 was reconditioning, retraining, and redeployment, but apparently he's proving difficult. The head of the PsiCorp also testified that the Subject has always had an undesirable temperament that limits his value. At one time they would have tried harder with behavioral modification, but they're afraid, and…"

He trailed off, eyes now firmly on her feet. Kerelle's stomach clenched with dread, but they had to keep going. "And what?" She prompted quietly.

The man's voice wavered slightly as he said it. "On the recommendation of the head of the PsiCorp, the board voted this morning to lobotomize the subject and extract what remaining value they could from DNA donation."

Shock seared Kerelle's vision dark, and for a moment she thought she was going to vomit. She felt Galhen's steadying hand at her wrist, banishing the physical symptoms of horror -

likely to keep his own in check. She took a shuddering breath and forced it all down, deep into a box she could deal with later. Ilyen needed them, *now*.

Assuming it was real, and not a trap meant to snare what remained of the psionic rebellion. She almost wished it *were*. That would be less awful.

"Why would you tell us any of this?" She made herself ask. "And how can we believe you? Is it just coincidence, that you're working late in a psiblocker the night we come here?"

"I work late *every* night," he answered with an unexpected touch of heat. "If you don't believe me, they're going to destroy your friend." He lifted his gaze to meet hers then, and took several quick, deep breaths. His hands had begun to shake.

"If you don't believe me," he repeated, "then read my mind and see." He removed the psiblocker.

His fear buffeted her like a stormy sea, but he held himself at attention, eyes never leaving them. Stars help them, they had to know the truth about this. Kerelle gave him a single nod, and stepped forward to rest her hand against his forehead. She dove in.

His name was Aureis Lenar Calduit, thirty-six years old, born in the most populous city in the Fandelas Cluster. He was the Director of Finance Operations for the Strategic Assets group, which included the PsiCorp. And earlier that day, he had attended a meeting about the latest developments in the psionic crisis. She accessed the memory, and watched it through Aureis's eyes.

THE BOARDROOM WAS SLEEKLY STERILE, *all clean lines and immaculate glass that crafted an image of expensive beauty while devoid of anything that might feel like a point of view. Being in it always made Aureis feel cold. Even now, part of him was wishing he'd brought his blazer, even though the number of people packed around the table meant it was going to heat quickly.*

He couldn't remember the last time the entire executive team had shown up to the same meeting. More or less on time, even. Besides their own meeting room, a number of video calls streamed in from SysTech offices across the galaxy, turning the wall-to-wall monitor into a mosaic of serious-faced people crowded around sterile glass tables of their own. All of them were listening intently to the man who now paced at the head of table, a few feet away from Aureis.

Kerelle's breath caught. Velrin, in the flesh. They'd missed him by hours.

"As I have said in the past, Subject A725 is a toxic asset. It is true that the company has made significant investments in his training, and his unique capabilities cannot be easily replaced." Velrin paused pacing and turned to face his audience. "However, I believe the events of the past year have made it painfully clear that we will never *see a worthwhile return on that investment."*

He made a few taps on his tablet, and suddenly the mosaic of conference rooms on the screen was replaced by a video recording. The clip was not high quality, obviously taken from a security cam, but it was clear enough to make out what they were seeing. Kerelle's gut clenched.

The armored, psiblocker-clad guards formed a ring around Subject A725, who glared back. He had been recollared, of course, and his hands and legs were shackled as well. Even through the grainy footage, there was no missing the dark bruises splashed across his skin. Aureis glanced at the rest of the table, who watched impassively. If anyone was bothered by the sight, they didn't show it.

Velrin was talking again. "A725 has proven time and again that his behavioral problems are not merely the product of youthful indiscretion, *as some have argued. Furthermore, his belligerence poses a risk both as an instigator of delinquent behavior among the other PsiCorp, and as a potential PR incident." He cleared his throat, and his tone took on a slight sneer.* "Another potential PR incident." *Velrin turned his gaze back on the video. "He is resisting all attempts at therapy."*

On-screen, the guards were attempting to move A725, who struggled in their grip. He managed to wrench out of his captors' grasp, and brought his bound arms around to strike the nearer one. The guard stumbled, and the others fired up their shock wands. A725 spat something at them, and didn't back down.

Aureis's stomach lurched as the first wand struck, and A725's whole body arced in pain. Again his eyes darted around the table, but the rest of the meeting sat as calmly as if they were watching a product pitch. When he looked back at the screen, A725 was on his knees and clearly losing consciousness. He still managed an obscene gesture at the closest guard; the video cut off right before the shock wand connected again.

Kerelle was aware that tears had started sliding down her face. That was their Ilyen - stubborn, defiant, brave to the end. Her chest ached.

Aureis struggled to keep his breathing steady - and the contents of his stomach in their place. He'd had some vague, abstract awareness that the PsiCorp could be a harsh place, and that there were things that went on there he did not want to know about. Watching it on stark display left him feeling deeply shaken.

All the more so, because no one else seemed to be. This wasn't new to them, was it? This is what you do, Calduit. This is what you're part of.

Velrin put his hands on the table, looking around the room and up to the camera that streamed them across the meeting call. "There would be greater value," he argued, "and less risk, in retaining A725 as a DNA donor and test participant, with surgical cognitive reduction to curtail his disruptive behavior. He is young and physically healthy, and with adequate nursing care there is no reason he would not live another several decades in a research facility. That's several decades of live samples to study his unique abilities and," his voice took on a conspiratorial shade, "Perhaps even crack the code of replicating them. Even if nothing ultimately comes of it, any additional learnings on psionic physiology would provide a greater return than continuing to pour resources into still more futile attempts at reform."

Velrin straightened again, and delivered his pronouncement. "Therefore, I am formally recommending that a full lobotomy be performed on A725 at the earliest date possible, and that he be subsequently transferred as an asset to the bioresearch division."

There were nods around the table. Aureis played with his shirtsleeve, a nervous tic he'd never quite managed to suppress throughout his career. He'd only gotten the promotion to Director three months ago, and this was just his second full exec meeting. He still felt like he didn't quite belong in here, and he knew it was somewhat against protocol for junior executives to speak without being called on, but...

"I...I have some concerns," he heard himself say. Stars, did his voice always sound so thin? Everyone turned to stare at him, and he forced himself not to wilt under the sudden weight of attention. "Performing a procedure like that on a nonconsenting human doesn't seem...ethical."

He knew he'd made a mistake as soon as he'd said it. He looked back on a table of stony silence, faces set in carefully neutral impassivity that reminded him of the room they were sitting in. The mosaic was silent as well, and the force of a galaxy's worth of stares hit his shoulders. They let the quiet stretch, the lack of response serving to emphasize how out of line he had been. From the other end of the table, his department head was giving him a venomous look that boded poorly for his performance review.

Aureis felt his face coloring with embarrassment. The best thing he could do was apologize immediately, but that insubordinate spark in his mind that had prompted him to speak in the first place refused to be extinguished. Well what did you *expect* they were going to do, give you a commendation? If anyone at this table cared the slightest bit about ethics, they wouldn't be sitting here like they were having tea. *He found he couldn't take the words back, no matter how negatively they might reflect on him. He'd meant them.*

"Thank you for gracing us with your wisdom, Director Calduit!" Velrin's tone dripped with all the gleeful derision of a bully who'd read the room and knew that his prey would find no help. "Legal approved it, the head of psionic psychology approved it, but certainly the opinion we

really *needed* was yours. *I don't know how we even* held *these meetings before you joined them last month."*

Aureis tried to look composed, though the intense heat in his cheeks told him he was likely red as a tomato. He wanted to argue despite it all, but his mind blanked of any response excepted a blurted it's wrong, *and that would only confirm that he didn't have a leg to stand on. From Velrin's deepening smirk, he knew as much.*

"If there are no further…independent analyses?" A few chuckles, without even a pretended cough to disguise them. Aureis focused on keeping his face neutral. There seemed an increasingly likely chance this would be his last *full exec meeting, and stars be damned he was going to leave with as much of his dignity as he could manage.*

His parents had been so very excited when he'd made Director. He felt slightly sick at the prospect of having to tell him he'd been demoted after less than a full quarter.

He snapped back to attention, feeling guilty at thinking of his own petty problems when the fate of A725 was a visceral demonstration in how bad life could actually be. Velrin was calling for a vote of approval.

Even if he weren't currently in disgrace, Aureis would not have a vote. Directors and Associate Vice Presidents might attend the executive meetings for information, and participate when requested, but real decision-making was reserved for the department heads and the C-level.

Aureis wasn't even disappointed when they approved the proposal unanimously. Disappointment implied there had been any chance it might have gone differently, and there wasn't. The decision had been final before anyone even bothered to raise their hands.

There was little left to discuss after that. No one would look at him as the meeting adjourned. Aureis resisted the urge to flee to the relative safety of his office, instead forcing himself to make the walk back to the second floor at a deliberate pace. He tried to use it to steady himself, to clear his mind of everything except the work awaiting him when he returned, but the sight of A725 bloodied on the floor of Oulemar refused to be cleared.

He was a part of this. He'd never thought of the work he did, of himself as contributing to the kind of thing he'd just seen on the meeting room screen. But somehow by balancing the accounts and initialling the requisitions and preparing the tax records, he was helping allow SysTech to murder that man onscreen, even though he wouldn't hold the knife.

But what could he do?

KERELLE CAME BACK TO HERSELF, and found her hand shook almost as violently as Aureis's. He was telling the truth. This was real.

"So." She took a shaky breath to steady herself. Feel later. "What can you tell me about Oulemar?"

"It's the most secure detention facility SysTech currently operates." He took a step back as she lowered her hand, still radiating fear like a furnace. Kerelle had to hand it to him - he'd clearly had to sum up a lot of courage to let her into his mind. "It's under the surface of a moon orbiting one of their deep-space mining interests. Most people don't even know it exists."

She raised an eyebrow. "Why do you?"

Aureis gave a short laugh in spite of himself, and a smile that was somewhere between wry and bleak. "Accounting knows where the bodies are buried."

This whole conversation was like some surreal dream. But she'd read his mind and sensed no deceit. Bizarre as it might seem, they really were standing in a SysTech office shortly after midnight, discussing secret moon prisons with a frightened accountant. It would be the kind of story to tell over drinks, if it weren't centered around one of her closest friends in horrific peril.

Galhen spoke first. "I imagine we'll need something more robust than borrowed cleaner uniforms to get in there."

"Yes," Aureis agreed. "The facility is designed to resist

assault, and the only thing that goes in and out besides guards and prisoner transport is the periodic supply ships."

"And how do they know if a supply ship is legitimate?"

Aureis met his gaze straight on. "I approve them."

Not much later, they were in Aureis's office, waiting tensely as he worked. The room was silent but for the light clacking of his keyboard. Nor was there much to see, besides the desk itself - none of the family photos or media stills she'd seen on other desks around the office. Apparently Aureis wasn't much for personal touches at work.

Galhen leaned against the wall, mental tension belying his relaxed posture. *Darling, you were the one in his head - on the spectrum of absolute fidelity to inevitable betrayal, how much do we trust this man? He's been quite cooperative thus far, but I can't help think of how simple it would be to summon security while we obligingly wait in one place.*

That's a concern, she acknowledged. *On this though, I am inclined to trust him. He…watched how they were treating Ilyen, and what they planned to do to him, and his horror was genuine. As was his feeling of helplessness at not being able to stop it. I didn't pick up any hint of intended deceit.*

He was quiet for a moment, wordless dread flowing through the bond. *And…how were they treating Ilyen?*

As you'd expect. She didn't want to share the image, didn't want to even recall it. She didn't need to - he understood. A brush through the bond like a squeezed hand, carrying reassurance that they would get through this and see their friend back unharmed. Kerelle knew Galhen worried as much as she did that such sentiments were hollow, but she appreciated the gesture all the same.

Aureis finished his forms with a final tap of the keys, and withdrew a small device from his workstation. He handed it over to them.

"Here's your transponder, all programmed and ready to go. When you get in range of the base, you'll show up on their scanners as a registered supply vendor. I put you in as a provider of general materiel, so you can make up whatever story you want about why you're there." His hands were shaking violently again, almost dropping the transponder as he placed it in Kerelle's open palm. Against her senses, his fear flared back up like a sudden bonfire.

"If…if it's all right," he stammered, eyes fixed on his desk, "Can I…message my parents first?"

Kerelle blinked at the sudden shift. "First?"

Galhen, as always, was quicker on the social uptake. He cut in smoothly. "Director Calduit, did you think we were going to kill you?"

Aureis swallowed hard and kept his eyes on his desk. "You kind of have to, don't you? I know where you're going and why. I could tell them to expect you."

Galhen raised a golden eyebrow. "Will you?"

Oulemar isn't just for psionics. The projection hit them both like a slap, overlaid with an all-consuming terror akin to looking under the bed and discovering that the monster of one's childhood nightmares was real all along.

"It was…very brave, then, for you to offer to help us."

Aureis gave a nervous half-shrug. "You were going to kill me either way."

Oh dear. "No," Kerelle answered carefully, "We weren't." She exchanged a sidelong glance with Galhen. "We aren't going to kill you *now*, either."

Rather than reassuring him, this sent another wave of terror through Aureis. His projected thoughts were almost deafening, even through her shields. *I can pretend they forced me into it, but I'll be on camera taking off my psiblocker and oh holy stars,* what if they send me to Oulemar for questioning -

"We can kidnap you, if you prefer," Galhen said, interrupting the other man's spiraling thoughts. "I can't promise you'll get your life back when all this is over, but you'll at least have some deniability."

Aureis went pale, but his brows furrowed together in thought. Another thought slipped out, before Kerelle upped her shields again with a faint trace of exasperation. For a mundane, Aureis projected strongly and often.

What in my life is worth going back to?

"I...I'll go with you," he said finally, his voice only wavering a bit. "I'll go."

"Excellent. Let's make a show of it for the cameras, then." He glanced over at Kerelle. "Darling, do something telekinetically intimidating?"

She flexed a hand and snapped the handles off his desk drawers, whirling them around her hand like makeshift projectiles. Aureis didn't fake his frightened step back.

Desk drawers?

Blame our new friend's neat office. I'm not exactly surrounded by potential material here.

We do end up in the oddest situations, don't we?

A sharp gesture to move, and they were herding Aureis between them out of the building. The accountant looked so miserable, Kerelle couldn't help a pang of sympathy. It felt foreign to have anything but contempt for a SysTech executive, but Aureis *had* helped them, at no benefit to himself. The faked kidnapping *might* help him avoid consequences, but there was no denying that he was taking a very grave risk. She hoped it turned out better for him than it had for Nalea, but somehow she suspected it would be much the same.

From his expression and his trembling hands, Aureis knew that as much as they did.

SEVENTEEN

SANDREL WAS NO LONGER surprised when Kerelle returned from a mission with more people than she'd left with. His dark eyes took in Aureis trailing behind them with a kind of tired resignation.

"Strap in. There's been no chatter around security, but I'd rather not invite risk. You can introduce me to your new friend when we're safe in hyper."

Kerelle didn't argue. She had a feeling that running into Aureis and getting out clean had just used up all their luck for the decade.

A short time later found them all gathered around the mess table, the ship now safely ensconced in the unnatural serenity of hyperspace. Sandrel's eyebrows lifted significantly as they introduced Aureis, and he gave Kerelle a look that assured her they would most definitely discuss this later.

But all he said was, "If those two say you're legit, then I'll trust that." Aureis mumbled thanks, eyes trained on his mug. Despite his earlier thoughts about having nothing to go back to, Aureis was clearly losing some of his equilibrium as the reality of what he'd done began to sink in. He clutched his tea like a life preserver.

She felt Galhen's flicker of guilt through the bond, at having to push Aureis when he obviously needed space and reassurance. But they didn't have time to make him comfortable. *Ilyen* didn't have time. Her eyes slid involuntarily to Nalea, sitting silent and withdrawn at the edge of the circle. She wished they didn't have to tell her this part. But there was no time for *her* comfort either.

"Now that we're all here," she started, "we would appreciate any additional details you have on Oulemar and Ilyen."

A momentary confusion crossed Aureis's face, and Galhen leaned in. "Ilyen is our teleporter friend," he explained gently. "Ilyen Kirana Vanadariel."

Of course. Aureis only knew him as Subject A725. From the faint expression of distress that crossed his face, Aureis had just made that realization himself.

Kerelle's stomach roiled again, this time as much with anger as with dread. SysTech would pay for it, someday. All of it. She forced her anger down - she needed to be sharp for this. They wouldn't get more than one chance.

"There isn't that much more to tell," Aureis confessed, "at least not that I'm aware of. Subj - *Ilyen* - was taken to Oulemar following his capture, along with the other high-value psionic detainees. I don't know precise details but the general plan was retraining, with the eventual goal of redeployment."

Hope pricked at her chest. "You say there were other detained psionics - was one of them Riyel Valessa?"

"Was Riyel Valessa your spy?" Of course. Aureis probably didn't know *any* of their names, only their detainee designations.

"He was." No use hiding it now - by all indications Riyel's cover was already well and truly blown.

Aureis nodded slowly. "There was a PsiCorp spy taken to

Oulemar after Velrin discovered him. Interrogation specialists were able to extract the location of the rebel base on Cashaal. That's how this whole thing started."

It was what she'd expected to hear, but still her heart sank. She didn't want to have to confirm Lilika's fears.

"You said the *high-value* psionic detainees were taken to Oulemar," Sandrel said slowly, a crease in his brow. "I'm assuming that's the C3s. But we've got a lot more people unaccounted for than just the top rankings. Where's the rest?"

It went quiet. Aureis wouldn't look up from his tea.

"You have to understand," he said finally, "I'm not *in* those meetings, exactly. I can't be certain."

"But?" Sandrel prompted. His eyes flicked over to meet Kerelle's, and she saw her own dread reflected there. This wasn't going to be good.

"But...from the records that came through..." Aureis swallowed. "My understanding is that many of captured rebels weren't considered to be worth the effort of retraining. The Class-3s were, and some of the stronger Class-2s. The Class-1s and the weaker Class-2s were shot."

His voice dropped to almost a whisper. "From what I've heard about Oulemar it...it might be better."

He trailed off, looking miserable, as the table digested that with dark expressions. Kerelle was starting to feel numb.

Galhen took pity on him. "Is there anything else you can tell us, to help save the people we still can?"

Aureis looked relieved to move on, though his body still radiated tension. "As I said, they took your friend Ilyen to Oulemar, along with the others, with the goal of retraining." His brows furrowed. "They hardly tried with him, though. Almost as soon as the teleporter was captured, Senior Vice President Velrin started arguing that he was untrainable."

"They have a history together," Galhen told him. "Velrin

managed the black ops division where Ilyen grew up. From what Ilyen has told us, there was no love lost between them."

"Ah." Aureis looked up for the first time. "That makes sense, actually. I *thought* it seemed overly personal. But of course, it would reflect badly on Velrin that his division raised a famous rebel, especially such a valuable one.

"At one time, I would have said he was *too* valuable for the company to do something like this," he added. "But the executive leadership is desperate to show the board that they're taking action. And, of course, spilling SysTech secrets across the datanet didn't exactly endear him to senior management. There are official inquiries open in three systems over that."

"Definitely Knives's fault there," Sandrel commented dryly, "and not theirs for arranging a bunch of assassinations in the first place."

Aureis gave a half-shrug. "That's not how the board sees it, and Velrin has a lot of pull with them right now. He's been pushing the view that the rebellion only happened in the first place because the PsiCorp are overly coddled. The board is eating it up."

"Are they." Kerelle couldn't quite keep the anger out of her voice.

"Previously, the accepted wisdom around managing the PsiCorp was that if you gave them enough carrots, you wouldn't need to use the stick, and you'd get higher quality work out of people who wanted to be there. Velrin's arguing that if you use enough stick, you can get the same results without any carrots at all. There's significant cost savings to eliminating PsiCorp benefits. If he can deliver what he says he can? Once the crisis is over, things won't go back to how they were."

He must have seen the eyebrows raise around the table, because he hurriedly moved on.

"Anyway the important part is that as you know, the board approved the proposal for Ilyen earlier to today. I believe the procedure is being scheduled for two weeks from now, when the specialist is available. He's being kept under heavy sedation until then."

Nalea spoke for the first time. "What do you mean, the *proposal for Ilyen?*"

This was the part Kerelle had been dreading. She exchanged glances with Galhen.

I'll handle it. And he did, giving her an impersonal but accurate accounting of events. Nalea's face drained white as bone, but she said nothing.

"So." Sandrel picked up the thread. He too was pale beneath his warm complexion, but his expression showed only determination. "Two weeks. Depending on where we're going, that's not a lot of time."

"It isn't," Aureis agreed. "But it should be enough."

NINE DAYS LATER, they were gathered around the table again.

"All right people. We've got a couple of hours before we'll be dropping out of hyper at the coordinates Director Calduit gave us." Sandrel gave Aureis a nod, and he gave a small nod back. To say Aureis had been *uncomfortable* being trapped on a ship with them for over a week would be an understatement. To his credit, though, he'd tried his best, even volunteering for a share of the ship's chores. Kerelle halfway suspected it was just to keep himself busy, but she couldn't blame him if it were.

"I think we all know the plan for getting in. We fly up to the front gate, pretend we're supposed to be there delivering supplies, get them to let us inside. Thanks again to Director Calduit, we've got a transponder that backs up our claim, and a manifest that's pretty much indistinguishable from the real thing. We've also got a good cover story for why they aren't expecting us."

He looked over at Aureis. "It wouldn't be the first time HQ fumbled communications on supply shipping," the accountant explained. "Captain Marene and I went over the most likely points of failure. It will sound plausible, because it's happened legitimately before."

Sandrel nodded. "Once we're actually in, I make a fuss about SysTech being a terrible client, and you two sneak off to find Ilyen. From there on it's all you."

"We'll find him," Kerelle answered, more confidently than she might under other circumstances. Failure was not an option here. She looked over to Aureis. "Any surprises we should know about?"

"You should expect a lot of antipsionic gear, but...that probably goes without saying by now. If there's more specific antipsionic defenses I don't know about them. But...I would expect that, psionic or not, most of the defenses will be more geared towards preventing escape, rather than stopping intruders."

Kerelle nodded her understanding. "Antipsionic gear complicates things, obviously, but we expected as much. We'll take conventional weapons, and we'll be careful. Hopefully," her eyes slid to Nalea, "our own defenses will prove useful as well." She didn't quite want to admit to Aureis that Nalea had developed protection against SysTech's psionic suppression weapons. He'd been very helpful so far, but there was no need to bare all their secrets just yet.

To her surprise, Nalea met her eyes. "I'm coming with you."

They all turned to stare at her. "You...what?"

"You heard me. I'm coming with you."

Kerelle recovered enough to respond. "Nalea, I understand you want to help, but I think you should stay at the ship, where it's..." She was going to say *safe*, but that was so blatantly untrue the words couldn't cross her lips. Nothing about this was safe. "Where it's *more* safe," she finished awkwardly. Nalea rolled her eyes.

"Like I was *safe with the ship* on Kalnis? Besides," she added briskly. "We know there's a lab here. We know there's anti-psionic equipment. What if you run into a prototype of something you need expert help to dismantle? What if you walk into some kind of trap for psionics?" Her eyes cut over to Aureis as well, then back to Kerelle. "Plus, I've got some new toys I've been working on."

Apparently she didn't want to go into specifics in front of their guest either.

"Nalea," Galhen tried, "There's an excellent chance this will get violent - "

"I know. When the shooting starts, I can shoot back." She was all ice now, voice cold and posture rigid. "Ilyen's been teaching me for months. He said I needed to know how, in case he wasn't here to protect me." The words were slow and deliberate, and after she'd said them, an awkward silence descended on the room.

Kerelle brushed thoughts with Galhen in silent conference. *She has a point, darling.*

Yes. From the emotional overlay, Kerelle could tell Galhen was even less enthusiastic about bringing his sister into danger than she was, but she also felt his acquiescence. *As reluctant as I am to put her in harm's way, we may very well need her skills before this is out. I only hope she does not need to use any skills related to firearms.*

Kerelle sent her agreement, and gave Nalea a single nod. "All right. The three of us will search for Ilyen after the ship lands."

She turned to Aureis. "You should stay with the ship, and out of sight." He nodded with undisguised relief.

Kerelle trusted Aureis to have been straight with them thus far. She'd seen his mind back at the headquarters, and during their brief time together since he'd given off no hint of deceit. She did *not* entirely trust him to lead them into Oulemar. If he *did* get cold feet about the entire venture, betraying them to

SysTech in the heart of its secret prison was probably the one thing he could do to guarantee he'd get back in good graces.

And if he didn't get cold feet, well, there was still a chance he'd be recognized by someone on the SysTech side, which would open an entirely new can of trouble. It was better for all of them if he stayed with the ship.

"I guess that covers it." Sandrel sounded tired. "I'll let you know when we're about to drop back to realspace. Let's all be ready when we do."

EIGHTEEN

THE MOON WAS dark on approach. It appeared nothing more than an empty rockscape indifferently orbiting a gas giant, and even knowing Sandrel had double-checked the coordinates she still had an involuntary flash of doubt that this was the place. She felt less guilty when she looked over at Sandrel, and caught him glancing back to the coordinates as well.

"This is it," he confirmed. "I guess if you want someplace to make people disappear, it's not a bad spot. Nothing out here but the mining platform on Veru," he indicated the gas giant, shining red like a baleful eye in the void, "and that's probably mostly automated anyway. Nobody to notice what's going on next door."

Kerelle shivered, the dark moon taking on an aura of menace as it sat quiescent in the vidport. Somewhere in those silent shadows was Ilyen, closer now but still too far out of reach. From the way Nalea's eyes fixated on its image, she was thinking much the same.

"All right." Sandrel stretched lazily, though his aura was anything but relaxed. "We're in range. I'll hail on the channel provided," he nodded at Aureis, who swallowed and nodded back, "and hopefully we get in according to plan." *And out according to plan*. His projection was strong enough to have been spoken aloud.

Sandrel looked around at all of them, gathered grimly in nav. "Any last concerns? Final issues? Second thoughts?"

"All right then," he said again into the resulting silence, and reached over to flick the comm.

"SysTech Frontier Outpost O7X53D, this is the freighter Starstream 6 on approach, requesting clearance to land." The comm crackled. "I repeat, SysTech Frontier Outpost O7X53D, this is the freighter Starstream 6, on approach as scheduled. Requesting clearance to land and dock assignment for unloading."

Even knowing the base was there, Kerelle still jumped when the comm lit up in response.

"Freighter Starstream 6, clearance is denied, we have no record of your scheduled arrival."

"SysTech Frontier Outpost O7X53D, I'm surprised to hear that. I have a manifest here for requisition 7102937D, and a hold full of cargo specifically for the facility at these coordinates."

The voice on the other line was still unconvinced. Nor did she sound particularly convinced when, after nearly ten minutes of back and forth, she finally relented and gave them a dock. Still, Sandrel wasted no time in bringing them down to the surface.

As they descended from the thin atmosphere, there was at first nothing beneath them but an endless dark expanse, the ship's spotlight revealing only barren patches of rocky wastes. There was no sign of a landing dock, or of *any* human habitation. Kerelle was just opening her mouth to ask Aureis, when suddenly the ground beneath them began to shake, and a door lifted from beneath the flat wasteland with a great grinding roar.

Sandrel expertly guided them inside, with only the tightness around his lips betraying his discomfort.

Kerelle had to suppress a shiver as they passed out of Veru's wan reflected light, and into the shadows of the landing bunker. Before she could suppress it, the thought fluttered anxiously through her mind - was this the last time they would see daylight?

IF ANYONE *on this ship should have taken up theater, it's Sandrel.* Even with the tension coiled around her like a tightly-wound spring, Kerelle had to appreciate the ease with which their smuggler stepped into roles. In this case, it was the role of aggrieved businessman, and he did it very well.

As they'd touched down, a port manager flanked by several guards had come out to continue the argument they'd begun from orbit. Sandrel soon had their attention completely focused on him.

"I had to jump through hoops for *months* to get clearance for this job!" His voice rose with indignation, drowning out the port manager's attempt to interject. "I passed up another paying job to go through all the bullshit for this one, I've got six mouths to feed, and you don't even have it together on *your* side!"

"Captain Florinde, I understand - "

"See, this is the problem with the galaxy today, you get these big corps that think they can jerk around small business. I've got twenty-five years hauling freight and…"

"Captain Florinde!" The port manager sounded exasperated. "I understand there was a miscommunication with headquarters, and I can *see* you have documentation from our purchasing department, but this is still technically an unscheduled shipment and *I have to inspect cargo.*" Her voice rose in volume at the end, and Kerelle got the impression she was refraining from smacking the side of the ship in emphasis. Sandrel made a disgusted noise and threw up his hands.

"Fine then, come in and *inspect* so I can get unloaded. Right now I'm paying those lazy assholes in my crew to sit around and watch the show."

It was quite simple, after that. The port manager and her guards came aboard for an inspection. A short time later, they were tied up and unconscious in the hold, while the rescue team adjusted the fit of their uniforms. On close inspection, it was apparent Nalea was shorter than the guards they'd purloined the clothing from, but they had to hope nobody would look that closely.

Aureis tapped at the manager's datapad. "We're all set," he announced. "I've marked in the logs that the shipment is legitimate and no further action is required. That should buy us some time before anyone comes to investigate further."

Kerelle nodded, meeting his eyes and then Sandrel's. "Stay out of sight, and stay safe. We'll see you when all this is over."

Kerelle took a deep breath and opened the hatch. With Galhen and Nalea at her heels, she descended into the halls of the Oulemar prison.

<hr>

KERELLE HAD EXPECTED A DARK DUNGEON, complete with flickering lamps and crumbling stone. Instead, Oulemar was a nest of neatly tiled floors and fluorescent overhead lights, its concrete walls painted a bland beige that wouldn't be out of place in an office. Knowing what went on here, the outward normalcy of their surroundings only increased the menace of the snaking halls and nondescript locked doors.

Naturally, it was still built like a maze. Even with Aureis's schematics giving them a vague sense of direction, Kerelle found herself struggling to keep her bearings as they made their way to where the cell block should be. She had to hope they could find Ilyen and the others without too much backtracking. And that, after they did, they could make it out again in the hurry.

They saw other uniformed guards, and non-military personnel hurrying about as well, but they walked past with purpose and no one challenged them. *For now*, her mind couldn't help but supply. The only somewhat encouraging part was that not *everyone* they encountered was wearing a psiblocker - in fact, most of the civilian personnel were not. But it seemed as though every guard they passed was wearing antipsionic protection, and she had to assume they had antipsionic weapons as well. Getting out with a group of injured psionics in tow would be non-trivial.

The best plan they'd been able to come up with was to pretend to be moving the prisoners. Plan B, which Kerelle privately suspected would very quickly become Plan A, was simply to blast their way out. Ideally their rescued comrades would provide additional firepower, but there was no knowing what kind of condition they'd be in. Kerelle had to assume their escape would rely entirely on the three of them.

She wasn't going to let herself think about what the odds looked like for a single telekinetic in a field of psiblockers, backed up by two noncombatants with guns. They'd make it. They had to.

The hallway ahead of them abruptly ended in a large concrete door, that even from a distance Kerelle could tell was reinforced. It was flanked by two armored, psiblocker-clad guards.

And our first obstacle is sighted. Galhen's tone was calm, though Kerelle could feel his suppressed nervousness through the bond. *Bluffing or guns, darling?*

Bluffing, she returned. *We can always fall back on guns.*

She stepped up purposefully, ready to put their move-the-prisoners plan into action. To her surprise, however, one of the door guards spoke first.

"You here from Dr. Loune's group again? We were just about to power the gates back up. Thought they had the one they needed."

Kerelle thought fast. "Yes, Dr. Loune wants more of them. Not sure why they couldn't just get them all the first time, but..." She tried a long-suffering eyeroll, careful to keep her concern from showing. Who was Dr. Loune?

The guard looked somewhat surprised, but gave a world-weary shrug. "What, they give up on this whole batch then? It'll sure make this job easier, I guess."

She made herself laugh along with him as he keyed in the sequence to open the door. She and Galhen exchanged bursts of anxiety - this did not sound good at all. The door opened, and the guard waved them in ahead of him.

The cell block itself was closer to Kerelle's expectations for Oulemar, a dark passage of dim light and unpainted concrete, noticeably colder than the hall they'd just left. Both walls were lined with endless rows of heavy doors, anonymous but for the numbers spraypainted above them like an afterthought.

Their people were here. Friends and colleagues were shoved in these rooms, locked alone in the dark and chill. She couldn't think about it right now; to help them, she had to focus.

The guard was regarding it all with an air of resigned indifference. "Might as well get the weaker ones out first, a couple of them are pretty feisty still. Retraining specialists are getting soft." He glanced back at them quickly. "They send you with any kind of conveyance? Or you just want the ones that can walk?"

She forced herself to stay steady. "All of them, please. The instructions were very clear."

The guard gave another shrug and started fishing around in his pocket. "Well, don't want to keep Loune waiting." He took out a small security card and raised it up towards the first cell's lock. Then paused.

He looked back over again, and seemed to really *see* her for the first time. Kerelle got a bad feeling. Nalea leaned over to whisper something to Galhen.

"Who did you say your instructions were from, again?"

Love, there's a security cam over the door behind us. Push it out of alignment?

Kerelle tried to keep her manner nonchalant, and her attention on the suddenly-less-friendly guard as she surreptitiously reached for the security cam. There - she could just tilt that lens up, just a bit...

"Someone in a lab coat?" She answered him with a shrug and a smile, trying to grasp at the bored camaraderie they'd managed outside. "I didn't get a name, all those science types look alike."

He didn't smile back. "I'm going to have to call in for specific clearance," he said shortly. His hand dropped down closer to his weapon. "If you could just step outs-"

His eyes glazed over, mouth working soundlessly for a few seconds before he dropped senseless to the floor. Nalea impassively withdrew her syringe from the back of his neck.

"It's an adaptation of what they used on us," she explained, unruffled. "He should be paralyzed for at least an hour, and he won't remember anything from shortly before then."

Kerelle and Galhen stared at her. She stared back, eyebrows raised slightly, and Kerelle was struck by just how far her sister-in-law had come since that bunker on Zharal V.

"Well done then," she said finally. They didn't have time to waste reminiscing. "We need to keep moving. We probably don't have a great deal of time before someone comes to investigate our situation in here, not to mention the other guard outside. We need to get our people out of here and back to the ship."

"Well," Galhen answered, kneeling next to the fallen guard,

"needs must." He unclipped the guard's psiblocker and clapped a hand to man's forehead. He was still for several long seconds before resurfacing.

"Whatever is going on, this Dr. Loune's assistant Canvel is the one coordinating things," he told them. "That's the name we can drop to the guard outside. Perhaps we can - "

Kerelle's comm lit up. Galhen cut off as the three of them looked at each other. The ship wouldn't comm them in here unless it were absolutely dire.

Kerelle flicked it on with a nervous glance at the door behind them. "Evandra here."

"She's already here!" Aureis sounded slightly panicked. "I checked the records on the port manager's data pad. The specialist they needed for Ilyen is here, they must have moved up the procedure date. We're out of time, it might already be too late!"

Kerelle's stomach dropped. That's who Dr. Loune was. That's what the guard meant by "the one they needed."

They'd already taken Ilyen for surgery.

She fought down the hyperventilating panic that threatened to flood her body. Her own, and Nalea's, buffeting her like a hurricane as the scientist struggled to stay calm. Panicking wouldn't help anything; they needed to problem solve.

Galhen reached over and took both their hands; her physical shock symptoms dropped away. She gave his hand a grateful squeeze and turned back to the comm.

"Thank you, Aureis." Her voice sounded remarkably calm, given how she actually felt. "We'll handle it. Stay in contact."

"We'll have to expedite this," Galhen said briskly as she closed the comm channel. "I'll deal with the situation here, you and Nalea need to get to the medlab and save Ilyen."

"We can't just *leave* you here -"

"And we can't just leave our *people* here, either. I'll be fine, I've got an idea. Tell the guards outside you've been called for another errand by Canvel, and that Sergeant Rembsen here and I have it under control."

At her expression, his voice softened. "It'll work, darling, and if it doesn't you can rescue me later. Ilyen doesn't *have* a later."

Her eyes stung as she gave him a nod, and on impulse a hard embrace.

"Make it back," she whispered fiercely, then strode for the door, Nalea close behind.

The guard on the other side looked surprised to see them. "Just you? Thought you were collecting the leftovers?"

She made herself grimace and roll her eyes. "Got another comm from Canvel, needs me to bring a few things. Man can't be bothered to do anything himself, apparently." From the other guard's amused snort, he was buying it more than the one inside had. Thank goodness.

"Anyway, my colleague can handle it with Sergeant Rembsen," she said lightly, hooking a thumb back at the now-closed cell door. "Have a good one."

He waved them off. Walking toward the corner at a leisurely pace was one of the more difficult things Kerelle had done on this trip, but nonetheless they made it safely out of sight. As they turned the corner into the empty corridor, Nalea and Kerelle exchanged glances. They both started to run.

The lab seemed impossibly far away, down yet more of those bland, empty branching halls. Per the schematics, they had to be getting close -

They both stopped short as an alarm shrieked to life, flashing lights leaping to life in time with its piercing blare. But the alarm pattern - that wasn't an intruder alarm. Suddenly she felt the force of dozens of panicking thoughts, projected wildly by everyone in Oulemar who wasn't wearing a psiblocker. All had one overriding focus.

Radiation breach.

Before it could fully set in, Galhen's voice cut into her mind. *All according to plan, darling. Get Ilyen.*

She met Nalea's wide eyes. "Galhen says it's a fake alarm." *At least I sure hope that's what he was saying.* She didn't want to find out if Galhen could heal the kind of injuries they'd get if it wasn't. "We need to keep going."

"Then let's go." Nalea took off running again.

The halls quickly filled around them, coming to life with chaos as people fled for the evacuation shelters. No one noticed one more running pair of guards amidst the sea of tumult, all too preoccupied with their own survival to realize those guards were running a different direction than everyone else.

When they finally reached the medlab wing, the doors were thrown wide open, one hanging at a slight angle that suggested it had been forced backwards enough to damage it. That solved that problem of how they would get in - and hopefully indicated that the staff had all left in a stampede. Kerelle's boots clicked on the coldly immaculate tiles, and she had to blink to keep her eyes focused as the strobing alarm lights made the corridor almost psychedelic. There - the surgery theater. They burst through the swinging doors.

The surgery theater had clearly been abandoned in a hurry when the alarms started up. Scrubs and tools were scattered haphazardly across its surfaces, gloves discarded on the floor as if their users had been running as they removed them.

The staff had abandoned more than their tools. In the central bed, still strapped down with bright lights trained on his face, was Ilyen.

Nalea made a strangled sound between a sob and a shriek, and surged past Kerelle to his side. Kerelle hurried after her.

He lay unresponsive as Nalea's hand brushed his face, still tethered to numerous IV drips that likely kept him unconscious. Kerelle's eyes darted upward - they'd shaved his head and inked lines to cut, but the skin was unbroken, and there was no blood.

She was nearly bowled over with the sudden weight of relief. They'd made it in time.

In time to ultimately save him, yes. But as her gaze traveled back to his face and down his form, bile rose in her throat. His normally golden skin had taken on a grayish pallor, and the marks on his body told a clear and horrifying story. Ilyen had endured a great deal of pain.

The shiny new collar was the final indignity.

With an exasperated noise, Nalea pulled up her removal device and fitted it against the collar. Suddenly she gasped, and jerked her hand away. Even under sedation, Ilyen's entire body clenched.

A woman's voice suddenly echoed from behind them.

"I knew it was too convenient to be a real alarm."

NINETEEN

THEY WHIRLED TOWARDS THE DOORS. Unhurried, the speaker stepped out of the shadows of the hall. She looked dreadfully familiar, though Kerelle couldn't place her at first. Then she turned her head slightly, and from the right angle it all snapped into place.

Phaera Beniwell, the mysterious executive's daughter. The secret telekinetic. Kerelle had last seen her over a year ago, trying to lure Nalea on to her yacht back on Xan Xaldanan. The guards there had said something about her father being an important executive - what had her patronymic been again?

It hit her like a thunderbolt.

Velrin.

Phaera Velrin Beniwell.

Shit.

Phaera advanced slowly, the collar control card in one hand and a gun trained on their direction in the other. She held up the card.

"Don't try it, Evandra. We both know that if I hit the kill switch, my shields can hold you off long enough to finish the teleporter. Stay powered down, and I'll keep my fingers from slipping."

Her eyes cut over to Nalea. "And Dr. Ambrel. Lovely to see you again. Good to see my father's instincts were right, and you *are* a lying terrorist sympathizer." Ilyen's body clenched again, a soft whimper escaping his unconscious lips. Nalea's eyes locked on the control card.

"Stop hurting him," she growled, her posture defiant despite her corona of fear.

Phaera smirked. "I'm hurting *you*. Think of it as a little preview. A725 was always too stubborn to respond to the usual retraining methods, but once we deal with this," she waved her hand, "little incident, and we hook *you* up to the electroshocks instead, I suspect he might prove a usable asset after all."

She laughed and took another step forward. "Cheer up, doctor, you saved your boyfriend. Just probably not the way you had in mind. And I promise," she added, her voice dropping as if in confidence, "once we have A725 fully reconditioned and we don't need you anymore, we'll finish you off quick."

Nalea drew herself up to her full diminutive height as her aura shifted abruptly. The scientist was suddenly too angry to be afraid.

"His. Name. Is. Ilyen." Despite Phaera's superior firepower - conventional and otherwise - Nalea looked ready to take a swing at her. Phaera's smirk deepened, and her attention focused on Nalea.

Kerelle took her chance.

The most frustrating part about fighting opponents with psiblockers was how much extra force was required to achieve an effect, accounting for the psiblocker sapping your strength. Phaera had telekinetic shields, but she couldn't wear a psiblocker without cutting off access to her own abilities.

It was almost refreshing to aim a telekinetic blow and have it connect with full force.

It didn't break Phaera's shield, but it pushed her off balance. The other psionic swore and steadied herself, fingers reaching on the control card.

Kerelle didn't give her time to activate it. Instead she struck hard, centering the force on Phaera's hand. The shields held, but the jolt was enough to make her drop the card.

Game on.

Kerelle sent the card skidding away under a cabinet, then barely blocked in time as Phaera hit her with a tightly focused blow of telekinetic force. Kerelle tucked into a roll, trying to deflect the blow by following its momentum, and narrowly missed slicing her shoulder open on a discarded scalpel. She snatched it up and flung it at Phaera with the force of a speeding bullet.

The other woman dodged and deflected as well - but instead of turning the blade back at Kerelle she sent it hurtling over her shoulder towards Nalea. With a burst of near-panic Kerelle reinforced her shield, and the scalpel clattered harmlessly to the floor.

Almost before it hit the ground, Phaera followed up with a hard wave, targeted on Nalea and Ilyen. Kerelle swore as it hit her shields; she was going to feel that one later. She swung back with a wave of her own and this time sent Phaera staggering into a wall, but her opponent quickly recovered.

It was a deadly back-and-forth, then - Phaera targeting her attacks at Nalea and Ilyen in the center, Kerelle defending them and trying to find an opening to strike back. The lab around them was quickly reduced to rubble, broken lamps sparking at shattered furniture thrown haphazardly across the ground.

Neither of them were holding back. Kerelle had twice faced Phaera and let her go, and each time the other woman had only used her mercy as an opportunity to attack again. Phaera couldn't control how she'd been raised, what she'd been brought up to believe, any more than Kerelle could. But she could choose what to believe *now*. She wasn't simply complicit in SysTech's abuse of its psionics, she was an active participant. What SysTech was attempting to do to Ilyen was a gross defiance of all human decency, and Phaera was here to ensure it happened as planned.

And that was beyond Kerelle's capacity to forgive.

Still, it wasn't easy. Kerelle gasped under a particularly hard hit, and tried to turn the momentum back toward Phaera. She was fairly certain she was still the stronger psionic, but Phaera was either a soft C3 or a hard C2, and she was very well trained. When she struck, it was with precision force that hit all the harder for being concentrated, and she knew how to defend without losing her own momentum. She might not ever have been PsiCorp, but Kerelle was certain she'd been trained by a few.

She wondered what those erstwhile tutors had thought of her situation, and what had happened to them afterward.

Kerelle rolled to avoid another hit, then struck back with a precision blow of her own. She didn't need to take down Phaera's entire shield, just weaken it enough for a gap -

There. She felt the other woman's shield fragment, and flung the scalpel again straight for her chest. Phaera spun and caught it, a handbreadth away from its target.

When she screamed suddenly and fell to her knees, Kerelle was as surprised as she was. But it seemed that along with PsiCorp training, Phaera had picked up a common PsiCorp flaw.

She underestimated mundanes.

The gun shook in Nalea's hands, the scientist's eyes gone wide. But judging by the blood rapidly soaking through Phaera's jacket, she'd scored a vital hit.

Phaera coughed and dropped hard to her side, crimson dripping from her lips. She reached out, fingers scrabbling for the gun she'd dropped earlier in their battle. Kerelle kicked it away.

"How could you *do* this? To your own *people?*" She couldn't keep the anger out of her voice, the adrenaline still coursing through her veins as she advanced. "You're a psionic! This could be *you!*"

Phaera was gasping for breath, but she still looked up at Kerelle with a sneer on her bloody lips. "I don't...give a shit... about some psionic identity bullshit." Her anger still burned clearly, despite her voice going ragged. "You aren't...*my people.*"

"No," Kerelle answered. "We aren't." The adrenaline was fading, and now all she felt was ice. "But we could have been."

Snap.

She left the body where it fell.

IT TOOK some time to extricate Ilyen from the surgery table. The physical restraints Kerelle could simply snap off, but the chemicals keeping him under needed to be turned off gradually to avoid injury. The collar, too, was a new design, and did not immediately respond to the removal device.

Nalea was hunched over it with Phaera's since-retrieved control card, jaw clenched as she fiddled with something in the wiring. Whatever she was trying to do, her still-trembling fingers weren't helping. But there was no time to unpack and process what had just happened, not while they were burning through borrowed time in the heart of enemy territory.

And so Nalea kept her focus on freeing Ilyen, and Kerelle kept watch with mounting anxiety. They had been lucky to be undisturbed so far, but there was no way that luck could hold. The radiation breach alarm had bought them time, certainly, but it couldn't take *that* long for the SysTech staff to realize no breach had actually occurred. It was virtually guaranteed that security forces would intervene soon, especially if any security cams had caught their battle with Phaera.

Nalea wasn't the only one with feelings to unpack about

that. Kerelle could tell it would hit her later, and at some point she'd have to deal with it, but now wasn't the time. For now, she thought with another nervous glance at the door, they *really* needed to get moving.

As if on cue, Galhen pinged her through the bond.

Status report please, darling.

We've located Ilyen, in time. She couldn't bring herself to say unharmed. *We're having some difficulty with extraction. We also had a bit of a complication. It's been resolved.* She shared a quick impression of what had happened with Phaera. Like feelings, the full details could wait.

He paused. *I appreciate you and Nalea are doing all you can, but if there's any way to expedite, now would be the time. I have all the others back at the ship, Riyel included, but we attracted some attention on the way in. And by now they will be realizing that the radiation alert was a false alarm.*

Understood. We're coming.

Aloud, she said, "Nalea, we're out of time. We need to work on the move."

"This is harder than it looks," Nalea snapped back. "I can't run and disarm a fucking *time bomb* at the same time."

"Then we get back to the ship and disarm it there," she answered evenly. Nalea's hostility was a screen for her stress and anxiety, and both of them knew it. Kerelle wasn't going to waste time snapping back. "Galhen says they have everyone else back at the ship, but we're likely to have company soon. If we don't get out now, we won't be able to."

She didn't have to elaborate on what was likely to happen in that scenario. Nalea grumbled but hurriedly gathered up her tools. The control card, now partially disassembled with a mass of wires hooked around it, was shoved unceremoniously into her pack. The dials on the IVs she checked much more carefully.

"I think he's okay to disconnect now," she said. From her

tone, there was a margin of error there that Nalea wasn't entirely comfortable with, but they had little choice. As she watched Nalea gently withdraw the needles from his veins, a grim part of Kerelle's mind reflected that Ilyen was *already* going to need Galhen's help; any damage from premature disconnection might just roll in with all the rest.

Nalea looped her lover's arm over her shoulder as if to carry his limp body on her back. Kerelle waved her off and simply picked him up with her telekinetics, careful to float him high enough that his feet didn't drag.

"We'll move faster," she told the other woman. Nalea's lips compressed, but she couldn't argue. "Let's go."

She wanted to run, but Kerelle forced herself to move deliberately as they retraced their steps through the hall. The frenetic alarms that had covered their entry were now ominously quiescent, and the corridor was silent but for the clacking of their boots on the tile. Kerelle's sense of vulnerability intensified.

As they approached an intersection with another corridor, a sudden scuffing noise caught her attention, out of cadence with their own echoing footsteps. She held up a hand to stop Nalea and threw up a shield around the three of them, her senses straining for the source of the noise. She couldn't sense any presence, but if they were wearing psiblockers…

They were.

The security troops flooded out of the other corridor, a hail of projectiles pinging against her shields. Blood and flame, the paralytic darts again. Give her straight bullets any day.

Kerelle shoved Nalea and Ilyen behind her; it would be easier to maintain the shield with a smaller surface area. She sent a hard wave pushing ahead of them, seeking to throw their foes off their feet. Some stumbled and fell, others managed to regain the balance and fire back. Kerelle's jaw clenched. Any time they spent here engaged with this group was time more groups could come in to reinforce. They couldn't afford to be bogged down. And after the things they'd seen here, she wasn't inclined to grant mercy to people *just doing their jobs*.

She struck hard at the floors beneath their feet, shattering the ceramic tiles and ripping up their sharp-edged shards like makeshift knives. Two she was able to impale before they could react, the force behind her throws carrying the tile shards even through the psiblockers' dampening field. The others scattered, some aiming now for the weaponized tiles instead of her. Kerelle hit them with another wave, this one carrying hurricane force behind it. The sheer strength of the push tore still more tiles from the floor behind them, punching holes in the otherwise-featureless walls. The survivors stumbled again, more falling to the ground this time, and she was on them with the tiles almost before they could scream.

Almost. Now they *really* needed to get out of here.

"Keep up," she barked back at Nalea, and started to run.

Subtlety was behind them at this point. Kerelle collected more broken tiles as they ran, thankful for their sharp tips and jagged edges. At first she tried to fight her way through the next group that engaged them, but then more and more joined the fray and she realized their only chance was to try to clear a path and run for it. She changed tack to trying to blast enemies out of their way, using her tile-knives to deal with anyone who got too close.

It would have been a lot to deal with *without* having to over-compensate for the psiblockers. With them, she wouldn't be able to keep this up all that long. The knowledge gave her a frenzied kind of strength, and she found herself sundering the walls to crush their foes with. Behind her she could hear Nalea beginning to flag, the punishing pace more than her physical fitness could keep up with. A split second to consider, and Nalea yelped as Kerelle picked her up as well. She took off at speed then, Nalea and Ilyen floating right behind.

She imagined Nalea would have something to say about this later. If it meant they *made* it to later, Kerelle would gladly endure the earful.

They were getting closer, she knew they were. She could sense everyone back at the ship, like beacons of safety in the surreal nightmare-world that was Oulemar. She kicked her speed up to a sprint, though she could feel her own body protesting. Maintaining the shield, too, was getting harder.

Ice overwhelmed her, and Nalea shrieked as she and Ilyen hit the ground. Kerelle herself stumbled forward, filled with the horrified knowledge that the shield had been faltering more than she'd realized. The dart in her shoulder had found a gap in her shield, and now she could feel that terrible numbness of the suppressant oozing through her veins.

She could feel it…but she did not go totally numb. She could move, and her powers were still there, though accessing them felt like calling across a chasm. Still - she *could* access her psionics.

Nalea's inoculation had worked.

The SysTech group was advancing recklessly now, secure in the knowledge that Kerelle was defanged. She closed her eyes and dug deep.

It was hard enough to get her sluggish powers to respond; there was no way she could summon up enough force to make it through the psiblockers. She didn't try.

Instead, she shoved down as hard as she could manage on the ceiling above them.

The collapse took them all by surprise, a flood of rubble coming down on their attackers' heads. It sufficed for a distraction and a barrier all in one. She pulled herself back up to her feet.

Nalea had regained her feet as well, Ilyen draped over her shoulder. The teleporter stirred slightly, but remained limp and unresponsive against her. Kerelle reached to lift him again and realized just as swiftly that she couldn't afford to spend the strength, not if they needed to fight again before they reached the ship. Instead she slung his other arm over her shoulder, and the three of them started again toward the ship. The pace was painfully slow.

Her psionics still felt like they were underwater; she felt Galhen's urgent inquiry through their bond, more as a feeling than as actual words. Feelings were all she could manage in response, but he must have understood, because the response was clear: reassurance that help was coming.

More footsteps, this time from in front of them. Kerelle drew a shaky breath and gathered her strength. She wondered if she could drop a ceiling on *this* group too.

Suddenly the entire corridor went bright, a flash approaching before any of them could react. Kerelle threw up a shield in reflex, but though she could feel the heat of the fireball, its deadly flames stayed well away from their little group.

The guards weren't so lucky, and Kerelle closed her eyes as they screamed and suddenly cut off. The fireball died, leaving only ash behind. Her stomach churned, even knowing what they'd been complicit in, even knowing what they would have done to her and Nalea and Ilyen if her defenses had been over-whelmed. *Feel later.*

If they ever made it to later, there was going to be a lot of *feeling*. Yet another problem to deal with then instead of now.

Elinea stood at the far end of the hall, her outline aglow. Even battered and dirty, she blazed like an avenging spirit, fury and defiance etched on her face. Kerelle had never been so happy to see her.

"You almost made it, Evandra," she remarked lightly as they caught up. From her slight limp and the dark bruising across her face, Elinea had endured her own suffering in Oulemar, but her spirit still burned bright. She too was likely *feeling later*. "I left

Jesara guarding the entrance to the hanger, we'll catch up with her soon. Captain Marene's ready to take off as soon as we're in."

"That's welcome news," Kerelle answered with a grunt as she shifted Ilyen's weight against her shoulders. "Let's not keep him waiting."

She could sense the telekinetic Jesara not far away, and Galhen was close behind her. Just a little bit further now…

Ilyen's sudden scream in her ear stunned her, and when he thrashed violently against her shoulder it sent them both crashing to the floor. His eyes had flown wide, and for a split second they met hers before his entire body clenched and then convulsed. Nalea began to swear incoherently as she dove for his collar.

Kerelle watched in helpless horror. Phaera's card wouldn't have been the only one synced to Ilyen's collar. Whoever held the master had flipped the kill switch.

The time bomb had gone off.

Ilyen's eyes were unfocused now, staring blankly at the ceiling as he began to gasp for breath. Nalea's face hardened, and she darted a hand in her bag to withdraw a pair of wirecutters and two little vials, both with syringes attached. The inoculations she'd developed to counteract hemindrium.

Nalea had said she didn't know if they'd be fully effective. Kerelle realized with a sick twist in her gut that they were about to find out.

Kerelle swooped in to help the best she could, holding the thrashing teleporter down so that Nalea could get a clean shot at a vein. The scientist gave him both doses in rapid succession, then reached up and snapped the collar off with the wirecutters, perhaps before she could reconsider.

Ilyen's eyes rolled back up in his head and he collapsed limply again - but his breathing quickly steadied. Nalea gave them a quick nod and slung him back over her shoulder, ignoring the tears that had begun to escape her eyes. Kerelle grabbed his other arm and they resumed the painful trek onward.

They were pursued, but Elinea was merciless. Kerelle's powers were slowly bubbling up from the icy lake the suppressant had submerged them in, and she could sense the pyrokinetic's vicious, personal satisfaction flare up like one of her fireballs whenever her erstwhile captors were reduced to ash. It was disturbing to feel in proximity. Kerelle couldn't judge her for it.

Jesara met them with palpable enthusiasm. She too was heavily bruised, with a burn mark across her cheek that looked like it had come from a shock wand, but she didn't hesitate to grab Ilyen from Nalea and Kerelle's flagging grasp and sling him over her own shoulders instead. They ran for the welcome glow of the ship's open hatch, tantalizing in its offer of safety. Already it hovered slightly off the ground - Elinea hadn't been exaggerating that Sandrel was ready to go.

Galhen and Aureis met them at the door, pulling them in and hurriedly closing the hatch. The ship rocketed forward almost as soon as the lock light engaged. Aureis ran up toward the cockpit as they picked up speed.

Galhen took one look at Ilyen and began to swear almost as intensely as Nalea had. "What's happened?"

"We had to pull him off the sedative drip on the early side, then his collar went off and I had to double-dose the hemindrium dampening agent before brute-forcing it. He hasn't been conscious and coherent since we found him." Nalea's voice started to choke, everything that had happened catching up to her now that they had made it back. "Galhen, *please* - "

"Everything I can," he cut her off. "Help me get him to the medbay."

Before Kerelle could offer to help, Sandrel's voice cut over the intercom.

"Any telekinetics with juice left, I need you up here stat."

She started to run. Thank goodness the adrenaline hadn't worn off just yet - and that the earlier suppressant was fading fast.

She skidded into the cockpit, and the reason for Sandrel's call was immediately clear. The great bay doors were open - *how did they get open?* - but were grinding inexorably inward to close.

"We just need enough of a gap to get through," Sandrel told her brusquely. He was outwardly calm, but his knuckles were white around the controls. "Break it, hold it, I don't care, we just need to get out and into open air."

Kerelle drew everything she could. Even with the suppressant fading, her strength was seriously depleted from the battle with Phaera and all that happened after it. But if they couldn't get through the bay doors, then it was all for nothing anyway. She braced herself and shoved against the doors.

The resistance nearly threw her to her knees. Burning void, this was insane, there were thousands of tons of metal and concrete there, she could never hold it. If she didn't, they all would die. She tried again.

The weight lessened as Elinea took up a place beside her, and again as Jesana caught up. Kerelle couldn't spare the concentration to look behind her and see who else had joined them, but she could sense the additional assistance from other telekinetics clustered in the cockpit and corridor. The doors were still moving, they were too much to stop, but slowly, slowly, still too fast...

Kerelle gritted her teeth and pushed with everything, everything she had. Metal screeched, and the doors shuddered as their mechanism began to spark.

Their jaws scraped the top of the ship with a teeth-rattling shriek as the ship slipped through. Sandrel gunned it, and the force threw them all backwards as the ship rocketed into empty space.

Kerelle's head was screaming, and she was vaguely aware that there was something hot and metallic dripping from the area of her nose. The soft blur of the ship entering hyper was the last thing she registered before everything went black.

TWENTY

THE FIRST THING Kerelle became aware of, even before she fully came to in the cabin she shared with Galhen on Sandrel's ship, was the throbbing, burning pain in her head. She squinted groggy eyes open and immediately squeezed them shut again as the harsh light flooded her temples with renewed pain, bright in its intensity. Her body's instinct was to pull the sheets up over her eyes and try to retreat back into sleep, in hopes that her affliction would fade with rest.

But no - as more of her mind came fully awake, she realized that was unlikely to accomplish much. The events of the previous - *hour? Day? What time was it, anyway?* - were coming back to her in a rush. She'd pushed way too hard, and at the very least she was probably severely dehydrated, at worst...

Nalea would probably tell her that using her psionics in this condition wasn't advisable, but *advisable* or not she had to know. Cautiously she reached out a small telekinetic push against the bedsheet. When it moved she almost passed out again, this time in relief. Her psionics were sore to the touch, but they were *there*, and responsive. She wasn't burned out.

Slowly and painfully, Kerelle levered herself upright. Her

eyes were adjusting to the light - which was not actually harsh at all, was actually keyed to its dimmest setting - and though the effort of sitting initially sent knives through her head again, after some careful breathing the burst faded. It was then that she noticed the glass of water on the bedside table, next to two pills and a neatly lettered note.

Darling,

I'm sorry I can't be there with you right now, and that you likely have a terrible headache. You should be all right with some rest and rehydration, however, and I've left some painkillers to help in the meantime. Take those, and when you're feeling up to it, go down to the mess to get yourself a pot of tea. Keeping drinking tea or water throughout the day, and try to avoid using your psionics for at least the next day or so.

I'll check in with you when I get a chance. Until then I'll be doing what I can in the medbay.

All my love

- Galhen

The effort of focusing her eyes to read the note sent her head flaring up again, this time with a burst of nausea as well. Kerelle set the note aside and downed the painkillers, taking care to sip the water slowly instead of chugging it all in one go. By the time she'd finished the glass, the painkillers were beginning to do their work, and she was feeling like some approximation of herself again.

She reread the note, more able to focus on what it actually said. The last bit sounded rather ominous, all the more so that he left her a note in the first place rather than just checking in telepathically. It likely meant he was going to need everything he had for healing.

Sure enough, the bond was closed from his side, likely to conserve energy and avoid distraction. The implication sent another curl of nausea through her gut. Ilyen had obviously been tortured; if Galhen was this heads-down in the medbay then he likely hadn't been the only one.

If that was the case, there was nothing Kerelle could do to help right now except stay out of Galhen's way, and be ready to defend against any further threats. And since threats were unlikely to materialize in the temporary sanctuary of hyperspace, the best she could do was rest up and recover for when they dropped back into realspace again.

***

THE SHOWER WAS worth the effort of dragging herself down to the lav. Besides just the revivifying effects of the steam and heat, it felt good to wash Oulemar's air off her skin and hair. It was almost like a ritual cleansing, leaving the last trace of that horrific place behind.

Catching sight of herself in the mirror afterward - clad in lounge pants and one of Galhen's knit shirts, damp hair pulled roughly back - Kerelle observed with weary amusement that she looked more like a university student on the weekend than a rebel leader coming back from a successful raid on a secret enemy prison. But there was no way she was putting on the clothes she'd worn yesterday until they had a good wash (or two), and she really couldn't be bothered to hunt for something more professional-looking, so "university student" it was.

Besides, she doubted anyone else would have the energy to care either. Time to see about that tea in the mess.

It took her quite some time to *get* to the mess, for the best possible reason. The ship was gratifyingly full.

Packed into common areas were roughly twenty faces she'd thought she wouldn't see again. She could scarcely go a few steps without a greeting and a hug, and by the time she finally made it to the mess her face was wet with tears.

The good kind, this time.

Elinea was already brewing tea when she got there. Kerelle gratefully accepted a cup.

"So," the pyrokinetic said as they settled into their seats. "You're up again."

"Yes," Kerelle answered, not really sure how to respond. "Are you surprised?"

"Eh. You were looking pretty bad after that last bit with the doors, but I figured if you were *actually* in danger Ambrel would have been a lot more agitated about it. Of course," she added with a grimace, "he's been pretty busy."

Which segued into what Kerelle *really* wanted to know. "What's happened since the escape?" On further thought, she added, "and how long was I out, anyway?"

"Since yesterday," Elinea confirmed. "You probably slept around 14 hours." She looked over her cup at Kerelle, expression cautious. "Are you...is everything...okay?"

"I'm not burned out," she answered quickly. Relief flooded the pyrokinetic's face.

"Thank stars for *that*. I mean, it would be awful for you, of course, but..." the other woman's jaw tightened. "It'd be pretty awful for the rest of us too. We need your firepower. Especially now."

Elinea ran a hand through her bright hair. "Look, I don't want to talk specifics, but that was...that was real rough. On all of us. I can still fight. I *want* to fight." For a moment, her eyes glowed bright as her flames. "But I can't speak for everyone else."

Kerelle nodded slowly. "Of course." Elinea was right that they needed firepower, but they weren't SysTech. Their people were more than tools. "We'll do everything we can to protect the injured." She pursed her lips - part of her was afraid to ask, but she had to know. "Speaking of..."

"We haven't lost anyone else so far," Elinea answered bluntly. "Ambrel did a triage on who was the worst off, then got to work. As far as I know he hasn't left the medbay since we hit hyper."

Kerelle's question must have been plain on her face.

"Vanadariel was first up," Elinea confirmed. "Sounds like Ambrel got him stabilized and then took care of some others. I haven't heard much on updates there."

Kerelle digested that. It didn't sound promising. "I'm assuming Nalea is in the medbay as well?"

Elinea shook her head. "Ambrel kicked her out. She's been locked up in her lab ever since."

Oh dear. That didn't sound promising at all.

Kerelle sighed deeply. "I'll go check on her later, then. Anything else I should know?"

Elinea shook her head. "No, but…I'm hoping there's something you can tell *me*." The pyrokinetic leaned forward, uncharacteristic anxiety in her eyes. "Anniya and Teriel. Did they make it off Cashaal?"

"Yes," Kerelle replied, and some of the tension went out of the other woman's shoulders. Kerelle swallowed and made herself continue. "Anniya escaped without injury, but Teriel… was badly hurt. I don't know details, only that…only that Lilika wasn't sure he'd make it. That was over a week ago; I'm sorry, I don't know any more."

Elinea nodded heavily. "Then I guess we find out when we get where we're going." She stood up suddenly then. "I'm going to get some rest. Call me if anything needs to be on fire."

Kerelle let her go. Some time to process would probably do them all good.

THERE WAS no word from the medbay as the day went on, and Kerelle didn't want to interrupt. Galhen knew better than any of them how to approach things, and her presence would only be a distraction. Instead she occupied herself with checking on the welfare of the others, answering what questions she could and ensuring everyone was as comfortable as they could manage.

Perhaps unsurprisingly, Nalea didn't answer the door when Kerelle knocked. Kerelle couldn't help but worry, but at the same time she knew her sister-in-law. If Nalea wanted to be alone right now, she would be. She called an offer to talk any time through the silent door, and left the scientist to her own devices.

It was towards the end of the day that Kerelle came across Aureis, perched awkwardly in a corner of the mess. He was, she sensed, trying to make himself as small as possible.

He'd gotten a change of clothes at some point, and his hair was loosely combed rather than carefully styled. Despite herself, Kerelle was struck by how much younger and more vulnerable he looked without the suit.

She briefly considered continuing on her way. She appreciated all that Aureis had done for them, but she wasn't quite sure what to say to him now that his part in it was over. A small part of her, too, rebelled at the thought of fraternizing with a SysTech executive, however indirectly he had been involved in her people's suffering. But that wasn't entirely fair - SysTech executive he had indeed been, but Aureis had recoiled when he realized just what he was abetting, and he'd put his life in danger to help them.

She wasn't entirely sure what to do with him now, but surely she at least owed him a check-in.

"Hey," she greeted him quietly, sliding into the adjoining seat. "How are you?"

"I'm fine." His eyes stayed glued to his tea. "Captain Marene has been very kind."

"Sandrel is good people," she agreed, mildly surprised they'd had much interaction. But she supposed she shouldn't be; they'd collaborated on the Oulemar plan, and Sandrel was good with strays. She was probably proof of that.

Awkward silence lapsed between them. Aureis still didn't look up at her, and his posture was tense. When he wasn't fired up about something, it seemed their accountant was actually rather shy.

A moment's guilty wish that Galhen were handling this instead, and Kerelle rallied.

"Thank you for your help," she said sincerely. "I know it wasn't easy, and that the consequences for you are significant."

She got a darted glance upward for that, and a quick nod. She tried again.

"Have you thought about what happens next?"

His laugh sounded slightly hysterical. "I've been trying not to. I don't know, really. I can't go back now though, not after how things went at Oulemar."

She looked at him quizzically. "Things at Oulemar?" He'd been in the ship the whole time.

"They'll review the records and see that it was my override access that triggered the alarms, and bypassed the lockdown to open the hangar doors when we left."

Kerelle blinked in surprise. "I didn't realize that was you."

"Well, the alarms were Dr. Ambrel's idea, I just made it happen. It still might not have worked if Dr. Ambrel hadn't used telepathy on the people without psiblockers, to push them into panicking." Aureis took a shuddering breath. "But either way. They'll know. I can pretend you forced it out of me, but..." he shrugged miserably. "Best case I get a polite pretext and a respectable severance package. Worst case I get arrested and shot."

From his tone, Aureis thought the second one was much more likely. Kerelle wouldn't patronize him by arguing otherwise.

"Even if it *was* the severance, I'm not sure what I would do." Aureis was still staring at his tea, but now that she had him talking it seemed like they'd opened some kind of floodgate. "I gave SysTech the last fifteen years of my life. There was never time for anything else, didn't feel like there *should* be anything else, not when I was lucky enough to get one of the internship slots out of university."

"Internship slots are hard to get, then?"

He blinked at her. "Stars, yes. There's thousands of applicants for just a few spots every year. It's different if you're a legacy at the firm, obviously, but I wasn't. My parents were SysTech, at least, but they were in lower administration."

The explanation was, if anything, more confusing. Aureis must have picked up on it from her expression, because he immediately clarified.

"Being a *legacy* means your parents are executives at the firm. It also means guaranteed internships and fast track to promotion." He tilted his head. "Didn't you run into this when you worked there? The head of Tallimau's PsiCorp unit was a legacy, if I recall correctly."

She shook her head. "We didn't exactly get bios on the SysTech staff we worked with. They gave us missions; past that it was none of our business." A strange thought, though. She recalled Director Cafora as intimidating, but generally fair and competent. It was a bit startling to hear he'd gotten his position through family connections.

"Well, it's not impossible to do well if you aren't a legacy, but it's harder. I was lucky enough just to get *into* my program, and then to have my work recognized and move up from there. All the way to *Director*, even. It felt like I'd done so well, like working hard and doing the right thing and always putting the company first had paid off."

He leaned his head back then, eyes closed. "And that's kind of the worst part, actually. The *right thing* for what? What did any of it *mean*?"

Kerelle wasn't sure how to respond; after a moment's quiet Aureis answered himself.

"I don't think it meant *anything*. When we….first met, in the office, and I thought you were going to kill me? I thought it was my last 15 minutes of life, and I was trying to think of things I'd leave unfinished, people I'd leave behind, *anything in the world* that would be poorer for my absence. There wasn't anything.

"The nice apartment I only ever slept at will be re-rented by the end of the month, and I hardly even left anything for the landlord to throw away. My team won't notice one less face at the weekly happy hour, and there's no one else I see regularly."

His laugh was more bitter than anything. "I think the last non-SysTech person I spent any real time with was my girlfriend from university, and we broke up a week after graduation. There was this lawyer in the contract division for awhile, we got drinks together a few times, but half the time I'd have to cancel because of work, or else he would, and even then we never had much else to talk about besides our projects. When Caslen transferred offworld the worst part was how much I didn't miss him."

He finally looked over at her, eyes bleak. "I realized, today, that if you shot me in the head right now and threw me out the airlock, aside from my parents there's not a single living crea-ture who would care. Or even *notice*. I should be upset that I can't go back, that my career is over, that the life I had is *gone* but…" His voice cracked slightly. "What was the *point* of my life? What was the point of *anything*?"

Aureis leaned forward, resting his forehead in his hands. "I don't know why I'm telling you this."

In brutal honesty, Kerelle wasn't sure why he was either, but he was clearly distressed. Kerelle desperately wished he was having this conversation with Galhen, or Sandrel, or literally anyone who knew what to say when people were upset. But they were all busy, and he was going to have to make do with her.

"Sometimes you just need to let things out," she responded slowly. "I'm sorry things happened like this for you. But…" she didn't quite know how to say it, so instead she gently tugged his hand away from his face. "Look around you. Look at all the people who are alive and free because you helped save them."

His grey eyes passed over the room, though Kerelle couldn't tell if he really *saw*. Still, he nodded slowly.

"I guess…I'm glad I could do something, in the end."

"It doesn't have to be the end." She tried to smile encouragingly for him. "You're welcome to stay with us, Aureis. We're happy to have you here."

His brows lifted a fraction. "Does your…movement…take non-psionics?"

She patted his arm. "We can start."

TWENTY-ONE

IT WAS late before Galhen joined her in bed. She'd slept only fitfully, and the quiet swish of the opening door was enough to bring her back to full awareness. For his part, Galhen barely paused to kick off his shoes and leave his clothes piled on the floor before collapsing onto their bunk. The sharp scent of Sandrel's preferred soap met her nose. He must have come straight from the showers.

Kerelle was dying for updates on Ilyen and the others, but she could tell immediately that Galhen was in no shape for a question-and-answer session. Their bond was finally open again, and it thrummed with stress and exhaustion. She didn't need to ask details - she *felt* how hard it had been, felt all the horror he'd suppressed throughout it all to focus on doing all he could to help. Felt the aches settling into his muscles as the fatigue crept in. The hot water had done a little to relieve the knotted tension in his back, but not enough.

She felt his need, too - for comfort and solace and *life* that wasn't in danger of winking out. He didn't want to wake her, not when surely she needed the rest as much as he did -

Almost before he'd settled into the bed she rolled to pin him beneath her, and fiercely met his open lips with her own. His earlier line of thought cut off abruptly, at the answer to the question he hadn't yet asked.

They'd barely finished when Galhen drifted into sleep, Kerelle's hand softly stroking his hair. In the morning, he was gone before she woke up.

Worry bubbled up in her again as she stared at the ceiling of their cabin, arm stretched across the empty spot beside her. He'd left early enough that the sheets were already cold. Not for the first time, Kerelle wished this was something she could help with, that she'd been gifted with the ability to heal instead of destroy. But she hadn't, and there wasn't anything she could do but continue to stay out of the way.

That, and she was long overdue to check in with Sandrel. Not that he was likely to need her help either, but she ought to at least find out where they were headed next. Kerelle heaved herself out of bed.

SANDREL WAS IN THE COCKPIT, where she expected to find him. She was rather surprised to find Aureis there too, perched in the copilot's chair with a steaming cup of tea.

The accountant stood hastily as she entered the room, nearly spilling his tea in the process.

"Commander Evandra! Good morning." A faint blush spread rapidly up his cheeks, and she caught a burst of mortification about *blathering on like an idiot yesterday about my stupid problems, what was I thinking, what must she think of* me-

"Good morning, Director Calduit," she responded, hoping her smile looked nonthreatening. "And please, just Kerelle." She wanted to joke that hearing his life's story put them on first-name basis, but she suspected it would only make him *more* uncomfortable.

He looked plenty uncomfortable already, but she wasn't sure if it was her specifically or just the situation in general. He gave her a quick of nod agreement.

"Thank you, Commander Ev- *Kerelle*. I'm sure you and Captain Marene have important business, I won't get in your way."

Sandrel called out as he retreated from the cockpit. "Thank you for the tea, Director." He lifted his own mug. "It's good."

Aureis's flush deepened and he was gone with a whispered thanks. Kerelle sat down into the copilot seat he'd vacated.

"He's...a lot more skittish than I would expect, for an executive," she observed. Sandrel shrugged.

"Can you really blame him? His entire world's turned upside down, the company he spent his whole life at probably wants him dead, and he's stuck in an enclosed space with a bunch of people who probably scare the shit out of him."

He took another sip of tea. "I mean, you scared the shit out of *me* when we first met, and it wasn't exactly my first time in a dicey situation. Two weeks ago the biggest danger in *his* life was making a mistake in the budget projections." He considered. "Or maybe an early stroke from working too hard. I might bring that up to him, actually."

"I didn't realize you two were talking so much," she commented. She wasn't sure a few conversations over tea really counted as *talking so much*, but compared to Aureis's interactions with the *rest* of the crew they were practically best friends.

Sandrel quirked a grin. "I'm currently the only other mundane on the ship. Pretty sure that makes me the least terrifying person available. But joking aside," he added more seriously, "he was a big help when we were getting ready to take on Oulemar. He's bright and a good problem solver, and I think he'll be a good fit for the team once we get him comfortable."

Kerelle glanced at the comm. "Speaking of the team...?"

"I figured you were here to ask about that." Sandrel drained the last of the tea and set the cup down near the comm button. "Some good news there. I've had contact with the rest of our people. Lilika's got everyone who's left hunkered down on some backwater with a tapped-out mine. Doesn't sound like a long-term hideout, but it's keeping them off the radar for now. We're on course now to join them."

"Apparently Oliven has really stepped up," he added with a ghost of a smile. "Lilika says his shuttle only made it out because he did some fairly fancy flying to get past the enemy. Now that they're settled for the time being, he's been organizing repairs to the shuttles and working on emergency piloting lessons for anyone who's interested. Our lost kid is all grown up."

"So he is," she agreed, a bittersweet smile on her own lips. She was proud of Oliven, but she wished he'd never had to do any of this.

She was afraid to ask the next question, but…"Any updates on the wounded?"

"Not a lot. You know Lilika, she's not big on discussing things we can't control. I did ask about Teriel. She said he's still alive, but the way she said it sounded bad. Hopefully Galhen can do something."

Kerelle only nodded; she hoped so too. But that had been far too common of a refrain lately.

Sandrel shifted, and his eyes slid over to hers. "On that subject…"

"I don't have any updates on Ilyen," she confessed. "Galhen was too tired to talk last night. All I know is he's been in the medbay pretty much since we left Oulemar."

"How's Nalea handling it?"

"About usual," she answered with a sigh. "She's been locked in her lab and won't answer the door."

"About usual then," Sandrel agreed. He stretched and gave the viewports a baleful glance, as if there were anything to see but the soft nothing of hyper. "Let me know if anything changes?"

She nodded her agreement and got up to leave. "Likewise. In the meantime I'll be doing the rounds." The cockpit doors swished shut behind her, and she hoped that next time she passed through them she'd have better news.

———

THE TEA KETTLE was almost done brewing when the ping came; she nearly dropped it in surprise.

Darling. A soft overlay like a quick kiss on the cheek. *I'm about to bring Ilyen out of sedation. Can you fetch Nalea please?*

On my way.

Kettle abandoned, Kerelle practically ran to Nalea's cabin, dodging curious stares as she did. There would be plenty of time to fill everyone in later.

"Nalea!" She banged her hand on the closed door. Externally nothing had changed from her last visit, but Kerelle was certain she could be heard. "Nalea, open up please! It's about Ilyen. We need you." The door wrenched open.

From the look of her, Nalea had slept little since their escape from Oulemar. But her bloodshot eyes lit with a kind of desperate hope when they met Kerelle's.

"Is he - "

"Galhen's getting ready to wake him up. Come on."

She didn't have to say it twice. Nalea sped toward the medbay at a pace Kerelle struggled to match.

Galhen gave a nod of acknowledgement as they entered, his fingers still resting lightly on Ilyen's temples. They both looked awful, frankly, but Ilyen's skin had recovered some of its healthy color, and the ugly marks had faded. To Kerelle's surprise, he also had a full head of shoulder-length hair again, the raven strands pooled around his face like fine silk.

Her surprise must have echoed through the bond. *It's no effort at all to regrow hair,* Galhen told her shortly, *and a small price to give him back some dignity.*

Aloud he only said, "We've made good progress. I've taken care of the worst of it, and the rest he'll be able to recover from on his own. I'm going to give him a dose of suppressant and bring him back to full consciousness."

Nalea stiffened. "I think he's had enough suppressant lately. Why dose him again?"

Kerelle felt a wave of exhaustion through their bond, but Galhen's tone stayed professional. It was a reasonable question, as much as he just wanted to get through this so he could sit down. "Ilyen's time with SysTech was clearly horrific, and he's had a lot of drugs in his system. If he's confused or frightened when he wakes up, he might teleport on instinct."

More gently he added, "Seeing you will help him feel safe."

Nalea nodded tersely, her brow tense with the effort of holding back tears. Kerelle pretended not to notice. Let Nalea keep *her* dignity, too.

Galhen nodded back. He carefully gave Ilyen the injection, then lifted his hands and stepped back. Nalea twined her fingers with her lover's, and carefully watched his face.

It felt like hours passed then, though it couldn't have been more than a few minutes. Suddenly Ilyen's breathing changed, and his eyes snapped open. His heart rate spiked, sending the medbay's little monitors into trilling alarm.

The suppressant was probably a good idea, Kerelle observed.

I know.

Meanwhile Nalea stroked his hand and murmured reassurances, her demeanor softer than Kerelle had ever seen her. Tears slipped openly down her face as she kept up her gentle, cooing litany, that he was safe now and everything would be all right. The monitors fell silent as Ilyen's heart and breathing slowed, his eyes blinking rapidly as if to clear them. His gaze locked on to Nalea's face.

Hesitantly he reached out to brush her cheek. She leaned into the touch, lifting her other hand to cover his.

"You're real," he whispered, and then his lips were on hers.

Kerelle glanced away, suddenly embarrassed to be intruding on the tender moment. There were tears on Ilyen's face also.

The teleporter pulled back after a moment, shifting himself closer to sitting upright. His gaze suddenly sharpened on his and Nalea's entwined hands, and Kerelle felt the projected realization that he had fingernails again. Ilyen blinked again and looked around, noticing her and Galhen for the first time.

Galhen leaned forward slightly. "How are you feeling?"

"Shitty." Ilyen's eyes cut to his hand again. "But not as shitty as I should be." He lifted one of his fingers, examining the neat row of nails. "This was you, wasn't it."

"Yes, among other things. I was able to heal the worst of your injuries, and get your body's natural healing underway a bit faster. I also gave you a dose of suppressant so you wouldn't vanish on us as soon as you woke up, so don't panic. You should be able to access your psionics again in an hour or two." He withdrew a small packet from the cabinet behind him. "From here we should be able to manage your recovery with painkillers. There's instructions in there, but let me know if you have any questions."

Galhen grimaced slightly as he handed the painkillers off to the teleporter. "Ordinarily I would just finish the job, but there are others who need tending as well, and I've only so much energy to go around."

Ilyen nodded his understanding, leaning back. His initial burst of adrenaline seemed to be fading, leaving only the exhaustion of his ordeal behind. "Who else were you able to get?"

"Everyone who was left." There was a note of satisfaction in

Galhen's voice, despite it all. "We have eighteen survivors from Cashaal counting yourself, plus Riyel Valessa."

Kerelle snapped to attention on that. No one had been able to tell her anything about Riyel, except that he was present and in the medbay.

"Not bad, Ambrel," Ilyen replied with a ghost of his usual smirk. "You managed to not fuck up without me."

He sobered quickly, however, and when he spoke again his tone was unusually subdued. "Were you able to do anything for Valessa?"

"Some. I've been alternating between the two of you. You were in better shape; now that you're at baseline functionality I can focus on him. It's going to be a...longer process."

Oh sweet stars. She'd *seen* Ilyen...and Riyel was worse?

Ilyen just nodded, his gaze far away. Nalea stroked his hand, and he came back to the present with a small smile.

"In the meantime, you're out of the woods," Galhen told him. "You'll need a lot of rest over the next few days, but your body is healing itself and you'll fully recover. We can actually move you to your own cabin from here."

"I'll take you up on that." *Anywhere that doesn't smell like metal and antiseptic.*

Kerelle avoided glancing at Galhen. That last thought was not something Ilyen had meant to share.

Any discomfort he may have had with the current setting, Ilyen kept hidden. Instead he swung himself off the medbay bed, swearing as he landed a bit more wobbly than he expected. Nalea darted in to take his arm over her shoulder.

"You only *just* woke up!" Kerelle heard her hiss as they headed towards the cabins. "What *is* it with you psionics and not resting?"

Ilyen just laughed in response, the sound rusty but genuine. He might currently be wobbly, but the sparks of his usual self were there. At the end of everything, Kerelle reflected soberly, Ilyen was a survivor. He'd get through this and recover.

Riyel, though. That had sounded bad.

She turned to ask, just in time to see Galhen sit heavily down, eyes closed and head leaned back against the wall as if he lacked the strength to lift it.

Alarm surged through her. *Darling?*

"I'm fine," he replied aloud. "Or I will be, rather. Don't worry, love, I know how far I can push myself before risking collapse. Even if," he admitted, "I'm skirting the line right now."

Kerelle wanted to disapprove of how he was exhausting himself, but she could not. The plight of their rescued comrades demanded every resource they could offer it, and in his shoes she would have done the same.

Galhen sighed, not opening his eyes. "You were going ask about Riyel, though." It wasn't a question. "It's bad. Worse than Ilyen, and less recent, so it's harder to heal."

Her stomach turned. "Can you...?"

"Yes. It *will* take time, however, and that's just for his physical state. Stars know what kind of mental condition he's in, or what constant suppressive exposure for such a length of time might have done to his psionics."

Kerelle didn't know what to say to that, the sick feeling spreading through her gut.

"I'll have to wake him soon," Galhen told her. "I'd been putting it off until I could reduce the pain he'll be in, but I've already done most of what I can in the immediate term."

The air thickened as she sensed his hesitation. There was something else, something he wasn't sure if he should say.

What is it, darling?

Some of the long-term work had been started already. They intended for him to survive, and be functional, and we know damn well it wouldn't have been for any humanitarian reasons.

It was silent a beat before he spoke aloud again. "We should speak to Lilika as well. We can confirm he is safe, and alive…"

"And you want her to be prepared when she sees him," Kerelle finished quietly.

"Yes. I'm sorry to ask it of you, darling, but can you contact her in the dream? I would be the one to do it, but…"

But he needed all his strength for healing. She ignored the pit in her stomach and nodded.

"Of course, I'll try to reach her this evening. In the meantime, Sandrel says we have eight days before we get to the rendezvous point. Hopefully you can make some progress by then?"

"Hopefully. I'll do what I can." Galhen stretched and levered himself up from the chair. "For now, though, I need a cup of tea and a few hours' rest until my psionics are recovered enough to dive in again."

He paused to kiss her cheek on his way out of the medbay. His vibrant eyes were bloodshot and heavily shadowed, but warm nonetheless. "We'll get through it, love. All of us."

TWENTY-TWO

AS IT TURNED OUT, they didn't need to wonder why SysTech had begun healing Riyel's injuries. Once he was awake, he told them.

Or told Kerelle, at least. She doubted Galhen was listening - her husband was deep in his work. He'd been sitting motionless with eyes closed and Riyel's right hand cradled gently between both of his for the better part of a half-hour, and probably wasn't aware of the conversation at all.

As she watched Riyel awkwardly sip tea with his off hand, Kerelle realized with a jolt that this was her first time actually seeing him in person. It was intensely surreal.

The thin man sitting across from her was a pale shadow of the warm, quietly confident telepath she'd gotten to know over a year of dream meetings. Riyel had been withdrawn since he'd woken up, not that she could blame him. The truth was she had no idea how to help him, except keep him company while Galhen worked.

That, and keep him fed. She tried not to eye how his shirt hung off his shoulders as she refilled his teacup.

"They were hoping I could still be of use to them," he told

her frankly. "They brought a C3 regenerative in, a few times, to help ensure I would be able to perform the task that was required of me."

She didn't want to ask. "And what task was that?"

His eyes met hers. "To infiltrate the psionic rebellion as their agent. I was held at Oulemar for...retraining." A small shiver wracked his frame, but his voice stayed steady. "After they were finished with me, I was meant to 'escape' and contact Lilika for help." He closed his eyes. "And then I was meant to kill her."

Kerelle's stomach lurched, and she knew her shock must have shown full on her face. "*Kill* her? Kill *Lilika?*" It fit, with what she would expect of SysTech - to learn of their loving, devoted relationship and see it as a weak point to exploit. It still sent her recoiling with disgust.

"That was their intention. Possibly you and Galhen as well, but I think they preferred you both alive."

"Alive? Us, but not Lilika?"

"They probably hoped to use you against each other." He took another awkward sip of tea. "They also theorized that the rebellion would collapse without her leadership."

Well, Kerelle had to admit, they probably weren't wrong.

A terrible thought surfaced unbidden in her mind, one that she crushed mercilessly as it did. But Riyel must have read it in her face - or it was on his own mind as well.

"I didn't agree," he said quietly. "Not that it was ever presented as a *request*. But I'm not here as a sleeper agent. You rescued me, legitimately, and I'm very happy you did."

Heat flooded her face. "Riyel, I'm sorry, I know you would never - "

"No," he said firmly. "After what happened, you can't simply take my word for it." He held her gaze, warm brown eyes deadly serious. "Look in my head. I'm practically burned out. I couldn't hide anything if I *wanted* to."

"That's not necessary - "

"It is. And Lilika will say the same. We both know how SysTech plays this game." He stretched out his hand. "Please, Kerelle. Look, so that she doesn't have to."

She didn't want to, not really. But if this was as bad as it sounded...Lilika shouldn't have to be the one to see.

Kerelle laced her trembling fingers with his.

It all went by in a horrible blur. How he'd been working with another C3 telepath on recruitment, and she'd betrayed him to SysTech. How hard he'd tried to hold out in interrogation until he finally, simply, couldn't. The isolation after that, irregularly punctuated with meager rations. Finally the "retraining specialist" with her bland smiles, the extra food and healing when she approved of him and the electroshocks when she did not. The fog that settled as he was regularly denied sleep. The gnawing fear for Lilika. The terrible, grinding despair as time lost meaning, and he began to realize he would not see the sun again.

The truth of it all reverberated through her bones. A very strong telepath might be able to fake it. Lilika likely could. Riyel might have been able to, before. But Riyel's assessment of his own condition had not been exaggeration. His mental defenses were all but gone, and he felt horribly similar to how Galhen had, after the escape from Dalanva. The long-term suppressive exposure *had* damaged his psionics, in a way she could only hope was temporary.

She was shaking as she broke the connection. "I'm sorry. I'm so sorry."

"It was my fault for trusting Asela."

"It was Asela's fault for betraying *you*." It came out a bit more as a growl than she'd intended, but the shock of experiencing it all, even secondhand, still echoed down her nerves. He looked away.

The silence threatened to stretch, when suddenly Galhen's breathing changed, and he opened his eyes for the first time since they'd all sat down. A triumphant grin danced around his lips.

"Try wiggling your fingers for me? I think I have everything repaired."

Riyel cautiously did as he asked; the movement was much more nimble than it had been that morning.

He wiggled them again, and broke into the first real smile Kerelle had seen. Galhen returned it with an almost giddy enthusiasm, though Kerelle silently noted the tremor in his hands as he removed them from Riyel's.

"We'll get there," he assured Riyel warmly. "One day at a time, we'll get there."

MORE THAN ANYTHING, what told Kerelle they had turned a corner was when Galhen finally let himself rest. He'd taken snatches of respite here and there, of course - naps between patients, periodic stops for tea, restless sleep after late nights. But it had always been a brief intermission between work sessions, a necessary accommodation to keep his psionics functional. This was the first time she'd seen him actually step back since they'd left Oulemar.

Kerelle could tell it was well overdue. Galhen had repeatedly reassured her that he was fine and her worries were groundless, but the bond betrayed him. Beyond the fog of exhaustion that had started to creep over his senses, a deep ache had settled in his muscles, and his migraines were approaching blinding. Even if he were to keep pressing on, they were well past the point where he was likely to start making mistakes.

And so he was finally propped in bed in the mid-afternoon, sipping an herbal tea blend while Kerelle did her best to massage some of the tension out of his shoulders. He probably could have taken care of that himself without too much strain on his powers, but she felt through the bond that he was enjoying her touch. The quiet intimacy was helping him relax, more effectively than any physical benefits.

He stretched beneath her fingers and turned in her arms to face her.

"Naturally, darling, wake me if there's a crisis. But..." He finished the last of his tea and set the mug on the nightstand. "I've repaired any critical injuries, and everything else should be manageable with painkillers. Everyone should be well enough for the time being." He sounded like he was trying to convince himself more than her.

She kissed his nose and pulled him down gently, so they were lying side by side. "Everyone will be fine. And you need to *sleep*. Your head hurts so badly *I* can feel it."

"Apologies for that," he whispered back with a rueful smile. He brushed her hip lightly and closed his eyes; within minutes his breathing had slowed, and his hand on her hip became dead weight. Kerelle lay there like that for a few minutes more, letting herself enjoy the closeness, before she carefully extracted herself and left him to sleep.

As it happened, he slept for nearly all their last two days in space. Ilyen, on the other hand, was taking progressively fewer naps, as he recovered in leaps and bounds.

On the morning of their last day, she was startled in the mess by his sudden appearance at the coffee machine. Ilyen poured himself the last of the brew, replaced the now-empty carafe, and popped away again without starting a new batch. Kerelle couldn't help the laughter that bubbled up past her lips. Normally she'd be annoyed. This time, she was just happy he was feeling better enough to resume his obnoxious habits.

Still smiling, she set a new batch of coffee brewing herself. He got a pass on this one. Next time, it was back to lectures again.

CLOSING in on Lilika's coordinates reminded her uncomfortably of the approach to Oulemar. From space, the small planet looked like a desolate rock orbiting a fading star, its surface dull and pocked with craters. They broke atmosphere shortly before its dawn, and the view hardly improved with proximity. The planet below them lay still and silent as they soared over its scrubby fields, with no pinprick lights to promise relief from the gloom. The atmosphere was livable, according to the charts, but there was no indication anyone was *actually* living here.

As they drew nearer to the rendezvous point, some signs of human habitation grew visible in the dim light. Or rather, Kerelle soon realized, *former* habitation. Ramshackle buildings dotted a canyon, assembled from corrugated metal or poured concrete, painfully like the ones she'd seen a lifetime ago on Elekar. Some had partially collapsed; those still standing were streaked with rust, and many had holes in their roofs or siding. It was obvious that no one had lived in them for some time.

"We go to the nicest places," Sandrel commented under his breath as he took them in a bit lower. Ilyen snorted, glancing over from his spot by the vidport.

"What's wrong, not excited about landing in a haunted industrial site? Didn't take *you* for the type to be afraid of ghosts."

"With you back, Knives?" Sandrel's eyes glinted. "I think they're more likely to be afraid of *us*."

Ilyen grinned, and Kerelle did too, creepy haunted industrial sites aside. The teleporter seemed very much recovered from his ordeal; whether he was *really* all right or just faking it convincingly was his own business.

She couldn't deny how good it felt to have him back again.

The ship descended a little lower, and Sandrel gave a little *ha!* of triumph. As they swung back around the canyon, they caught sight of five little ships nestled under its overhang.

Kerelle's heart sped up. She hadn't realized until now how badly she'd needed to *see* they were alive.

As Sandrel brought them down, a small crowd surged out of the mine's entrance. Kerelle could sense the excitement bubbling outside even before the hatch opened. Excitement, tinged with nervousness. By now it was likely well known that not everyone taken at Cashaal had survived captivity; Kerelle had given Lilika the names of those on the ship, but seeing them actually here would make it real.

The hatch opened, and her little group began to stream out to rejoin their people.

The canyon itself was undeniably creepy, dark and silent and pockmarked with the structural detritus of the abandoned mining operation. All shadows were banished, however, by the sheer joy radiating from the scene before her, the reunion of friends and lovers who had feared they would never meet again.

Elinea paused next to Kerelle on the way down, but whatever she was going to say was cut off as Anniya launched herself into her arms. The two pyrokinetics were both crying as they kissed fiercely, Kerelle forgotten entirely. She smiled and made her way toward the throng.

Tears were a common sight; even Lilika's face was wet as she clutched Riyel tightly. Kerelle's heart ached for them; their fierce spymistress had truly believed she would never see him again, and even now he was wounded in more ways than one. They would help him recover, Kerelle vowed to herself. Riyel, and all their injured friends. They were all still alive, and where there was life there was hope.

A slight movement from the corner of her eye caught her attention. Aureis was hovering awkwardly near the hatch, literally radiating uncertainty at whether he ought to be here or not. Kerelle felt like she should intervene there, but at the same time

Aureis seemed nervous around her still, and she wasn't sure her presence would be much of a reassurance.

She was saved from having to make a decision when Sandrel approached him instead and gave him a clap on the shoulder, gesturing toward the crowd. Aureis flushed and said something quickly; whatever it was, Sandrel shrugged it off and gestured again. Kerelle caught something about introductions, then Sandrel was making a grinning beeline for Oliven, Aureis following uncertainly.

Kerelle sensed rather than saw Galhen's approach then; he threaded his fingers with hers and watched from her side. The few days of rest had worked wonders for her husband's wellbeing, and he leaned gently against her now in affection rather than exhaustion.

He said nothing in words, aloud or otherwise, but she felt his warm emotion through the bond. All the headaches and pains and fatigue were a small price to pay for the scene before them, and one he'd gladly pay twice over.

She squeezed his hand and rested her head on his shoulder. There would be decisions to make, and soon. But let tonight be for celebration.

THE NEXT DAY, work began again.

"We lost a lot of people on Cashaal," Elinea said bluntly. "Do we even have the manpower to keep up an offensive?"

She looked around the room; the whole of their group was gathered near their camp in the main mineshaft. Lilika was leading the meeting, but everyone would have a voice. The subject was too important for anything less.

"What choice do we have?" Koren's mouth was a grim line. "We can't just run away. There's nowhere we can go that they won't follow us. Not with how much trouble we've caused them."

Ilyen's brows pulled down. "So what then, we go down in a blaze of glory? We just die and hope the next generation of PsiCorp have better luck? Because I'm not voting for that plan."

"Luck wouldn't help them anyway," Aureis's voice was so quiet Kerelle almost missed it. Heat climbed rapidly up his face as she and many others turned to look at him. Aureis had been clearly uncomfortable to be included in the meeting at all, but Lilika had insisted. He was the freshest source of SysTech intel they had.

Kerelle was surprised he had spoken at all, and half-expected him to shrink under the sudden attention. Instead he straightened a bit and firmed his jaw before continuing; she saw a flash of the determination that must have helped him climb the ranks at SysTech.

"Luck won't help the PsiCorp who come after you," he repeated. "Velrin argues the rebellion was inevitable because they allowed you too much autonomy and too much leniency. He says psionics are a tool, and tools don't make their own decisions. The board agrees."

He paused, as if unsure if he should say more, but went on. "There was…discussion, when I was still there, about what Velrin wanted to do instead. What he got approval to do. The next generation of psionics will be raised in isolation cells, and they'll only see the sun when SysTech has a mission for them. They won't have your education, or your world experience, or your resourcefulness. Things might relax again eventually, when people forget enough, but…" He shrugged helplessly. "It will be decades, maybe centuries before another group of psionics has the chance you did. If any of this is going to mean anything, you have to finish it."

The silence stretched after that, tense and fraught. Aureis's discomfort grew but he did not retract his words.

They all knew they were true.

It was Elinea again who finally broke the quiet. "So where does that leave us? Licking our wounds and waiting for another chance?"

Tempting as it sounded, Kerelle knew it wasn't a viable choice. "That won't work in our favor," she pointed out. "As we try to regroup, SysTech will keep up the pressure. The longer this conflict drags on, the more they gain an advantage."

"So how do we stop it from dragging on?" That was Melaris. "What does our endgame even *look* like?"

"Right now?" Lilika's voice cut through the room, commanding the attention of all present. "We *have* no endgame."

Silence fell again, and she continued. "We cannot realistically hope to best SysTech militarily. They are too large, the resource gap too wide. And even if we did, we would have to fight the other multigalactics after them. A freed PsiCorp threatens *all* their interests. We gave SysTech a bloody nose, and stars know it needed to be done, but we're at the limit of what that can do for us."

Lilika stepped into the center of the circle, looking at them each in turn. "If we're going to win this, *really* win it, we need political engagement. And we need mundane allies. The multi-galactics are able to enslave us under treaties signed by the Council of Interplanetary Governments. We need to get those treaties overturned."

It was quiet again, as everyone absorbed what she'd said. What she proposed was so momentous, it seemed ridiculous on its face, like declaring they would all sprout gills and live under the sea. But Lilika did not traffic in dreams and optimism; Kerelle knew if she'd said this, it was because she believed it was doable.

Still, when Ilyen broke the quiet, his voice was laced with skepticism. "The CIG can't even order lunch without five years of debate, and half the planetary governments are in bed with the multigalactics anyway. How exactly do you think we're going to get them to help us?"

"I never said it would happen *quickly*. But if we get the CIG involved, SysTech will be forced to stand down until the issue is resolved. As you say," she noted with a ghost of a smirk, "that may take decades."

Lilika raised her voice to address the assembly again. "If we keep on as we have been we'll spend the rest of our lives huddled in foxholes and safe houses, until eventually we slip up or SysTech picks us off one by one. A pointless, soon-forgotten martyrdom. Even if the CIG argues until we're all old and grey," she urged, "it's the best shot we have at a future, if not for ourselves then for the ones who come after us."

To Kerelle's surprise, Aureis spoke again.

"You'll need someplace to stay, though, and a sponsor to get you a speaking slot to address the general assembly."

Lilika raised an eyebrow. "You know someone?"

"There's a SysTech base on Amaecea. It's out of the way, significantly understaffed, and the only reason it hasn't been shuttered is because the terms of SysTech's contract with the colony's government stipulate that it stay open. They've been trying to get out of that contract for years."

"Why are they even *in* that contract?" Sandrel asked. "Doesn't seem like the kind of thing that's their style."

"Amaecea has significant delciral deposits, and since it was a bootstrapped independent colony the government actually owns their own resources." Aureis was warming to his topic, his nervousness fading as his voice gained volume and enthusiasm. "They sold the mining rights to SysTech, but to protect the local economy the contract required them to keep a base open there for several decades, with a certain percentage of jobs going to Amaecean citizens."

"That was back when delciral was supposed to be the next

big thing in fuel, so SysTech signed it. To be honest," he added somewhat conspiratorially, "I think they signed as much to keep ConEn out as anything. Of course, then it turned out delciral wasn't so great for fuel efficiency after all. The market collapsed, and SysTech was stuck with a useless outpost on a world with no other significant interests."

"When they lost the last appeal to get the contract annulled, they went for passive-aggressive pressure instead. The base is still open and functional per their obligation, but it's down to a skeleton crew. I think it provides a single local job. If anything, though," he shrugged, "that just made the Amaecean First Ministers more determined not to back down. They'll probably hold SysTech to the full term just out of spite."

Aureis had become rather animated during this story, and colored again as he seemed to abruptly realize he'd been talking for some time. Granted, everyone was also staring at him. It was the most any of them had heard him say at once, excepting that one time he and Kerelle had talked after Oulemar.

Aureis, it seemed, was a drought-or-flood kind of speaker.

"Erm, my point is," he said, suddenly awkward again, "It's an independent world, and SysTech isn't very popular with the locals."

"That sounds...kind of promising, actually," Sandrel mused. Several people nodded agreement.

"They might not be any happier to see *us*," Nalea pointed out. "SysTech's done their best to make everyone think we're a menace."

"It's not hopeless," Lilika responded. "My agents report that our counter-propaganda has been having some effect. People are debating about psionics, which is better than just accepting that we're monsters. There's still a sizable contingent that thinks we should all be locked up or shot," she conceded, "but it's not everyone."

"Hopefully Amaecea isn't in the lock-up-and-shoot camp," Nalea muttered. Again, there were several nods.

"We could appeal to the First Minister for asylum." Galhen had been listening silently, but now he spoke up as he met Lilika's eyes. "We'll need the support of Amaecea's government anyway, if we're to gain an avenue to the CIG."

She nodded firmly in agreement. "Indeed. It would be far wiser to secure his blessing before we show up in force. And for now," she acknowledged with a nod at Aureis, "Amaecea is the most promising lead we have."

TWENTY-THREE

SECURING an appointment with Amaecea's First Minister proved much easier than Kerelle had expected. One of Lilika's surviving agents acted as the go-between, and a few nerve-wracking days later they received word that the Minister had agreed to meet with them, discreetly.

Kerelle had no idea what to expect, or what the Minister expected. She doubted Lilika's agent had been so blunt as to openly call them the Psionic Rebellion, but surely the idea had gotten across. That he was willing to talk to them at all seemed like a good sign already.

As always, of course, there was the possibility it all was a trap. First Minister Haskrai might well have called SysTech the minute they were on his calendar. They hoped the meeting was legitimate, but they were coming prepared for a fight none-theless. Nalea had given each of them a new dose of her anti-hemindrium inoculation, and they all kept senses open and shields up.

The party was small - only Lilika, Galhen, Kerelle, and Ilyen. Lilika had included the teleporter very reluctantly, and only after a great deal of consideration. But the facts were, if things went sideways, outside of Kerelle herself Ilyen was simply the best equipped to handle it. And so he accompanied their group to meet the minister, under strict orders from Lilika that he was not to talk, at all, to anyone.

Kerelle knew Lilika was still nervous about that.

They'd landed on Amaecea uneventfully, as just another commercial freighter, and now made their way to the address they'd been given as an anonymous group on the city streets. Kerelle kept her senses open for signs of trouble, but thus far everything seemed normal. Amaecea's eponymous capital city was on the small side, with buildings that topped out at five or six stories rather than the hundred-floor behemoths of Tallimau or Astallia, but its streets bustled with a lively energy all the same. It made it easy to blend in.

"So," Kerelle murmured to Lilika as they crossed the street and turned off the wide boulevard into a small street lined with residences. "Do we know anything about the man we're going to see?"

She did, naturally. "The First Minister is Kolren Haskrai. He's held the office since succeeding his mother 28 years ago."

Kerelle started. "The office is hereditary?"

"Unofficially. When a First Minister dies or resigns there's a confirmation vote on the proposed successor, but it's mostly a formality at this point. The Haskrai family bankrolled and led most of the founding expedition, and a Haskrai has held the First Minister position since the colony's establishment."

That made sense. To come out and *say* it would be highly unusual, but in practice a lot of prominent positions in the galaxy seemed to be unofficially hereditary - including in the multigalactics, per Aureis's comments about legacies.

"In any case," Lilika continued, "Kolren has led Amaecea for nearly half his adult life. I have no personal experience with the man, but I did some investigating before our arrival, and he has a good reputation in the colony for being fair-minded." She quirked a half-smile. "He's also gained popularity for taking a hard line against SysTech. Aureis was correct about that.

"Apparently, however, he's retreated a bit from public life lately to deal with a family crisis," Lilika noted. "Reportedly his young granddaughter is an invalid with some sort of debilitating condition that keeps her confined to a care suite. Nobody seems to know details, and she hasn't been seen in public since the onset of her illness."

Kerelle glanced involuntarily back at Galhen, who seemed to be talking to Ilyen. *I wouldn't want to take advantage of a young girl's illness.* In fact, just thinking about it made her feel guilty. But...*If it's something we can heal, that could only strengthen our position with Haskrai.*

Indeed. I was tempted to offer it up as a bargaining chip, but I know Galhen would never stand for it. He would insist on doing his best to help even if Haskrai wanted to truss us all up and send us back to SysTech. Her thoughts were colored with shades of affectionate resignation.

The residential street narrowed, winding up out of the neatly ordered downtown blocks into more spacious estates in the hills. The designated address turned out to be a stately mansion, with "Haskrai" engraved above its wrought-iron gate.

His residence, then, not the office, Lilika mused. *I'm not sure how that bodes for us, though I imagine it's more discreet than ushering us into City Hall during business hours.* She glanced back at the men behind her, who both nodded. They were ready for anything, too.

But no ambush leapt forth as Lilika rang the bell. Rather, the doorman was expecting them, and they were whisked into an elegant parlor. Waiting for them inside was the First Minister himself.

Kolren Haskrai was probably in his early sixties, well-dressed and seated with the kind of casual confidence of someone who was accustomed to giving commands. He offered no hint as to how this was likely to go; his features were arranged in serene impassivity to mirror Lilika's own.

He *was* wearing a very nice psiblocker, which gave her some pause, but that alone didn't indicate trouble. Given the circumstances, it might be simply a prudent precaution on *his* part. He had no reason to be any more sure of their sincerity than they were of his.

Haskrai didn't blink as he was introduced to some of the more notorious leaders of the psionic rebellion, nor did his expression give any clue to his thoughts. Instead, when Lilika finished introductions and the usual politeness about thanking him for the meeting, he offered them tea and got down to business.

"I'm not entirely sure why you're here, Ms. Charyth." He inclined his head towards the rest of them, seated in a half-circle beside her, but he had clearly picked up that Lilika was the one who would do the talking. "I am aware your group has had some difficulties, but I don't see the connection to Amaecea."

She offered him one of those serene mask-smiles. "Allow me to explain, First Minister."

Lilika succinctly laid out their side of the story - their determination to escape forced service and mistreatment by the multigalactics, albeit with many of the details skipped over. Instead she finished by laying out their case for asylum, and the hope of gaining an audience with the CIG.

Haskrai listened impassively throughout. When she'd finished, he took a long sip of tea before answering.

"I understand your need, and why you would come to us with this request. However, you must *also* understand that sheltering a terrorist group would have a negative impact on Amaecean interests."

The words were out of Kerelle's mouth before she could stop them. "We aren't terrorists! We've gone out of our way *not* to hurt people, unless they were trying to hurt *us*. And even then, we've always tried to minimize casualties."

An amused projection from Ilyen, that *he* hadn't been the one to speak out of turn after all. Kerelle's eyes darted towards him involuntarily; the teleporter's lips were curving into a slight smirk. A telepathic nudge from Galhen, then - *steady, love.*

Lilika gave her the barest glance, accompanied by a rather more forceful telepathic reminder to *let her do the talking*.

Outwardly, she remained unruffled. "Ms. Evandra is correct that we have dedicated considerable effort to conducting our activities responsibly," she took over calmly. "We have also never attacked a civilian target. Senator Dalanva may claim herself as such, but we have been very clear that our purposes there were to extract Dr. Ambrel from being held against his will. There were few injuries to any of her guests, and Dalanva herself was struck in self defense."

Haskrai raised his eyebrows slightly. "That's not how the Senator recalls the incident."

"Yes," Lilika agreed. "She has thus far omitted how she attempted to end Dr. Ambrel's life rather than allow him to escape her. Ms. Evandra acted in defense of her partner, which regrettably necessitated violence. Indeed," she continued firmly, "Violence has only ever been an unfortunate means to protect ourselves."

Haskrai sipped his tea. "Can you offer any proof of that, Ms. Charyth?"

"The proof is in how many SysTech people are still alive," she answered bluntly. "We *have* done them injury. Many have recovered. If we truly had no principles to restrain us, if our only goal was vengeance and hurt, we would leave no survivors when we fought. We would strike the civilian offices, at the height of their business hours. We would stalk the executives and their families like prey, and let the bodies tell the story of how little we could be stopped."

Kerelle glanced over in alarm. None of that had even *occurred* to her; the very thought made her feel slightly sick.

Lilika met Haskrai's gaze straight on. "We have done none of those things. That is your *proof*."

He nodded, and Kerelle got the sense they'd passed a test of sorts.

"Amaecea is not a world with a lot of pull," he responded. "We have a relatively small population, and while our economy is self-sufficient we are not a major exporter. My support won't win you your war.

"However," he continued, "as you are aware we *are* an independent colony. Our *business relationship* with SysTech," he said the words deliberately, with a touch of irony, "does not rise to the level of corporate patronage, and so as head of state I do have the legal standing to put you on the agenda for a session of the CIG general assembly. To do that, however, I would need to know more about what you intend."

Lilika tilted her head slightly, the image of elegant poise. "What we intend, First Minister?"

"I understand that you want your day in court. But the arrangement you are proposing is more than simply a speaking slot. You're also asking for asylum, presumably indefinitely. I'd like to know what it is you're hoping to find on Amaecea."

He sipped his tea deliberately. "There is also the matter of how we benefit. The benefits to *you* are apparent. Amaecea, however, will be taking a considerable political risk, with strong potential for financial and diplomatic repercussions. Why should we take that risk?"

"Quite reasonable questions, First Minister." That polished smile again. "To the first, we are hoping to find a safe haven, with legal status, that Amaecea as an independent colony is in a unique position to provide.

"This is not a war that can be won by armed conflict," she continued seriously. "To accomplish our aims will require political and social change. If Amaecea provides a sanctuary for psionics, it give us an opportunity to prove psionics and mundanes can live side by side in peace. To that end," she acknowledged with a slight nod, "we would consider the colony's interests to be our own interests as well."

Haskrai's face gave nothing away. "And then what? You talk about psionics in bondage to the multigalactics. Will you simply watch from afar as that continues for those psionics who did not escape with you?"

"We will work to overturn the laws that permit it. We will campaign to help the people of the galaxy understand who we are and why we deserve freedom like anyone else. And yes," she answered, head held high. "We will help our brothers and sisters when they need us."

Haskrai was quiet as he finished his tea. Finally he rose. "There's something I'd like to show you."

Kerelle's curiosity intensified as they followed him deeper into the mansion. She kept her senses open for trouble, but still she sensed nothing amiss. Any attackers would be in psiblockers, naturally, but Haskrai's staff were not, and she did not detect the kind of discomfort or fear that might project from the household if there were armed commandoes lying somewhere in wait.

"Have you heard anything about my granddaughter Jannea?" Haskrai's tone was conversational, as if they were discussing the weather.

"We've heard she's quite ill," Galhen answered, speaking for the first time. "Actually, I was going to ask if I could see her while we were here. There may be something I can do."

Lilika's mental snort to Kerelle carried an unmistakable overlay of *told you so*.

"Thank you, Dr. Ambrel, but I doubt there's anything you can do for her, at least not in the way you're thinking." Haskrai paused before a door that Kerelle suddenly noticed was secured with a small panel softly glowing red. He withdrew an access card. "You'll understand when you meet her."

Haskrai's card flicked the lock panel green, and he ushered them inside.

A small child's boisterous laughter rang through the hall, and small footsteps pounded rapidly towards them. A grinning, very healthy-looking girl, probably five or six years old, rounded the corner at top speed.

"Grandpapa!" She squealed, launching herself into Haskrai's arms. It was then Kerelle realized there were several dolls floating in the air behind her.

Oh.

"Oh shit," Ilyen whispered from behind her. Kerelle gave him a nudge, but the little girl was thankfully ignoring them as she eagerly rattled off her dolls' latest adventures to Haskrai. The last thing they needed was to teach the First Minister's grand-daughter to swear.

Lilika linked with her and Galhen immediately. She was as surprised as they were.

This certainly explains the sudden onset of her "illness." She's squarely in the average age for psionics to manifest.

Her control of her dolls is quite good for her age, Kerelle noted. *She may well grow up to be a C3, or a hard C2.*

Which would only increase SysTech's interest in her, if they knew. Galhen's thoughts were overlaid with a grim understanding. *At best, she'd be a bargaining chip to get their contract annulled, but if she has that much potential they might just prefer to take her outright.*

The girl's nurse caught up with her then, freezing as she saw the small group gathered. Haskrai gave her a nod and she relaxed slightly, though her gaze remained wary.

When Haskrai set his granddaughter down and turned back to them, his next words confirmed their earlier suspicions.

"We're trying to keep Jannea out of public view until she learns to control her powers. Regardless of colony status, our entire sector is considered SysTech talent rights territory, by those same treaties you want overturned. If her abilities were discovered, I could not stop them from taking her."

He watched the little girl spin around, her dolls whirling with her. "Jannea is my son's eldest. When her father and I are gone, by right she should be the First after us. That can't happen in the universe as it is today." He turned back to them, his face set.

"I wanted to you see her, because I want you to understand why I'm going to give you my support, and what I expect in return. I will grant you your asylum. I'll let that sanctimonious ass from their legal team annul the contract for Epsanal Base, and your group can move in once they leave. I'll arrange for you to address the CIG."

"What you will grant me in return," he said deliberately, holding Lilika's eyes, "is your investment in Amaecea's future. You will help defend us if SysTech retaliates. You will use your gifts to help our people as needed. And," he glanced at Jannea, "you will teach my granddaughter and any other psionic children among our people how to control their gifts, and use them for the good of Amaecea."

Lilika paused, her jaw firming almost imperceptibly. "We are always happy to help our friends, First Minister. But we will be no one's servants, not ever again. If we stay, we will be equal under the law."

"Asylum, and provisional citizenship," he replied bluntly. "I will require a written commitment on the training and the mutual defense."

We can work with that, Lilika said internally. Kerelle's pulse picked up.

Externally, she smiled genuinely for the first time, and held out her hand. "That sounds acceptable, First Minister."

Haskrai shook her hand, and the world changed.

TWENTY-FOUR

EPSANAL BASE HAD UNQUESTIONABLY SEEN BETTER days.

When it was built, it had likely been cutting-edge. The sweeping lines of its architecture were the height of fashion a few decades ago, and its interiors were elegantly designed with high-quality materials. If Kerelle squinted just right, she could almost picture its halls vibrant and alive with bustling workers, as it must have been back when it first opened.

Any bustle was long gone, however, and the Epsanal Base of today was more like a corporate-office version of the rusted-out industrial site Lilika had chosen as a hiding spot. It was painfully obvious that it had been many years since any significant maintenance was done, and even then SysTech had probably pinched every credit. The sleek lighting fixtures were hung with grimy cobwebs, and most were missing one or more of their bulbs. Whatever their original color, the carpets were gone mottled grey with accumulated dirt, and in several spots were worn through to the concrete beneath. Here and there a broken window was haphazardly patched with ugly plywood - plywood that, judging by the stains of rain and mildew, had been there for quite some time.

It was easy to identify the handful of offices that had still been in use when SysTech had finally pulled out completely - they looked like someone had cleaned them in the last decade. Everything else, all around the base, was abjectly filthy.

Abjectly filthy, and now their problem. Haskrai had done his part in agreeing to annul the SysTech contract, and allowing them to quietly move into the base once the last of its few employees had left. The condition of the base, however, he left up to them.

Kerelle understood the logic - they had agreed to keep their presence on Amaecea confidential until they secured a hearing with the CIG, and a flurry of official activity at the defunct base would raise questions. Looking around at the derelict facility, however, she couldn't help the uncharitable thought that he just didn't want to deal with it himself.

Chin up, darling. Galhen's fingers threaded with hers, that soft half-smile on his lips. *At least there won't be scorpions this time. And the electricity works from day one.*

As if on cue, one of the remaining bulbs in the nearest lighting fixture sparked and died.

Mostly. Almost certainly *no scorpions, though.*

She couldn't help returning the smile, as much as she wasn't looking forward to this. *I'll try to think of it as building my resume for when we start our janitorial service.*

His laughter shimmered through the bond, and Kerelle's heart warmed. Despite the onerous task ahead of them, this was the most relaxed and cheerful he'd been since Oulemar. She suspected their rescued comrades' continuing recovery played a large role.

That's the spirit. Shall we decide which bedroom is worth challenging the spiders for?

TWO WEEKS LATER, Kerelle had to admit that they'd done a good job. The fixtures were still aged, and the carpets were still threadbare, but they were *clean*. As she wandered slowly down one of the wide corridors that bordered the inner courtyard, she saw no signs of the dirt-streaked, dust-covered battles they'd recently fought there. If she didn't know what it had looked like before, she wouldn't have guessed.

They all had quarters again as well, and rather nicer ones than Kerelle had slept in for some time. The base had included a dormitory wing for essential personnel, and now they all had proper bedrooms instead of converted closets and storage rooms. Granted, one look at the bedlinens and Elinea had burned them on the spot, but such things were easy enough to replace.

The cleaning itself hadn't been the hard part.

As they wrestled with transforming Epsanal from a derelict base to a livable home, it was impossible not to recall doing the same with Cashaal. Physically, of course, Epsanal was much easier. Temperatures were reasonable, fresh food and water were easily accessible, and as Galhen had so cheerfully noted, there was a merciful lack of aggressive poisonous wildlife. The physical wasn't the problem.

Using her powers to run a sponge along the tops of the tall windows beyond her reach, she was reminded that she'd last done this side by side with Flaveren. They'd chatted about food and life in the PsiCorp and the things he hoped to do when the war was over. Things he'd never gotten to do, before the hail of SysTech bullets. When she passed Peralen and the other students perched together with tea, all she could see was the empty space next to them where Helia should have been. Their friends may have fallen at Cashaal, but it was Epsanal that felt haunted.

A peal of laughter pulled her out of her dark thoughts, and as Kerelle got closer she saw the small group gathered on the sunny patio. The base's courtyard was as sterile as the interiors, just a few long-dead shrubs and rusted picnic tables scattered across grey paving stones. Now, though, brightly-colored planter pots dotted the space, transforming it as much as the cheerful chatter of the people gathered around them.

Teriel still tired quickly, but his breathing was much easier than it had been, and Galhen had cleared him for light activity that morning. *At this point, good company and sunlight will help his recovery more than sitting in the medbay,* Galhen had said. Kerelle could see what he meant. Sitting propped in the center of the circle, carefully mixing soil to plant the small seedling beside him, Teriel looked better than he'd been since Cashaal.

Elinea and Anniya were sitting with him working on plants of their own, as were Oliven and Aureis, somewhat to her surprise. But then, maybe she *shouldn't* have been surprised - Aureis had been living and working alongside with the rest of the group to clean up Epsanal. It was only natural that he get more comfortable with the psionics, or at least less intimidated. After you've swept floors and chased spiders and hauled trash with people, they tended to lose their mystique.

He certainly *looked* happy, chatting with the others while he patted the dirt around his little seedling into place. Aureis had a charming, open smile, one that made him look younger, and Kerelle realized she was happy to see it. Freedom from SysTech, she mused, looked good on *everyone*.

The door on the other side of the courtyard opened, and Sandrel walked in with what looked like a box of pastries. The group greeted him cheerfully; he passed out pastries and made his way to sit down next to Aureis. The accountant's warm smile broadened.

She continued on her way then, with a lighter heart. Cashaal would probably be with her the rest of her life; she knew that, and she could only face it as it came. But there was hope in the present day too, and hope for the future.

Cashaal would not, could not be in vain.

RAISED voices drew Kerelle's attention. Curious, she moved closer to the source - a small office at the end of the hall.

"The hell I'm filling out paperwork!" Ah, that was Baneten, one of her telekinetics. "We always just buy what we need."

She was surprised to hear Aureis answer him back. "That's exactly why the purchase requisitions are necessary. How do we know what we need? How do we keep track of what we've spent and accurately project what we'll spend in the future? How do we make sure we're allocating resources appropriately?" He didn't sound like he shared Baneten's annoyance - in fact, he sounded rather excited.

Kerelle turned the corner to find the two of them in a lively discussion. She was struck by the scene, almost in spite of herself - and how far their wayward accountant had come. The Aureis she first met couldn't even hold eye contact with a psionic. This Aureis was carrying on an argument with a C2 telekinetic without a trace of fear.

Aureis had his tablet open to a complicated-looking spreadsheet, gesturing at it while he countered Baneten's arguments. Sandrel sat in the other chair behind the desk. He simply leaned back, watching the dispute with open amusement.

"The idea isn't to stop anyone from getting what they need," Aureis explained patiently. From his tone, he'd repeated this more than once. "The idea is to ensure we're getting the maximum value from our expenditures, *while* fulfilling the team's needs. This is to *help* the team."

Baneten muttered something noncommittal and spun on his heel, stalking out of the room with only the barest nod to Kerelle. She made a mental note to check on him later, though hopefully all he needed was time to cool down.

Aureis, on the other hand, lit up when he saw her. "Kerelle! Just who I was hoping to see. Let me show you some of the changes I've made to our procurement processes."

She blinked. "We have procurement processes?"

"We do now!" Aureis's enthusiasm seemed more appropriate for a holiday than anything involving accounting. "Sandrel and I have been discussing our little group's finances."

"Namely that we don't have any," Sandrel interjected.

Aureis's slight cough might have covered a laugh. "Yes, well. We were discussing how resources were limited, and I think part of the problem is the lack of controls in place. We need to be sure we're managing our funds optimally.

"Also," he added, "The First Minister implied there might be employment opportunities for some of our people, which could mean additional income for the group if we wanted to go that route. This is where things get rather intriguing, actually."

Intriguing was not a word Kerelle would use for this subject, ever, but thank goodness *someone* did. She did her best to look encouraging. "Oh?"

"Well, I looked over the records."

Kerelle raised her eyebrows at Sandrel, who smiled blandly back at her. Aureis was too absorbed in his topic to notice.

"I looked over the records, and up to now the rebellion has really functioned as a single unit. It's been highly informal, but everyone seems to have kicked in to a common pot for supplies and so on. Now that we're settling on Amaecea, at least for now, we have an opportunity to discuss how we want to move forward and codify any kind of arrangement."

Aureis flicked to a different page in his spreadsheet, holding it out for her to see. "We could draw up a charter as a formal collective, with a certain percentage of earnings to be contributed for the needs of the group. Like taxes, really, but more flexible for our arrangements."

Kerelle dutifully took the tablet and looked over the spreadsheet, thought she struggled to make much sense of what she was seeing. Aureis's eyes, on the other hand, were positively shining.

She got the distinct feeling he was going to talk about this for as long as she let him. Kerelle was beginning to like Aureis, but not enough to listen about fiscal processes for the next hour.

"This is a very interesting idea," she said carefully. "You really ought to bring it up with Lilika. I have to go...check the equipment."

"That's a great idea," Aureis agreed, presumably about talking to Lilika rather than her limp excuse to extract herself. She had a feeling he hadn't even noticed that part. "We'll want to do a bit more refining first, but I think we can have it ready for review by tomorrow."

He glanced over at Sandrel, who nodded back with a warm smile. Apparently it was a joint project between the two of them. Kerelle had never taken Sandrel for the spreadsheet type, but she supposed it made sense. Illicit business was still *business*, and Sandrel had been a very successful *businessman*.

"I THINK IT'S A GRAND IDEA," Lilika told them the next day. She'd gathered the small group Kerelle had begun to think of as the inner circle - herself, Galhen, Ilyen, Nalea, Sandrel and Riyel. Kerelle was half-surprised Riyel was there; since the rescue he had been frequently withdrawn. He *was* there, though, and engaged in the conversation, so he must have been having one of his better days.

Lilika continued. "Aureis is correct in that we need more structure around our finances, particularly now that we are settling into a hopefully more permanent home. That's actually part of a larger issue that I've been considering how to address."

Kerelle cocked her head. "A larger issue?"

Lilika nodded and glanced around. "We need more structure around *everything*, particularly how we organize ourselves. The CIG won't listen to a loose collection of misfits. When we address them, we'll need all the legitimacy we can muster."

"We basically *are* a loose collection of misfits," Ilyen pointed out. "And weirdos." He glanced at Galhen, though the look was more playful than challenging. "And bleeding hearts."

Lilika almost smiled. "All the more reason, then, to construct a convincing facade. And besides," she added more briskly, "We need this ourselves. It's a miracle we haven't had more internal conflict already, given the informality of our command structure. With the removal of imminent danger from our common enemy, such conflict is practically inevitable. We need to have a mechanism for making decisions, and handling disputes, that goes beyond simply 'Lilika said so.' And we need to get it in place when the group is still small enough to *make* decisions."

She looked over at Sandrel. "My dear captain, does your financier friend have any experience drawing up charters?"

Sandrel smiled. "Even if he doesn't, he'll be excited to try. But next time," he added gently, "why don't we have Aureis here to ask him ourselves?"

AUREIS TOOK to the charter proposal with enthusiasm, and with an auditor's obsessive attention to detail. A few rounds of debate later they had a draft charter for the new Psionic Union, outlining the governance, rights, and responsibilities of its members. A few rounds of debate after *that*, and it was put to a general vote. Kerelle was not at all surprised that the vote ended with the Psionic Union's official ratification, and that Lilika Anhei Charyth walked out as its first elected Premier.

She was *rather* surprised, however, to immediately afterward find herself General Evandra, Chief Minister of Defense.

The title seemed rather…grandiose.

"It's nothing you aren't doing already," Lilika told her when she expressed concern. "In practice, you have been leading our military operations since the beginning. Now you have a title to reflect that, and which will force the CIG to take you seriously."

Lilika suddenly looked tired then, her eyes far away. "Haskrai says he will make the request to the CIG at the end of next week. We're about to need all the *serious* we can get."

TWENTY-FIVE

IT WASN'T PARTICULARLY surprising that the appeal to the CIG, and with it the reveal of the Psionic Union, sent the galaxy into a tizzy. Once again, their faces were plastered across round-the-clock news outlets, with datanet reactions ranging from pious applause to frothing apoplexy. The news channels owned by multigalactics naturally tended towards the latter. Kerelle had half-expected one particularly vocal talk show host to burst a blood vessel.

The reaction on Amaecea itself was more muted, but still mixed. There were some people who welcomed them with open arms, and some others who vehemently protested outside Haskrai's office and Epsanal Base. It was hard to tell which was more prevalent; both claimed to represent the silent majority, who simply averted their eyes and kept walking.

It also wasn't particularly surprising that, after the CIG announced that they would hear the psionics' case, SysTech ramped up its propaganda. The upcoming hearing effectively prevented them from direct attacks, but the news was suddenly full of heartfelt tributes to Phaera Velrin Beniwell, cruelly murdered by psionic terrorists in revenge on her father.

Nor was it surprising that their response video, detailing Phaera's role as a SysTech agent and her involvement with Oulemar, was one of the most widely viewed media of the week. Kerelle had mixed feelings about killing Phaera - or rather, she had no regrets, and felt somewhat guilty that she didn't. But burning stars, if SysTech wanted to play her up as an innocent martyr, then she would tell the world who Phaera Beniwell *really* was. Not to mention that Velrin, the great champion of psionic subjugation, was a hypocrite with an uncollared psionic daughter.

Somehow the multigalactic news programs always left that part out.

What *was* surprising, however, were the children.

THREE MONTHS before their scheduled hearing, the ping from Lilika came as Kerelle was sitting down with tea. She'd found herself at rare loose ends; at Haskrai's request, she spent much of her time these days training the Amaecean defense force to fight alongside psionics, but today the Amaeceans had an inspection scheduled instead. She was just contemplating what to do with her morning when Lilika's voice popped into her head.

Kerelle, are you terribly busy? It was a courtesy question, they both knew she was off today. Unlike Lilika herself, whose role didn't seem to come with an "off" setting. *Haskrai is requesting our presence at City Hall and he's being rather cagey about why. Simply that there's* someone here who's demanding to see us.

Kerelle blinked. *That's rather cryptic.*

Indeed. I don't suspect foul play, not at this late stage, but given the mysterious status of our someone *I would prefer to greet them with a variety of talents.* She paused. *Pity Galhen is occupied, but I'm sure if it's something that needs his attention they would have gone to the hospital first.*

Kerelle agreed, and a short time later they found themselves ushered into a small meeting room at City Hall. Kerelle didn't know who she'd been expecting to find here, but it wasn't a well-dressed woman and a fidgety young boy. She was about to express her confusion to Lilika when the boy interrupted her instead.

Hi, I'm Darial! I'm not supposed to talk to people but Mom said we came here so I could talk to you. Do you want to play lizards? It was a child's unskilled projection, all blunt force and forthright emotional overlay. He was bored waiting here, he had enjoyed the sweet tart his mother bought him on the way to City Hall and would like another one, he was vaguely uncomfortable with his mother's obvious worry, he was eagerly hoping that they would take him up on his offer to play with the toy lizards, already clutched tightly in his small hands.

Kerelle and Lilika exchanged glances. Whatever they'd been expecting, it wasn't this.

"It's nice to meet you, Darial," Kerelle said carefully, aloud so that his mother knew that they knew. "We have to talk to your mom right now, but maybe we can play lizards later."

Lilika was speaking quietly to the boy's mother. "How long have you known?"

The woman swallowed. She was clearly nervous, though Kerelle was carefully avoiding reading whether she was frightened of them or simply stressed at the situation itself. "Six months. I...I don't know, maybe there was something before then, he always seemed to know when I was upset. But six months ago is when he started...talking."

The woman's eyes darted between them, anxiety knotting her brow. "We've been moving around ever since, trying to lie low, but I can't keep this up forever. When I heard that your people were here, I had to come. You'll protect him, won't you?"

Naked pleading bled into her voice. "He's one of your people, you *have* to. I saw your videos about what life in the PsiCorp was like. I can't let that happen to him."

Her projection burst in before Kerelle could block it - her terror for her gentle, happy son, who loved everyone and didn't have a cruel bone in his body, being taken and broken and re-formed into something to serve a corporate profit. It was mingled with a desperate flavor of hope - *please, please let them agree, please let them be what they say they are, even if they tell me I can't stay with him, I'd do anything to know he was safe from those monsters -*

Kerelle blinked rapidly and upped her shields again.

"This is not strictly our decision to make," Lilika was telling her. "Members of the Psionic Union are currently guests of the First Minister, and it will be his final say. However," she added, as the woman's brows drew in, "if First Minister Haskrai permits it, we would be happy to extend you our welcome. *Both* of you," she added.

They left shortly after to track down Haskrai himself, as there was little else to do without his decision. Lilika was thoughtful as they headed back down the hall.

I am not often surprised by possible outcomes, she said finally, *but I will admit I did not foresee this one. Apparently our counter-propaganda worked rather better than we thought.*

Apparently so. The whole discussion felt surreal. *She was really willing to leave her son with us, to keep him away from the multigalactics.*

Indeed. Fortunately, I suspect Haskrai will consent to both of them remaining at Epsanal Base. We can't very well just send him back out into the cold, and none of us know the first thing about babysitting.

HASKRAI DID INDEED AGREE to allowing Darial and his mother Lenya to stay; as it turned out, they were only the first. There soon was a steady stream of parents and psionic children arriving on Amaecea, seeking the same refuge.

Stigma or not, many families in the galaxy were clearly not happy to give up their psionic children to the multigalactics.

"This is likely the tip of the iceberg," Lilika commented one morning over coffee, six weeks before their hearing. "The ones coming to us are the families with the resources to do so. They have the savings to cover uprooting their lives and coming to Amaecea, or jobs that allow them to take enough time away to do so. Although," she acknowledged with a tip of her head, "I expect those with positions at the multigalactics, won't much longer. But regardless - the families that have joined us are the affluent ones. If we've seen this many from just that group, it suggests there may be a much higher number overall who would but lack the opportunity."

Nalea nodded and grabbed for the last two pastries, passing one to Ilyen. Kerelle laughed inwardly - the teleporter was wearing off on her.

"I think you're right," the scientist posited around a mouth full of pastry. "It's pretty much the opposite of what the norm is, but..." She swallowed her pastry and washed it down with another glug of coffee. "It's starting to look like the 'norm' wasn't really normal at all. Growing up it always felt like you were supposed to be okay with giving up psionics, like there was something wrong with us for being upset." She glanced quickly at Galhen, though the look held significantly less discomfort than it would have a year ago. "Maybe that was just what SysTech wanted us all to think, and everyone was upset the whole time."

"The more recent propaganda would suggest that." Riyel's voice was soft, but self-assured. He had made significant progress in recovery - both physically with Galhen, and emotionally with an Amaecean therapist who specialized in helping trauma victims. Dr. Kalutra had actually taken on a number of their people, though not everyone who likely needed her help was willing to admit it. Kerelle's eyes flicked involuntarily to Ilyen, demolishing his second pastry with enthusiasm. She'd caught something about *nightmares* in a low conversation between Nalea and Galhen, followed shortly by *stubborn*.

Riyel was continuing. "There was an interview yesterday morning with the parents of a conscripted telekinetic about how proud they were that their daughter could serve in the PsiCorp, and another one with that man they keep bringing out to talk about how we're scientifically disposed towards sociopathy." He sipped his coffee with rather more restraint than Nalea had. "It seems they're trying to reinforce the narrative that our families should be happy to surrender us."

Lilika smiled. "That it *needs* reinforcing is promising it itself."

Despite the uptick in propaganda - or perhaps because of it - the families kept arriving, young psionics in tow. Initially, they'd set up one of the more sociable C2s as a private psionic tutor for Haskrai's granddaughter Jannea; soon, Palira found herself teaching an entire class. They were mostly telepaths and telekinetics, but there was even one little regenerative. It was too early to know how powerful she would be, but even a C1 would be an asset to the community.

Kerelle could see why Haskrai was willing to fund the psionic school.

An even bigger surprise soon followed, in the form of a quiet man in his early forties who had been concealing his telepathy nearly all his life. Nor was he the only one - several adults joined them over following weeks, psionics whose parents had managed to evade detection.

Common knowledge had always been that resistance was futile, and that the multigalactics would take what they were due in the end. But clearly it *wasn't* impossible. How many other psionics, Kerelle wondered, were out there hidden across the galaxy?

If they ever found out, it would be just the latest in a string of surprising events. And one evening, three weeks before the hearing, was the biggest surprise of all.

"DR. AMBREL?"

Galhen and Nalea both looked up. They were most of the way through dinner; one of the major advantages of Epsanal Base over Cashaal was its proximity to food the group didn't have to cook themselves. Kerelle was finishing her third of the dumplings Galhen had picked up on his way home from work; Ilyen took advantage of the table's distraction to secure a fifth.

Peralen shifted from foot to foot. "Um...Ma'am," he clarified with a nod at Nalea. "There's...there's visitors. Asking for you."

Nalea quirked an eyebrow, and straightened from where she'd been slightly leaning against Ilyen's shoulder. Since their reunion, the two of them had been markedly less reserved in showing public affection. "Are these visitors with *names* or are they selling something? If they're selling something I'm not interested."

"Um...they have names, ma'am. Alhren Tarau and Mirilesa Ambrel. They're in the office by the fountain."

Nalea looked like she'd been slapped. "I...I see. Okay. Thanks." Peralen took the dismissal and left with a flash of relief. Nalea still looked slightly stunned.

"My *parents* are here." She looked over at Galhen, who'd gone pale as snow. "*Our* parents are here."

Nalea sat blinking, half-eaten dumpling forgotten. Finally she took a deep breath and let it out.

"...Okay. I don't know why they're here but...I should go see them. Galhen, you...should come with me." She turned to Ilyen. "I want my parents to meet you too, but...maybe a bit later."

Ilyen glanced between her and Galhen; Kerelle caught an

uncharacteristic projection of guilt. He would have gone to support Nalea if she'd asked, but this promised to be weird and awkward and he felt bad for how relieved he was that she *didn't* want him there.

Galhen, on the other hand, was radiating need. Outwardly he'd retreated into his serene mask - though that itself was a warning, for those who knew him well enough to recognize it. Internally, he was a storm of conflicting emotions, that he for once struggled to put into words. Kerelle reached for his hand and offered him the open bond, letting his feelings simply wash over her.

He should be happy. He wasn't. He wasn't sure *what* he felt, except that he felt like he was eight years old again and watching his home recede from the back of a corporate car. No, his *house* - home was inside with his parents and siblings, who'd drawn the blinds and locked the doors behind when the men in suits had taken him outside.

Intellectually, he knew that giving him up without a fight was the best option they had. He thought he was fine with it, that he understood why his parents had chosen as they did and bore them no resentment over it. But the prospect of seeing them again, that they would *actually* be there, was surfacing all kinds of things he thought long buried.

Amidst his whirling thoughts, one rose beseechingly above them all. *Darling, please, I don't want to do this alone.*

Kerelle squeezed his hand and flooded reassurance through the bond. *I'm with you, love. Now and always.*

"-think the telepaths need a minute," Ilyen was saying. He and Nalea were both watching them; Kerelle got the impression they'd been waiting for a response. Nalea's brows were drawn together.

"Are you going to be okay?"

Galhen met his sister's eyes and gave her a strained smile. "I suppose there's only one way to find out. Shall we start this reunion, then?"

AS NALEA OPENED the door to the office, Kerelle had no idea what to expect. The entire situation felt utterly surreal, as if at any moment the laws of reality might break down altogether into primordial chaos.

But no chaos awaited them on the other side of the door; just an attractive older couple who held out their arms when Nalea walked through. Focused on them, she didn't notice Galhen had stopped following her.

"We were so *worried*," the woman - Mirilesa, Nalea's mother, *Galhen's mother* - admonished her tearfully, arms tight around Nalea's shoulders. "Not a *word* from you! All those terrible things on the news, then those people from SysTech asking over and over again if we'd heard anything from you - "

"That's why I didn't *write*, Mom." Nalea's tone was faintly exasperated, but her aura belied her prickly demeanor. She was happy to see them too, and happy they'd been worried about her, and relieved they were safe.

From her vantage point near the open doorway, Kerelle couldn't stop staring. Nalea and Galhen had their father's vibrant green eyes - *the Tarau eyes*, Galhen had called them once. She wondered if he had given them their golden hair as well, or if that had been their mother.

Behind her, Galhen hung back in the shadows of the hallway, his feelings a paralyzing mess. They were so familiar, and yet not. They'd gotten so *old*. The loving home, whose treasured memory had helped him stay *himself* through a subsequent decade of PsiCorp indoctrination. The strangers in front of him, who'd surrendered him to monsters without a whimper of protest.

The bond was fully open, and she could feel his emotions almost as strongly as her own. He clung to it like a telepathic lifeline. Kerelle sent him all the reassurance she could.

Nalea's father hugged her too, though he was more outwardly restrained. Nalea looked between them.

"But what are you *doing* here?"

"We didn't even know if you were *alive*, Nalea," her mother answered with a hint of acid. "First we hear about that awful attack on the conference, we knew you were there but no one can tell us what's going on. Then we hear you're going to be evacuated, but the ships landed and you weren't on them and *nobody could tell us what happened to you*. We were in contact with the University, and they finally said they'd found you and then the next thing we hear the *police* are after you - "

"I'm sorry you were worried, Mom, but I couldn't exactly call home and tell you where I was."

"And then it was on all the news channels, that you were *here*, and that..." Mirilesa faltered for the first time. "And that your brother was with you..."

"He is! He's right here - " Nalea turned around to gesture, blinking for a moment at the empty space behind her. She leaned back to look down the hallway, confusion furrowing her brow. "Galhen?"

He took a fortifying breath and stepped through the door.

Sudden silence descended as he entered the room, surprise written across Alhren and Mirilesa's faces. Surprise, and a hint of uncertainty. For a terrible moment they all just stared at each other.

This was a mistake. So many emotions overlaid his thoughts, Kerelle could hardly discern them all - shock that this was happening at all, mortification at the awkwardness of the scene, nervousness at facing them, beneath it all a primal kind of hurt, deeper for being long-buried and long-denied.

When SysTech had demanded him, they hadn't even tried.

I shouldn't have come. They didn't ask for me.

He was just starting to edge backwards, when Mirilesa slowly stepped forward.

"Galhen," she whispered. "My little boy." She lifted a hesitant hand to brush his face. Kerelle sensed his breath catch, though he didn't outwardly react.

"I saw you, once," she said, so softly Kerelle could hardly hear her. "I was on Tallimau for business. It had been years, at first glance I thought it was Balheren. You look so much like your brother. But you were too young to be Balheren, and I knew he was at university, and when I looked again and I saw *it*," she lowered her trembling hand to trace the spot where his collar had been, "I knew it was you."

"You were with a group of others, all in collars and school uniforms. I...I followed you eight blocks, pretending I was just walking the same way. Then your group went into a SysTech base, and all I could do was watch you vanish again."

She blinked rapidly, eyes bright with unshed tears. "You seemed happy. You smiled and laughed with the other children. I told myself that that had to be enough."

Suddenly Mirilesa threw her arms around him, the squeezing embrace almost uncomfortably tight. "It was *never* enough," she whispered fiercely, her voice breaking as she lost the battle against tears. "Every day we thought about you. Every day we missed you."

Galhen was still for a moment before he awkwardly returned the embrace, tears starting down his face as well. He wanted to forgive her. He wanted this to be a joyful reunion where the past was past. But the hurt was there, raw and ugly, and the words that left his mouth were not the ones he wanted to say.

"But you didn't come to see *me*." It was a question and an accusation in one.

She pulled back to meet his eyes. "We *hoped* to see you." Her voice was soft and sad. "But we weren't sure you would want to see *us*."

He stared back at her searchingly, echoing through the bond that even *he* didn't know what he hoped to find in her face.

"You let them take me," he stated quietly. "You know what they were, and you didn't stop them. You didn't even *try*."

"We couldn't," she whispered. "We knew we couldn't stop them. If it were only our own lives, we could have tried to run, but…"

"But you had Balheren and Nalea." His tone was dull, an uncharacteristic coldness threading the words. "You sacrificed me to keep them safe."

The statement dropped like a stone into the room's sudden quiet.

Alhren stepped up beside his wife, a hand of support on her shoulder. He had been silent and stoic throughout the exchange, but Kerelle could sense the emotion radiating off him just as strongly. This meeting was fraught for all of them.

"Yes," he answered simply. "We did." He let the stark admission settle before he spoke again. "We thought we couldn't protect you all. I hope that someday you can forgive us for it." His gaze was steady as he met his son's eyes. "We've never forgiven ourselves."

Galhen was silent, staring at them through tear-filmed eyes. Something broke, then, in the maelstrom of emotion that swirled through the bond. He stepped forward, and wordlessly embraced them both.

They hugged him back, and a bit of the room's tension dissipated. Nalea glanced at Kerelle.

Is he okay? The scientist mouthed, gesturing toward the group in the middle.

I think so, she mouthed back. That was only partly true; she was still getting very mixed emotions through the bond, and she suspected Galhen was going to be sorting out his feelings for some time. But he was going to try, and Mirilesa and Alhren were going to try, and that was the best anyone could do at this point.

Galhen released his parents and stepped back, slipping his hand into Kerelle's.

"Mom, Dad." He said the words carefully, as if testing how they felt. "Allow me to introduce my wife."

TWENTY-SIX

There had been considerable debate over who to send to the hearing. Lilika was going, obviously - as official leader of the Union that had never been in doubt. Haskrai would attend, as their sponsor. Kerelle, Galhen, Ilyen - they were all well-known, thanks to SysTech's propaganda and their own responses to it. Lilika would do most of the talking, but they could provide valuable supporting testimony.

Kerelle was initially surprised that Lilika would willingly include Ilyen as a possible speaker. When she said as much, the Premier's lips twisted.

"Ilyen offers his thoughts freely, and is either unwilling or incapable of tempering his bluntness with any sort of regard for others' political sensibilities. And that is precisely why I want him with us. What happened in Oulemar does not deserve to be cushioned in diplomatic niceties. I would have him tell it to the Councillors in his own words."

Nalea had initially insisted that she was coming as well, refusing to be parted from Ilyen. Lilika was firm on that, however, and at length the scientist was reluctantly convinced.

"Those of us who escaped the PsiCorp are assured safe harbor while the CIG hears our appeal. You are not former PsiCorp, and so your legal status is muddier. SysTech has already tried to arrest you once, Dr. Ambrel, and I do not intend to give them a chance to do so again. We're already taking a risk bringing Director Calduit."

"If you're bringing Aureis, you can bring me," Nalea had muttered, but even she recognized the difference. Nalea had been utterly indispensable, since the very beginning. But she'd had little real interaction with SysTech, and her work was not directly relevant to their appeal to the CIG. Aureis, on the other hand, had been a SysTech executive just a few months earlier, with firsthand knowledge of PsiCorp administration. It was why they were taking the risk of bringing him along.

And even then, it was less of a risk than bringing Nalea. As far as anyone knew, *Aureis* didn't have a current writ out for his arrest.

Aureis had swallowed hard when Lilika asked him to join them. A jagged projection, *what if there is a writ out for me, what if I'm seized in the hallway and hauled away, down into the dark of another Oulemar, except no one would come to save me, I'm not really one of them and even if I was they wouldn't know where to find me....*

He set his jaw, and his determination to see this through projected almost as loudly as his fears a moment before. "I'll go. If I can help, I want to."

His nervousness lingered, and apparently it didn't take telepathy to see it. As Kerelle left the room after their little meeting's adjournment, she caught low voices from down the hall.

"You don't have to do this," Sandrel said seriously. "You don't owe us anything, Aureis. If you'd rather stay on Amaecea, no one will argue." There was a curious quality to his tone - a protectiveness Kerelle wasn't used to hearing from him.

"I *do* have to do it. And...I want to." His voice softened. "I was a part of that, Sandrel, even if I didn't realize what that meant. I want to do anything I can to make sure what happened to those people never happens again."

Sandrel drew him into his arms. "You've done a lot for us already," he whispered. "Never doubt that."

Aureis returned the embrace and was quiet a moment, simply resting his head on Sandrel's shoulder.

"Will you be there, when I have to speak?"

"*Of course* I'll be there. Aureis, you didn't even have to ask."

A burst of warmth from Aureis's aura, like a rising sun. "Then I can face anything."

"YOU'VE ONLY *JUST* NOTICED THIS?" Galhen's tone was faintly incredulous. "Darling, they've been gazing longingly at one another for weeks." They were once more ensconced in their cabin in Sandrel's ship, settling in for several days in hyperspace. Thinking about what awaited them on the other side of the jump tied Kerelle's stomach in knots. She was trying not to focus on it.

"I've been a bit preoccupied with everything *else* that's been happening." Her retort had no fire in it. Now that he mentioned it, Sandrel's recent good moods took on a new light.

"I've been working shifts in surgery, and *I* noticed."

"Yes, well." She shifted to snuggle closer. "You *would*."

He didn't disagree. "I'm glad for them." His voice was quiet. "Sandrel has always taken a great deal onto himself. He deserves someone who can be a true partner to him." *And Aureis as well,* he added. *I can't hold his service to SysTech against him. He did what he was brought up to do, the same as any of us. And when he realized the truth of things he tried to make it right. If he can do that, so can others.*

He didn't have words for the next part, more a swirl of feelings related to hope that enough other people in the galaxy could be open to change, so that one day the Psionic Union would be unnecessary.

Kerelle could only share her agreement - and hope that enough of those kinds of people would be hearing them at the CIG.

SHE DID a good job of keeping her mind on other things throughout the journey, so that she didn't have time to get nervous about the hearing. When they broke atmosphere, however, the sight of the CIG's sprawling headquarters stretched out beneath them made that impossible. This was really happening. And it was happening *now*.

The next hour passed in a whirlwind. They landed, were greeted by a blandly smiling group in suits, and were escorted to their assigned guest rooms to refresh themselves. In what seemed far too little time afterward, they were gathered once more in the hallway, waiting for their escort to assembly hall.

Lilika gave the group a critical once-over. At her insistence, they'd all gotten a wardrobe upgrade before they left Amaecea, and Kerelle had to admit it had been a good idea. Well-tailored and cleanly understated, the suits lent all of them an elevated credibility. They didn't look like a *loose collection of misfits*, now. Now they were a serious force to engage with.

Even Ilyen, with his hair tied up and his blazer buttoned, looked positively respectable.

Lilika seemed to agree; her lips cracked in the hint of a smile. "Here we are, everyone. I won't pretend the stakes aren't high, but we're ready. All of us." The smile widened, and her dark eyes flashed with an almost predatory light. "Now let's go out there and make them regret they ever tried to take us on."

Their escort arrived. The ornate, towering doors were opened. They filed in.

The sheer volume of humanity took her by surprise, and Kerelle upped her shields on instinct as they crossed to their table. CIG delegates often didn't attend all meetings on the calendar, Kerelle had learned that in the runup to their hearing, but it seemed no one had wanted to pass up the chance to see the notorious Psionic Union in the flesh. She forced herself to keep her gaze level and her expression unchanged, as she took a seat with the eyes of thousands of planetary government representatives watching her. More than just that; cameras were trained on them from every direction, most likely streaming live to the datanet. The galaxy, quite literally, was watching.

Galhen gave her a soft pulse through the bond as they took their seats. He was nervous too, and just as determined not to show it.

If Lilika was intimidated by the enormous crowd, she gave no outward sign. Head held high, she strode up to the podium when the assembly chairman invited them to make their opening address.

The whispers died out. She began to speak.

Lilika had always been a good speaker; certainly, she would have been Kerelle's first choice for this, even if she *hadn't* been elected their political leader. But as she delivered her opening speech in a voice that rang through the hall, Kerelle's only thought was that *good speaker* had been a severe understatement.

Dignified without seeming haughty, passionate without seeming overwrought, Lilika commanded the room as she laid out the case for why psionics should have the same rights as mundanes. Many of the delegates present, Kerelle knew, were aligned with the multigalactics, yet even they were listening in riveted silence.

Lilika concluded, words echoing through the vast chamber of the assembly, and made an unhurried walk back to their table. Her face was serene, but her thoughts held a thread of vicious glee.

Game on, bastards.

IT WAS the opening salvo in a long war of words, played out in the hearings that dragged on over the next weeks.

SysTech had sent its own representatives to the assembly. Soon its lawyers argued to the delegates that the practice of mandatory contracts was well within the law, and that overturning those contracts set a dangerous precedent that could threaten businesses and the economy. Nor were they alone - perhaps sensing a common threat, the other multigalactics had sent legal support as well. There was even a small contingent of ConEn lawyers, seated at the other end of the table from their employer's archrival.

The CIG heard from PsiCorp program managers at several companies, who testified to how well the PsiCorp were treated, with a higher standard of living than many "free" mundanes. The SysTech contingent had come armed with old credit records, from their time with the PsiCorp, and read aloud the extravagant things purchased with SysTech money by the very same psionics who now sat here claiming oppression. Kerelle suppressed a wince as a man read off, with a slight sneer, just how *much* she and Galhen had once spent on whiskey.

Worse, at the time she hadn't even *realized* it. When getting something she wanted was simply a matter of scanning her payment card, the value of money had been rather more abstract.

Naturally these were followed by the "psionic psychology experts" who had been making the media circuits, full of regretful but confident pronouncements that psionics were simply incapable of empathy and bonding. That they could be charismatic and eloquent, as we'd seen in these hearings, but ultimately any positive social behaviors would be a tool to manipulate others into giving them what they wanted.

The low point, in Kerelle's mind, came on the fifth day, when Senator Dalanva took the podium.

Dalanva had lost none of her charisma in the past two years. When Kerelle had first encountered her, thrown off balance by the chaos at her party, she had thought the senator seemed smaller and more frail in person than in her media appearances. Here, in an environment that was practically her home ground, Dalanva seemed larger than life once more. She was smaller in stature than the security detail that accompanied her in, but carried herself with an unshakable self-assurance that dominated the space around her.

She ascended to speak with a regal serenity, sweeping her gaze unhurried across the chamber. As her head turned towards the psionics' table, she made deliberate eye contact with Galhen.

Kerelle sensed his pulse spike almost immediately, felt his struggle to conceal his body's panicked response to being in the same room with that woman again. She tamped down her own anger at Dalanva to send him calm and safety, to help shore up the rational part of his mind that was trying to convince the rest of him that she was no longer a threat.

To her surprise she felt Lilika's cool touch as well, sending him her own encouragement. *Breathe, Galhen. Don't let her see it. She's trying to intimidate you and* stars and blood *we won't give her the satisfaction.*

A mental handsqueeze, to both of them, and he stared her down without flinching. Dalanva's eyes flicked back to the assembled delegates as she began her speech.

It was more of the same from her media interviews, that same constructed narrative of the psionic viper she'd allowed into her home, of how when compassion failed to moderate his behavior she had been forced to rely on sharper discipline to protect herself and her staff.

Kerelle wasn't sure which of them reached out, but at some point her fingers had become entwined with Galhen's. When Dalanva gravely recounted how her psionic assistant's defiant refusal to treat an injured child had led to the girl's death, his grip on her hand became almost painful. Kerelle returned his grasp and kept her eyes glued to the senator's face throughout, as if the force of her gaze could bore through the other woman's lies.

Alas, her lies continued unabated. There was no examination of her testimony when she finished, only grave thanks from the assembly chairman for her trouble in making the trip.

Lilika's mental voice was all ice. *This isn't the end of it.*

And it wasn't. Galhen was called afterward to give his own version of events; his earlier distress had given way to a core of anger as he detailed Dalanva's callousness towards her staff and their lives. Kerelle herself was called later, to explain once again the series of events that had led to their escape and the Psionic Union's formation. Standing at the podium, facing the sea of people who held their lives in their hands, was more terrifying than heading into combat; she felt as though she'd dissociated for the entire interview.

There had been a barrage of questions from the delegates, about her escape, about the Ash and Bones, about Elekar. She'd answered as best she could.

Lilika told her afterward that she'd done well, and Kerelle would take her word for it. The entire session was a blur in her memory.

In one of the more lurid sessions, Ilyen gave a clinical recounting of what had been done to him in SysTech custody. Murmurs arose throughout the chamber, though the examination period made it clear not everyone was convinced.

"This is a very *dramatic* story you've told us," commented one of the delegates, his tone shot through with skepticism. "I just find it remarkable that you could have gone through all of what you said you went through, and be sitting with us here looking like you're ready for a fashion shoot. Particularly," he inclined his head toward the SysTech table, "in light of everything we've learned about psionic manipulative patterns. It seems you're asking for a lot of credulity from this chamber."

"That's a great question, representative!" For those that knew him, Ilyen's bright tone was a warning sign. His hands started fiddling with something near his shirt collar. "You all get to enjoy my pretty face because Galhen Ambrel is an overachiever, even by C3 standards." He shrugged his jacket off. "But there are some bits he hasn't gotten to yet."

Kerelle heard Galhen's sharp hiss from beside her, as he realized what Ilyen was going to do a half second before he did it. Smirking slightly, the teleporter undid the last button and slipped off his shirt.

It was true that Galhen had been conscientious in working to eliminate scarring, for Ilyen, Riyel, and all others who had suffered in Oulemar. It was also true that the process was slow, and he'd prioritized areas that were usually visible. Ilyen's face and hands were unmarked. The rest of him still bore signs of what he'd endured.

Chaos erupted in the chamber. Cameras flashed and a clamor arose from the delegates - some in shock at what they were looking at, others in protest at the gross breach of decency caused by the speaker's *partial nudity*. The session dissolved with the chairman's increasingly frantic calls for order.

Ilyen looked sardonically pleased with himself as he rebuttoned his shirt on the way back from the podium, his jacket slung casually over one shoulder. Lilika's expression was a mix of exasperation and pride.

Well, she commented silently to Kerelle, *I did say I wanted his disregard for niceties.*

"CHAIRMAN, WE MUST *PROTEST* THIS." Outrage threaded the SysTech lawyer's tone as she rose up sharply from her seat, punctuating the statement with an emphatic gesture at the psionic table. Aureis froze, still standing beside his seat. Even from a few seats away, Kerelle could see his hands were trembling.

"Steady," she heard Sandrel murmur. Aureis's eyes were glued to the head of SysTech's legal team as she continued.

"This man is *not* a psionic and does not have a legitimate reason to speak on the behalf of the *Psionic Union*." Her tone conveyed SysTech's opinion that the Union didn't have much legitimacy to speak either. "Furthermore Aureis Lenar Calduit is under investigation for corporate espionage, abetting terrorism, and as accessory to murder. He *should* be arrested immediately."

"SysTech's counsel is poorly informed," Lilika cut in coldly. She had risen from her seat as well, and stared down the other woman like she was a misbehaving student. "Aureis Lenar Calduit is a citizen of the Psionic Union, and holds the position of Minister of Finance. He is appearing today not only as an expert on SysTech's PsiCorp practices, but as a representative of the Union government. As such he is covered by the Union's immunity for these hearings, regardless of any *investigations - "* Lilika let her own contempt show through "that SysTech may have taken upon itself to pursue."

A susurrus of conversation rose about the chamber - this was the first any of the delegates had heard about the Psionic Union offering citizenship to mundanes, or about Aureis holding a government position.

Probably because, as far as Kerelle knew, Lilika had just appointed him on the spot.

Aureis had gone pale, but he had the good sense to nod along with Lilika's pronouncement. The assembly chairman banged his gavel and declared he would allow it.

Kerelle held her breath as Aureis ascended to the podium. His hands were still shaking, but he kept his head high.

He still looked slightly shocked as he took his place to speak under the gaze of gathered assembly, and for a horrible moment Kerelle thought that words might fail him. Their financier swallowed, took a deep breath, and leaned in to give his account.

He didn't falter once.

Over the next hour he gave a matter-of-fact overview of the business management of the PsiCorp, including the recent initiatives to curtail autonomy and enforce harsher punitive measures to ensure discipline, and the cost savings SysTech hoped to realize. Much of what the psionics had asserted, Aureis confirmed in quotidian details of policies and procedures. Speaking before so large and august an audience was nerve-wracking for him, Kerelle knew, but at the same time she could sense him shedding some of those nerves as he warmed to his topic.

Aureis would never be a firebrand revolutionary, but in a way he was in his element here. His careful explanations of SysTech's business processes and analyses of their outcomes, delivered with the quiet confidence that came from having run the numbers several times, held the chamber's attention throughout. He finished with a full confirmation of Ilyen's story, and how it led to his own departure from SysTech.

It was that last part that he received the most questions on, naturally, some from delegates obviously hoping to trip him up on details. But if there was one thing Aureis Lenar Calduit excelled at, it was details. When the session finally adjourned for a recess, a half-hour of determined questioning by hostile delegates hadn't managed to uncover any inconsistency in his statements.

Their shy, nervous accountant had done them proud.

The Union had been granted use of an adjoining office during their hearing, and they all filed into it for the recess. As soon as the door was shut, Aureis practically collapsed against it.

"Burning stars," he groaned. "I think that was the worst thing I've ever been through. Including that time when we first met and I thought you were going to kill me."

He squeaked in surprise as Sandrel swept him into an embrace. "Aureis, you were *brilliant*," the pilot emphasized. "Absolutely brilliant. That was a bloody nose they won't shake off easily."

"I don't know," Aureis protested, "They'll probably just explain it as - "

Sandrel cut him off with a kiss. "Absolutely brilliant," he repeated softly, and their newly-minted Minister of Finance melted against his shoulder.

FOR THE FINAL testimony of the hearing, SysTech brought out the big guns: the CEO herself, surrounded by a buzzing swarm of aides and bodyguards.

Lysendra Ulnor Ardast had the air of a woman who'd been born wearing a suit. From her meticulous appearance to the way she carried herself with effortless authority, every inch of her screamed *senior executive*, to the point that Kerelle couldn't really imagine her relaxing into anything else. Even at the beach, she suspected, Ardast wore a blazer and took calls from her cabana.

There was certainly no hint of leisure in the Ardast who strode up to the podium. She thanked the Assembly for the opportunity to speak with due respect and gravity. Her brisk tone, however, clearly implied that these hearings were taking her away from important business functions, and left no doubt that she felt the psionics were wasting everyone's time.

Her speech itself was fairly standard - "typical executive bull-shit," as Ilyen might describe it. There was a lot about SysTech as an innovator and generous community partner - *reminding them of all those campaign contributions*, Lilika commented snidely - with some noble-sounding bits thrown in about balancing the wants of psionics against the best interests and overall safety of the community.

Ask Elekar how safe they were, Kerelle thought darkly, *with SysTech holding our leash.* But there would be no more opportunity to offer rebuttal on the Assembly floor; any further arguments would have to be made directly to the public on the datanet.

But it wasn't the words of Ardast's speech, that drew the psionics' attention like moths to a light cube. It was what she was wearing on a lanyard around her neck.

From far away the control card might have been mistaken for a statement pendant, or some sort of VIP identification. To the psionics, intimately familiar with what the control cards looked like, there was no mistaking it.

Ilyen leaned over to Kerelle's ear. "Is that..."

"I...I think it is."

It is, Lilika sent her abruptly. *I suspect she's flaunting it to intimidate us - or make a point that she can threaten us even here with no consequence. I doubt she makes a* habit *of wearing the Prime Card around her neck like a convention pass.*

Kerelle almost couldn't believe she was this close to it. Seeing the regional manager's master card, the one they'd used to free an entire PsiCorp group at once, had already felt surreal. Now she was looking at the master card with control over the entire SysTech PsiCorp. Supposedly only two copies of the Prime Card existed; the CEO kept one on her person at all times, and the head of the PsiCorp kept the other.

She wants to remind us how easily she can snuff out the psionics still under their control. Lilika's anger sparked as though her thoughts were threaded through with lightning. As always, however, her face stayed schooled in serene neutrality.

When Ardast wrapped up, their Premier met her eyes and did not look away.

But our days of cowering are over.

NERVOUS BUTTERFLIES LEAPT in Kerelle's stomach as they took their seats in the Assembly chamber for the final time. After three long weeks, the hearings were over, and the CIG would finally put their questions to the vote. In a few short hours, there would be a decision made on the legitimacy of the Psionic Union, the overall legality of mandatory psionic contracts, and the multigalactics' legal recourse against contract breach.

Everyone was trying to stay nonchalant, but from the silence over their barely-touched breakfast, Kerelle knew she wasn't the only one with apprehension.

Lilika had been the only one to speak, shortly before they were due back in the chamber.

"Remember our objective in all this is to begin a path towards recognition and international acceptance," she'd told them bluntly, "and to create barriers to SysTech's ability to attack us with impunity. The CIG is not a fast mover, and we should not expect to leave this building with all of our goals fulfilled."

Kerelle wasn't sure it made her feel any better, that Lilika obviously had concerns about the vote too.

She could scarcely breathe when the votes were finally called. It turned out to be rather anticlimactic.

The legality of the mandatory contracts, it was decided, required more deliberation and study before a final decision could be made. The Assembly passed a vote to begin consideration of forming a series of committees to examine the issue in greater rigor.

The legitimacy of the Psionic Union would remain undecided as well. The Assembly's conclusion was that they made compelling arguments, and that some of their assertions about the PsiCorp were concerning. But if the CIG were to step in to deprive some of the galaxy's largest entities of their assets by fiat, it would set a precedent with problematic social and economic implications. Some of the delegates, too, were very concerned about the psionics' extralegal activities. More debate would be needed, and committees might be formed to recommend a procedure for setting milestones towards official recognition as an independent entity.

In other words, they're not going to do anything, are they.

They didn't rule that we were naughty children who should be packed up and sent back to our parents, Lilika answered. *That's the best we were ever going to do today.*

Kerelle sighed mentally as the Chairman wrapped up. *It would have been nice, though. To have them* actually *take our side.*

It would also be nice to have SysTech suddenly overcome with collective remorse and resolve to change its ways. And about as likely. Chin up, General, she added with a faint smiling overlay. *We've accomplished what we needed to, for now. We've bought time.*

THERE WERE no real words to describe Kerelle's relief that, after several weeks shuffling between the hearings and their guest suite, they were finally going home. The hearings already felt like some bizarre dream, like something that happened to somebody else. Getting back to reality again felt like the first time she could really relax since all this began.

Judging by the expressions around the mess, she wasn't the only one. They all clutched their tea in exhausted, staring silence.

Part of Kerelle wanted to ask what happened now, what the

next move would be when they returned to Amaecea, but the rest of her opted against. Whatever came next would *still* be coming next after they'd all had a chance to rest, and they could talk about it then. Right now, she just wanted to sleep for the rest of the trip home.

She didn't even get to sleep through the first night.

Loud, persistent noise roused her from her scattered dreams; as her foggy mind reluctantly crawled back towards awareness the noise resolved into a frantic banging on their door. Beside her Galhen stirred, blinking in confusion as he came awake as well.

Kerelle heaved herself out of bed and went to the door, her mind rapidly clearing as alarm set in. That alarm curdled as the door whooshed open to reveal Lilika in the corridor, hand raised mid-knock. She was still in her nightclothes, and her brow was bent in uncharacteristic anxiety.

"I just heard from Riyel." Her voice was sharp with urgency. "Amaecea is under siege."

TWENTY-SEVEN

"UNDER *SIEGE*?" Haskrai thundered. "Those corporate assholes are trying to take *my colony* while I'm away?"

His face was all righteous anger, but Kerelle picked up the frantic worry beneath the bluster. Haskrai could thunder all he wanted, but if SysTech *did* take Amaecea, there wasn't going to be a whole lot he could do about it. The entire plan around the CIG hearings had been built on the assumption that SysTech would want to retain a veneer of respectability. It was starting to look like that assumption had not been correct.

If SysTech decided they didn't care about the PR, Amaecea and the Psionic Union lost a great deal of leverage. Judging by the bleak expressions around the room, Kerelle wasn't the only one who'd reached that conclusion.

"Taking the colony does appear to be their intent." Lilika had recovered some of her mask of poise - though anyone who knew her well enough could see the tightness around her eyes. It was Lilika's anxiety, more than anything, that set a curl of fear down Kerelle's spine. She went on. "According to Riyel, a detachment of SysTech ships entered atmosphere a few hours ago. The colony's comms are being jammed."

Kerelle pursed her lips. "This was supposed to be a surprise then, when we returned. Amaecea wouldn't be able to comm us, and we're far out of range for normal telepathy. They would have expected the colony to have no way to reach us."

"So it appears. Given Captain Marene's history of evading their spacecraft, they likely intend to meet us on the ground. And if Riyel did not have the ability to reach me in the dream, they very well might have succeeded."

"Did he have any detail on what the situation is?"

Lilika gave a terse nod. "Thus far the SysTech ships are sitting threateningly in the sky. They issued a broadcast a short time ago demanding the surrender of 'the psionic fugitives,' as well as the Haskrai family for aiding and abetting." Her brow tightened. "Apparently it was made by Velrin himself. It seems he's decided to lead the operation personally."

"Great, maybe he'll overrule the people who actually know what they're doing." Ilyen's tone was bitter with a thin veil of sarcasm. Agitation radiated from the teleporter like heat from a furnace. Nalea was on Amaecea, and he wasn't there to protect her.

"One can hope." From Lilika's tone, she didn't have much optimism for that. "There has only been bluster at this point, but no one doubts that violence will follow. Velrin's broadcast claimed that if the colony complies, no one will be harmed, but no one on the ground believes that. They also don't believe that SysTech will simply leave again afterward."

"Nor should they," Galhen agreed. His eyes were far away; even without the bond, Kerelle knew they were both thinking of Elekar. "Amaecea will become a de facto corporate property, even if it takes their lawyers a bit longer to sort out a formal annexation."

Lilika gave a terse nod of agreement. "Riyel said that Amaecea has not issued a response yet, but they're preparing for the worst. The First Minister's son Talien Haskrai," she inclined her head towards the elder Haskrai, "has assumed the position of Acting First, and is organizing what resistance Amaecea can offer. Civilians are being evacuated to any shelter available, and the colony's defenses have been activated."

Kerelle glanced over to Haskrai. "What defenses are those?"

His jaw was tight. "Shielding around essential government facilities and designated shelters, some anti-aircraft weapons. Sufficient to handle pirates. Not nearly enough for a corporate assault."

From Lilika's expression, Riyel had already said as much. "Those psionics who have combat abilities are preparing to assist in the defense. Dr. Ambrel has also volunteered any help she might provide. But I see no point in pretending the situation is not dire." A moment of uncharacteristic hesitation. "Riyel described it as a last stand."

From her brittle expression, Kerelle suspected there had been more to the message, for Lilika alone.

"We could go back to the CIG," Aureis offered halfheartedly. From his expression, he didn't have any more confidence in that option that they did. "If we explain what's happening..."

Lilika and Haskrai shook their heads in unison. "It won't be in time," she responded. "SysTech will probably have some thin legalese to explain why they're entitled to their actions, and by the time the CIG bestirs itself to form a committee the whole issue will be moot." Her brow tightened again. "They were probably hoping the CIG would shut us down in the hearings, and they could swoop in afterward with no consequences. But if they've decided to act now regardless, they've clearly decided they can take the heat."

If there even is any. If Kerelle did not already realize how serious things were, the rawness in Lilika's thoughts would have driven it home. *They might just appreciate one less controversy to deal with.*

It was the closest Kerelle had ever felt her to defeat. Lilika wasn't bothering to shield at this point, and the weight of nearly two years of being the one to always have the answers, two years of *being strong, for everyone,* was suddenly threatening to crush her. They'd come so far, she had done *so much,* and it wasn't going to be enough. It was *never going to be enough.*

Without thinking, Kerelle reached out to take her hand.

You've been more *than enough, Lilika.* She wasn't good with words, not for things like this, so Kerelle just let her feelings flow through instead. If this was how it was all going to end, she was proud to stand beside her.

But as she did, another thought bubbled up in her mind, the hope it offered almost more painful than inevitable defeat. Kerelle drew back, letting it take shape. It was completely insane, but what else did they have to lose?

"Velrin is leading them," she said slowly. "We know he's there, with the invasion force."

They were all looking at her now, unsure of where she was going with this. She swallowed. "Velrin is there, and his Prime Card will be there with him. If we take it from him..."

"We can free SysTech's entire PsiCorp, across the galaxy, all at once." Lilika's eyes were wide, but already the fire was back in them. There was a path forward again, and she would march through the burning void to reach it. "We would take SysTech by surprise, and most of their antipsionic troops are probably here. There would be little stopping a mass escape."

"And freaking out about *that* would make it hard for them to get reinforcements put together." Ilyen met her eyes. "If we can take out the forces that are here, we'll have time to get ready before they send more."

That was still a big *if,* but it was all they had. "It does give us a chance to ward off the invasion," Kerelle agreed. "And even if we die here, we give the rest of our people a fighting chance."

IT WAS a grim group that settled in to plan.

"So we know where Velrin is, and we can probably even guess which ship he's on," Sandrel pointed out, "But that doesn't help us get to him. We don't have the firepower for a boarding action, and it's pretty damn hard to sneak onto a ship while it's actually in space. Even for my special talents."

Kerelle suspected his circumspection in mixed company was more habit than anything. It seemed unlikely that Haskrai would give a rat's ass right now what illegal modifications Sandrel had on his ship.

But all she said was, "Then we need to make him land."

He raised his eyebrows. "You think he'll put down in port if we ask nicely?"

"He might," she answered quietly, "if it was to accept our surrender."

The room went silent for a moment. When Ilyen finally broke it, he sounded thoughtful.

"He might go for that, actually. He's a self-righteous asshole who likes to pretend he's hot shit. If Amaecea says it'll only surrender to him personally, he might not be able to resist going down there to rub it in."

Kerelle turned to Sandrel. "If Amaecea can lure him down to the surface, will you be able to sneak us past the SysTech ships to touch down first?"

He glanced over at Haskrai and seemed to come to the same conclusion Kerelle had earlier. "Probably, if I'm careful and we keep the stealth field up. Hard to say what we're in for without seeing their fleet, but I haven't met a blockade yet that I couldn't run." She nodded her agreement, both with the statement and with the unspoken mutual decision not to mention that slipping the Zharal V blockade had not gone smoothly at *all*.

"Well, that solves the cold-vacuum-of-space problem." Ilyen

sounded almost cheerful. "Once we're on the ground we'll have a lot more options for getting close to Velrin." *And killing him.*

Kerelle suspected Ilyen would not have bothered to shield that projection, even if he'd had the ability.

"All right then," she said finally. "Let's have Riyel convey the plan to Talien Haskrai and the others on the ground, then reconvene for any adjustments on our side. We won't get another chance."

THE SYSTECH SHIPS orbited Amaecea's soft blue in deceptive stillness. Kerelle was reminded of the vultures on Cashaal circling a weakened animal, their patient presence a pronouncement that its struggles were futile.

She clenched her teeth. That was not how this was going to end.

They'd hammered out a plan in conference with Riyel the night before. It was, admittedly, far from a sure thing, and carried considerable danger for themselves, the ground team, and Amaecea itself. But it was still the best shot any of them had to survive this. They weren't rolling over for the vultures just yet.

Sandrel was outwardly composed, but Kerelle caught his eyes flicking back towards the sensor readings with unusual frequency. She didn't blame him. Even with the stealth field engaged at its maximum, being this close to the SysTech fleet was unsettling.

He maneuvered them into orbit, spaced far enough from the other ships to be invisible to their sensors.

"We're in position," he said quietly. "Whenever they're ready."

Lilika nodded tersely, her lips compressed. She linked with

Kerelle and Galhen, and then with Riyel, kilometers below them on Amaecea's surface.

We're here, she told him simply. *You can tell Talien Haskrai to go ahead with the call.*

Riyel's acknowledgement echoed back to them. Through his eyes, Kerelle saw him relay the message to a man who could only be Kolren Haskrai's son. The Acting First responded, features grim, and keyed in a sequence on the conference room's screen. The screen came to life moments later as the call went through to the SysTech flagship. Riyel waited discreetly in the hallway, in earshot but out of sight from the camera.

"Well this isn't a surprise," Velrin sneered. *"Realizing it's not so fun to play games when they end in getting bombed into gravel?"*

Talien ignored the greeting. "I've come to ask for terms," he said stiffly. *Velrin laughed gratingly.*

"Terms!" He echoed mockingly. "The terms are that whatever I say goes." He leaned into the camera, eyes dancing with vicious glee. "We'll take all those renegade psionics. You and your family will never see the outside of a detention center again. The new SysTech governor will make this miserable little backwater regret it was ever incorporated. And if anyone tries to resist, the only thing alive down there by next week will be the cockroaches. Those are the terms."

Talien's restrained fear and anger weren't faked. They didn't need to be. There was still a very good chance all of that would come to pass.

"Amaecea will accept the terms," he answered through gritted teeth. *"We will mark space for your ship to land in Civic Square. I will make the formal surrender to you in person."*

"You don't get to make demands, Haskrai. I can take your surrender from here."

"Amaecean law requires an in-person signing to cede control of the colony. It will prevent any misunderstandings from the populace." Talien's jaw twitched, and a thread of emotion leaked into his voice. "And I want to see the man who is destroying everything my family has built."

Velrin's sneer widened, and Kerelle got the impression he'd taken that last bit as a compliment. As they'd hoped he would.

But all he said was "We'll see," and killed the call.

"OF COURSE HE DID," Ilyen said soon after, when they all were gathered again. "If he agreed right away he might look like a pushover. He'll wait a few hours to 'make them sweat.' But," he shrugged, belying his tense aura. "I think he'll take the bait. Humiliating the Haskrai kid, in front of the whole colony his family has run since forever? He's probably furiously jacking off right now just thinking about it."

Lilika pinched the bridge of her nose. "*Speculative vulgarity aside,*" she said with a long-suffering sigh, "We can only hope you're right."

He was. Right before sunset in Amaecea City, Riyel pinged Lilika to let them know that Velrin had agreed to the in-person transfer with much gloating.

"I guess that's one problem solved then," Sandrel noted solemnly. He triple-checked the stealth field, and carefully started their descent to the surface.

TWENTY-EIGHT

THE DAWN CAME clear and chill. Kerelle shivered slightly in her borrowed uniform, not quite enough to ward off the sharp air. Scattered murmurs and rustled clothing sounded around Civic Square, breaking up the quiet that had otherwise settled on Amaecea like a fog. Even so, the sounds were faint, and subsided nearly as soon as they were heard. It was as if the entire colony were holding its breath.

Soon they would know if all their frenetic preparations were enough; there was nothing to do now but wait.

The city was emptied, as much as they could manage. The citizens that should have filled its neighborhoods and boulevards were instead packed into the emergency shelters beneath the city, to await whatever outcome emerged from the day. The shelters had been built with natural disasters in mind, not bombs or invasions, but they were large and shielded. Kerelle had to hope that would be enough to keep the city's populace safe in the coming attack.

Those same shelters held a fair number of psionics as well. Anyone without combat talents had been evacuated along with the civilians - though not always without protest.

Oliven had been particularly reluctant to take shelter, rather than staying to fight. He'd only gotten more mulish as Kerelle had tried to reason with him; it was Sandrel who'd finally got through.

"Nobody thinks you don't have the courage for this. But if this goes bad enough that all those high-powered telekinetics can't handle it? Then all of us on the ground are getting killed, and the only way any civilians get out is with a pilot skilled enough to outrun the SysTech ships."

"But if we win then we won't *need* to run! How can you tell me to just *hide* instead of - "

"Oliven. *Captain Zharus.*" Sandrel's voice went quiet and serious, with none of the usual layer of levity. "This isn't about having something to prove. We all intend to win this, you know that. But if we don't? Not everyone gets the same chances in life, Oliven, and nobody here knows that better than you and me."

He'd leaned forward, holding the younger man's eyes. "Lady Haskrai and her kids will have their bodyguards with them, and they've probably got a private craft to try and get off-world if things fall apart. But the only hope for regular people, like that pretty girl you keep taking to dinner, is going to be *you.*"

Suppressing another shiver in the cold morning air, Kerelle hoped fervently it wouldn't come to that. But as she swept another glance around the square, she knew they'd done everything they could. Everyone was in their appointed places, all the preparations had been finished, now they just needed to see if it would be enough.

"The waiting around is kind of the worst part," Ilyen murmured in her ear. She nodded back. Like her, he was in an Amaecean military uniform, indistinguishable from the soldiers around them. The troop was arranged in inspection formation for the surrender ceremony, visibly unarmed. The rifles they should have been carrying were neatly stacked in a conspicuous pile across the square for confiscation or destruction, as the new regime saw fit. Opposite from that neat, conspicuous pile was a neat, conspicuous grouping of psionics, binder cuffs restraining their arms in front of them.

Less conspicuous were the psionics hidden among the Amaecean troops, or the Amaecean commandos interspersed with the psionic group. Less conspicuous also, that none of the binder cuffs were locked. When Velrin landed, he should see roughly the number of people he expected to see, where and how he expected to see them.

They didn't intend to give him time to look more closely.

The dull roar of the engines came first, then dark spots above that slowly resolved into a small fleet of shuttles. Kerelle held her breath as they landed one by one, the large Civic Square suddenly feeling too small.

This was it.

The shuttles opened, and a torrent of anti-psionic troops surged out, weapons ready. When no one sprung forth in ambush, they took up position in a formation not so different from the Amaeceans, a well-ordered sea of black uniforms spreading out from the shuttles. After the soldiers came a flurry of administrative personnel, and finally Velrin himself.

It was almost impossible to believe he was actually here, that she was actually *seeing* the man responsible for so much suffering. Velrin was not short by any means, but he still seemed too small; it seemed almost absurd that his venom and cruelty could be contained in the middle-aged man of average build who emerged from the ship.

But there could be no doubts about his identity, even without Ilyen's searing projection of antipathy. The SysTech force saluted as Velrin stepped onto the top of the shuttle ramp, decked out in combat fatigues. He was wearing a psiblocker, naturally, but it didn't require telepathy to see that he was relishing the role of the victorious general.

"As if he did anything," Ilyen muttered, "besides sit on the bridge and tell people to do shit they were going to do anyway."

Velrin made his way down the ramp with a swagger in his step, a smug grin on his face as his eyes swept over the Amaeceans. The grin widened when he caught sight of Talien Haskrai in dress regalia, all stoic elegance as he waited at the head of the troops. As he came closer, Kerelle felt a wave of relief wash over her - yes, there it was. Hung from his neck like a trophy, the Prime Card.

She didn't realize until then, how much she worried she might have been wrong about that.

Velrin paused at the foot of the ramp, and four of the antipsionic soldiers fell into place around him like an honor guard. They each withdrew a small device, and a faint blue energy field sprung to life between them and their leader.

Ilyen swore softly and leaned into her ear. "Psiblocker field. They were working on those back when I was in the black ops, but the tech wasn't there yet. They must have accelerated development when things heated up."

Kerelle watched the faintly-visible shimmer with a sinking feeling. "Is it what it sounds like?"

"Yep." Ilyen sounded faintly disgusted. "Like a psiblocker, but affecting an area of space. I won't be able to port into the field it's covering, and *you* won't be able to grab the prize from a distance. We'll need to knock it down before we can get to him."

Well, that was delightful. Five minutes in, and Plan A had already gone straight to the void.

Kerelle reached out, feeling an answering ping from Galhen at the field hospital, and Lilika from the makeshift command center she and Kolren Haskrai had set up in its vicinity. She got straight to business.

We've had a setback.

Already? If Lilika were sitting there in person, her eyebrows would have gone up. *Is he even off the ship yet?*

Just disembarked. He's got some kind of new tech with him, like a psiblocker but covering a field of effect. The snatch-and-run option isn't going to work. We'll have to take him down and grab it once the shooting starts.

Understood. Be careful. We should be able to proceed shortly.

Kerelle sent back acknowledgement and returned her attention to the scene in front of her. Velrin had made his way to where Talien stood in front of the Amaecean troops; once again, his vanity was working in their favor. He was several minutes into a gleeful speech about how stupid the Amaeceans had been to throw in with the rebels, and how he was doing them a favor by removing the nest of vipers that Talien's senile old father had welcomed in.

Those several minutes were giving them all the time they needed to finish up.

The ping came from Lilika. *Confirmation from our team. The sappers are ready when you are.*

Kerelle eyed Velrin. He was finally wrapping up his monologue, and produced a pair of binder cuffs with a melodramatic flourish. Talien impassively offered his wrists.

Talien was placing a great deal of trust in the psionics, and this had gone on long enough. She tapped Ilyen's wrist and he nodded sharply.

Do it now, Kerelle sent, and threw up her strongest shield.

The shuttles erupted in a deafening blaze, the force of it shaking the earth beneath their feet. The SysTech troops were thrown to the ground, and even through Kerelle and Ilyen's combined shields the Amaecean force wobbled. Across the square the other group swayed but kept their feet as well, protected from the shockwave and shrapnel by their own telekinetics' shields.

Flaming bits of the SysTech shuttles bounced heavily off her shields to clatter harmlessly to the street. Other pieces, though, sailed over their heads into the empty city, and ominous smoke began rising almost immediately from the nearby buildings. The small detonator bombs, painstakingly hidden beneath the paving stones by the Amaecean military the night before, had worked almost a little too well.

But they *had* worked. The SysTech troops were in disarray, and their escape route was now cut off. Velrin wouldn't be fleeing back to his flagship.

The smoke and dust kicked up by the explosion started to thin, and a lot of things began to happen at once.

In the "psionic" group, the unlocked binder cuffs were hastily discarded, and the telekinetics among them hastily whisked over the rifles that had been sitting harmlessly across the square. Kerelle's group pulled out small arms of their own, or caught rifles and hurriedly flicked them to the ready setting. For their part, the SysTech force quickly recovered. The two sides started firing without hesitation.

Kerelle realized almost immediately that this battle was not like the previous ones. There were no clattering darts intended to incapacitate; only live rounds intended to rend flesh. This time, SysTech wasn't taking psionics alive.

The chaos of pitched battle washed over the square, all blood and screams and gunfire. The element of surprise had worked in the Amaecean's favor, but they were still outnumbered. Outgunned, as well - the colony's defense force existed to fight off pirates, and while their weaponry was serviceable, it couldn't match the SysTech elite for calibre. The open ground favored their enemies.

But Kerelle couldn't worry about that - she had to trust their people to follow the plan and retreat to cover. She had to focus on hers and Ilyen's task. And their task was becoming hard to spot, as his bodyguards tried to hustle him away.

Ilyen swore viciously. "Can't get a clear spot to port closer like this. We need better line of sight on him." He took off into the melee, Kerelle close behind.

They both had shields up to deflect attackers, and they avoided engaging enemies as they tried to slip through towards Velrin. Sometimes engagement was unavoidable, and then they were forced to deal with their assailants as quickly as possible as precious seconds ticked away. Kerelle let her frustration lend her strength - each SysTech fighter that stood in her way lengthened Velrin's lead on them. Psiblocker or no, her blows landed with force.

Ilyen was even more efficient; the close-quarters combat played to his strengths. Psiblockers were effective at blocking telepathy and dampening telekinetics, but they offered no protection against a knife through the ribs. And Ilyen was intimately familiar with the weak points in SysTech body armor. Together they were a whirlwind of destruction, and inch by inch they gained on their quarry. Velrin was a faint blue light ahead of them - his psiblocker field ironically leading them like a beacon.

A ping from Lilika. *Anniya reports the main force is falling back to the neighborhoods as planned. What's our status with Velrin?*

Still in progress, she sent back distractedly, dodging a SysTech rifle butt aimed at her head, and sending a retaliatory blow at her assailant's knees. *He's running for it but we're on his trail.*

Acknowledged. Keep me informed. She said nothing more, but the reply was overlaid heavily with *don't fuck this up.*

Working on it.

Ilyen finished the one she'd knocked prone, and then they were moving again. The battling crowd around them was beginning to thin, as the Amaeceans and psionics scattered into the empty city and the SysTech forces streamed out to pursue them. The blue glow grew larger. Kerelle started to sprint.

She felt Ilyen's surge of triumph. He vanished from beside her, and she broke out of the disintegrating melee to see him reappear in a leap on the back of one of Velrin's bodyguards, his knives opening a crimson fountain across the man's throat. She didn't waste the others' momentary surprise, sending a hard shove against the nearer one to knock him off his feet.

She took a step forward to press her advantage, when liquid agony wrapped around her arm.

The scream ripped out of her throat as she stumbled and lost her feet, only sheer base instinct keeping her flickering shields in place. The sound of the bullets bouncing off them barely registered. The pain was everywhere, crowding out her thoughts, and it felt like scrabbling at slippery ice to try to collect herself. It was like nothing she'd experienced.

Except once, echoed through Galhen's collar, collapsed on the floor of Dalanva's estate.

Teeth clenching so hard they ached, she dragged her gaze over to the source: a dark whip curled around her forearm, irregularly studded with blue-illuminated LEDs. The handle was clutched in one of the remaining guard's hands; his finger nudged something and the pain intensified. Kerelle heard herself shriek as her vision spotted.

She couldn't pass out...she couldn't...she had to...

Scuffle. Shouts. Hot splatter of blood.

The pain receded like a retreating wave, leaving her shaking on the cobblestones.

Kerelle forced her breathing to slow. They weren't finished. She had to get up.

Ilyen crouched next to her, his brows pulled together. "We have to move, Evandra."

She nodded, still working on getting herself together. Now that the whip-weapon was out of contact, her body was beginning to recover - though she suspected she'd be sore for some time.

The whip itself was on the ground between her and the body of its wielder. Its LEDs had gone dark and the handle of it was crushed, as if someone had repeatedly bashed it with a blunt object.

Glancing from a loose cobblestone nearby to the pinched worry on Ilyen's face, she suspected someone had done exactly that.

"What *was* that?" She couldn't keep the dread from her voice.

Ilyen's nose wrinkled in distaste, and she sensed his telekinetic push as the whip flipped over, exposing the thin metallic seam on its slightly flattened bottom side. It seemed he didn't want to touch it either, even as it lay inert.

"I helped Nalea pull out the hemindrium layers from old PsiCorp collars," he answered. "They looked like this. It probably works the same way, except way easier for them to hit us. Since, you know, they don't have to collar us first." His lip curled slightly, and the ruined handle shattered further. "Hopefully we just fucked up the only prototype."

He glanced back quickly at her. "So I know you probably feel like shit right now, but..."

"But we can't stop and wait," she finished. As much as she'd like to sit here and catch her breath, there was no time. Kerelle grabbed his hand and painfully clambered to her feet.

The square around them was all but deserted. Of the living, at least - debris and bodies littered the ground, and she couldn't look too closely at whose bodies they were. Not now. There would be time to count and mourn later.

"Did you see where he went?"

Ilyen scowled. "He threw a flashscreen grenade and took off while we were busy with his goon squad. But I think he went down that way." He gestured irritably at one of the boulevards leading away from the square. "He's had plenty of time to double back, though. He could be anywhere by now."

"We'll find him," Kerelle answered firmly. They couldn't

afford *not* to. "With his shuttles down, he can't escape. We know he has to be somewhere in the city."

She took a shuddering breath and tested her feet. Yep, definitely sore - but she was rapidly recovering function. She gave Ilyen a sharp nod. "Let's go flush out a sociopath."

They set off at a jog down the empty boulevard, into the looming silence of the city.

TWENTY-NINE

IT WASN'T SILENT LONG. The Amaecean retreat from Civic Square had been strategic; with the city emptied of civilians, they could use its alleys and edifices to their advantage. The pitched battle of the square had atomized into a hundred smaller struggles, and house-to-house fighting echoed in the streets. The Amaeceans made brutal use of their home ground familiarity, laying traps and dropping ambushes on the pursuing corporate force. For their part, SysTech was taking no pains to avoid collateral damage, and the cityscape was punctuated with dark smoke and licking flames.

It reminded her horribly of Elekar - a mirror-world version, where the guerrillas were on her side and neatly uniformed soldiers she might once have led were the targets.

She shoved that comparison deep down into the *feel later* compartment. Preferably *feel never*.

She and Ilyen tried to keep moving; if they stopped to aid with every skirmish they encountered they would never catch up with Velrin, and none of this would matter. And tracking Velrin was hard enough as it was.

She could catch no glimpse of his fleeing thoughts - hardly a surprise, since he was practically guaranteed to be wearing one of the best psiblockers on the market. Instead they were relying on guesswork as they sped past flaming buildings and knots of battling soldiers.

Most bullies were cowards, when you stripped away their advantage. Velrin would want to put distance between himself and danger, so he'd be more likely to run deeper into the city than stop to hide somewhere he might get caught up in the fighting. On that premise, Kerelle and Ilyen kept moving deeper in themselves.

She kept her senses open, both to detect nearby trouble and in the faint hope that she could pick something up from *someone*. From a group of Amaeceans near a major intersection, she caught a break: they had briefly seen a blue glow like Velrin's shield, moving rapidly toward the arts district.

She tugged Ilyen's wrist and they changed course. The sounds of fighting and the roar of flames faded behind them; this was further from Civic Square than most skirmishing groups had come. By the time they reached the museum plaza that anchored the district, their surroundings were blanketed in an eerie silence, broken only by their footsteps.

A terse ping from Lilika interrupted her. *Kerelle. Status.*

Still on his trail. We've tracked him to the arts district.

We need to end *this.* Tightly controlled worry underpinned her thoughts. *There are more of them coming down from the blockade fleet, and doubtlessly they've called for aid. The Amaeceans are holding on but we'll be crushed if SysTech brings in reinforcements.*

A sudden boom startled them, and Kerelle looked up to see a flaming shuttle streak across the sky. The colony's defenses were back up.

Yes, they are, but Amaecea's handful of anti-aircraft guns won't be enough to fend off a secondary invasion force. You have *to find Velrin before we're overrun.*

I understand the urgency. Lilika could probably pick up her thread of frustration, but whatever. *But he's wearing a damn psiblocker and I can't exactly track him the usual way.*

Well, you need to -

Ilyen gasped and staggered forward, and whatever Lilika was going to say receded as Kerelle's attention wrenched away. She whipped her head up just in time to see a faint blue glow on one of the museum's balustrades, vanishing backwards into the building.

Crimson was spreading from Ilyen's left shoulder. She hesitated a half second, a quick worried glance from him to the building.

"Go," he gritted out. "I'll be right behind you." Kerelle took off like a shot.

Found him, she sent Lilika hurriedly. *Will update when I can.* Shields woven tightly around her, she barreled through the double doors to his hiding place.

***

HER FOOTSTEPS ECHOED in the darkened atrium. It was cavernous around her, ceilings stretching into murky gloom and loud, polished tiles lining the floor. Numerous hallways branched out to the exhibit wings like the points of a star, and a large, elegant stairway swept up to a spacious landing on the second floor.

It had been too much to hope for that this could be a museum for minimalism.

She hesitated a moment, then headed for the stairs. The faint glimpse of Velrin's shields that she'd had from outside was on the second floor, so she might as well start there. Inspiration struck then, and she sent her telekinetics to snap the doors' heavy locking mechanism, jamming them closed. He wouldn't be able to slip out this way behind her.

Kerelle kept her senses open as she ascended to the landing, and her shields up. And so the bullet, when it came, pinged harmlessly off her shields to skitter on the tiles below.

She sprinted towards the direction it had come, the gun's sharp retort still a deafening echo in the empty hall. She skidded into a long room full of looming shapes.

Some of the shapes were taxidermied animals, surrounded by plaster rocks and ersatz plants depicting their native habitats. Others were recreations of large beasts who predated humanity on Amaecea, near jutting bones that were all that remained of them now. A giant timeline took up one wall, noting when each creature had roamed the world.

With the lights out, the only illumination came from small windows near the top of the high ceilings. The jumbled and overlapping shadows of the exhibit's stuffed inhabitants created ample space to hide. She stepped forward carefully, her eyes scanning what she could see and hoping to catch something out of place.

"I was expecting more from you, Evandra." The room's acoustics sent his voice echoing from every wall, the direction of its source unclear. "Disappointing. You could have *been* more, if they'd let me train you like I wanted to."

Kerelle advanced slowly, scanning her surroundings with careful attention as she moved deeper into the room's dim murk. *Keep talking,* she thought. *Keep talking so I can find you.*

"I tried to get you *twice,* actually, back when you were a whelp on Hasha. But that asshole Cafora wanted you for the Tallimau set, and he was Yuzene's little golden boy. You know what he said about you?"

Velrin's tone was conversational, though it still held that smug, mocking note she associated with him. Kerelle tried to ignore his words; they both knew he was trying to get in her head to distract her. Instead, she tried to focus on where his voice was *coming* from. She took another step in.

"He said you were *unsuited for the subtlety required of my group* and you'd be a better fit for the Security Force. I could have *made* you subtle, but no, you got Cafora's coddling and now you're not good for anything but blunt force. But we'll get our chance still, won't we Evandra?"

There - she thought the echoes sounded slightly louder towards that corner.

"Maybe I won't *start* with retraining you though. Maybe I'll start with one of the other ones, and you can watch. You know, breaking regeneratives is always *fascinating*. They're so used to just fixing anything that hurts, they don't really know what pain *is*. A few shots of suppressant, and you get to open up their world to a whole new range of experiences."

Louder, louder....a twitch of movement behind the giant aurochs, so faint she nearly missed it. Deliberately, Kerelle turned her head the other direction, as if she hadn't seen, and judged her angle to strike. Another step or two and she'd have a clear path back at him.

"So I think we'll start just strapping you into the chair across, and you can watch as I work on your pretty - "

She pivoted sharply and lunged in his direction, just as he fired a barrage into her shields.

He'd probably hoped she'd be preoccupied picturing his grisly scenario. Instead, the bullets clattered harmlessly to the floor, and she leapt the last few feet to grab his arm through his anti-psionic shield. He managed to jerk himself free of her grasp like a slippery goose, and sprinted through an arching portal to another exhibit. Kerelle followed close on his heels. She wasn't going to lose him again.

She followed him closely, dodging glass-encased rock samples and a large exposed geode on a pedestal. Suddenly Velrin drew up short and spun to face her, scattering his shield devices to form a small antipsionic field surrounding him. The exhibit hall dead-ended behind him in a large, sweeping cross-section of a tree. She had him cornered.

Cornered, but not yet down. He kept his gun trained on her as she advanced slowly closer. They were at something of an impasse, here - if she stepped into his antipsionic field, he would shoot her, and she would be unable to deflect. If he stuck a finger outside that small shielded area, she would drag him out and end him before he could blink.

For a moment they just stared at each other.

Her eyes flicked briefly to the bisected tree towering behind him. This would be much easier if she simply wanted him dead.

But crushing him with a destabilized tree exhibit risked also crushing the Prime Card, still dangling before him like a medal. And without the Prime Card, none of this would matter.

The flicker of fear wiped from Velrin's face. His customary smirk reasserted itself as he gripped the card, though his eyes sparked with a certain wildness that sent unease skittering down her spine.

"This is what you want, isn't it? This is what that whole ridiculous show was for. You want to use it to let more of your little friends out." His eyes bored into hers, shining with malevolence. "Well, maybe *I* should use it first."

He made a show of lifting it up, and Kerelle became aware of two things. The first was that this was not a feint. Velrin was trapped, and he knew it, and if Kerelle was going to kill him then he wanted to die with the satisfaction of knowing he'd forced her to watch him mass-murder the SysTech PsiCorp.

The second thing was that she and Velrin were no longer alone in the hall. And she needed to buy just a tiny bit more time. She needed to distract him, as he'd tried to distract her.

She took a gamble, and prayed it didn't backfire.

"Is this about Phaera?"

The raw pain on his face made her falter, even with what he'd been about to do. *What he could still do.* She thought of thousands of psionics dying in sudden agony and forced herself to go on. She had to keep him focused on her, just a few seconds more,

"I didn't want to have to kill her. I let her go, twice, and hoped I'd never see her again." She drove forward before he could interrupt. "*You* are the one who brought her to Oulemar. Who brought her in to *all* of this. You kept her out of the PsiCorp, that could have been enough!"

She still didn't regret killing Phaera in their battle in Oulemar; it had been Phaera's choice to stay on the path that was set for her. But it was Velrin's doing that she had been on that path at all.

"You could have just sent her on to university like a mundane, and she could have gotten one of those plush management-track internships, and *lived out her whole life in peace.* But it wasn't enough for you." She didn't try to keep the accusation out of her voice. "Even your own daughter had to be a tool."

His face flushed crimson, though with rage or shame she would never know. From the high branches of the tree exhibit, beyond the antipsionic field's reach, Ilyen dropped soundlessly from the spot he'd appeared in just moments before. He landed hard on Velrin's back, the ready knife in his good hand sinking deep into his target. Kerelle looked away as Ilyen yanked it free to stab him again, and again. The agonized gurgling fell away sooner than the squelching thrusts of the knife.

When she turned back to face him, Ilyen was staring down at the ruined mess of Velrin's corpse. His expression was unreadable, but the rapid rise and fall of his chest, and the blood spattering across the floor from the knife that shook in his hand, betrayed his calm facade.

Cautiously, she laid a hand on his arm. "Are you all right?"

He inclined his head slightly, not looking at her. She suspected he wasn't, not really, but in this context "all right" was probably a relative term. She didn't need telepathy to know he had a lot of feelings about this.

Stars, *she* had a lot of feelings about it, and she hadn't spent most of her life subject to Velrin's petty cruelty.

A second drip of blood, this time from the saturated sleeve of his shoulder, jerked her out of it. They didn't have time for feelings, not now. Ilyen should probably get himself to the field hospital.

And, of course, what they came for.

Kerelle knelt and carefully extracted the Prime Card, deliberately not noticing anything else as she retrieved it from the corpse. She handed it to Ilyen.

"Get this to Nalea?"

He nodded, his icy eyes for once deadly serious. "See you on the other side."

He vanished.

THE MUSEUM WAS SUDDENLY TOO silent and empty, as she stood alone with Velrin's ravaged body in the blood-spattered exhibit hall. Kerelle left it where it lay and headed back toward the entrance, her footsteps a fast-paced staccato on the tiled floors.

There would be time to collect the dead later; she'd tell Haskrai to make sure they didn't leave the mess for some hapless museum docent to find.

She was almost at the bottom of the stairs when Lilika's voice rung sharply in her mind.

Where are you? Tension overlaid her terse question. Another knot of worry formed in Kerelle's gut. Lilika didn't sound victorious.

Arts district, she answered, picking up her pace. She flung the broken doors off their hinges and jogged back into the midday light. *Velrin is dead. Did Ilyen arrive with the Prime Card?*

Yes, and Nalea is working on it now. But we have a more immediate problem - a wing of bombers just broke atmosphere. They're coming down from the battle cruiser. We have to do something!

On it.

Kerelle took off at a run toward Civic Square. Before she'd gone more than a few meters, a deafening boom shook the ground beneath her feet. At least one of the bombers had dropped its payload. Another one nearly sent her sprawling as she neared the square, and the dark blotches of the bomber craft grew more visible.

The sharp, cracking boom of an anti-aircraft gun, and one of the bombers exploded midair in a searing flash. That was one less to worry about, then - but at the same time, the AA guns had noticeably slowed. Either they were running low on ammunition, or they were running low on personnel. She hoped the SysTech troops had not managed to capture any.

But either way, it seemed the AA guns wouldn't be enough.

As if cued by her thoughts, the bomber formation turned north, towards the shielded civil office they'd appropriated for the command center and field hospital.

Those civil office shields were never built for something like this. The bombs would punch holes in them in minutes, and rain death on the people inside. On Lilika and Nalea and Ilyen and Galhen.

Kerelle would not allow it.

She watched, waiting, as the formation flew nearer. This was bigger than anything she'd ever attempted, and probably quite ill-advised. But these most certainly qualified as desperate times. Desperate measures were on the table.

The bombers were close, now, and she could make out the details on their individual shapes. She gathered all her strength, and grabbed one.

The sheer *force* was unlike anything she'd experienced. The ship strained violently against her, and she nearly let go immediately as the effort threatened to send her tumbling backward. But instead she braced herself against a wall and *held*, her breath coming in sobs as the ship's thwarted momentum built.

Trajectory, trajectory, trajectory. She repeated it like a mantra in her mind. So close now…there!

She released the bomber, with just a slight push to alter its path as it shot forward with pent-up force. It smashed violently into one of the other craft, another bright explosion consuming them both.

Two down, four remaining.

Smaller dark shapes flooded down from one of the bombers - it was dropping its payload. Kerelle growled and grabbed as many as she could, flinging them back upwards towards their originators. They missed, of course, but she caught them again on the way down, and this time she was better prepared. She split them into clumps and guided them behind the ships, tailing close behind the bomber craft like some sort of deadly aerial dance.

She was faintly aware that her ears were buzzing, and that there was a steady hot, metallic dripping from her nose. *Feel later.*

One didn't bank fast enough, and her cluster of bombs struck its tail.

Three left.

Another boom from the AA gun.

Two left.

Another well-aimed floating bomb cluster.

One.

It had seen her, now, and realized what was going on. The last ship turned in a swoop, its guns trained on her.

She was out of bombs; the wreckages of the other ships was out of sight; there was nothing for her to grab and fling at it that would damage it thoroughly enough, quickly enough, to keep those ship-grade bullets from shredding her in seconds. Unless it simply couldn't fire.

Her hands were already shaking, but she spread them wide anyway, planting her feet and drawing up everything she had. She reached out with her powers, feeling over the body of the craft - the wings, the fuselage, the engine, the guns. It was almost on her now, guns spinning up to fire.

With a sudden lightheaded burst, she ripped it apart.

There was a terrible screech of metal as the craft was sundered midair, its pieces tearing away from themselves to fall in jagged shreds to the earth below. There would be no more bombs on Amaecea.

Kerelle was falling too. That buzzing in her ears was more like a roar now, and what had started as dark spots in her vision were now a rippling curtain of black. Her head was screaming, or it should be, but at the same time she felt light and disconnected, as if something that was holding her in place had *snapped*, and she should probably be worried about that should probably be worried about a lot of things but she just couldn't focus long enough to worry-

Something hard and rough under her hands and knees, then on the side of her face, *pavement, it's called pavement, that seems important to know.* Some kind of sound, too, maybe voices, but it was hard to hear anything over the buzzing and trying to focus on the sounds made her head hurt and she just wanted to lie down and *sleep sleep sleep it's already so dark*

THIRTY

SHE DRIFTED.

It wasn't a bad sort of drifting. The world was soft and fuzzed around the edges, and Kerelle was actually rather content. Sometimes a thought would push at the edge of her mind, that there was something she ought to be doing, some reason she *shouldn't* be content simply floating in a vague nothingness. But it never fully formed and always faded soon, and then she was back to simply drifting. She was never quite sure if she was asleep or awake, but that didn't really seem important either.

It was a pleasant kind of emptiness.

She didn't have much sense for time, so she wasn't sure how long she'd been there when Galhen first appeared. He wasn't there, and then the next moment he simply was. She smiled and reached for him; he reached back, and the sensation was quite unlike anything else in the floating world, but she thought she liked it.

Then he was trying to say something to her, but the words sounded harsh and discordant and loud and trying to understand them made her head hurt. Trying to speak back, too, felt impossibly complex. At last he seemed to understand, because he stopped talking and simply held her, and they floated together. She liked the feeling, of drifting in his arms, and when he finally let her go and vanished she felt a twinge of something like regret. It passed quickly, however, and she was content once more.

He came to visit her often after that, or so it felt, though it was hard to say how much time had passed. At first he just stayed near her, holding her hand or cradling her against him, and there was something extra-pleasant about that, something that made the floating world seem less comforting once he was gone.

Eventually he tried words again, slowly and carefully, and Kerelle found that words were maybe not so impossible after all. She could decipher them, now, even if she didn't always understand what he meant. Still, it was nice just to listen to his voice, and so she drifted with him and closed her eyes and listened to something about friends, and rebuilding, and an apartment he lived in and hoped she would live in too.

"Are you ready to come back with me?" He asked it in the soft, careful voice he always used in the floating world, but she sensed something stronger behind it, sensed that the question was important. Still, the thought of leaving the floating world made her scrunch up her face in dismay.

"All right," he answered, but she could tell somehow that he was sad. He kissed her cheek. "Maybe next time. I love you." He was gone then, and something hurt in her unexpectedly, and for a fleeting moment she was sorry she hadn't said yes.

But she said no again, the next few times he asked, because it was safe and quiet and comforting here and she didn't quite remember what outside was like, except that it was not those things. Gradually, though, the safety began to feel like enclosure, the quiet like emptiness. She still floated, but she found herself growing restless with it.

"Are you ready to come back with me?" Galhen asked, his hand gentle at the small of her back.

"Yes," she said.

———

THE FIRST THING that hit her was the glare of the lights. Kerelle groaned and squinted, turning her head to one side to avoid it. When she ventured to open her eyes all the way, it was to a vast blur, as if they had to remember how to focus. When they finally did, her vision cleared to a sparse hospital room, and Galhen sitting beside her.

He looked terrible. It was obvious at a glance he'd lost weight, and his always-fair skin seemed especially wan in the room's fluorescent lights. The dark circles under his eyes only further emphasized how pale he was, and there were new threads of silver in his golden hair.

His bright eyes met hers with a kind of desperate, aching hope.

"Is everything all right?" She asked uncertainly - or tried to ask, as she found her voice was a hoarse croak.

He burst into tears.

Kerelle tried to sit up, and discovered sitting up was much harder than she remembered it being. She also discovered that she was connected to an alarming number of tubes and wires.

"Careful, darling, *careful!*" He was on his feet in an instant, gently laying her back against the bed. "Don't try to move just yet." He gave her a faint smile, a few wet rivulets still working down his face. "Give your body a chance to catch up."

She did as he told her, focusing on deep breaths as he tapped a few buttons to shift her bed into a slight incline. It wasn't quite sitting upright, but it was a start. As her head started to clear somewhat, Kerelle concluded that she felt awful. Judging by their surroundings and Galhen's reaction, she was guessing that feeling awful was probably about right.

Actually, it was odd that she wasn't picking up more from Galhen. His physical tells all indicated that the bond should be fairly bursting with emotion. She knew he shielded around patients, but surely that didn't mean *her*. She reached out.

Except that she didn't, because there was nothing to reach out *with*.

Panic lit along her fragile-feeling nerves. She tried again, nothing, just a gaping hole where her psionics should be. She struggled to breathe as one of her bedside monitors trilled in alarm.

"Kerelle!" Galhen was beside her again instantly, clasping her hands in his. "Kerelle it's all right, you're safe here, it's not forever, everything is fine. I need you to breathe with me. Can you do that? We're going to breathe in right now, and hold it."

She let him lead her through the breathing exercises, slowly in, slowly out, until gradually her racing heart slowed and rational thought reasserted itself. One of the first of those thoughts was that Galhen didn't seem surprised, by any of it.

"How did you know I was—burned out?" She had to fight the last words out. Saying it made it real.

Galhen paused a moment, as if considering how best to answer. Finally, he gently asked, "Darling, how could you not be?"

She stared back at him in confusion. He tried again. "Do you remember anything, from the invasion of Amaecea?"

"Of course I do. Ilyen and I chased Velrin through the city and secured the Prime Card, and then..." she faltered as the memories filtered back. "And then there were those bombers, and I couldn't let them reach you, and I..." she glanced over at him. "I think I rather overdid it."

"Just a bit," he agreed, his short laugh sounding more

desperate than amused. He leaned in then, letting their still-entwined hands rest against his chest.

"Darling," he told her slowly, "You were unconscious for nearly two months. There were times - " he choked slightly on the word and looked away, blinking rapidly to dispel a fresh wave of tears. "There were times we did not think you would awaken."

She stared back at him in shock. Two months, *two months* she had been asleep. And her friends thought she might have died. Not physically, but *her*, the parts of her that were Kerelle and not simply a functional body. That *could have happened*. Thinking about it felt like she might start hyperventilating all over again.

"You were badly overextended," he continued "in ways that I couldn't repair. I was able to heal your physical injuries, of course, but your mind..." he looked like he might cry again. "Your mind had to decide on its own."

"That *was* you, when I was floating in...in whatever that was. That was you who kept asking me to come back."

He inclined his head slightly. "It was. I won't pretend I wasn't discouraged the first few times, but as you got stronger... I had to hope, love. You've never been the sort to lie down and die."

She lifted their hands and kissed the tips of his fingers. "I'm sorry I worried you. Thank you for not giving up on me."

He laughed then, and it sounded rusty but genuine. The smile he gave her was real. "Kerelle, darling, you should know by now that that's one thing I could never do. I wouldn't even know how to start."

SOME TIME LATER, she sat propped up in her bed with a weak cup of tea, as Galhen filled her in on the last two months.

"We aren't dead, or worse," she commented, blowing on the tea to help it cool. "So I'm guessing the plan worked?"

"Better than we could have hoped for. The Prime Card wasn't a standard architecture, naturally, but Nalea's tricks still worked. Roughly when you brought down the last bomber, every psionic in the SysTech PsiCorp was freed."

She exhaled. "*All* of them?" It seemed too big to be real.

He squeezed her hand that wasn't holding the tea. "Every one. It was mass chaos, across the galaxy. There were no reinforcements that SysTech could spare."

"And by evening," he added, "Lilika's people made sure that the everyone in the galaxy knew what had happened here. The top datanet vid sites all crashed under the traffic. SysTech couldn't come back, not with all those eyes on them."

He smiled slightly. "They've disavowed Velrin - the official story is that he went rogue and attacked Amaecea without management approval. It's all rubbish, of course, but they're under extra scrutiny, and it will be some time before they can openly move against us again."

She made a face as she sipped her tea. "We thought they wouldn't dare at the hearings as well, and look how *that* turned out."

"Ah, but it's a rather different situation now." He paused for several seconds, and she raised a quizzical eyebrow.

"Forgive me, darling, I'm trying to think where to begin. As I said the Prime Card gambit worked brilliantly, and we were able to free the entire SysTech PsiCorp at once. Some chose to stay with SysTech, others vanished, and a few have unfortunately taken after Klai - and granted we'll have to deal with those, and soon. But many of those freed chose to join us here on Amaecea."

He smiled again. "Our little group is no longer quite so little. We've grown to where the CIG was forced to acknowledge us."

She almost choked on her tea. "What? What does *that* mean?"

"Lilika said it means we got too big for them to sweep under the rug, and I've no reason to doubt her analysis. She's been buried in negotiations with them since almost the moment the battle ended."

"What are we negotiating *for*?"

"Freedom from mandatory contracts, for one thing." He held her eyes. "And in this sector, at least, we have it."

Kerelle stared at him, her heart pounding loudly as she processed what he'd said. "Are you serious? Here, right now, if a multigalactic acquisition squad showed up, they would have no right to take us?"

"No right to take anyone," he confirmed. His eyes almost glowed. "We've been officially declared a special interest zone. In this small corner of the galaxy, involuntary psionic recruitment is no longer legal. The initiative was ratified yesterday morning."

Kerelle set her tea down carefully, then flung her arms wide and leaned up as much as she could manage. Galhen swooped in to meet her embrace, and she clutched his shoulders fiercely.

Her head hurt, she was getting tired just sitting upright, and even *she* could tell she very much needed to shower, but Kerelle couldn't help the grin that stretched almost painfully on her face.

Hot damn. They actually won.

EPILOGUE

Six months later

KERELLE STOOD in the center of the living room with a critical
eye, trying to decide if she liked how they'd arranged the furniture. She finally decided that she did, just that the couch needed
to be ever so slightly to the left. She reached out with her telekinetics and carefully lifted it up, setting it down gently a few
centimeters away so as not to scuff the hardwood floors.

Her lips curved in a smile - it was good to be back. As
Galhen had predicted, the burnout was a temporary condition of
overstressing her powers, and she'd recovered normally in the
subsequent weeks. Long, frustrating, helpless-feeling weeks.

She would never take her gifts for granted again.

Kerelle pushed the unhappy memory away. A lot of good had
happened in those weeks, too. For one thing, they'd bought this
flat.

As she looked around the living room again, the smile broadened to a grin. It was still strange and wonderful, her and
Galhen's own space, that *belonged* to them. Furniture, dishes,
appliances, linens - all things they'd chosen for themselves. The

dog bed, acquired in anticipation of their appointment next week at the animal shelter. The balcony where they sat with tea in the evenings to watch the sun set over the city. It was missing the beach from her old PsiCorp fantasies, but that was all right. The wooded hills were a nice substitute.

Sometimes she still had trouble wrapping her mind around it, that they had a permanent home now. With a postal address, and their names on the property record. Their *own* names, no less - Karia Vela Vendrys and Garyth Dala Avlor were officially retired. They would never have to hide behind an alias again.

It was quite a feeling.

The faint squeak of a knob, and the sound of running water ceased. A few minutes later Galhen emerged from the shower, the tips of his hair still dripping onto his hastily-fastened jacket. He'd been held up at the hospital later than anticipated, which meant they would be pushing the definition of "on time" for Sandrel and Aureis's housewarming party.

Kerelle didn't mind, and she knew Sandrel wouldn't either. Being the head of Amaecea General's trauma unit might be stressful sometimes, but they all knew Galhen loved it.

He crossed the room to give her a quick kiss. "Sorry for making you wait, darling. Hopefully we won't be the *last* ones to arrive."

Kerelle just smiled back. "There's no rush, we still have plenty of time to make it, and everyone knows the hospital can be unpredictable. Besides, we'll never be as late as Lilika. She had another late-afternoon call with the CIG, and it's practically a given to run over time."

"In that case, we're lucky that we're seeing her at all." Galhen paused to consider their delightfully well-stocked wine cabinet. "Do I recall correctly that Sandrel prefers dry reds?"

"Sounds right," she confirmed, and he grabbed a bottle that fit the description. A quick ride down the building's lift, and they were outside.

The metro was running again, but it was a pleasant evening, so they walked instead. They weren't the only ones out taking advantage of the weather, and they received numerous waves and greetings from the other pedestrians. *Their neighbors.* It was still a strange word.

The streets of Amaecea were still scarred by the SysTech assault, but all around were signs of rebuilding and renewal. Ruined buildings were demolished, and new ones rose in their place. New businesses sprung up in empty storefronts. The city would never be the same, but it would recover.

Just like the people who lived in it.

SANDREL AND AUREIS'S new address turned out to be a lovely top-floor apartment overlooking a park, with a rather enticing-looking pastry shop at ground level. It was closed for the day, naturally, but enough fresh-bread scent lingered that Kerelle made a mental note to impose on Sandrel for brunch at some point.

Aureis opened the door at the second knock and ushered them in, eyes sparkling.

"You're the first ones here! Our first guests ever, actually." He sounded excited, and Kerelle was reminded that Aureis's career with SysTech hadn't left much time for entertaining. This was as novel to him as it was to the psionics.

"They got here first because they think ahead," Sandrel called from the kitchen, "and they knew it was the only chance of getting to try these dumplings before Doc and Knives show up and eat them all." He turned the corner with a tray and a grin. "And if these came out anything like the practice batch, you'll want more than one."

"You *practiced* the dumplings?" Kerelle winced slightly as she snatched one off the tray; it was hotter than it looked. She settled for floating it while she waited for it to cool down.

"First time I've had an oven in almost twenty years. Haven't lost my touch though, apparently."

Her dumpling cool enough that she could dare a bite, Kerelle had to agree. It was filled with a light, savory herbed cheese, and it was *perfect*.

"You're right," she told him, "These will last about three minutes once Ilyen and Nalea get here. Hopefully they weren't meant to feed a crowd."

"Nah, we wanted to keep things small - just the old crew. Lilika and Riyel should be by at some point too, otherwise that's it, since *Captain Zharus* is on a job."

"Have you heard from Oliven since he left? How does he like the freighter business?"

"Quite a bit, it sounds like. He sends me updates every couple of days, his first solo shipping run is going great." Sandrel smiled broadly, pride infusing his tone. "He asks me questions now and then, but really I've taught him all I can at this point. Now he just needs to get out there and get experience for himself."

Kerelle glanced over. Aureis was animatedly discussing something with Galhen; for the moment she and Sandrel were more or less alone.

"And how is it for *you*," she asked quietly, "living planetside after all this time?"

"An adjustment, honestly," he admitted with a rueful chuckle. "Waking up to the same scenery every day, I don't know if I'll *ever* get used to it. Sometimes I want to call Oliven up and tell him I changed my mind, he can take the logistics-director desk job here and *I'll* go do the legwork.

"But at the same time," he added, "it was time for a change. I did just fine working solo for years - and I liked it, don't get me wrong. But it'd be hard to go back to that, after I got so used to having you lot around. Ship would feel pretty empty, you know? And besides," his eyes lingered on Aureis, who noticed and gave him a sparkling smile. "There's things worth staying put for."

"No arguments on that," Kerelle agreed. "And…I'm glad you're staying, too." It came out more awkwardly than she'd intended, but Sandrel only grinned and gave her a playful nudge with his shoulder.

"Yeah? I'd miss you too, Fury. I'm looking forward to spending time together like normal people, with nobody trying to kill us. It'll be a fun new change."

The doorbell rang, and Ilyen and Nalea were ushered in. She carried a small succulent in a bright pot.

"Happy housewarming!" Nalea announced. She handed the pot to Aureis. "The guy at the garden store said these were really hard to kill."

Aureis looked nonplussed. "Um…thank you?"

"Great vote of confidence there, Doc," Sandrel answered with a grin.

"I'm just looking out for you. High-maintenance houseplants are a menace."

"Ours lasted like two days," Ilyen confirmed cheerfully. His eyes caught on the tray still in Sandrel's hands. "Hey, are those dumplings?"

They migrated to the table then, and in short order everyone had a glass of wine.

"I saw the forms come through for your new venture at Epsanal," Aureis commented to Nalea. "How are things going with that?"

"Really good, actually. Plans for the research institute are really coming along," Nalea answered between bites of dumpling. Kerelle surreptitiously helped herself to two more while her sister-in-law continued. "Kolren Haskrai really liked the idea when I pitched it to him, and he's even thinking of providing an endowment."

Sandrel clinked his glass against hers with a warm smile. "Congrats, Doc. Quite an upgrade from your little table in one of my aft cabins."

Nalea grinned back. "Let's not go too crazy on the 'upgrade' thing, it's still Epsanal Base, and it still looks like my grandparents did the interior design. But at least I'll have space for a real equipment array - and an excuse to tear out all that terrible carpet."

"Plus, we've already cleared out all the spiders for you," Galhen noted, a teasing glint in his eyes. "*And* the mold."

"Pretty sure the fact that we'd already done half the work on renovating helped convince Haskrai, actually. The family's already put up a lot of money to help rebuild, but he said that given the industry and investment that could follow a successful research lab, he sees it as a bet on the future."

Ilyen piped in. "That, and if we build a successful bioresearch competitor in their old base, it's kind of a giant fuck-you to SysTech." He glanced over at Nalea. "Don't tell me he wasn't thinking it."

"Honestly? He probably was. But if it means we can start hiring by fall, then cheers for revenge."

Sandrel leaned back. "So what's first up for researching, once those sweet government funds start rolling in?"

"Well, I mostly worked on prosthetics tech before my life got weird, and I want to get back into that field again. But..." She swirled her wineglass, expression thoughtful. "The last few years have been interesting, too, and I think there's a real opportunity to build on that, and continue research around psionics. There's been a lot of work done over the years, usually funded by the multigalactics, but psionics have always been the test subjects, not the lab partners." She looked up. "Here on Amaecea we have a real opportunity to change that."

Kerelle blinked. "You're hoping to recruit psionic scientists?"

"Or at least create opportunities for some. Maybe get some

ideas for psionic problems that science can solve, instead of just new ways for psionics to solve problems for other people."

Nalea shrugged. "I'm also hoping to get a partnership going with Capitol University to place their grad students. I know Lilika's talking with them about opening slots for our people, and I wrote Teriel a letter of recommendation for their botany program. If he still wants into research when he's done, I'd love to hire him."

"Speaking of upcoming events," Aureis ventured, "Is there a date we should save for the wedding?"

Nalea and Ilyen made disgusted noises in unison.

"Not yet," Nalea acknowledged. "We're...working on it."

"Oh?" Sandrel's eyes danced. "What have you gotten done on it?"

Nalea stuck out her tongue at him and poured herself more wine. "I already *did* the hard part, the rest of this is just insult to injury."

Ilyen's eyes gleamed. "Yeah, not going to lie, might not have said yes if I knew how much hassle it was going to be to actually have a wedding."

Nalea grinned back at him. "That's why I didn't mention it. But you *did* say yes, and now you're stuck with me." His answering grin was electric, and they both leaned in.

"No making out at my dinner table, please," Sandrel interjected.

Ilyen smirked. "What, that reserved for residents only?"

"Yep," Sandrel answered cheerfully as Aureis turned red. "If your name's not on the lease, then no dice."

Ilyen snorted but leaned back in his chair. "I keep saying," he declared, "it would be a lot *less* work to just skip it, and do the courthouse thing like *they* did last month." He jerked his thumb at Kerelle and Galhen.

"Kerelle and I have been married for over two years," Galhen commented mildly. "All we did here was clear up some paperwork."

Kolren had not-so-gently suggested that settling permanently as citizens of Amaecea was a good time for the psionics to get their legal affairs in order, including things like papers filed under false names. There was a marriage document now in Amaecea's civil archives that said *Kerelle Evandra* and *Galhen Tarau Ambrel*.

It was nice to have, another one of those things that meant here was home and they did not need to hide who they were. Galhen was right, though - it was only formality. They'd said their real vows on Xan Xaldanan, regardless of the names on the form.

Nalea rolled her eyes. "I told you, my parents would be upset, and I don't want Mom to bring it up every year at holidays for the *rest of our damn lives*." She cocked her head. "That reminds me, I should tell them we're engaged before they come out for New Year."

"You haven't *told your parents yet?*" Aureis looked absolutely scandalized; Sandrel less surprised.

"You should get on that, Doc," was all he said.

Galhen only sipped his wine, expression pleasant. But Kerelle sensed a familiar, bittersweet twinge through their bond. He'd seen his parents once more in person since the victory, and there were now semi-regular video calls in which he made small talk with Alhren and Mirilesa about their retirement, and they asked him about his day at work, and the three of them quietly tried to puzzle out how to rebuild a shattered bond.

Their calls were strained and awkward, but Kerelle knew he appreciated them anyway. All three of them were trying, and hoping that one day they could be easy with each other.

The door chimed then, and Aureis darted up to answer it. A few moments later, he returned with Lilika and Riyel.

"Apologies for our tardiness, though you probably expected

as much," Lilika announced as she took her seat, hand already extended for a glass of wine. "If the CIG ever ends a call on time, the world might end on the spot." She smiled beneath her long-suffering tone - the call must have gone well.

"No worries, Chief," Sandrel replied with a smile. "I understand that getting on the calendar for the Head of Psionic Affairs is quite an achievement in the first place." He held out the bottle to pour her a glass. "Tell me when to stop."

Lilika gave an amused huff and watched it fill significantly past a standard wine pour. "There, that's a good start." She took a deep draught and looked over her glass at Sandrel. "And don't be ridiculous, my dear Captain Marene, I *do* have my priorities straight. If that meeting had looked likely to run any later, I would have cut that blowhard Senator Couru off mid-drivel and told her I had a more pressing engagement."

Riyel glanced over as Sandrel offered him the bottle. "About half that much for me, thanks," he said dryly. "*I* didn't have to spend two hours on a call with Couru."

"No, you got to take a group of children to the park to practice telepathic location, then get ice cream afterward," Lilika grumbled. "When Haskrai asked me to take this role, I really should have refused and become a primary grade teacher as well. The maturity level on some of these committees is roughly the same."

Kerelle had been surprised to learn that while she had been under, the Psionic Union had officially ceased to exist. Or rather, it had merged with the Amaecean government. Understandably, Haskrai and his advisors had been reluctant to cede the new arrivals a wholly separate government for their people alone; if they were staying on Amaecea, they needed to commit to it. Lilika now held one of the top posts in Haskrai's administration, and made no secret of her goal to integrate more psionics into local affairs.

Besides representing psionics' interests in government, her

other primary duty was, as Haskrai put it, to "wrangle the CIG into accepting that this isn't going away." It was a great deal of work, but Kerelle knew she relished it. There was a certain softness to her edges now, as if for the first time Lilika could let down her guard and look to the future with hope.

Kerelle understood the feeling entirely.

Riyel only smiled and sat back with his own glass. Out of all their friends, he had changed the most dramatically during her absence. Riyel had regained the weight he'd lost in Oulemar, and that personal warmth she'd always associated with him in the dream was once again back in his demeanor. He was apparently one of the more popular teachers at the psionic school, and Kerelle could see why.

She suspected Oulemar would always haunt him, the way Cashaal would always haunt her, but he no longer lived in its shadow.

"Was it a productive call, at least?"

"It was," Lilika conceded. "The CIG is very interested in our proposal for a specialized team to deal with psionic criminals. Elinea did brilliantly handling that psionic gang that was terrorizing Balarn, and they'd like her to head it. I have a provisional charter back at my office."

"That's great news," Kerelle responded, and it was. The idea had been hers, originally - some of the former SysTech psionics persisted in dangerous behavior, and it seemed irresponsible not to help solve problems the Psionic Rebellion had unleashed. All the same, Kerelle had known she didn't want to lead it. She would, if there was no one else to help. But Kerelle couldn't help but feel that she'd done enough violence in her lifetime, even if now it would be for a good cause. She'd been utterly relieved when Elinea had stepped up instead.

"It *is* great news," Lilika agreed, "and it can only help our standing with the CIG. They're warming up to us, in their own way."

Galhen raised an eyebrow. "Does that mean our passports might be good outside of Amaecea soon?"

"I wouldn't go *that* far, we'll likely be fighting this fight for decades. It takes time to change the world, and we've made quite a bit of progress already." She swept her hand around the table. "The fact that we're all here living our lives, having a party even? With no fear that someone is about to swoop in and arrest us all? Honestly, it's more than I had hoped for in our lifetimes. All the more so that we have the full rights of citizenship."

Her glance caught on Riyel, and a burst of warmth passed between them. There was a document in the civil archives now too that said *Lilika Anhei Charyth* and *Riyel Ceilas Valessa*.

"But enough about work," Lilika declared with a genuine smile. "How is everyone doing?"

The conversation moved on, but Kerelle's thoughts stayed on what she'd said. *More than I had hoped for in our lifetimes*, to be simply living quietly in the open, without contracts and without fear. It was more than she'd ever hoped for too, more than, deep down, she'd ever really believed possible. But here they were.

A smile crept over her lips, and she slipped her fingers through Galhen's beneath the table. He sent a faint questioning thought, but she only responded with a telepathic kiss on the cheek. No making out at the dinner table, after all.

It wasn't perfect - there would be struggles ahead, both against encroachment by the multigalactics and against generations of social norms. As Lilika said, one did not change the world overnight. But she had a home now, where she could live in peace with her husband. She had the family they'd built for themselves, and a future she was free to choose. That they were *all* free to choose.

It was enough.

THANK YOU FOR READING!

We've come at last to the end of Kerelle's adventure! Thank you for coming along on this whole wild ride, and I hope the conclusion was satisfying.

So what now?

Join my newsletter to get the latest on what I'm working on (plus a free Gift of the Stars prequel story!). I promise I only send newsletters when I have things to say!

Follow me on **Amazon**, **Goodreads**, or **Bookbub** to get alerted when I have a new release.

And finally, if you enjoyed this series, please consider **leaving a review**! Reader reviews are the single best way a new book can find its audience.

ACKNOWLEDGMENTS

I started working seriously on Gift of the Stars in the summer of 2016. The scope was initially much smaller (I like to describe it as a short story that got completely out of hand) but it quickly became clear that this was going to be a much bigger project than I'd ever done previously. I might not have had the courage to tackle that project, or the fortitude to see it through, without the love and support of some incredible people in my life.

In no particular order, none of this would have been possible without:

Mike and Kathleen, who have tirelessly cheered me through every milestone, and whose feedback significantly improved the final draft of this book.

The enthusiasm and support of my book club (Kalyani, Eugene, Sean and Tiane), who keep letting me come to meetings even though I usually forget to read the books.

Susan and Beth, who provided countless hours of support - listening, reading, editing, and generally encouraging when the whole thing felt too big.

My parents, who always told me I was good enough, right from the crayon-scribbled beginning.

And finally Ryan, who test-read drafts, helped me work through thorny plot problems, talked character development over dinner and morning walks, and reminded me to be kind to myself when things got hard. You were exactly what I needed, when I needed it.

ABOUT THE AUTHOR

Lena Alison Knight grew up reading space opera and high fantasy, and started writing her own as soon as she could hold a crayon steady. She lives with her husband in the San Francisco Bay Area, and when not writing she can be found taking brisk walks, haunting local coffee shops, or sprawled on the couch playing video games.

Lena can be found online at lenaalisonknight.com. Join her newsletter to get a free Gift of the Stars short story, and keep up with what's coming next.